Kiss Me, Maybe

OTHER BOOKS BY GABRIELLA GAMEZ

The Next Best Fling

Kiss Me, Maybe

GABRIELLA GAMEZ

FOREVER

New York Boston

Forever
Hachette Book Group
1290 Avenue of the Americas, New York, NY 10104
read-forever.com
@readforeverpub

First Edition: May 2025

Forever is an imprint of Grand Central Publishing.
The Forever name and logo are registered trademarks of Hachette Book Group, Inc.

The publisher is not responsible for websites (or their content)
that are not owned by the publisher.

The Hachette Speakers Bureau provides a wide range of authors for speaking events. To find out more, go to hachettespeakersbureau.com or email HachetteSpeakers@hbgusa.com.

Forever books may be purchased in bulk for business, educational, or promotional use. For information, please contact your local bookseller or the Hachette Book Group Special Markets Department at special.markets@hbgusa.com.

Print book interior design by Jeff Stiefel

Library of Congress Cataloging-in-Publication Data

Names: Gamez, Gabriella, author.
Title: Kiss me, maybe / Gabriella Gamez
Description: First edition. | New York : Forever, 2025.
Identifiers: LCCN 2024053637 | ISBN 9781538726655 (trade paperback) | ISBN 9781538726662 (ebook)
Subjects: LCGFT: Romance fiction. | Lesbian fiction. | Novels.
Classification: LCC PS3607.A436 K57 2025 | DDC 813/.6--dc23/eng/20241118
LC record available at https://lccn.loc.gov/2024053637

ISBNs: 9781538726655 (trade paperback), 9781538726662 (ebook)

Printed in the United States of America

LSC-C

Printing 1, 2025

For the real Natalia <3

So, yeah, about TikTok...

If you're reading this on or after May 6, 2025, TikTok *might* be banned in the US. As of January 30, the day I'm writing this, we still don't know!

Much of *Kiss Me, Maybe* is about Angela's journey on Tik-Tok. It's the driving force that launches her into a whole new era of her life as she navigates dating, identity, and romantic love for the very first time, much like I've seen it do for many creators on this app over the course of five years. Life inspires art, and art in turn inspires life. This has been true for centuries and will continue to be true with or without TikTok. No one can take that away from us, no matter how hard they try.

So, readers from the future, tell me—is TikTok finally officially banned for good, or was it all merely an elaborate scheme from the government to mess with our minds? Would love a crystal ball right about now...

One

The last time I went viral on TikTok was from an accidental thirst trap. This time, it's so much worse.

By no means am I an influencer or anything of the sort, so you can imagine my surprise when a lip-syncing video of me in my pajamas did numbers—especially when it was the first video of mine to ever do so. Perhaps it was the consequence of using a trending sound coupled with the fact that my sleep tank was apparently tight enough to inspire the imagination that ultimately caused thousands of strangers online to have the sort of reaction only someone like me couldn't understand. At least, that's what I've gathered from the more indecent parts of my comment section.

I may be asexual but I'm not a prude. I'm familiar with sex, even if only in the abstract sense. When I look back at that video, I don't see the sexualized woman they see. I could understand how people found me cute or pretty or sexy, but what I couldn't understand was the number of men incapable of keeping their disgusting imaginations to themselves. Most of all, I couldn't understand why their overblown sex drives were now *my* problem.

Even my boss thought it was my problem, according to the lecture she gave me last week.

"What's so inappropriate about it?" I was *this* close to crying in Erika's office, and maybe I would've been if she and Marcela hadn't made it clear from the beginning of the meeting that I was in no danger of losing my job. "It's a lip-syncing video for god's sake. I'm barely dancing, and you can only see the upper half of my body. Sorry if I didn't know my flat boobs were so boner-inducing."

There was a long, awkward pause where Erika cleared her throat and Marcela's stunned expression quickly morphed into a stern look I rarely see from my best friend. That's when it dawned on me that I'd actually used the phrase "boner-inducing" in front of my boss. If I wasn't in danger of losing my job, well, at least I could prove that the day was still young.

"I don't think your, um, chest is the problem," Marcela said, pulling up the video on her phone. And thus began a worthy contender for most humiliating moment of my life: my best friend and boss explaining detail by detail what strangers on the internet found so titillating about a video that should've stayed in the drafts. "It's everything in concert together. Scantily covered, conventionally attractive woman on the internet pretty much does it for every lowlife, cis straight man. The hip roll might've been the final nail in the coffin."

It was on the tip of my tongue to argue the "scantily covered" bit of her description, but I knew it wouldn't do me any good. I'm flat enough to wear most shirts without a bra, have no cleavage to speak of, and the black tank top I was wearing in the video is thick enough to hide my nipples in even the coldest temperatures, but none of that ultimately matters when your workplace's reputation is on the line. As much as it sucked, what's considered "appropriate" wasn't up to me.

"The hip roll certainly wasn't great, but it's the strap falling off your left shoulder that got me a call from a board member." Erika broke eye contact in favor of staring down at the keyboard on her desk, her discomfort a physical tension in the air I could feel. "I'm very sorry, Angela, but regardless of whether or not you see how this video looks, it has to come down."

It's not that I was angry about having to delete the video. If anything, it was a relief to not be bombarded by sexually explicit comments and messages from men that I neither asked for nor wanted, even if that meant giving up the largely positive reception from people who hadn't sexualized me at all.

But if I'm being honest with myself, I *was* a little disappointed. While the attention from men was unwelcome, and even creepy at times, the attention from queer women had been…unexpected. While their numbers weren't nearly as overwhelming compared to the men's, they still came in at a steady pace.

At first, it was hard to discern whether the wows and fire emojis and "looking respectfully" comments were purely innocent praise, or something deeper, but a closer look into those accounts told me I was, in fact, also desired by the sapphic community.

And I didn't mind one bit.

"It's a shame you had to take down the video," Marcela had told me after the meeting, during our lunch break. In the Whataburger parking lot, she didn't have the awkward job of talking to me as an authority figure. "Otherwise, you could've moderated the comment section and capitalized on the moment."

"Asexual thirst trapper does have a paradoxical sort of

ring to it." I tapped my chin, pretending to think. "It might have been a nice side hustle. How much money do you think I could've made?"

"Don't even go there." She threw a fry in my lap. "Erika will have a heart attack if you put her through this a second time, and then we'll get stuck with a micromanaging branch manager who'll move our desks apart."

"As if that'll stop us from yapping." I smirked at her, picking up the fry and popping it into my mouth. "Is it bad that I kind of loved the attention? Not from the ones who took it too far, but..." I sighed. "I don't know. I hate dating apps, but how else am I supposed to find women to date? That video was the closest thing I've ever had to a dating pool."

A few of them had even slid into my DMs with compliments that turned to friendly conversation. Even if it was through small talk, it was a relief to finally tell people other than my parents or Marcela I was an asexual lesbian, maybe even more so than coming out the first time. Maybe because I'd reached another first: I was being welcomed into the community I belonged to, and perhaps even on track to building my own.

"You've never been on a dating app." Marcela rolled her eyes at me.

"Correction: I hate the *idea* of dating apps."

"What about a lesbian bar?" Marcela asked. "I can help research if there are any in town that are good."

"As if we'll go anywhere that isn't Havana Bar," I huffed, ignoring the knowing look she gave me. We both knew why I wouldn't go anywhere else, and it was all thanks to the beautiful, bisexual bartender I can never seem to get out of my head.

"Krystal could probably give us some good options," Marcela pointed out. "If you stopped pining over each other for longer than ten minutes, I mean."

"We do not *pine*." She doesn't, at least. Me? Pining is all I know how to do when it comes to Krystal Ramirez.

"You could always try asking *her* out," Marcela suggested, and not for the first time. "You never know. She might say yes."

"Too real." I shook my head, and she sighed. "I'm not ready to be rejected in person, especially not without options, which brings me back to the dating pool."

"You've shot my suggestions down and it's not like you can date a TikTok comment section that doesn't exist anymore, so I'm all ears," she said. "What's your plan?"

I didn't have one, but I was starting to.

I didn't really think about what I was doing a week later, only that I was overcome with the need to do *something*. I hadn't planned on making a follow-up to the video I'd deleted, but I wasn't content to leave it at that either.

Which brings me to now, in the aftermath of hitting post for a second time without thinking it through. I played the video back, watching the number of views climb with a lump in my throat.

CAPTION:

AN UPDATE OF SORTS

@ANGELA CLOSED CAPTIONS: So, I had to delete my last video for work, which…is whatever, at this point. No one's surprised that Texas has an ultraconservative code of conduct in *and* out of the workplace, just like no one's surprised by a cis straight man's capacity to ruin things for everyone, so it's honestly good riddance to all those gross comments I was getting from them. I'm an asexual lesbian, I don't want that.

As someone who's only recently come out to a handful of people in my life, I've realized a couple things after the shitshow that was that video. Number one: I'm tired of being seen as a sexual being by men. Period. Number two: what I crave more than anything right now is community. I don't have a lot of asexual friends—or even queer friends in general—in my life yet, and I'd really like to change that sooner rather than later.

Finally, number three—and maybe this sounds like an oxymoron if you don't know anything about being asexual—I am so fucking tired of being single. I've been single my entire life, all twenty-seven years, and I've never come close to dating, let alone *kissing*, which means I'm starting late and have no idea what I'm doing. So if anyone has any suggestions for me, please help a girl out. Otherwise, I'm *this* close to making another thirst trap—tailored entirely to the sapphic community and as appropriate as I can make it without getting fired—and dating the internet.

That's all for my update. Goodbye.

I nearly let out a scream when the video ends. What in the world was I *thinking*? I'm already in hot water with Erika, and I know firsthand how fast things can escalate on the internet. I'm sure Marcela will let me know exactly how much I've fucked up the next time I see her. But as the first comments start to flood in, the adrenaline rushing through my veins seems to slow, and something like calm washes over me.

> @Alisha: I'm also 27 and haven't dated anyone! I have no idea if I'm asexual tho, how did you realize you were?

> @LetilsTrying: Dating as an ace person is HARD. Lmk when you figure it out, I need all the help I can get too.

More comments echo the same, and I'm more relieved than I probably should be. None of us have it figured out. *I'm not alone.*

> @Priya: I'm curious how you would go about dating the entire internet lol

> @Connor: You're 27, look like that, and have never dated? Something has to be wrong with you

That spike of fear is back even as anger rushes to the forefront, the tips of my fingers itching to type something nasty back to the latest commenter. I stop myself, though, because as untactfully as he might've put it, he's not wrong.

It's hard to say why I've been holding myself back for so long. Maybe part of it was coming from a homophobic family, even if my parents ended up changing their minds on that issue. But the biggest reason was that for so long, I wasn't sure what I wanted from a relationship. There was always this part of me that saw sex as an inevitability in romantic relationships. Even though I've always wanted romance in my life, I was never sure if sex with another person was something I wanted—or something I *could* want.

Realizing I was on the ace spectrum put a lot of things in perspective for me, even if I still have more questions than answers about certain aspects of myself. It was the final key to unlocking something vital about my identity, who I am on an intrinsic level. After so many years of fighting this feeling I didn't have a name for inside of me, of questioning myself the same way other people who claimed to care about me did, of not belonging anywhere…I had an answer.

It took me a long time to get here, but I'm ready for more than I've allowed myself to have up to this point, and I'm not letting anyone stop me this time.

"How do you feel about online dating?"

"Mija, I'm married." My mom rolls her eyes at me as she packs my dad's suitcase. My father, meanwhile, is pretending to nap on the other side of their king-sized bed. To get out of helping prepare for their San Juan trip, no doubt. "To a man who doesn't know how to pack for himself. Lucky me."

"I mean, if you guys hadn't met at that…dance hall." I'm old enough to know "dance hall" is code for "dive bar," but I let my mom have her version of the story. "Would you have downloaded the apps? Do you think you could meet someone that way and fall in love and get married, and live happily ever after?"

She zips up the suitcase and then turns to me. "Is that how Marcela met her football player? Could be worth a try. You should let Julian help you while he's here. He's always going out on dates."

My cousin doesn't know this, but he's the reason I found comfort in the idea of coming out to my parents. Though deeply Catholic and previously known for the occasional homophobic comment, they didn't bat an eye when Julian brought another man as a date to our tía's birthday party two years ago. But the same couldn't be said for everyone, including Julian's father.

An ache formed in my chest when my dad stood up to Tío Manuel, partly for Julian but selfishly for myself too. It was strange, the feeling that had come over me, because I hadn't fully realized my identity then. I only knew that I was different, even if I couldn't put my finger on how yet. For so long, I let myself believe that being the queer daughter to two Mexican parents in Texas would lead to nothing but endless fighting, heartache, and inevitable separation. They'd lose me and always ask themselves where they went wrong. I'd lose them and always wonder if I made the right choice in cutting contact.

Luckily, it never came to that. When I eventually did sit them down for the conversation two months ago, they made it clear in no uncertain terms that they would accept me no matter what, but they couldn't hide their relief when I told them I wasn't ready for the rest of the family to know yet. They also couldn't hide the fear reflected in their eyes when they thought

I wasn't looking. Those wordless glances between them said enough.

They loved me. They accepted me. But they'd never stop worrying about me, and I'd just given them a new reason to.

"No, she didn't," I tell my mom. "And Julian's only been out on a few dates, as far as I know."

"So, I'm your last resort for advice." My mom smirks. "Is it easier for women to meet other women online to date?"

"I have no idea." I shake my head. "Maybe dating is a hopeless endeavor once you've reached a certain age without any experience. Plus, everyone is disillusioned with dating apps these days. Makes the whole prospect seem bleak."

"Angela, you can't give up." My mom's stern face brings me back to the time I stole one of her box hair dyes during my middle school emo phase. Really, anytime she looks at me like that makes me feel like a teenager all over again. Ah, the perks of still living at home. "You haven't even tried yet."

"But—"

My father interrupts the moment with a yawn and stretches his arms over his head. Maybe that nap was more real than pretend after all.

"What'd I forget to pack this time?" my dad asks, rolling over to face us.

"Towels, underwear, your medication, toiletries—" Sensing she could go on, my dad waves her off.

"If this is what I'm missing out on in marriage, I think I'm okay with that."

My mom laughs and shakes her head at me, but a look passes between my parents that gives me pause. *Uh-oh.* I know this look.

"We just worry about you being alone here while we're gone, that's all," my mom says, but I can tell it's not the whole truth.

"You're not leaving for another couple days. And Julian will be here, too, so I won't be alone."

It was my dad's idea to let my cousin stay here for his final semester of college. The teaching semester doesn't leave room for many part-time gigs (not that that stopped Julian from trying), which meant he couldn't renew his student housing lease. That left Julian with two options: his parents' house or mine.

"No one asked you to flee, by the way. If you're so worried about me being lonely, why are you leaving for three months?"

I already know the answer—both versions, actually. My mom's is that she hasn't seen her side of the family in ages and she's overdue for an extended stay. My dad's is that he's giving me and Julian "space" to do our own thing without the house getting too crowded. But the real reason is that he doesn't want to answer to his brother if Tío Manuel figures out where Julian's staying.

My family has never dealt with conflict well. Avoidance is a trait my father and I have always shared, not that it's served either of us well over the years.

"We just wish you'd go out more. Go on some dates, meet someone special," my mom says. "Even join a dating app if you have to. We don't want you to be lonely."

"Have some fun while we're gone," my dad adds. "You and Julian look after each other. Don't hole up in your room like you have been all winter."

I bite my tongue before I blurt out that the only reason I've been isolating lately is because of the shame and humiliation that comes with reaching viral fame from the toxic half of the internet. That, and the last historical romance series I binged was so good, the only time I left my room for an entire month was for work.

But maybe I still haven't kicked that avoidance trait like I thought. The last time I spoke to the internet, I said I was sick of being single. An entire week has passed and my views have since surpassed the accidental thirst trap, but have I done anything about it?

No. Not unless you count talking to my mom about online dating. Because despite how tired I am of being alone, am I ready for all the ways my life will change once I find someone? Or worse—what if I put myself out there, then find out I'm a terrible dater and fail to find someone I click with? What if it happens over and over again?

"When was the last time you saw Marcela outside of work?" my mom asks. "You should go out, get some fresh air. You never know, you might even meet someone."

My phone beeps before I can reply, and when I glance down at it, my blood freezes. It's a notification from a group chat that hasn't been active since my cousin Briana's birthday a few months ago. *Oh no.* I'm praying that the video isn't the reason my cousins have revived the chat, but a quick scroll tells me otherwise.

Esme: What do you mean you've never been kissed????? WTF Angela
Esme: *Video attached

Bri: WHAT
Bri: Wait, this is a straight up lie!

Julian: Leave her alone
Julian: This isn't our business

Esme: LOL Julian she posted it on the internet
Esme: It's everyone's business now

I stop reading, heart pounding. Suddenly, I'm back in tenth grade, hiding in the bathroom of my own home out of sheer humiliation, body curled on the cold tile. My dad found me later, and when he asked me what was wrong, I burst into tears. I didn't tell him. I didn't tell anyone about all the ways my cousins bullied me for being different, but when my parents finally caught on, they wrote it off as harmless teasing.

Which is why I lie and say it's Marcela when my mom asks who's texting me. It's just the excuse I need to get out of there and back to my bedroom. As soon as I hop onto my bed, some strange masochistic tendency keeps me scrolling through all the messages, before going back to the top again. I have to reply, but I have no idea what to say. In the end, I throw my phone across the room and scream into a pillow.

I knew oversharing on the internet would have consequences. I can't be the real me without my past catching up to me.

Two

I t's really not that bad."

Marcela is lying through her teeth, and not for the first time this week. When it's clear from my face that I still don't believe her, she heaves a sigh.

"At least it's not as bad as the first video. The chances of Erika pulling you into another meeting are low. She's not one to police our personal social media usage unless she gets a call from a board member." She sips her raspberry mojito with a thoughtful look. Her jeans-clad legs are crossed at the knee, and she's leaning back against a red upholstered chair. "Has anyone you know seen it yet?"

I haven't told her about my cousins. If I'm being honest, I don't really want to. Ever since I made the mistake of telling Esme I'd never been kissed back when we were teenagers, anything to do with my cousins has become my greatest source of shame. I know Marcela would never judge me the way my cousins do, but it's too painful for me to talk about them. If I start crying and Krystal sees from the bar, I'll die of mortification.

"Not that I know of," I lie. "And I hope you're right. I can't take another half hour of facing Erika's disappointment."

"And yet, that didn't stop you from posting an update video."

"It's not a thirst trap!" I pull up the video on my phone and point to myself on the screen. "I'm fully clothed! You see that turtleneck I'm wearing? It hasn't seen the light of day since at least 2017."

"Is this going to be a regular occurrence with you?" she asks, her tone as serious as it was back in Erika's office. "You know I'll support you if it is, but, Angela...you have to be more careful about what you post."

"I know. You're right." I take an invigorating sip from my drink as I mull over an answer. I have no idea if I plan to keep this up. Hell, I hardly know why I started in the first place. "Would it be so bad if I did keep posting?"

"No," she says, despite the concern shining in her eyes. "Not if it's something you feel like you need to do."

It's a relief to hear her say that, even if I'm not sure I'm going to keep posting. After the first day's outpouring of positive comments, I got anxious the tide was about to turn like it did last time and haven't checked my notifications since. When I tell Marcela as much, she says, "Here, I'll look for you," and holds out her hand for my phone. I let out a sigh of relief once it's out of my hands.

I might still be anxious, but at least I'm not holed up in my bedroom and anxious. My parents were thrilled to see me dressed up at eight p.m. on a Saturday, but I felt like an imposter in skinny jeans and a lace blouse that gives the appearance of more cleavage than I actually have. Before I came out, all it took was a little lean over the counter, a smile for the male bartender, and I wouldn't have to open my wallet all night. It's something I've worn a thousand times, and I've never thought to question it until two months ago when I came out to myself. I don't feel like that person anymore, but I'm still trying to figure out who I am now. What does the right wardrobe for *figuring it out* look like?

I soaked up my parents' compliments the same way I always do and watched as they exchanged conspiratorial glances when I told them I was meeting Marcela, no doubt thinking their little "talk" was the cause of my going out for the first time in a while. Little do they know what the internet has gotten me into.

"Bless you." I finish off my drink and rise from my seat. "I'm getting another. You good with yours?"

She glances at her drink, which is still three-quarters of the way full, then back up at me with a knowing look. "No need to use me as an excuse to talk to Krystal," she says with a wink.

I roll my shoulders and give her my best oblivious look. "I have no idea what you're talking about."

I turn away from her before she has a chance to get another quip in, moving through bodies on my way to the bar. Backlit by a row of red lighting, Krystal spins a bottle of whiskey behind her back before depositing the liquid into four shot glasses lined up on the countertop. Her dark brown hair is tied back with a red bandana, but a riot of curls cascade down one shoulder. When she looks up, her eyes meet mine immediately.

Her mouth forms a crooked grin, and if I hadn't seen her

smile that same way at a hundred other bar patrons, I'd swear it was just for me. Still, I doubt I'm imagining the way her gorgeous brown eyes light up when they lock on me. At least I can say I have that over the regular bar patrons.

"Look what the cat dragged in." She comes around from behind the bar and wraps an arm around my shoulders in a cordial side hug. I've never really considered myself tall, but my five foot five inches is practically giant to her five foot zero inches. Her head is directly under my nose, giving me perfect access to the smell of her coconut shampoo. "I haven't seen you in a couple months. I was getting worried."

Not for the first time, I'm grateful for the dim lighting that hides my pink face.

"Oh, you know. I've been…busy." I look away from her, willing my nervous heart to stay still in its cage. *Busy reading romance books and worrying my parents over my lack of social activity.* No need to let her know how uncool I really am. "Work is busy, grad school is busy. You know how it is."

"Sure," she says. "But you're not too busy for TikTok."

"What?" My head snaps up. "You saw that?" I'm so shocked, I don't even know which "that" I'm referring to. Which would be a worse video to come across Krystal's For You page, my accidental dabbling into thirst-trap territory or my spur-of-the-moment confessional where I detail not only how sick I am of being single, but also that I have zero romantic experience whatsoever?

"Sure did. It's a bummer you had to delete the first video. You looked *hot*." Her grin is teasing. "You're full of surprises aren't you, Angel?"

It's easy for the compliment to go right over my head, mostly because I'm still reeling over the fact that my crush of five years knows I've never been kissed. The cheesy nickname helps to soften the recoil, though.

"I'm a little *too* angelic for my liking." I groan into my hands. "How are you always a witness to my most embarrassing moments?"

"There's nothing embarrassing about sharing your experience," she assures me, and a rush of gratitude fills my chest. "Now, getting drunk and telling the bartender how beautiful her face is, on the other hand—"

"Stop!" I shove at her shoulder, and that teasing grin of hers returns in full force. "You're never gonna let me live that down, are you?"

"Not a chance."

"I should've stopped coming here a long time ago," I grumble. Even through the noisy crowd that surrounds us, she hears every word.

"But you won't." She sounds so confident about that. "You just can't get enough of me, can you?"

Thankfully she doesn't give me a chance to try and sputter out a response. She walks behind the bar and gets started on my usual. *It's her job to know what her regulars order*, I remind myself. That's the only reason she has mine memorized. She knows Marcela's order too.

"Malibu sunset." She hands me a glass once she's finished pouring. "I'll update your tab."

"Thanks." I take a sip from my drink, hiding my disappointment that our conversation is over so soon. A line formed behind me as we chatted, and now she has to get to them. I take one last glance as she dashes to grab the Tito's bottle off the shelf before turning to leave.

"Took you long enough," Marcela says, handing my phone back as I return to our table. "How's your girl?"

"She's not my girl." I shake my head at her, then let out a groan as I recall our conversation. "And she saw the video. *Both* videos."

"You're kidding." Marcela cringes in solidarity. "That's rough."

"Did you see if she commented or followed or anything?"

"I didn't see her name. I did see that Alice commented with the emoji that goes like—" She mimes her head exploding.

"I miss Alice." I take another sip. "I don't have anyone to hang out with on a regular basis anymore now that you're all booed up."

"I'm sorry, Angela." She reaches for my arm and squeezes. "I'll ditch Theo next weekend. We can get lunch or something."

"No, no." I wave her off, and the immediate objection that follows. "Don't ditch him. I'm just feeling extra sad and lonely lately. You know it's bad when I'm turning to the *internet* for companionship."

"You do seem to have a love-hate relationship with Tik-Tok. At least this time there were more positive comments than negative ones," she says. "There has to be someone else we can befriend."

"Maybe." It's not a bad idea, but making new friends as an adult is almost as hard as dating. The other library assistants are so much older than us, and the three aides we have are all in college. I'm almost tempted to ask Erika to hang out outside of work, but I can only imagine how awkward drinking with my boss would be, no matter how much I like her.

One dramatic sigh later, I go for another sip only to find my glass empty. I give Marcela a knowing look, waggling my brows at her. She lets out an exasperated sigh only someone who's known me for a decade could make.

"Again, Angela? Really?"

"You're right, okay? I'm obsessed," I tell her as I get up from my seat. "Obsessed and unashamed!" I call over my shoulder. She casts me an amused look and shakes her head.

"Back again." Krystal is less busy this time around, no signs of the earlier crowd as she wipes the counter with a rag. She nods at the empty glass in my hand as I approach the bar. "That was fast."

"I hope you don't think differently of me after that video," I blurt, probably because I've become something of a lightweight in my old age. I can't handle my alcohol the way I could a few years ago. "I didn't expect that many people to see it. It was just supposed to be a one-off thing after deleting the accidental thirst-trap video, you know?"

"You brought up the idea of dating the internet as a one-off?" She raises a brow at me.

"It's just talk. As if dating the entire sapphic internet is plausible." I let out a huff. "I didn't actually mean any of it."

"Are you sure?" she asks as she pours grenadine into a fresh glass. "I thought it was brave of you to put yourself out there like that."

"Really?"

She nods as she slides a new drink across the counter. I take a careful sip, ignoring her burning gaze until I can't take it anymore. "Brave in a good way?"

"I never took you for high-strung." Krystal laughs at whatever offended expression is on my face. "You're kinda cute when you're stressed."

"I'm not high-strung. It's much worse than that," I say gravely. "It's TikToker's remorse."

"Come on, Angela. The way I see it, you put yourself out there for a reason." She rests her chin in her hand and levels a thoughtful look at me. "What were you hoping to get out of it?"

I consider her question for a moment. What *was* I hoping to get out of posting that video? I already knew I wasn't the only person my age lacking in romantic experience. I've found plenty of videos online of other people like me sharing their experience—or rather, their *inexperience*. Videos I've bookmarked, saved, and even commented on a handful of times.

"I think I've been hiding." This is a fourth drink kind of revelation, and yet I haven't even started my third. I thought I knew what would happen if everyone knew the truth. They'd treat me the way my cousins did, with disbelief and cruel jokes and disdain. Pressure me into doing something about it until I gave in, the way I almost did my senior year of high school.

When I have my first kiss, I want it to be on my own terms. I want it to be what *I* want, not what anyone else wants. I've been holding on to some of these firsts for so long because I wasn't sure what I wanted. Others I held on to just to spite my cousins and ended up spiting myself instead. Holding myself back from opportunities I've always dreamed of experiencing.

"You know, a couple months back, I saw this other girl on TikTok who had never been kissed," Krystal starts, pushing a stray curl behind her shoulder. I almost miss what she's saying because I'm too distracted, daydreaming about doing just that. Of reaching out, curling my fingers around her hair, pushing it back from her face. "She was so busy focusing on other stuff up until she turned twenty-four and realized she'd been putting her love life on the back burner. So, she had a couple guys apply to be her first kiss and picked the best candidate."

"Apply?" I ask. "What, like a *job*?"

"With a Google Form." She smirks. "It worked for her. I think she may have even asked for references."

"That's so unromantic," I scoff. "There's nothing special about a Google Form. It's so...*clinical*."

"I think it's kinda sweet." I let out another scoff, and she laughs this time. "People put too much pressure on themselves when it comes to this stuff. She got her first kiss the way she wanted. There's something commendable about that."

"That may be true, but 'sweet' is not the word I'd use. I don't want to put my first kiss on a checklist. That's the last way I would ever imagine being kissed for the first time."

"You may have a point there." She laughs. "Plus, you'd probably want it to be with someone you know rather than a stranger."

I'm about to agree, but then I think about it. "Actually, I don't think that part bothers me as much."

"Really?" She looks at me curiously.

"If they're not a stranger, chances are they're a friend and that comes with its own set of problems. If I meet someone at a bar, they're still a stranger before I decide to go on a date with them. But dating apps?" I shudder from the mere thought.

"That's a resounding no, huh?" Krystal crosses her arms over her chest. "What's so bad about them?"

"It's like the girl with the Google Form. At the end of the day, you're just choosing between the least offensive matches."

"I never thought about it that way. But if you're on them long enough, they can turn you into a cynic. Believe me."

"I'm not a cynic, and I've never used a dating app. But I'm not gonna start now just because I'm desperate to be kissed for the first time."

As soon as the words are out, I know they're a mistake. Krystal's mouth quirks up, eyes glittering. Heat crawls up my cheeks, my entire face, truth be told, the longer she looks at me like that, but I refuse to back down.

"Yeah, I said it. I'm *desperate to be kissed*. So what?" I try to shrug nonchalantly, and if my shoulders weren't so stiff, it would've worked. "You would be, too, if you'd gone twenty-seven years without having the ever-living shit kissed out of you."

"I didn't say a thing, but it was low-hanging fruit, anyway." She chuckles. "So, no dating apps and no Google Forms. Got it. What would you have done instead if you were her?"

I tap my nails on the glass, thinking. When an idea pops into my head, an excited gasp leaves my lips. Krystal leans toward me, intrigued. "I'd turn it into a scavenger hunt."

Her brows scrunch together. "Explain."

"A scavenger hunt where each clue would be centered around aspects of my personality. The last would lead directly to me, and it'd be something like..." I purse my lips, thinking. "Find me in a house painted blue, where the smell of aging paper envelops you and books line every wall."

"Cheever's," she guesses right away.

I fight the smile threatening to take up my entire face. "Maybe that one was too easy."

"So the first person to solve all the clues wins...you?" Her smirk turns sly.

"That's the general idea." I nod. "Or at the very least, the honor of becoming my first kiss. Ideally, whoever wins would be someone I'm most compatible with. If we have the same interests, they're bound to solve the clues quicker. If the kiss is any good, we could start dating?"

"Is that a question?" She grins so I know she's teasing. "That's...not a bad idea."

A noise that sounds suspiciously like a huff leaves my lips. "And here I thought you'd be impressed. I just came up with this on the spot, you know."

"I am." Her smirk is nothing short of amused. "You are very impressive."

Her tone is dry, but that doesn't stop me from taking it as the compliment it is.

"Totally better than a Google Form, right?"

"You got me there." She laughs. "But how would you get people to participate? Would you use your newfound viral fame?"

Before I can answer, a group behind me waves for her attention. She tells me to hold that thought as she pours them drinks. It didn't occur to me that my having gone viral—twice—could ever be useful, but I might have enough engagement to pull something like that off.

"Sorry about that," she says as she returns. "Where'd we leave off?"

The ways to spread the word are endless. My video could be a stepping stone to something bigger. If I filmed the entire process, made it into a series, would people keep watching?

"Angela?"

I snap my head up, but I'm still only half present. "Sorry. I was just…thinking."

She stares at me for a moment, expression unreadable.

"What?"

"Nothing." She shakes her head. "So, a scavenger hunt, huh? You should do it. If anyone could pull that kind of thing off, it's you."

"I don't know." But even as I say the words, a buzz of excitement zings through my veins. I can't remember the last time I was this excited about something, much less the possibility of dating. "Maybe."

It's certainly a possibility to consider, which is more than I had yesterday.

"I thought I lost you." I'm snapped out of my thoughts by a hand on my shoulder. When I turn around, Marcela's face comes into view. "It's getting late. Are you ready to head out?"

I nod at her, downing my last drink of the night. "Let's go."

We wave goodbye to Krystal after catching her eye. She returns the gesture, that same Cheshire cat grin pinned perfectly in place, aimed directly at me. I aim mine back at her, because two can play this game.

Three

HOW I REALIZED I'M AN ASEXUAL LESBIAN

Replying to @Alisha's comment
I'm also 27 and haven't dated anyone! I have no idea if
I'm asexual tho. How did you realize you were?

@ANGELA CLOSED CAPTIONS: On some level, growing up, I always knew I was different from my straight friends and family members. Yeah, I found some guys cute, but I never wanted to kiss or date any of them. When it came to girls, there was a lot of mental gymnastics going on in my mind to "explain away the gay," so to speak. It didn't occur to me until I was older that it maybe wasn't straight to imagine romantic dates or holding hands with other girls.

As far as being ace, I've found it really hard to explain my identity without falling into TMI territory, so bear with me. I once heard someone say that sex for aces happens almost exclusively in our heads, and it's like a lightbulb went off. Then I read a passage in *Loveless* by Alice Oseman that echoed the same thought. For me, what that means is I've never been actively turned on by another person, even someone I've had a crush on, or had sexual fantasies that include *me* in them. But I have had fantasies and I do have a sex drive; it's just not activated by a desire to have sex with a specific person, if that makes sense.

So when you put together my history of romantic attraction to women and femme presenting people with my lack of sexual attraction, you get something like me: an asexual lesbian.

The first week of February, my parents leave for San Juan. Julian arrives the week after.

I almost don't recognize him when I answer the door. His black hair is a bit overlong and curls against the collar of his T-shirt and a thick layer of scruff covers his cheeks. The bags under his eyes and dirty sweats tell me he's been through it. I tilt my head before letting him through the door, not used to him looking anything other than clean-shaven and put together.

"Is that a hot Cheeto stain?"

He cracks a grin as he swats my hand away from the red patch on his shoulder. "Nice to see you again, too, cousin."

"No prima? What happened to your Duolingo streak?" I

ruffle his hair as he passes by me with a duffel bag. "And while we're at it, when's the last time you got a haircut?"

"That stupid green owl needed to die. If that means I'm a no sabo kid till I die, then so be it. And I'm a broke college student. You think I have money for haircuts?"

"Is that what this new look of yours is? Broke college kid couture?" When he avoids my gaze, something nags at me. "Are you doing okay, Julian?"

I meant it when I called him my favorite cousin, though maybe that's not saying much. He's the only one who never made fun of me when Briana and Esme found out I'd never been kissed. While they cackled behind their hands as they told the rest of our family, Julian was the one who found me crying in the guest bathroom. To comfort me, he confessed that he'd never been kissed either. Though it hadn't meant much coming from a preteen, it was still nice to hear.

Maybe that's why it's hard for me to see him as anything other than that thirteen-year-old kid. It kills me that he felt the need to strike out on his own when his father refused to accept his identity. Lots of kids his age work through college, but I hate to think that he cut himself off from accepting help from anyone else in the family because of what his father said.

"Of course I am." He finally looks at me, but I'm not sure I believe him. Less so when he diverts the conversation away from him. "I mean, I'm not TikTok famous or anything, but I'm getting by all right."

"Julian—"

"How many followers are you at now?" he goes on before I can answer. "Just promise me you won't forget the little people in your life once you're rich and famous and too good for us common folk. You'll need us around if you want to stay humble."

"You're hilarious." I shake my head at him. "Where's the rest of your stuff?"

"Storage." He shrugs, a maddening gesture that has me reaching for my phone. "I'll get it later. Who are you calling?"

"Reinforcements," I answer. "My best friend is dating a former Dallas Cowboy, so that ought to do it."

"You're *friends* with an NFL player?" His eyes bug out at me before he shakes his head with a bone-weary sigh. "We've already lost you to the fame monster, I fear."

Marcela and Theo arrive twenty minutes later. With all our combined strength (but mostly Theo's), it doesn't take long to empty Julian's storage unit and set all his belongings into the guest bedroom across the hall from mine.

"Moving sure takes a lot out of you," Julian says once he's all settled in, limbs sprawled on the living room couch in a dramatic show of exhaustion for someone who left most of the grunt work to the athlete in the group. Not that Theo complained once. In fact, he even offered to rearrange Julian's guest room so the bed wasn't blocking the desk.

"Glad to see you're already making yourself right at home." I smile dryly at him.

"Thanks again for letting me stay here," he says, sincere for the first time since showing up. "I managed to find a part-time job that doesn't conflict with my school hours. You'll hardly know I'm here."

I'm struck by a sudden wave of disappointment. It's been months since we've gotten to hang out. I'd assumed we'd have more time to catch up while living together.

We don't want you to be lonely.

I shake my mom's voice out of my head. Whatever. I have my own life too. I have a new semester of school and work, though since all my classes are online I'm usually able to kill two birds with one stone by completing assignments during downtime. But I have friends I see every day—well, one friend, and Marcela has meetings that occupy most of her days. And now that she's with Theo, I try not to ask her to hang out as much as I used to. As it is, I feel bad calling her for an emergency two weeks in a row.

"What about weekends?" I ask Julian. "I hope you gave yourself a break somewhere in your schedule. I burned out to a crisp and ended up switching fields after graduation, and that was without an extra job on top of student teaching."

Plus, I don't like the thought of being in the house by myself all the time. Maybe my parents are right to worry about how their trip will affect me. I'm desperate for human interaction, and I'm not even alone yet.

"I have Sundays and every other Saturday off. Though I imagine most of that time will be occupied grading and lesson planning. I can't believe I willingly signed myself up for this stress." He laughs good-naturedly.

"Kinda sucks that we'll hardly see each other," I say glumly. "We should find some time to catch up."

"Definitely." He grins slyly. "The only two queer cousins in this family need to stick together."

I couldn't agree more.

"But speaking of cousins…" His tone turns hesitant, and I know exactly what's coming next. "Did you leave the chat?"

Marcela and Theo bound down the stairs before I can

reply. My best friend always knows when to save me, even if she doesn't actually know she's doing it. Theo's steps slow as he makes his way toward us, eventually stopping right in front of Julian. He looks sheepish as he rubs a hand on the back of his neck. "So, I sort of accidentally broke your dresser."

"It's a piece of crap." Julian waves him off. "Don't worry about it."

"Are you sure?" he asks. "I can buy you a new one. The thing just came apart as soon as I set it down—"

"Seriously, you don't have to worry about it," Julian says with a laugh. "It's from Walmart, and it's been with me since my first move. I was due for a new one anyway."

"Well, let me at least give you my number in case you change your mind." I watch them exchange numbers in awe. Theo and Julian don't have enough in common to be friends, but I thought the same of Theo and me once.

"I hear you're student teaching at Jefferson. I'm a football coach there," Theo says, and there it is. The start of the most unexpected friendship I've ever borne witness to. "If you have fourth or sixth period off, we can get lunch together sometime."

"I have fourth off," Julian replies, eyes lighting up. "I'd love that."

Marcela and I exchange glances as the guys trade phones to input their information into, and then again when Theo enters the garage and comes back with my dad's toolbox and a look of determination.

"Your boyfriend destroys someone else's property and makes a new best friend," I tell Marcela as they head upstairs. "Should we be taking notes?"

"Probably. Especially since Theo's school is getting a new assistant librarian, and I heard she's our age."

"Really?" I rub my chin in thought.

She nods. "I already sent her an email and followed her on Instagram. That's not creepy, is it?"

"A little try-hard, maybe." Her face morphs into panic. "But if we're lucky, she'll be as desperate for new friends as we are."

"If it wasn't for your little inconvenient crush, we could bring Krystal into the fold. I've almost invited her to brunch three times."

"What? *When*?" I ask. "Have you been going to the bar without me?"

"No." She shrinks beneath my accusing gaze. "We just message back and forth on Instagram."

The gasp I let loose is rife with betrayal.

"It's nothing! We just reply to each other's stories every once in a while."

"You follow each other?" My voice is so quiet, I barely hear it myself. "*And* DM each other?"

"I mean…"

"Where else do you follow each other, huh?" I cross my arms over my chest. "Do you send each other funny videos on TikTok too?"

"Angela, why are you so upset?"

A bone-deep sigh sinks my shoulders. From the outside, my life doesn't look any different, but *I'm* different. I'm out. I'm not living the lie I once was for so long. But am I any closer to the life I want for myself? Is my mom right—should I be trying harder to find someone so I don't end up alone?

"My mom is right. I'm going to be alone forever."

"No, you're not." She takes a seat next to me as I plop onto the couch. "Why the hell would she say that to you?"

"She didn't. Not in those exact words, anyway. Maybe it's all in my head, but sometimes it just feels like my parents are pushing me into something I'm not ready for." Though maybe it feels more like something I'll never have than anything else. It's been twenty-seven years and nada, after all.

"So what if you're not ready for what your parents want?" Marcela says. "In all the time I've known you, you've never done something unless it's what you wanted to do."

I shouldn't be surprised that's how she sees me. I haven't shown her, or anyone for that matter, the truth, have I?

"That's not exactly true," I say. "I waited twenty-seven years before coming out, Marcela. Maybe part of it was not knowing what identity fit me perfectly, but that doesn't mean I haven't been lying to everyone, including myself, for *years*."

"Oh," Marcela says, looking surprised. "You never told me you felt that way."

"Yeah, well. It was hard enough admitting as much to myself, let alone my best friend. You're the one person who's supposed to know me best, but how can you when for so long *I* didn't even know who I am?" I pull in a shaky breath. "I've wasted so much time pretending to be someone I'm not. The amount of catching up I have to do feels insurmountable sometimes."

"Angela, no one knows better than I do about wasted time," she reminds me. "Does ten years pining over a complete douchebag ring a bell?"

"Right." I return her smirk. "I guess we do have that in common, huh?"

"When it comes to experiencing romance, sex, or even your first real relationship, there isn't a right or wrong timeline to follow. It's okay to take your time until you figure out what you want."

"I've taken more than enough time, Marcela. I've had literally *nothing* but time, and you know what? I'm over it. I'm ready for the next step."

"What's the next step, then? What do you want?"

If anyone could pull that kind of thing off, it's you.

I can't get Krystal's voice out of my head, or the idea I pulled out of thin air after two and a half drinks. She's right about one thing. There's a reason I put myself out there, and I think it's because I'm finally ready to *do* something. I want to be kissed. I want to experience all the romance I've carefully curtailed for years. I'm ready for *something*.

"I want…" I trail off, knowing Marcela is hanging on every word. That she'll help me in any way she can, and I plan on cashing out the first chance she'll allow. My smile must be as devilish as my thoughts, because her sympathetic expression is steadily ebbing to one of exasperated weariness. "To finally get some firsts out of the way."

A plan not unlike the one I described to Krystal is forming in the back of my brain. *A scavenger hunt, and the final clue leads directly to me.* Five clues and five locations in total. A whole city to work with. But where to start?

I've gone twenty-seven long years without a trace of romance in my life. If I'm going to be getting all the firsts out of the way, they're going out with a bang.

"I'm gonna do it." I jump off the couch. "I'm gonna *do it!*"

"Wait, what?" I can hear the confusion in Marcela's voice as I run up the stairs. She reaches my room by the time I've opened my laptop. "Angela, what's going on?"

"One second." It's only after I've finished typing that I can finally put my idea into words. "Okay, done! I'm not simply going to get my first kiss out of the way. There's no romance in that. I'm going to make them *earn* it."

She looks at me sideways. "Come again?"

"The person I share my first kiss with will first have to prove themself worthy of my hand in a series of trials."

"I'm sorry, when did we travel back into medieval times?" Marcela teases. "Trials? *Worthy of your hand*? Who are you, a runaway princess in a fantasy novel?"

"No, not a fantasy novel. They're all running away from weddings and arranged marriages in favor of independence." I smile smugly. "I'm a wallflower, but I'm tired of sitting in the corner of every ball year after year. I want to be courted. I want *suitors*. A whole flock of them."

"Wallflower." She puts her hands on her hips, a flabbergasted expression firmly in place. "You really think that's an accurate depiction?"

"You haven't read a single historical romance I've lent you, have you?"

"Excuse me if dukes don't quite do it for me," she huffs, sitting at the end of my bed. "But go on. What scheme have you come up with, exactly?"

"Not a scheme. A scavenger hunt." I turn my computer around so she can see the screen. "The first clue will be found at the bar in the form of a riddle that leads to a second location, where the next clue can be found. The third location will have another clue, and so on and so forth until the first person to reach the final location—where I'll be waiting—wins my first kiss."

I don't need to tell her which bar. Havana Bar has been our regular haunt for years. And Krystal is the one who helped me come up with the idea in the first place. Maybe she'd be willing to help me pull off the first clue.

"Take a risk at the tallest point in the city," Marcela reads from the Word doc I've been typing my ideas in. "The tallest point being, what? Tower of the Americas?"

"Bingo," I say. "From there, they'll spot the next clue in the form of my favorite art piece. Last time I was there, it took my breath away." I scroll through my phone for the photo and then hand her my phone. "The picture doesn't do it justice. We have to go back in person."

The day my parents left, I also needed to leave. Just the house, at least. The walls were too empty, the halls too silent. So I drove downtown to do some sightseeing.

At the highest point of the tower are the city's most breath-taking views. Some would argue it's more beautiful at night, when the city is aglow with lights from other buildings downtown. I went during the day, which proved to be almost as monotonous as people say. There was nothing to see but concrete roofs and tall metal buildings, low-hanging gray clouds and no sun in sight whatsoever. Until I spotted a flash of purple graffiti on the side of a concrete building.

The mural was of a woman with a torn chest, holding out her own heart in raised palms. The offering in her hands was a slash of color—purple and black, more bruise than organ. Despite the wound in her chest bleeding white, she was smiling, almost wickedly. There was a knowing gleam in her painted eyes, as if she were all too aware of the power of what she held in her hands. As if she was daring the unknown person before her to take it.

"Wow." Marcela tilts her head at the image. "That's…Okay, yeah, I'm not even gonna try to understand what this painting means."

I let out a laugh, unsurprised. "It's okay. I'm probably interpreting it in a way that would make the artist cringe anyway."

I take my phone back from her. I stare down at it again, flooded with a feeling I'm not sure how to name. "This is probably going to sound weird, but I feel like I can see myself in this woman."

"The woman who tore out her own heart?" Marcela's face twists with incomprehension.

"That's not the way I see it. She's raging into love the way soldiers rage into war. Love is an act of bravery to this woman. It doesn't make her weak or vulnerable. It makes her powerful. She's offering up her heart like it's a challenge to be conquered."

Marcela nods in understanding, even as her gaze turns wary. "She's you."

"She's me," I say. "And it's not something I imagine many people will understand. To the people who do, they'll dig deeper and discover the artist is local and showcases her work during First Friday. I haven't figured out what comes next yet."

"It looks like you're really set on this wild-goose chase," Marcela says. "You couldn't just join dating apps like the rest of us?"

"Not a chance."

"Are you sure this won't have the opposite effect and put too much pressure on your shoulders instead? First times are awkward. Take it from the girl who accidentally shoved her tongue down her first boyfriend's throat in an attempt to impress him with her nonexistent kissing skills."

"You were also a teenager and didn't know any better."

"I was eighteen!"

"Nevertheless, I've wasted too much time to have all my firsts be *that* awkward." I shudder. "How about we put it to a vote? Let's see what my new followers have to say about this."

"I can't believe I know an influencer now." There's equal parts rancor and pride in her tone. But it only lasts for a moment before she says, "I know you joked about dating the internet, but are you sure you want to invite social media into this?"

I've made a few more videos since going viral, but they haven't been nearly as successful as the update video I put out after deleting the accidental thirst trap. I wasn't surprised. I never thought that I'd suddenly get a massive following and every video I did afterward would get the same numbers. However, I am gaining an audience. In the past month, I already have almost seven thousand followers.

"I get that you're searching for community," Marcela goes on. "I really liked the last video you put out, about figuring out your identity. I just don't want to see you get hurt."

"I'd hardly call myself an influencer." Though I'll admit, the prospect does sound exciting. "But I want to do this. I *need* to do this."

Marcela heaves a long-suffering sigh. "There's no chance I can talk you out of it, is there?"

"Not at all," I say, pointing the camera at us. "Besides, what's the point of searching for love if there isn't any flare to it?"

CAPTION:
SCAVENGER HUNT: YAY OR NAY?

@ANGELA CLOSED CAPTIONS: I know I joked a couple weeks back about dating the internet, but I have an idea that just might be bonkers enough to work…if there's anyone watching who'd be interested in being my first kiss, that is.

I explain the idea in much the same way I did to Krystal last week and Marcela now. I'm not sure what I'm expecting to happen once the video is posted. Definitely not to go viral again, but after two hours I have twice the normal amount of engagement.

Notifications flood my lock screen like a dam has broken. I'm stunned by all the attention, but far more pleased than anxious. Even so, I can't help the niggle of anxiety that makes goose bumps erupt across my skin. Marcela's nervous glances don't help either.

@LetIlsTrying: This sounds incredible! Dying to join!

@Kylie: I love the scavenger hunt idea! What city is this happening in? How do we sign up?

@Priya: Wow, you really were serious about dating the
internet. Hyped to see how this all turns out!

"Looks like I win," I say, scrolling through the comments
with a ridiculously wide smile on my face. The same rush I felt
when I first came up with this idea hits me again.

But there's also a pang of regret weighing on my chest.
Here I am at almost twenty-eight years old, and it's taken me
this long for the shame I've harbored for years to finally begin
to abate. I needed this normalized a decade ago, when I was
made to feel embarrassed for my inexperience. When I made
the choice to hide behind facades instead of embrace who I
really am, unapologetically.

And then, inevitably, I scroll down to a rude comment.

"What's wrong?" Marcela asks. When I don't answer, she
grabs the phone from my hands. "'Who makes it to her age
without being kissed? Don't fall for it, she's lying for attention,'"
she reads aloud. Then she scoffs. "How do you delete comments
on here?"

"Don't delete it," I say. "Five new ones will pop up in its
place, anyway."

"People online truly are the scum of the earth, aren't they?"
She hands me my phone. "So, you're really going through with
this?"

I nod, excitement and something else building in my chest
again. Determination. "I'm gonna do it. Now I need to start
planning."

Four

CAPTION:

**CONSIDER THIS MY OFFICIAL APPLICATION TO BE
YOUR INTERNET GIRLFRIEND**

VIDEO DESCRIPTION:
A slideshow of five of Angela's best pictures with text
overlaid at the top of the screen.

POV:
You're the girl who's trying to date the internet because
you've been single for so long you have no idea where to
start and dating apps are the place where romance goes to
die so your solution is to plan an elaborate scavenger hunt
to finally experience your first kiss.

DM EXCHANGE:

@LetiIsTrying: It's painful how much I relate to your
videos sometimes. Dating in the real world is AWFUL.
Really hope your scavenger hunt idea works.

@LetiIsTrying: Really loved your last post btw. Respectfully, I nearly spat out my coffee when those photos hit my fyp. Girl, you are HOT!!! 🔥 🔥 🔥 🔥

@Angela: Thank you!!! You're too sweet 🫶

@Angela: And when I get messages like these, I'm never sure if I should apologize or feel relieved I'm not alone. I'm here if you ever need to talk.

@LetiIsTrying: My one "relationship" barely counted as a relationship, and that was five years ago. I'm sick of being single, but I'm not like you. I struggle when it comes to putting myself out there.

@Angela: It's the worst, especially when you feel like you're falling behind everyone else. And you don't seem to be struggling when it comes to gaming content. Your nose scrunches up in the cutest way when the green serpent thing kills you in your *Stardew Valley* playthroughs. Someone in the gaming community could be crushing on you already.

@LetiIsTrying: Couldn't agree more, being the last single sibling is the worst. And gaming is different, especially the guys I'm interacting with on that side of things. You don't want to know how many creepy gamer dudes I've had to block on here. How my biromantic ass is still attracted to men, I will never know.

@Angela: Oof, why must men ruin everything? If worse comes to worst, maybe we should just go out with each other 😆

@LetilsTrying: If it'll get my parents to stop asking when I'm going to find someone, I'm in.

@Angela: Who knew dating was this easy?

It takes me a couple of days to work out the finer details. Once I finally do, I film an update post and save it to my drafts folder. If this idea is going to work, I'll need to enlist help from people at each location. And who better to enlist in my schemes than my favorite bartender?

An afternoon glow sets Havana Bar on fire. The six o'clock sunset casts orange light through the windows. The bar is abandoned at this hour and will likely continue to be until night falls. When I walk in, Krystal sets down her rag and looks up at me from behind the counter.

"Look who's come in to day drink." Her mouth curls into a half-smile. She leans forward on the bar, crossing her arms in front of her to support her weight. "Miss me already?"

She raises a brow, intrigued. For a moment, I'm struck again by how pretty she is. I've been coming here for years, so you'd think I'd know this by now, but somehow it catches me by surprise every time.

Dark brown curls fall over one shoulder, the lighting setting her hair ablaze. I've had plenty of daydreams where I sink my fingers into the soft tendrils, tugging behind the nape of her neck until we're eye to eye. Once I bend my head until our faces nearly touch, I inspect every line, from the black wings lining her wide brown eyes to the perfectly contoured brows I'd trace with my thumbs if I weren't worried about ruining her makeup.

Kissing is purely a romantic endeavor, at least in my mind. Eyes flick to mouths, the room around us stills, and only when we can't take it any longer do we lean in and touch lips. The daydream could go on for hours, but it never goes past that. *Just kissing.* Not that any of it matters, since I've never come close to kissing anyone I've crushed on. The probability of Krystal and me kissing for real is about 0.2%, and the probability of me kissing someone *in general* is about 0.0%.

"If I say yes, would you be willing to do me a favor?"

"For you?" Her eyes look me up and down in a way that warms me from the inside out. "Anything."

Okay, maybe it's more like 0.5%.

"Do you remember what we talked about last time I was here?"

She rests her cheek in a raised hand, elbows propped on the counter. "Of course." She nods sagely. "I remember any time my customers tell me about their love lives."

"Nonexistent, you mean."

"But not for long, if your newest post has anything to say about it." *Shit.* I forgot that there was a possibility my videos would come up on her For You page. Her grin is nothing short of shit-eating.

"How do you keep finding those?"

"I follow you." She shrugs at whatever shock must be written on my face. "It's the only way I can keep up with your shenanigans."

'When she turns to put away the cleaning supplies, I pull out my phone. I've gotten an influx of new followers this past week, so searching for her name isn't pulling any results. And then, just as I'm about to give up, I come across a profile that makes me pause. At first glance, the picture is innocuous enough. Boring black paint on a boring white wall, until I click the circle for a closer look.

That's what I thought. The bar's name is cut off, but I can just make out the painted *H* at the edge of the circle. There are no posts on the account or bio information, nothing that would clue me in aside from a single name at the top of the screen. *Bingo.*

"HavanaGirl1015."

She turns around, eyes sparkling at the use of her username. "Wow. You're good at this scavenger hunt stuff already."

Are her cheeks pink, or is the sunlight filtering through the window making her glow like that? Her smile spreads.

"It's too bad you're not competing…Which brings me to the favor," I say, getting us back on track. "As you already know, I've decided to go through with the scavenger hunt."

She nods. "Sounds cool. Come to thank me for the idea?"

"If I remember correctly, *I'm* the one who came up with the idea," I remind her. "You just told me I should do it."

"True, but I'm curious." She leans over the bar. "Which part comes first, the scavenger hunt or dating the sapphic internet? Or is the scavenger hunt just a means for you to date the sapphic internet?"

"Oh, I'm already way ahead of you," I say as another message from Leti lights up my lock screen.

@LetiIsTrying: Too soon to tell my family about you?

Oops, just did, they're dying to meet you 😉

"I always knew you were a player, Angel," Krystal teases after glancing down at the screen. Then she looks back up at me and puts a hand to her chest. "And here I thought I was the only woman you flirted with."

"If it makes you feel any better, you'll always be my first." I smirk at her. "Besides, it's all harmless. She's not even the first person I've messaged like this today."

"I hate to think how many virtual hearts you plan on breaking once this is all over," she says, sighing wistfully. "Are you messaging any San Antonio locals?"

"I don't think so, no."

She lets out a breath and if I didn't know any better, I'd say she was...relieved? "Not that we've really talked about where we live, but if I'm getting serious about the scavenger hunt, I probably should start searching for—"

"Potential suitors?" Krystal's brows furrow. "Suitoresses? What's the femme equivalent of a suitor?"

"Beats me." I shrug. "Anyway, I thought it might be a good idea to start the scavenger hunt off here at the bar."

"Okay." She nods. "I can talk to my boss about hosting the event. She'll probably be on board if it brings in more customers."

"Thank you. Would you mind giving me your number so I

can send you the details later?" I hand her my phone. She takes it, fingers tapping on the screen, and all I can think is, *We're exchanging phone numbers.*

"You want to stay for a drink?" she asks as she hands my phone back. "It's on me."

This isn't the first time she's offered me free drinks, just as this isn't the first time I refuse her ("Oh, no, I couldn't possibly—") and she refuses to be refused ("I'm already pouring, here, just take it"). The bar is still dead, giving us a rare moment of undisrupted time to talk.

"So, what made you decide to be an influencer?" Her brown eyes twinkle with amusement. "I want the longest version possible." She walks around from behind the bar and pulls me toward one of the upholstered couches. "Tell me *everything.*"

"It's not like I planned for any of this to happen," I divulge. "All of this started with an accidental thirst trap. I just wanted to set the record straight and get some things off my chest. I never expected anyone to actually be listening."

"Well, you can always come to me, you know," she offers. "If you ever need to talk or vent to someone who understands. Don't be a stranger."

"Thanks, Krystal. I appreciate that."

I can't remember the last time I was this excited about the prospect of dating. Maybe I never have been. Just in the past couple weeks I've gained an influx of new followers, experimented with my style to the praise of online strangers, and casually flirted with people through DMs.

Putting the pictures up on my last post was no small feat, not when all my old pictures show a woman who no longer feels like me. Reinventing my style and raiding my father's closet for the sole purpose of a TikTok post might seem rash, but even before I took those photos I knew I was on to something much bigger. It was a subtle change to slick my hair back in a low ponytail to show off my cheekbones, skip my usual makeup routine for a simple tinted sunscreen and lip balm, and finish off the look with a pair of bootcut jeans, sneakers, and a plain black T-shirt. It's a similar look to what I'm wearing now, only with my hair down.

Sipping on my drink, I tell Krystal about the clues and locations I have planned out so far. When patrons begin to trickle in, Krystal returns behind the bar. I join her at a corner stool, staring covertly at her when she's busy and not-so-covertly when she returns.

"I think what you're doing is really cool," Krystal says when the crowd dies down a little. "Is there anything else I can do? I can help you secure the second location if you want."

"Really?" I glance over at her. "You'd do that?"

"Sure." She shrugs easily. "This sounds fun. I want to be part of it any way I can."

"Of course. Yeah, I'd love your help."

"You think you'll find your soulmate at the end of this?" she asks, her tone teasing.

"*Ugh.*" The sound bursts out of me with a force I can't contain. "No, probably not. I couldn't possibly be that lucky to get it right on the first try."

"Then you're going through an awful lot of trouble for... what, exactly?" Her brows crease as she leans over the bar, her crossed arms pushing her ample cleavage up. It's like an extreme sport, pretending I don't notice. "Someone you'll date for a while?"

"I'm not stressing it," I say as her eyes grow wider. "I'll be satisfied just to lose my K-card."

She drops her head onto my shoulder with a groan that sinks its way into my chest. I freeze, breathless from the way her curls whisper against the edge of my cheek. The contact only lasts a second, but I still can't manage to catch my breath. "You *can't* call it that. Take that back right now."

"Is it really that bad?"

"Just awful." And yet, she can't stop smiling. "Why don't you think you'll find your soulmate?"

"Bold of you to assume I believe in the concept."

She pins me with a knowing look. "Says the woman planning to lose her 'K-card' in the most elaborate way possible."

"Fair point." I roll my eyes. "I'm not opposed, exactly. That'd be the best-case scenario, right?"

"It's a good story," she says. "One you can tell your kids."

My parents would love that. First a partner, then marriage, then kids. But I haven't done anything relationship-wise…ever. How do I know I'm ready for that type of commitment?

"That kind of life…" I shake my head. "It feels worlds away from where I'm at right now."

There's an expression on her face I can't make out. Then she says, so quiet I barely hear her, "I know the feeling." Before I can ask what she means, she continues. "What do you want to get from it, then?"

"You mean besides losing my—" A warning look stops me in my tracks. I roll my lips inward until they're no longer visible.

"Besides your first kiss," she says. "Is that all you want? Nothing else?"

"What else is there?"

"Someone you connect with," she says. "Someone you could love, if you're interested in finding that kind of thing."

"There are people who aren't?" The question is light, but from the way Krystal's shoulders tense and she averts her gaze, I get the feeling I've hit a nerve. "Are *you* not?"

"This isn't about me," she deflects.

But maybe it should be, because now it's all I can think about.

When my parents, along with the rest of my extended family, found out I'd never been kissed, I got a lot of pitying looks. I was only sixteen, but that didn't stop them from overwhelming me with heteronormative clichés every time they saw me.

Once you stop looking for it, love will sneak up on you.

The longer you wait, the greater it will be when you finally meet the right guy.

He'll be worth the wait.

I never looked for love. Never even tried. Maybe somewhere in the back of my mind, I was hoping everything they said was true. That I'd meet someone amazing in an organic way, and they'd enter my life when I least expected it. Maybe I'm still hoping for that, for this scavenger hunt to be a vehicle to lead *the one* directly to me without having to do any of the work.

But it *is* work. This entire week planning has been nothing but work, and I'm nowhere near done.

"Maybe it's just me, but I sort of feel this pressure to find the right person off the bat," I admit. "Because I've waited so long, you know? It's like…what was the point of holding off all this time if the first person I date is awful?"

She bites her bottom lip, and for a moment I'm fascinated by the view until her teeth pull away from her lip. I glance up at her eyes, but I'm not sure what I find there. If it's that same understanding, or something deeper.

"Right," she finally replies.

"It feels a bit superstitious, searching for love myself. I keep being told love will come when I least expect it. All my life, people have actually said that."

"It's bullshit," she says. "There's not some greater power at work here. Just misogyny. Women aren't allowed to have agency, remember?"

Her grin comes full force.

"That makes a lot of sense, actually." I let out a laugh. "Thanks. I needed to hear that."

"Welcome." She takes my empty glass and deposits it into the sink. "Besides, how can you expect to find love if you're not searching for it? That's a dumb thing to say to single people."

"*Exactly.*" I throw up my arms. "And it's not as if I'm expecting to find love right away. I want to dive headfirst into the dating pool. Have all the fun I've apparently missed out on all this time before settling down with someone."

"Not a bad plan."

She smirks as she places a glass of water in front of me.

"Thank you." The air grows tense the longer we stare at each other. I want to say something more, but nothing comes to mind that holds the weight of the gratitude I feel for her in this moment. Not just her willingness to jump into this with me, but also understanding why I need to do it.

Her gaze pins me in place. "You're welcome, Angel."

I try to say something, even just her name, but my tongue feels like sandpaper. I clear my throat and take another sip of my water. Tip my head in a nod when I don't trust myself to speak.

"You get more and more interesting every time we meet." Her smile is so dazzling, I nearly topple over in my seat. "There's no way I'm missing out on this. I can't wait to see how your scavenger hunt turns out."

Five

When I walk downstairs to the kitchen on Friday night, Julian is sitting at the table with his laptop and two stacks of worksheets.

"How was school?" I ask him. "Did you see Theo?"

"Good," he answers without looking up from the screen. "And yeah, we got lunch off campus. He hit the truck parked next to me with the passenger door."

"It's nice that you're making friends with people who continue to accidentally damage your property. Most people would steer clear at least, file a restraining order at worst. That's very magnanimous of you."

"Lucky for him, my car and everything else I own is a piece of shit. Besides, the school has a new position opening next year. Schmoozing with the staff isn't a bad idea in my book."

"So you're using my best friend's boyfriend for your own gain." I tsk. "I knew you had an ulterior motive all along."

"Speaking of questionable motives…" He shuts his laptop before staring at me head-on. "We need to talk about the group chat thing."

"That's not even a good segue," I scoff.

"Well you'd know, being the queen of avoidance and everything." His piercing look tells me I won't be getting out of the conversation this time. "You ghosted the chat for a week, and then you just…left. You had to know they'd react badly to that."

"I don't really care how they react." I cross my arms over my chest. "I'm not giving them the power to hurt me over something that has nothing to do with them. Not anymore."

"You never told them how much their teasing hurt you," he pointed out. "You should talk to them. Clear the air."

It wasn't just teasing to me. They made me dread school and family barbecues. I grew cautious of every interaction with them, waiting for the other shoe to drop and for them to make me feel like shit again. That's how it's always been with them, until the summer after high school graduation when I got so sick of them that I lied and said I finally kissed someone just to get them off my back.

The lie was a spectacular one too. I told them about Will Mora, a cute boy in my first period who I caught staring at me every day (truth), how I asked him out after catching him looking at me for the umpteenth time on the last day of school (truth), how magical our first date was (the magical description was a lie, but the date was unfortunately true), that it turned into a summer fling (a more blatant lie that I'm not proud of) where I lost my virginity on the shaggy carpet of his bedroom floor because his bed was too squeaky and we didn't want to wake his parents (the biggest lie I've ever told to date, inspired by a conversation I overheard in the girl's restroom).

I meant to kiss Will for real, just to get the first kiss thing out of the way, but after an hour-long date spent looking at the time on my phone more than his face, I couldn't force myself to go through with it. His lips were mere inches from mine when I brushed him off, said I saw him more as a friend—even though that much was generous; I didn't see him as anything at all.

But that wasn't even the worst part. It was Esme's squeals of joy, the way Briana's arms wrapped around me in a bone-crushing hug, and their shared excitement over my having *finally* experienced this so-called important milestone. Guilt churned in my belly as they asked to see a picture of Will and I was finally invited into their inner circle. Later on, Briana even told me she was jealous I "lost" my virginity before her.

I hated myself for the story the more their excitement grew. As soon as they started treating me like a friend, I knew I couldn't take it back. It was the first time they were actually nice to me since the whole first kiss debacle, the first time they saw me as someone they could relate to, and it was based on a lie.

Since they've seen my videos, Briana and Esme must now know I lied to them. Or worse, that I made it up for attention. I'm almost tempted to ask Julian to show me the chat, but I know reading their messages won't make me feel any better. It's easier to let it go, to not know what they're saying about me, and to ignore them for the rest of eternity. Or however long they'll let me, anyway.

Six

**APPLICATION TO BE YOUR INTERNET GIRLFRIEND
PART 2**

@ANGELA CLOSED CAPTIONS: If you were to come across my profile on a dating app, it would probably read something like this: Hi, I'm Angela. I'm a twenty-seven-year-old asexual lesbian who's never been kissed, let alone been in a serious relationship of any kind. My interests include obsessing over obscure art pieces graffitied on the sides of downtown buildings, reading YA fantasy and historical romance books, and spending way too much time on the internet.

I'm looking for someone kind, smart, and funny, who's not afraid of a little adventure. Dream dates include going to coffee shops and ordering coffee and dessert flights so we can share a little of everything, touring museums to interpret the art pieces in the most wildly and completely inaccurate ways that will surely make the original artists cringe if they heard us, and spending an entire day browsing every bookstore in the city.

If I sound like your kind of girl, let me know!

COMMENTS:

@LetIlsTrying: You already know you're my kind of girl (;

@Nikki: Your dream dates are my dream dates too!

@Alisha: Rooting for you to find someone great! Gives me hope that there's a chance for me too (:

In an effort to avoid talking the group chat situation to death, a few hours after posting my last video I stuff my current read into my bag, grab my keys, and then I'm out the door with hardly a goodbye to Julian. I don't make any promises to talk to Briana and Esme, but I do tell him I'll think about it. So here I am at a sports bar, reading yet another historical romance, thinking about it despite trying desperately to put the situation out of my mind.

Extravert though I may be, this isn't the first time I've brought a book to a bar. Unlike Havana Bar, the place has TVs on every corner displaying sports games I don't care about and an outdoor seating area on its second floor. I didn't bother changing from my sweatshirt and leggings, but I'm not out of place here. Everyone's in jeans and casual wear.

Two chapters later, a waitress appears to deposit sweet potato fries and a Malibu sunrise in front of me. I should be at peace. I'm reading a great book with my favorite drink in hand and an eight-dollar basket of fries that's worth every penny for the dip it comes with alone. But I'm not, and it has everything to do with Briana's last text.

> I'm confused by your video, and why you left the group chat. What happened to that summer fling you told me and Esme about the summer before college? Or all the free drinks and numbers you get when we've gone out with you? This doesn't make sense to me...Just tell us what's going on? We're...

The message cuts off from there, and I'm too chickenshit to read the rest without replying back or leaving her on read and risking another text from her. After my colossal lie, the three of us formed a surface-level closeness. We used to hang out a couple weekends a month, never talking about anything too personal or serious. Certainly not anything that mattered, for fear that they would stomp all over my vulnerability a second time.

Not once have I ever considered coming clean about the lie or coming out as an ace lesbian to them. They're not homophobic like their mom and Julian's dad and other older members of our family are. They've always been on Julian's side the way my parents and I have. I have other reasons not to trust them, and it's all to do with our messy high school history.

After polishing off the fries, I check the time on my phone. I've been here for about two hours, but I'm not ready to head back yet. If I'd brought my Kindle, I could continue reading outside until closing. As it is, I'll be lucky to finish the chapter I'm on before the sun fully sets, taking with it my only reading light. I let out a sigh and place the book down, face up, as I clean up my table.

A gust of wind pushes the napkins off my table, and I have to duck under to grab them, lest the staff think I'm a litterer. When I stand back up, my book is missing. *Shit.* How do I notice the trash being blown off my table and not my book?

I'm scanning the ground for any sign of the mass market, my focus fully concentrated on the act that I practically jump out of my skin at a tap on my shoulder.

"Whoa, Angel." Her voice is as familiar as the nickname. "Hey, it's just me."

What is Krystal doing here?

Her hair is down with nothing pushing it back from her face. I think this is the first time I've ever seen her like this. A riot of curls with a mind of their own, the wind making the edges brush my face. Somehow, she's even more beautiful like this—soft tendrils falling past her shoulders, a bright pink hoodie and light-wash jeans that hug her curves. The edges of her mouth curl up until dimples appear on both sides of her cheeks.

"Krystal. Wow. Hey." I'm so scatterbrained from seeing her, I don't notice the book in her hand until she's holding it out for me. "Thank you." I take the proffered mass market, ignoring the way my blood sings when our fingers brush.

"Regency, huh?" She tilts her head at me. "I think my mom has this book."

"Your mom has good taste." I mark my place before hugging the paperback to my chest. "What are you doing here?"

"Hanging out with some coworkers." She points to her table, where a few vaguely familiar faces sit. I never did learn any of their names, only Krystal's. "What about you? Are you with anyone?"

"Umm, no. Just me and my book." I glance up at the darkening sky. "But that's my cue to leave."

"Do you have to go so soon?" she asks, and I try to parse out the request in the simple question. No, I don't, actually. Julian has a late shift tonight, so he won't be home when I get back. Even then, he'll either go straight to sleep or plan out lessons for next week. And besides, if I'm being honest, getting the chance to hang out with Krystal outside of her workplace appeals to me on a level I'd rather not admit to.

I shrug, dripping nonchalance. "I can be persuaded to stay a bit longer."

"With another Malibu sunset, I bet." She laughs. "As long as I don't have to make it, that can be arranged."

"I'd never make you work on your day off."

She smirks. "I'll be right back."

She's not gone long. When she returns, Malibu in one hand, dark liquid in another, we don't join her friends. Instead, she pulls out a chair from my table and then takes the seat beside me.

"How's the planning going?" she asks. "What do you have so far?"

"Pretty good. I'm visiting the Tower of the Americas tomorrow to film some easter egg content for TikTok."

"Sounds exciting." She takes a sip from her drink. "Do you want any company? I don't work until five tomorrow."

"Oh. Sure." My voice sounds casual enough, but inside I'm short-circuiting. "Yeah, that'd be great."

For another few minutes, we chat about what I've planned so far, which admittedly isn't much. We talk through other possibilities before agreeing to meet tomorrow morning. I walk her to her coworkers' table and we wave our goodbyes as I head out.

The entire drive home, my body is buzzing.

I'm going to see Krystal tomorrow.

Seven

DM INBOX:

@Nikki: This is probably a longshot, but if you're ever in the Boston area and want to meet, let me know. I've been watching your videos since the accidental thirst trap debacle, and I resonate with your story so much. Plus, I think we'd make a really great match (;

@Jay: I could've sworn I passed by you in Dallas and it's driving me bonkers not knowing. Any chance you were at the Flagship Half Price? I know we're both readers lol

@LetilsTrying: Just got asked again by my sister when I'm finally going to meet someone. 🙄 Wishing our dating arrangement was real more and more every day.

I step out of the Uber, waving to the driver as he pulls away from the curb. Last night was my first time seeing Krystal outside of Havana Bar, and this is the first time we've made plans to meet up. I'm still not quite over the thrill of seeing her name on my lock screen. The message jolted me awake, this being the first time either of us has texted since exchanging numbers.

Excited to hang out today (:

Five simple words I've been unable to scrub from my brain all morning. Hell, the messages I've gotten on TikTok lately haven't made me smile nearly as hard as Krystal's text did. I thought about sending her a picture of the mural, but it's really something that needs to be witnessed in person. We agreed to meet in the lobby of the Tower of the Americas. There's a giddy anticipation building within me with every step forward.

Inside, she's leaning against a pillar, hair swept back in a high ponytail, wearing ripped jeans and a black tank top that shows off the floral tattoo sleeve on her right arm. Roses and a mix of other flowers on a leafy vine snake their way down her upper arm and stop at her elbow.

A navy flannel is tied at her waist. There was a slight chill in the air this morning, but now that it's noon the temperature has kicked up to blazing. The middle of February in Texas is more like a spotty, delayed winter until the sun comes out of hiding. If we came at night, I can imagine myself bundling her in that flannel, pulling it nice and tight around her body to keep her warm from the cold.

Gold hoops dangle from her ears, sparkling beneath the sun coming through the large windows behind her. As usual, the sight of her knocks the breath from my lungs, but this is different. This is the first time I've seen her in daylight, and I'm noticing things about her I hadn't before. The tiny freckle dotting the edge of her mouth, the purple shimmer lining her lower lash line, how smooth-looking her light brown skin is.

"There you are!" She rushes forward when she spots me, throwing her arms around me in a hug I don't expect, and I encounter yet another thing I never noticed about her: the fruity scent of her perfume. "Come on, I already got our tickets."

She pulls me forward, her grip on my wrist gentle but firm. All I can do is follow in her wake. I finally learn how to speak again when we reach the elevators. "I can pay you back for my ticket."

"Not necessary." Her grin is a brilliant red today. When she leans forward to press the button to go up, the edge of her ponytail touches my nose. I get a whiff of her shampoo this time. The coconut scent is familiar and I inhale on instinct before I realize what I'm doing and force myself to take a giant step back from her.

"It's totally necessary," I insist. "You're the one helping me, remember? I have to do something to repay you."

"Okay." The elevator dings its arrival, and she pulls me into the carriage. "You can buy me lunch. Does that make us even?"

"Definitely." I nod. "I can do lunch."

The metal carriage lurches upward, and just like the last time I was here, I have to resist a yelp. It doesn't help that we're surrounded by clear glass on three sides. I shut my eyes tight against the view outside growing smaller and smaller.

"Are you okay?"

I jump. Krystal's voice is right in my ear, her body crowding my space. The few times I've had crushes in the past, I dealt with them by avoidance and secretly admiring from afar. The same way I was content to deal with Krystal, until she offered to help with the scavenger hunt.

Crushes are inconvenient for me. There's no reason for me to be this nervous around Krystal when she's helping me find someone else to have my first kiss with. There's no reason for her mere presence to make my stomach swoop and bottom out when the view outside can do that just fine by itself. I'm messaging multiple women on TikTok, for Christ's sake. I should be over this crush I have on her by now, shouldn't I?

She rests a hand on my shoulder, concern lighting her warm brown eyes. I allow myself to take in a deep breath to ground myself, blowing it out through my nose.

"Sorry." I shake my head once I'm recentered. "I sort of hate heights."

Her lips twitch like she's trying to hide a smile. "And that made you think Tower of the Americas would be a good second location?"

"It's more of a stepping stone to the main event."

Her brows crease. "What do you mean?"

The smooth elevator doors slide open. I rush out of the carriage, Krystal on my heels. "Just as beauty is in the eye of the beholder, great art is in the eye of the interpreter. Find what moves you."

"What?"

"That's the second clue I'm workshopping." I glance back at her. "Let's see if you can solve it."

Her eyes glint with the challenge.

"You're on."

With a determined gait, she steps onto the balcony. Outside, a burst of cold wind blows my hair back. It's only warm with the sun out, but under the shade it's chilly. Krystal's gaze lands on the crossed arms over my chest and the goose bumps on my skin, and before I know it, she's untying the flannel from around her waist and offering it to me.

"But then you'll be cold," I tell her as she places the garment around my shoulders. Before she can offer to help my arms through the sleeves, I take a step back from her and do that myself. Her flannel is loose and oversized on me, but that just makes it cozier.

"Don't worry about me, Angel. I have a clue to find. That'll keep me occupied from the cold."

The difficulty with this clue is that art is subjective. To find the answer and get to the third clue, the participants would really have to find what moves *me*. I've given away the biggest clue in my last video, but there's a possibility that only those who've watched it and remember what I said will be able to catch on. Krystal's ability to solve the clue will give me a better idea of how it's likely to land in the scavenger hunt.

I spot the mural immediately, but Krystal's back is turned to it. Her eyes trace the windows, her hand resting on a metal scope. "I don't know where I'm supposed to be looking."

She turns around, and I catch the moment she spots it. A flash of recognition that rounds her eyes, jaw falling open slightly before she forces it closed with the click of her teeth.

My feelings exactly.

I can't explain what I felt when I first came across the mural, only that it hit me in the chest with the force of a ten-ton punch. *Moved, indeed.*

But just as soon as she spots it, her eyes slide past the graffiti up to the sky. "Find what moves you." The words are barely audible, but her lips move over them a second time, like a mantra. I try not to let the disappointment that blooms in my chest get to me. *It's right in front of you*, I want to tell her. *I thought you felt what I felt.* But I bite my lip to keep from giving her any more clues than the vague one she already has.

She places her eyes against the scope, moving it around until she spots something in the distance. I can't tell where she has it pointed to, but she lets out an "Aha!" like she's solved the entire thing.

She waves her arm for me to look, and when I place my eyes against the scope, still warm from her skin, I'm not sure what I'm looking at until the words on the sign come into view. It's an advertisement for First Friday, the art walk that takes place downtown every first Friday of the month.

She looks at me expectantly when I turn back to her. "Close."

"*Close?*" she guffaws. "Where else can you find art that moves you? Forget a museum, First Friday is *the* place to walk around and make inaccurate interpretations to your heart's content."

"You're still watching my videos."

"It's research."

Still, I can't help but delight in the way her cheeks turn pink.

"I have to see you the same way your followers do."

"Okay." I take a step closer to her. "What do you see, then?"

Her brown eyes track me curiously, rising to meet my gaze when I take up more of the space between us.

"Someone different than the woman I met five years ago."

I place my hands in the pockets of my baggy shorts. Technically, they're my dad's from the '90s. I've been raiding his closet a lot since my parents have been gone. I know better than to believe the clothes alone can do the work for me, but is that all she sees? The outward differences in the me I am now versus the me she met years ago?

"You've always been sure of yourself. Confident. But I don't think you've ever let anyone see you vulnerable until recently. Not unless you had a few too many shots in you, that is."

The facade I once created as a cover against my cousins' attacks, the one I carried with me all through college and after when I flirted with men for attention and free drinks just to end up ghosting them, has been effectively shattered with one singular video I posted to the internet on a whim. In all that time, I've only ever been honest with myself around Krystal. She was always impossible to shake, even when I didn't have a name for the way I felt about her yet.

"You bring that night up a lot, you know." I lean against the railing to avoid her gaze, but she follows in my wake. "I think it's time you return the favor. Tell me how beautiful you think *my* face is. We'll go back to the bar if you need some liquid courage first."

"I'll do you one better," Krystal says, smirking slightly. "I think you're beautiful, Angel. Inside and out, but more so when you're not afraid to be your truest self. When you're not afraid to put yourself out there. To be vulnerable in front of the entire world."

There's a lump in my throat I'm unable to dislodge for one long, charged moment. I have to glance away from her to recover, to shake off the effect her words have on me, because despite what she just said, I'm still a little afraid to be *that* vulnerable in front of her.

"I think I also mentioned a love of obscure art graffitied on the side of downtown buildings in my last video," I say. "Maybe the clue was misleading, but you were half right. The next clue is found at First Friday, but the sign isn't what's supposed to lead you there."

"What else would lead you to—" She looks up, her gaze aligning with the mural. Krystal bites down on her lip, staining the tip of her front teeth with her lipstick. "That's it, isn't it?"

The mural is far from the only graffiti, but it is the most intricate form of vandalism within view. From the scopes, lots of art pieces can be seen displayed on the city street, advertising next month's art showing.

Krystal squints at the slashes of purple, and then a soft sigh leaves her lips. She pulls out her phone, thumbs flying as she types.

"Natalia Aguilar. That's the artist, right?"

I nod, staring up at the mural again where her name is legible at the bottom of the woman's skirts in a swoosh of black ink.

"I only discovered her work recently," I say. "Figures she'd close her shop before I had a chance to commission something from her. From what I can tell, she's gone dark on social media. All her accounts are private despite having over two hundred thousand followers across platforms."

"You didn't hear?"

My brows furrow at her.

"She was dogpiled by people online after transitioning to queer art."

"What?" I shake my head. "Wait a second, how do you know all this?"

"I used to follow her years ago," she tells me. "She's locked her accounts on and off over the years. I'm not sure if anything happened recently, but watching everything go down the first time was sickening."

"What happened?" I ask before I think better of it. I'm more than familiar with all the ways people can act like vultures when they're safe and hidden behind a screen. "You know what? I'd rather not dredge up her past for the sake of gossip."

"I think she's talked about what happened in a couple of interviews," Krystal says as I pull out my phone and aim its camera toward the mural. "If you'd rather hear the story in her words, I can send them to you."

"Thanks." I nod. "I appreciate that. Do you mind if I record here?"

"You insufferable influencer," she teases, mouth spreading into a grin. "You're filming in public spaces already? Here." She holds out her hand for my phone. "I'll help you."

"I'll try not to be too obnoxious, but no promises," I say, readying myself when she gives the signal that we're recording.

Then I put on my most charming smile as I stare into the camera. "Welcome back to the scavenger hunt series. You might notice I'm in a different location today, and that's because I'm scouting potential locations and workshopping clues. What do I have ready so far?" I rub my chin in thought. "Not a whole lot. We're still at the beginning stages, but I can say that so far, it looks promising. More soon, until next time."

Krystal hands me back my phone once we're done and glances up at the mural again, looking contemplative.

"Why this mural? Is there a particular reason?"

I'm nowhere close to an art critic, and I can't quite explain what it is about the woman in the painting that speaks to me. If it's me projecting my own emotions onto the mural, or the artist's intent fully realized. Marcela didn't get it. Maybe Krystal won't either. I don't answer her right away, mostly because I don't have a coherent explanation. I'm used to tucking away the parts of myself I think people won't like or understand. If I'm being honest, it's probably why I came out so late in my life.

"What do you see?" I ask instead, tipping my chin up to the woman told in purple slashes of paint.

She turns back to the mural. There isn't much of a reaction on her face. Her throat bobs on a swallow. Lines appear on her forehead as her brows crease, but her mouth is an unmoving straight line.

"It's…intense, that's for sure."

"Yeah. That's one word to describe it." I laugh. "I don't know. Art's supposed to make you feel something, right? Something about it makes me feel…seen, I guess? Does that make sense?"

"How do you mean?"

"It's silly. I'm literally projecting myself onto a piece of graffiti." I shake my head. "I really only came out to a handful of people. My parents and Marcela. Then I made that TikTok update and started acting as if everyone knew. I let go of the front I used to put up. I'm finally the person I was so afraid to be, and I've never felt freer." I tip my chin up to the mural. "I feel like *her*. It feels like I'm holding my own heart in my hand, brandishing it like a weapon."

"A weapon." She glances up at the painting, arching a brow.

"Yeah." I nod. "I'm so used to breaking my own heart before anyone else gets a chance to. To believing there's something wrong with me. That I'll never be enough. That I may as well not even try falling in love if I'm not capable of it. I know better now. I know who I am, and no one can tell me otherwise."

There's something inexplicable shining in her eyes. She reaches for my arm, hand falling at my wrist. Her grip is firm but gentle, warm on my chilled, goose-bumped skin.

"My first thought was it made love seem brutal," she says, staring up at the mural. "I don't see what you see, but I guess that's the cool thing about art. Everyone has a different interpretation."

"I imagine fighting for it can be brutal. For love, I mean." I tilt my head at her. "From what I read on First Friday's website, Natalia Aguilar showcases her work during every First Friday. If I can get the timing right, I'm hoping to put on the scavenger hunt two weeks from now. Natalia's exhibit will be the third location. A lot of her recent work is inspired by queer identity, especially asexual and aromantic identity, which is why it feels important that she's part of the scavenger hunt. If she wants to be, that is."

"I like that idea," Krystal says. "Are you going to reach out to her? Do you know if she's still doing First Friday?"

"She's still listed on their website," I tell her. "But it could be an oversight. Getting in touch with her is a good idea. Maybe she has an email on her website somewhere."

She opens her mouth to reply when I catch a flash of metal from the corner of my eye. I turn around as what looks like scaffolding is elevated beside the building until it's aligned with the mural. I'm not sure what's happening until the man inside turns a nozzle.

"Is he—"

Krystal doesn't need to answer my unfinished question. A spray of water hits the mural, and paint begins to run.

Eight

No. No no no no no—

I rush back to the elevators, Krystal on my heels. I punch the button to go down, and when the doors don't immediately open, I punch down on it again. And again.

"We're not gonna make it in time." The doors slide open, as if to defy me. "What am I gonna do? This the only plan I have." More than that, the mural was the only plan I had my heart set on. So what if it wasn't perfect yet? I still had time to figure it out. Now I have nothing.

"It's okay, we'll figure it out," Krystal says, rubbing circles on my back to calm me. But it has almost the opposite effect, clouding my focus, every nerve ending in my body trained on that one spot where she's touching me.

Now is not the time.

"We can get there faster if we rent the bikes from the BCycle. They had some right outside the lobby."

"Okay, good idea." I haven't ridden in years, but what's that saying about never forgetting how to ride a bike? "Let's go."

The sun is oppressive when we get outside. I take off her flannel, tying it around my waist and promise Krystal to return it to her once we reach the mural. When she comes back with two bikes, we speed off down the street. Or Krystal does at least. I'm having a hard time adjusting my feet on the pedals, heart pounding so hard it's the only sound filling my ears. Once I get a good footing, I'm able to catch up to Krystal just before she turns down a side street. Her head turns over her shoulder, making sure I'm still behind her.

"You good?" she calls out. I'm still farther behind her than I should be.

"Yeah!" I pedal harder, gaining speed. She makes another turn. I try to follow, but it feels like I'm stuck on something.

What the hell?

As I glance down, the front wheel drops onto the street. Before I lose my balance and topple off, I force myself to stop with my left foot on the pavement. As I'm bringing the bike back onto the sidewalk, a car horn blares behind me, startling me out of my wits. I tip over, the bike falling on top of me until I'm nothing but a jumbled heap on the sidewalk.

Fuck.

A shock of pain ignites my shoulder when I hit the ground, and then again as the bike hits my knee. Someone calls my name, but I'm too disoriented to make out the sound. The bike is lifted off me, and then hands untie the flannel at my waist. I open my eyes as Krystal's arms circle my waist as she pulls me off the ground and settles me to a standing position. Behind her, there's a dark ring of water on the side of the building where the mural once was. A trail of purple-tinged water is the only thing left of the painting, droplets running down the brick.

We're too late—not that we would've been able to stop them anyway. Suddenly, this mad dash to the portrait all feels so pointless.

"I shouldn't have given you this stupid thing." She's bent over the bike, and that's when I notice the sleeve of her flannel caught in the front wheel. That's what I got stuck on. "Angela, are you okay?"

Her question snaps reason back into my brain. I stretch my arms above my head and wince. White-hot pain stings my left shoulder. She notices immediately and walks around to inspect the injury. "You're bleeding through your shirt. Goddammit, Angela, you could've gotten yourself killed!"

I flinch from a new pain coming from my leg, knees buckling, but she gentles her tone as if it was because of her. "Where else does it hurt?"

"My knee." I only notice the pain now that I've been standing on it. When I glance down, I spot the blood dripping in rivulets down my leg. "Ow, geez." I hunch forward, leaning a hand against the building next to me to take the weight off it.

"Hey, it's okay." Gently, she pulls me through the alley we just rode through. "Stay here, okay? I'm gonna return your bike and then we'll figure out how to get back."

She uses the flannel to apply pressure to the wound before leaving with one of our bikes.

"We're going to have to share a seat," she explains when she returns. "I'll mostly be standing on the pedals anyway, but we'll have to be careful with the added weight. Try to keep your body perched forward."

"This doesn't sound like a good idea." I blink up at her. It's not hard to imagine a second fall doing me in the way the first one almost did. "Me and bikes don't mix well, if you couldn't tell."

"It'll be a longer walk back, and you can barely stand," she says. "I'll ride slow. I'm not gonna let you get hurt again."

There's a steely determination in her eyes that tells me arguing with her would be useless. With a nod and a heavy sigh, I do as she says, letting her adjust me on the seat into a more comfortable position. Once I'm seated behind her, she swings a leg over and leans back until the edge of her butt hits the seat.

"Put your arms around my waist." After a moment of hesitation, I do as she says. "Tighter." As I wrap my arms tighter around her middle, the warmth of her body seeps into me immediately. The side of my head rests against her back as she propels us forward. Her heartbeat rushes through the ear pressed into her back, steady and sure. A contrast to my erratic heartbeat, though from the fall or her proximity, I can't say.

The ride back is clear and smooth, not a single bump beneath the wheels. I'm not sure how she's doing it, but I know I'm safe with this woman. This once, when no one's watching, I allow myself to breathe in her scent. It's more grounding than dizzying, almost enough for me to forget the aches and pains in my body.

"Almost there," she says. I blink against the black fabric of her tank top. Colored brick speeds past, and then the glass and steel of the Tower of the Americas fills my vision up ahead. We bypass it completely, and when I look up, I see she's taking us straight to the parking garage.

"Did you park here too?" she asks, swinging off the bike

before coming around to help me out of the seat. Her hands grip my sides, head bent down to make sure she's putting me down on the right foot.

I shake my head. "Uber." Downtown parking is a nightmare, but after my crash landing, I'm grateful one of us chose to brave it.

"I live ten minutes from here." Our faces are so close, I'm eye level with the freckle at the corner of her top lip. It takes all the self-control I can muster not to stare. Even then, I don't quite succeed. "I can stop by CVS for a first aid kit and bandage you up before I take you home. Does that work for you?"

"What about lunch? I still owe you—well, now I owe you double for saving me…"

"Hey, don't worry about it." She shakes her head, smiling slightly down at me. It's strained at the corners, not her usual flirtatious grin. "Here." She takes out her key and unlocks her car. "Lie down in the back for now. I need to return the bike and then I'll be back."

She opens the door for me, helping me in with more care than necessary and having none of it when I try to wave her off. In her defense, I do it with a wince of my shoulder. Her hands don't stray far past my waist, but somehow I feel her touch everywhere. I don't realize I've been holding my breath until her touch recedes and she's turning away from me, her form crossing the parking garage until she disappears behind a corner.

She isn't gone for very long. Once she returns, she helps me settle into a comfortable position in the front seat, and then we're off.

Nine

Under different circumstances, I'd already be snooping.

Krystal left me in her living room to grab alcohol wipes from the bathroom when she discovered the first aid kit she bought didn't have any. My eyes roam over everything in sight—the hanging potted plant by the front door, the TV stand with shelves displaying a small collection of books and DVDs. But it's the white stand in the corner that takes up the most space. A record player is placed on top of it, while a vinyl collection is housed on the two shelves beneath it. From the looks of it, there isn't a single inch of free space.

I scoot over the arm of the sofa for a peek at the record still sitting in the player. Selena's *Dreaming of You*. I nod to myself even as I wonder at the rest of her collection. Who are her favorite artists? What songs does she lose herself in when no one else is around?

"I'm back." Krystal waves the bottle of rubbing alcohol in the air. "Let's look at that knee first."

"I was really hoping you wouldn't be able to find any." I let out a groan, already anticipating the stinging pain. I know it'll be ten times worse than the stinging pain I'm already feeling. Now that I'm thinking clearly again, I'm completely mortified. I can't believe I crash-landed in the street and she had to come to my rescue. She probably thinks I'm an idiot. *I am* an idiot. What was I thinking, riding a bike when the last one I rode still had training wheels on it? And to ruin the flannel she let me borrow too.

"Can't you just throw a Band-Aid on me and send me home? I'm ashamed of myself enough as it is."

"No way." She kneels down on the carpet until she's eye level with my scraped knee. "I'm nursing you back to health, and I'm doing this right. I'm the reason you crashed in the first place."

"*Ouch.* Ow ow ow!" Every muscle in my body tenses as she pours a bit from the bottle directly onto my bloodied skin. She didn't even warn me first. After a heavy breath, I say, "Don't blame yourself. I haven't ridden a bike since I was nine. Even then, it was more of a tricycle." I wince again, tensing so hard my shoulder starts aching again.

"My flannel didn't do you any favors either." She meets my eyes. "I'm sorry about that, Angel. You have no idea how sorry I am."

"You have nothing to be sorry for," I tell her, because she hasn't smiled once since that strained one as she helped me into her car. Even then, I'm convinced it was for my benefit. "You were trying to keep me warm."

Once my knee is covered with a large, square bandage, she rises to her feet. "Turn for me."

I lean forward on the couch, turning to give her a better view of my injured shoulder. Gently, her fingers curl beneath my sleeve to carefully extract the fabric from the wound. I wince all over again, this pain somehow worse than the rubbing alcohol.

"It's too low." Her breath warms my skin, the crook of my neck. I shiver from the proximity, at the way the feeling warms my entire body. I haven't felt anything like this before. No, that's a lie. I'm only used to it under the cover of night, as I run through an assortment of fantasies in my mind that I've collected and sorted from various places.

Being asexual doesn't mean I'm repulsed or even averse to the idea of sex. Au contraire. Sex, at least in the abstract, has always been something that interests me, which is part of what made figuring out my identity even harder. It's just that when I fantasize about sex, I never imagine *myself* in that way. The bodies I imagine are usually nameless and faceless. Once, after a weekend binge session of *One Tree Hill*, Sophia Bush made a cameo.

As far as micro labels go, aegosexual has been the best fit for me. For aces with a regular to high sex drive, we're often aroused by sex acts in porn or smut or even just a particular sexual fantasy that looks good in our heads, with little to no desire to actually engage in sex ourselves. It was the first label to explain my relationship to sex, but I hesitate to call it a perfect fit (*Hello, Sophia Bush, what are you doing here?*). But if there's anything I've learned about labels, it's that there's always room for fluidity and change when something no longer fits like it once did.

Only now, with Krystal's warm breath on my skin igniting parts of me only porn, smutty romance books, and Sophia Bush have previously been able to, I've never felt more…fluid.

Even more when she says, "You're gonna have to take this off."

My heart is pounding in my chest, the sound so loud that it takes a second for the request to register that there's nothing sexual in nature about it. Even still, that doesn't stop a flare of heat from warming my cheeks. I want to fan myself, or at the very least wipe away the sweat beading my forehead, but I don't want to call more attention to the irregular temperature my body has taken.

"Is that really necessary?"

"I'm not going to be able to clean it otherwise." Her eyes skate over me carefully. "You could get an infection."

Without thinking too hard about what I'm doing, I pull the hem of my shirt up in one fast motion, only stopping when the part stuck to my shoulder refuses to budge. My vision goes dark as white-hot pain overcomes me, and I let out a loud screech as the fabric begins to slowly and painstakingly unstick from my skin.

"Hey, hey, it's okay. You're okay." Her voice is soothing as her arms circle me, cool fingers carefully extracting the remaining fabric stuck to the wound. "This is gonna hurt. Take in a deep breath for me, Angel."

I do as she says, breathing into the crook of her neck, inhaling her scent the way I've wanted to all day and I can't even enjoy it. She tugs the fabric up with a gentle but firm hand, doing everything in her power to lessen my pain. I grit my teeth until the shirt is peeled from my skin completely, and the only layer covering my torso is a black lace bralette.

I've always been self-conscious of my small breasts, but from the way Krystal's cheeks glow and her eyes look down for a beat longer than necessary, I take it I have nothing to worry about in that department. My stomach does somersaults as her stare lingers. I still can't get my breathing under control, and I can't tell if it's the toll my shallow injuries have taken on me, nerves, or something else entirely.

"Krystal Ramirez, you're no better than my comment section on a good day."

Her eyes snap to mine, face as red as mine is probably.

"I-I'm sorry," she stammers. "I didn't mean to stare. I just—"

"Yeah, I know what you were *just*." My smirk is devilish, and *lord* does it feel good to be the one throwing her off balance for a change. "Aren't you supposed to be taking care of me, not ogling me?"

"God, you're right," she says, tone miserable. "Taking you back here was a mistake. You're still breathing hard. I should've taken you to the emergency room."

"Krystal, I'm *fine*." I grab her arm as she starts to stand. "I was just teasing. I didn't mean to make you feel bad. I don't need the emergency room, and I need the bill even less."

"I'll pay for it."

"I can't let you do that." I shake my head. "As long as I don't need stitches, it's completely unnecessary. At least check out my shoulder first."

"I can do that. Turn around." I do as she says, letting her get a better view of the back of my shoulder. "I have to, um…" Her throat bobs on a swallow. "I have to pull down your bra strap to get to the scrape." I nod as two fingers hook beneath the strap. I bite down on a moan, but not because of any pain. Luckily, the material doesn't seem to be sticking to the wound.

But a new sort of pain is taking its place, more confusing and arousing than it has a right to be under these circumstances. I feel it low in my belly as her hands clean the wound on the back of my shoulder. Something must be terribly wrong with my nervous system, because I hardly feel the sting from the alcohol this time. Instead, I'm focused on the way her hands are moving against my bare skin. The light pressure of her left hand just below the back of my neck, keeping me still. The gentle, yet efficient movements of her other hand as she cleans and bandages the wound.

"You scared me today." There's a tenuous quality to her voice. I try to look at her over my shoulder to gauge her expression, but all I can see is the tip of her nose through a curtain of dark hair over her face. "I don't know what I would've done if you'd gotten hurt worse than this."

"It's not your fault," I tell her. "I was struggling on that bike long before your flannel got stuck in the wheel. So stop blaming yourself, okay?"

She doesn't respond as she finishes.

"Here, let me grab you another shirt," she says, heading down the hallway after inspecting my bloodied shirt. When she returns, she hands me a worn gray T-shirt. "Sorry if it swamps you."

I wave off her apology, not caring if the shirt hangs off me. It's expected for two women with two very different body types. I'm prepubescent, teenage boy skinny. She's mid-sized and curvy in all the best places. Silently, I vow not to ruin this particular article of clothing as she helps me into the T-shirt on my injured side. I try not to shiver at her touch. I don't succeed.

"How's the pain?" she asks once I'm sufficiently dressed. "I have some ibuprofen if you need it."

"I'll manage. You've done too much for me already." I stand up from the couch, carefully stretching out my stiff muscles. "Thanks for taking care of me. This goes far beyond your duties as my favorite bartender, I'm sure."

"Stop." She smiles, flashing white teeth. *She's smiling again.* "We're a lot more than that now." I forget how to breathe until she goes on, her smile falling as her expression shutters. "Angela...you fell off your bike in the middle of the street. I almost thought...Well..." She huffs a breath. Shakes her head and forces a brittle smile. "I'm glad you're all right."

"It's just a couple of scratches and bruises." I try to shrug before remembering my injured shoulder. Instead, it comes off as an awkward wince.

"You were almost hit by a car," she deadpans, her dark eyes catching my movement. "It could've been a lot worse. I'm glad it wasn't." She stares at me for a long moment, until I start squirming again.

"Okay. I'm sorry."

"Don't be sorry. I'm the sorry one, remember? Just don't do it again," she says, almost in a grumble. "You're not allowed to die on me yet. We just started getting to know each other."

"What do you mean *yet*," I counter.

"We all die, Angela," she informs me, like it's news to me or something. "But you're not allowed for another, oh, I don't know, eight decades or something. No more stupid stunts. You don't know how to ride a bike? You don't ride one unless you're covered head to toe in bubble wrap. Got it?"

Knowing she wants me around for at least another eighty years warms me from the inside out.

"I"—*am smiling like an idiot*—"will try not to die next time."

She gives me a look.

"*Fine.*" I let out a long sigh. "No more stupid stunts."

"Good." She gives a satisfied nod. "I'm gonna have to keep an eye on you. I have a feeling you're gonna be a handful."

I scoff good-naturedly, and she bumps her shoulder to my good one. "Come on. Let me get you home in one piece. You little daredevil."

Her eyes sparkle with mischief.

"No more Angel?" I pout, purposefully sticking out my lower lip.

A flash of surprise crosses her face, and then she lets out a light chuckle. Shakes her head. Places her hand on the small of my back as she opens her front door. Her lips hover over my ear, breath warm as she says, "Be good and we'll see."

There's that heat crawling up my skin again, making my heart pound everywhere, including more inconvenient places. What the hell *is* this strange feeling overcoming me, making me want to rush home and sort myself out under the covers?

But more than that, why do I like it so much?

Ten

B e good and we'll see.

Her voice low and husky, her breath warm on my over-heated skin. A hand I half wish was hers trails across my collar-bone. I'm alone in my bedroom, confused as all hell. A finger moves to trail the ear she whispered into, using my nail to graze the soft shell. When a shiver runs through my body, I can almost pretend it's her doing it. It's *her* driving me up the wall.

What the hell? I'm not sleeping anyway. I don't want to think too hard about what this means for my sexuality as I kick off the covers, cool air from the ceiling fan hitting my skin. Or what it means for everything I thought I learned about myself over the past year. If this will only place me a few steps back or straight to the drawing board.

All I know is I don't fight it when I turn over on my stomach and a hand roams my body. Up my stomach, strumming my already hardened nipples. Then back down, nails lightly grazing the hem of my underwear.

Lower.

I'm already wet, but that's not a surprise. For all the time I've known Krystal, pined for her from afar, I'm not sure I've ever been aroused by her. Not until today. It's not that I want to have sex with her, exactly. At least, I don't think I do. That's not the image in my head as my hand roams lower anyway. This feels more like a gray area between sexual arousal and sexual attraction—something new I don't have a name for possibly.

Masturbation is usually enough for me. Have I been curious what someone else's touch on my body would feel like? The sensation of hands and lips and tongues where only my own touch has been? Sure, but purely on a scientific level. My hypothesis: Would sex feel nearly as good as the way it looks in my head?

I have no idea.

Here's what I know so far. It started with her warm breath on my neck, her hands on my body stoking the fire, the scent of her perfume clouding my senses, our thighs pressed together on the sofa. A heady mixture I can't make heads or tails of.

That's it.

That's what's driving up my libido, all those remembered feelings that keep my hand traveling down my body, that has me spreading my legs and dipping two fingers beneath the soft fabric to the ache it's covering. A sigh leaves my lips at the first contact, but I can't come from those memories alone. For that, I have to cycle through the usual fantasies as my fingers work over my clit. But even still, I can't get Krystal's face out of my brain. My thoughts are a confusing jumble I don't understand until a wave of desire crashes over me, again and again. I collapse face-first onto the bed, my thighs shaking through the strongest orgasm I've had in months.

I roll to my side, avoiding my bad shoulder as I nestle back beneath the bedspread. It doesn't take long for me to fall asleep, but I don't have any answers by the time morning comes.

After starting a pot of coffee, I open my laptop at the kitchen table. I'm about to type into Google when I draw a blank. What am I supposed to put into a search engine to find the answers I'm looking for? *I thought I was asexual until my hot bartender breathed on me?* Please.

The sound of approaching footsteps startles me so bad, I close the laptop, revealing Julian's suspicious face.

"What was that?" He arches a brow.

"None of your business." I take a sip from my mug, avoiding his curious gaze. "There's coffee if you want any."

"Thanks." He reaches for a mug from the cupboard. "Did you talk to Briana yet?"

Nope. And I'm not going to. Maybe it's stupid, but I'm avoiding her and that whole situation for as long as possible.

"I know she texted you," he says before I can brush him off. "I don't know what happened between you guys, but you should probably clear it up before it blows out of proportion."

"You mean before *she* blows it out of proportion." I lift a brow and take another sip from my mug.

"You know how she is." He waves me off, but I'm sick of being dismissed. The only reason I lied to her in the first place was because I was tired of being dismissed, harassed, and made out to be a freak just because I didn't want to kiss a guy. "But she's family."

I don't need to tell him blood relation doesn't equal family. Not him, of all people. This is where we've always differed. He's far too forgiving of the situations our family members put him in, and I hold on to even the smallest of grudges until I'm buried with them.

"What did Briana tell you, exactly?" I ask cautiously.

"That you're lying on the internet for attention."

"I'm not lying."

"I know that," Julian says. "They're straight, so they don't get it. You haven't had any experiences that actually mean something to you. When I tried explaining that to them, they accused me of taking your side and then, well, it just got ugly from there."

"What do you mean?"

"Briana's hurt that she found out about your identity through the internet."

I'm taken aback by this information, though judging from Julian's reluctant expression, it has to be true. I kick out a seat and gesture for him to take it. He plops down with a raised brow.

"I lied to Briana and Esme the summer after high school," I confess. "That's why they think what I said on TikTok was a lie."

"What did you lie to them about?"

"Do you remember when they used to make fun of me for having never been kissed? When the three of us were in high school?"

"Sure." He nods. "They were kinda mean about it."

"It went on for two years, and I was sick of it," I tell Julian. "So, I lied about a summer fling to get them off my back. As much as I appreciate you giving me grace while defending me to them, I've never been kissed by *anyone*."

"Oh." He doesn't look at me any differently, which I'm grateful for. Only mildly surprised. "I can't say I blame you. They were pretty ruthless."

"I shouldn't have lied, though." I shake my head. "Hell, I shouldn't have told Esme I'd never been kissed to begin with. I should've just kept it to myself; then I wouldn't be in this situation in the first place."

"Yeah, I learned that lesson from you," he says dryly. When I cast him a look, he explains, "I didn't have mine till last year."

"Twenty-three's not so bad," I tell him. "Twenty-seven, on the other hand…"

"Is also not bad," he says, and relief fills my chest. "No matter what anyone says."

"They wouldn't agree," I reply. "So, Briana's hurt I didn't tell her, huh? Is Esme hurt too?"

"It's a mix of hurt and jealousy, I think," Julian says. "You know Esme's been talking about becoming a beauty influencer for years. She's still bitter her YouTube channel never took off. You should've heard her go off about the views you're getting."

"I'm glad I was spared that, actually." I laugh. "And what did Briana say?"

"She's confused and…angry. Not saying she's justified in feeling that way, just that she is." He shrugs. "She said she thought you guys were close enough that you would tell her something like that personally. That even a text would've been better than hearing it secondhand."

Oh, *she's* angry? What about *me*? What am I supposed to be after what they put me through all of high school?

"I don't owe her a goddamn thing. Either of them." I scoff.

"Even if I thought I did, if I tried to tell them the truth now, do you think they'll really believe me?" He stares at me for a long time, but he doesn't say a thing. "That's what I thought." Another sigh leaves my lips. "I don't know what to do here."

"I get where you're coming from, but I think you still need to try."

He's right. I know he is, but I hate the person I become when I'm around them. Small and invisible and juvenile. Less adult, less than them, period. I swore to myself a long time ago that I'd never be that girl again.

"I will," I tell him, even though I have no plans to. "Promise."

Turns out I'm not done lying yet.

Eleven

DM EXCHANGE:

@LetiIsTrying: Saw your last video, I'm sorry about the mural being washed off. It sounded like it meant a lot to you.

@Angela: Thanks, Leti. I appreciate it.

@LetiIsTrying: Of course. I'm here if you ever need to talk. But speaking of your last post, I did want to mention something...

@Angela: What is it?

@LetiIsTrying: I think we live in the same city.

@LetiIsTrying: It looked like you were filming from the Tower of the Americas. Do you live in San Antonio?

@Angela: No way! You live here too?

@LetiIsTrying: I do!

@LetiIsTrying: And suddenly I'm not so bummed about the prospect of someone else being your first kiss. I'm very competitive, you know.

@Angela: I gathered that from your livestreams. You're very...spirited when things don't go your way 😨

@LetiIsTrying: What can I say? I like to win

@LetiIsTrying: Btw, if the next time I say "Fuck me, Jesus Christ" on a livestream and you comment again with "He can't do that, Leti, he's a man of god" or something equally as quippy, you're going on my shit list

@Angela: Come on, Leti. We both know you love my antics. And when you lay it all out like that, I'm surprised you haven't gotten a TikTok violation yet

@LetiIsTrying: You and me both 😆

@LetiIsTrying: Get ready, Angela. I'm about to make this scavenger hunt my bitch.

⁕

My nights are spent online now more than ever. Except this time, I'm not posting or scrolling through comments. I'm searching for answers.

After hours of scrolling through @TheGreatAcecape's account, I'm more or less confident I'm still ace, which is a relief, but there's an ever-growing possibility that I'm not aegosexual like I once thought. @TheGreatAcecape doesn't use any micro labels publicly, but from their experience (or at least what they've shared online about it), they're the closest match to my own identity.

I just wish I could talk through the confusion of what I've been feeling lately with someone. I've chatted briefly with Leti about her graysexual identity, but the thought of talking to her about *this* doesn't sit well with me. It would mean admitting my feelings for another woman, which is an asshole move even if what we're doing is just harmless, flirty banter.

Then there's the added layer of us living in the same city. I should be more excited at the prospect of meeting one of my "potential suitors"—as Krystal calls them—in person. If anyone's a contender for my heart, it should be her, shouldn't it? Leti, with her sleek black hair, sparkling brown eyes, and dazzling smile. Leti, with her voice like velvet, despite her penchant for cursing out the screen when a playthrough doesn't go her way. Sweet one moment, borderline terrifying the next.

No doubt there's something intriguing about her, and maybe if it wasn't for the Krystal of it all, I would have a clearer head about where we stand. But I don't even have a clear stance on my identity at this given moment, so I'm hopeless either way.

I'm about to click away from @TheGreatAcecape's profile

when my gaze lands at the top of the screen. Where previously there was a checkmark, now there are two arrows indicating that we're following each other.

We're *mutuals*.

When I realized I might be asexual a few months ago, I binged every video on their account. If they liked or commented on any of my previous videos, somehow I missed it. Hell, I don't even know when they started following me back. The message button at the top of their account feels like a beacon. What are the chances they'd reply back to me?

Only one way to find out.

For half an hour, I craft out my casual-yet-thought-out message, switching over to the Notes app lest I accidentally hit send on an unfinished message. Once I'm confident in what I have, I copy and paste it into the message box and hit send.

@Angela: Are we really mutuals on here? I'm not hallucinating? I've been following you for months when I first realized I might be ace. Your account has been instrumental in helping me understand my identity better! I hate to bother you (feel free to tell me to fuck off at any time), but recently I've been going through a crisis of identity. Idk maybe that's a dramatic way to put it, but I'm sort of at a loss after dedicating so much time into finding an identity that fits my experience best, but something happened that's left me...confused. I feel like I just need to talk it out with someone who understands. I don't have any ace friends where I'm living, so any insight you have would be greatly appreciated.

It takes a few hours for them to reply, but I can't help smiling at my inbox when they do. The message they sent back is brief, but it's the opening I've been waiting for.

@TheGreatAcecape: Hi Angela! Love your account. I'm super invested in your scavenger hunt series. I'm open to talk whenever you need to 🖤

I take them at their word. I pour my soul into my next message, explaining about my time spent with Krystal, including my five years of crushing on her from afar. Their reply is fast, asking pertinent questions and helping to narrow down what exactly the issue I'm having is.

@TheGreatAcecape: A question you need to continually ask yourself is this: does this make me want to have sex with her? It can be hard pinning down which attractions you feel for someone, especially if you haven't been hanging out with them for very long. If you're not sure, the answer is likely no. Have you tried imagining it?

Imagining…me and Krystal in a sexual way? Not exactly. I fantasized about *her*, not me *and* her together. Is that where the difference lies? I close my eyes and try to picture it, but the second I include myself in the fantasy, it all falls apart. Another notification makes my phone buzz.

@TheGreatAcecape: What I find helpful for gauging my own attraction level is if I can't imagine myself having sex with someone, let alone fantasize about it for pleasure, then I'm probably not sexually attracted to them.

@Angela: What if I can't imagine myself having sex with her, but I might want to have sex with her anyway? My body physically responded to her touch, which has never happened with anyone before. Could that be sexual attraction?

Their reply takes a few minutes to come in.

@TheGreatAcecape: It could be. Let me ask you another question. If someone else in your life had been the one touching you, would you have had the same response? Would it have made you uncomfortable? Would you have felt anything at all?

I consider the question, even though my immediate reaction is that anyone aside from Krystal would've made me uncomfortable. At least, anyone but...

@Angela: The only other person I'd probably have had the same response to is Sophia Bush 😊 But we all have our exceptions, right?

@TheGreatAcecape: Personally all my exceptions are in theory rather than in practice, but I can see what you mean.

@Angela: Can I ask you one final, TMI question if it's okay with you?

@TheGreatAcecape: Of course, I don't mind oversharing.

@Angela: How did you know you were sex favorable? I feel like I could be, but it's hard to know when I haven't actually done anything. I just don't want to seem stupid whenever the time comes, but I have no idea what to expect or what the experience will be like for me.

@TheGreatAcecape: When I started dating my partner, I thought I might be demisexual because we only started having sex after I felt comfortable with her. I have a high sex drive, but until I met her I felt frustrated by all this pent-up sexual energy and having nowhere to release it. She could breathe on me and I'd jump her immediately. At the same time the most random shit could make me horny, and they weren't always instigated by my partner despite the fact that she was the one I was sleeping with.

It wasn't until a few months into our relationship after I'd gotten all that energy out of my system that I realized I wasn't demi and that I wasn't sexually attracted to her at all like I'd once thought. I can still be sexually stimulated and enjoy sex, if a bit less enthusiastically than I could in the past. It just takes a bit more concentration for me to come. I might not desire sex as often as I once did or be sexually attracted to her, but I do it because sex is important to her and the experience we share together in the moment is equally as important to me.

I know some aces who view it as a chore or as some menial, boring task because they don't have this overwhelming need to jump their partner's bones, but everyone's different, and everyone's enjoyment level of the actual act is different, and not at all dependent on sexual attraction.

I let out a laugh about @TheGreatAcecape wanting to jump their partner after she breathed on them. That's maybe a little too relatable for me. They've given me a lot to think over, despite the final answer I'm still lacking. I suppose I'll have to wait and see how differently I feel the next time I hang out with Krystal.

I send back a message thanking them for all the help. When I settle into bed, I'm still thinking over the possibilities in my head. It's a relief that I'm still ace, but my micro label might be changing. I'm just not sure what the right fit is yet.

Twelve

@Stephanie: Hey, Angela! Not sure if you saw my comment on your last video, but I'm friends with Natalia Aguilar. I was there when she painted the mural you love so much, actually. It's a shame they washed it off; it's one of my favorites of hers too. If you need anything, don't hesitate to reach out! I'm so invested in your scavenger hunt series. Rooting for you from the sidelines!

@Angela: No way! I fell in love with her portfolio after discovering the mural. Do you think she'd be interested in being part of the scavenger hunt? Or at least having her art play a role in any way possible?

@Stephanie: How do you feel about asking her yourself?

Krystal and I make plans to meet on Wednesday during my lunch hour. I spend nearly two hours getting ready, throwing aside articles of clothing until I finally land on a pair of black slacks and a white T-shirt with the library logo above my left breast. After pulling up my hair in a bun, I'm all set.

Marcela laments over her three back-to-back meetings and the fact that we haven't been able to get lunch together for over a week. On the bright side, our lack of socializing at work means I've had some extra time to catch up on class assignments. I'm weeks ahead on coursework without even meaning to be. I faux cry with her but am secretly glad I don't have to explain that I wouldn't be able to get lunch with her anyway because I'm meeting Krystal. Knowing my best friend, she'll press for details and I would have to tell her Krystal is only helping me with the scavenger hunt, and nothing more.

We decide to meet at a taqueria a couple streets down from work. When I arrive, she's already seated inside, head bent over her phone, bright blue nails tapping on the table. When she spots me, she rises from her chair and wraps her arms around me in a hug, careful with my injury.

"How's your shoulder?" is the first thing she asks me as we line up to order.

"Basically fine." I wave her off. "Same for my knee."

"I hope you're not lying so I'll stop worrying." She gives me a stern look before turning to order. "Thanks again for buying me lunch," she says once we're both done. We take seats across from each other at a table by the window. "Even though I'm not sure how much more help I can be. What are you gonna do about the scavenger hunt?"

"I have some options."

As bummed as I am about the mural being washed away, I was far more bummed about disappointing the internet. Or at least, this small community of people I've cultivated on my Tik-Tok page. I didn't give many details in my last update, just that there was an unforeseen setback along with a clip I managed to catch of the mural being power-washed off the building.

"A couple hours after posting the video, I got a DM from someone who recognized the mural and claimed to know the artist personally. We don't have any concrete plans to meet yet, but I'm hopeful we'll figure out something soon."

Krystal looks at me curiously. "What does that mean?"

"I don't want to jinx it. Either way, I'm not giving up yet," I say. "If I have to go back to square one, then that's what I'll do."

"You're awfully determined." Krystal's eyes settle over me in an assessing gaze.

"You said you'd been following Natalia for a couple of years." She raises a brow at my rerouting the conversation, but nods nonetheless. "Have you ever talked to her?"

"Yeah. I bought a piece of hers last year. Well, I tried to anyway," Krystal says. "She's a bit eccentric."

"Wait, you've *met* her? In person?"

"When she was still commissioning work, you could pick up orders at her studio if you lived in town. There was a mix-up with the art piece I commissioned from her. She never got around to finding mine, so she refunded me."

"Oh." I deflate. "That's a bummer."

"It seemed like she was going through something. I didn't take it badly." After a pause, she asks, "My turn to ask you a question?" When I nod, she goes on. "Why now, if you don't mind me asking? Why haven't you dated anyone until now?"

"I'm hardly dating," I grumble, sinking low in my seat. Her expression doesn't change. "I guess it's partly because I didn't know how my parents would react to having a queer daughter until last year. The other part was being too scared to evaluate what it is I really want."

"And now you've done some evaluating?"

"Evaluating, soul-searching." I smirk. "Pish, posh."

"I get that. It took me a long time to realize I was attracted to women, though I'm not sure it was entirely my fault. There are way too many articles on the internet dedicated to explaining away same-sex attraction, and I was a dedicated Googler in high school."

"We'd tell ourselves anything to explain it away too," I say. "Anything to keep us normal, right? Otherwise people might catch on and give you hell for it."

"Who gave you hell?" Her brows crease as the fillings of her taco start to fall out the other end from how tightly she's gripping it. "You know I'll give them hell right back."

"My cousins," I admit, taking a beat to consider if this is a story I really want to tell her. "They used to bully me a lot because I hadn't had my first kiss. The rumor spread like wildfire at our high school and before I knew it, everyone knew. At one point, they started giving my number out to random guys I'd never talked to before. But they're family, which meant I always had to forgive them no matter how far they went."

"That's awful," she tells me. "Tell me about these cousins. More specifically, where I can find them and teach them a god-damn lesson."

"You don't need to defend my honor." I smirk. "Your righteous anger on my behalf is plenty. Besides, I'd hate to see what you could do to them after watching you mangle that taco."

"You didn't deserve your fate," she says, scooping up the last bit of filling off her plate with a tortilla and popping the last bite into her mouth before cleaning her hands with a napkin. Then she glances at me and her voice takes an ominous tone. "Your cousins, on the other hand…"

I smile and shake my head at her. I kind of like this protective side of Krystal, even if it comes at the expense of her lunch.

"Do you still talk to them?" she asks.

"Here and there." I shrug. "They think I'm making it all up for attention because of an elaborate lie I told them the summer after high school."

"So they're still assholes, then."

"It's my fault for lying in the first place," I say. "And it was based on a half-truth. I went on a date with this guy who had a crush on me and tried to reciprocate his feelings. It never felt right, though. As soon as he tried to kiss me, I knew I'd made a mistake. It wasn't what I wanted, and when I tried to tell him that, he yelled at me for leading him on. I was so embarrassed. My parents were right on the other side of the door and heard the whole thing. When my dad asked me what happened, I burst into tears on the spot." I try and wave off the memory with a light laugh, but Krystal's horrified expression lodges it in the back of my throat.

"Angela." She stares at me for a moment, a flurry of emotion I can't read in her eyes. "High school was hell for you, wasn't it?"

"Understatement of the year." I say it casually, but the memory still stings. "It was years ago. He was a complete jerk about it, but he was kind of right. We shouldn't have gone out. I went about it the wrong way—"

"Stop." She places a hand over mine, her voice determined. "Don't you dare try to put the blame on yourself. If he acted that way, he's the one in the wrong. You didn't deserve any of that. And I want to strangle your cousins with my bare hands."

"Thanks, Krystal." She squeezes my hand tighter, and I let out a deep breath that deflates the tension in my shoulders. It's like her touch is anchoring me to the table, to this conversation, giving me the courage to keep going. "I only wish I was able to figure all this stuff out sooner. Sometimes I think if I knew myself better back then, I could've solved all my problems."

"I get that. Believe me." Her thumb has started to trace circles on my wrist. A shiver runs down my spine, and I try to gauge my body's reaction to her touch. The sensation isn't nearly as strong as her warm breath on the back of my neck, but I'd be lying if I said there wasn't some definite...stirring going on.

"I didn't come out as bisexual until three years ago," she continues. "I was already an adult and dating a man at the time. I almost didn't see the point."

There are so many tiny details in that one small statement, I almost don't know which thread to pull first. In the end, I latch on to the most pressing one.

"Was it serious?"

"Serious enough to consider marriage," she says, laughing derisively. "I thought I loved him. I just...couldn't see myself married. Even though it was something I tried really hard to convince myself I wanted."

Wow. This is probably the most Krystal has ever talked about herself. If we're exchanging confessions, hers comes in the form of a bombshell.

She was almost married.

"What happened?" I ask, ignoring the jump in my pulse. If she moves her thumb a fraction of an inch down my wrist, she'll feel it too.

"We were engaged for three months before I told him I was having cold feet," she says. "He took back the ring and we tried to salvage our relationship for six more months before he ended it."

I note the detail, that he was the one to end things, and wonder if she has any regrets. But it's not as if I can just come out and ask her.

"I'm still not really sure what I was so scared of," she continues, looking down at the table. "Why I couldn't just go through with it. I only know that I've never felt more stifled in my life than when I put on that ring."

"Was it the concept of marriage, or the thought of marriage with him in particular?"

"I've asked myself the same question so many times. There was nothing wrong with him. I truly did care about him and was open to sharing a future with him. I'm just not sure that's the same thing as love." She shakes her head. "He was a great guy. I should've loved him. I don't know why I didn't."

It's hard to imagine her in the life she's describing. There's nothing stifled about the Krystal I know, pouring drinks with a wicked grin, hair undone and as untamed as her soul. I can't see her wasting so much time trying to salvage a relationship with someone she didn't love.

I'm not sure what to do with this new information. We're in such wildly different places—I've never been kissed, and she was almost someone's wife. I've never been in her position, not even close, so I'm not sure what to say. I don't fault her for being unsure. It's a feeling I'm well accustomed to. The best thing to do in a situation like that is to step back. She did the right thing. I should tell her that.

Instead, what comes out of my mouth is, "Have you ever been in love before?"

For a moment, she looks stunned. She holds my gaze and then shakes her head, smiling ruefully. "No," she says. "If that relationship taught me anything, it's that love isn't really for me."

Wait, what?

My face must say it all. She lets out a laugh, but there's no mistaking the edge in it.

"Don't give me that look, Angela. Some people are meant for love, and others like me just…aren't." It'd be easier to believe her if she didn't sound so defeated. "I'm fine. I promise you."

"I don't believe that." I quickly backtrack, realizing what I said. "About the love thing, not about you not being okay." Although, maybe she isn't as okay as she wants me to believe.

"Listen, I know you mean well. Truly." Krystal squeezes my hand before pulling away. "But I've been through this conversation before in a thousand different ways, mostly from people content to talk *at* me rather than *to* me. The short version of this story is that I don't want to put another person through what I put Isaac through." *Isaac.* Her ex. "It wouldn't be fair to them, and I don't think it'd be fair to me either. Not when I already know what the outcome will be."

I don't say anything, not wanting to be another one of those people talking *at* her. But I don't understand how she can believe love isn't for her while actively helping me find it with someone else. All I can do is nod and bite my tongue, holding back any sort of reply that would tell her differently. No matter how much I may want to.

Thirteen

The DM I'm waiting for arrives the next morning.

@Stephanie: Why don't you swing by this weekend if
you're free? I'm sure Natalia would love to meet you.
Just let me know when you can make it.

We go back and forth about when a good time would be to
meet today, and then she sends me an address.

I'm going to meet Natalia Aguilar today.

"Tell me again why this artist is so important?" Julian asks
on the road. He'd insisted on driving us when he found out
Krystal and I were meeting an "internet stranger." "Can't you
just do the scavenger hunt without her? You don't even have the
rest of it planned out yet."

"For one, I want everyone to know that my asexual identity means just as much to me as my lesbian identity," I explain
to him. "I read a couple of interviews Natalia did back when
she was first gaining popularity. She talked about how she'd

get comments on social media that her identity was 'made up,' or that she was using it as an excuse to profit off the art she was creating with queer themes."

"The call is coming from inside the house," Krystal says from the back seat.

"Exactly." I nod. "It's like the handful of comments I still get on a regular basis. There are people who genuinely think I'm lying about never being kissed, who get so pissed every time I say I'm asexual. The other day, someone said it was because I'm afraid to call myself a lesbian with my full chest. That I need some kind of buffer between myself and the word. Others just think I'm a special snowflake."

"I'm sorry, Angela." Julian glances over with a frown.

"I could replace Natalia's work with something else that still tells people I don't give a fuck whether they believe asexuality exists or not. The problem is I wouldn't know where to start, and I can bet my entire savings account that nothing will be able to move me like Natalia's art." I shake my head. "There's also…"

"What?" Krystal asks when I trail off.

I have this absurd fantasy in my head of what it would be like to befriend her. Us hanging out, talking about our identities together and not worrying that she isn't going to know what I'm talking about, or that she won't be able to understand me. The same way I can talk to other aces online, except she's *here*. In the same city as me, where we can meet to go get coffee and talk to each other face-to-face, on a human level, without a screen between us.

It's too tempting not to at least try.

"Let's just see what they have to say," I tell them. "Stephanie reached out to me for a reason. Maybe they already have some ideas for how to incorporate Natalia's work in the scavenger hunt. If the vibe is off, we'll leave and you'll never hear me bemoaning the loss of the mural ever again."

Krystal nods when I turn to look at her, but Julian's expression doesn't change. Not even when he says, "She could be a serial killer for all we know. Yeah, online she's supposedly this great artist, but maybe that's just a cover for the murder house we're about to walk into."

I roll my eyes at Julian's assessment, but it's not lost on me that I could be completely delusional here. What do I really know about this person aside from how her art makes me feel? And is that enough foundation to build a friendship on, or is this a parasocial mess waiting to happen?

"She lives in a studio apartment," Krystal adds from the back seat. "And I've met her before. Didn't get any killer vibes from her."

"None you could pick up on, at least," Julian says. "But how much can you really learn about someone from one meeting?"

On that morbid note, Julian pulls into the parking lot of an old apartment building and stops the car a yard away. The building doesn't look much different from the Google street view I'd looked up earlier.

"This is it." Julian turns to me with a dry smile. "Try not to get killed. That'll be super awkward to explain to your parents."

"As usual, your support is unparalleled." I send him a sugary grin before opening the passenger side door. "Here we go."

"If you're not back in twenty minutes, I'm calling the cops."

"No interest in coming with us on the off-chance Natalia *is* a serial killer?" I narrow my eyes at him. "Here I thought you were playing the part of white knight in insisting you tag along."

"What's knight-ier than calling the authorities from the safety of the parking lot?" He rests a lazy arm against the steering wheel, flipping his phone in his hand. "There's no hope for you if I'm in that apartment when she's on her killing spree. I've got your back."

"A yard away from the building, you have our back," I deadpan. "Sure, Jules."

"So, we're agreed." He smirks. "Have fun."

In a couple of strides we reach the stairs, climb up the steps, and arrive outside apartment number 215. I'm bracing to knock when my mind blanks out.

"Do you know what you're going to say?" Krystal asks.

I shake my head, mind reeling. Damn Julian for getting in my head. It's not that I actually believe Natalia is a rabid murderer, but what if this meeting doesn't go the way I'm hoping?

"Come on." Krystal rings the doorbell and grabs my hand. She squeezes once, assuring me that everything will be fine. "You never know unless you try."

When the door cracks open, I recognize Natalia immediately from photos I've seen of her online. From what I can gather, she's around my age, and her dark hair is pulled up in a bun at the top of her head by a giant velvet scrunchie. She's wearing leggings and a tank top, and her feet are bare. She crosses her arms over her chest, face scrunched in confusion.

"Hi." I step forward, letting go of Krystal's hand to hold

out my own to Natalia. "I'm Angela Gutierrez. Let me just start off by saying I'm a *huge* fan of your work."

"I can't imagine how you found me, but I won't have any new pieces to share until the next First Friday."

I'm confused for a moment, and then flummoxed when she shuts the door in my face.

My confusion is echoed in Krystal's expression, so it's at least good to know I'm not the only one thrown here.

"What the hell was that?"

"You said she and Stephanie were roommates, right?" Krystal asks. "Did Natalia not know you were coming?"

I pull out my phone and read Stephanie's last message again.

I'm sure Natalia would love to meet you.

On my second read, it's not a definite indicator that Natalia was expecting me. It's not even an indicator that Natalia knows who I am, despite Stephanie's assurance that this meeting would be okay.

"I figured Stephanie told her about me." I shake my head. "Should we try again?"

A second later, the door swings open but it's not Natalia on the other side. "Angela! So glad you could make it."

"Stephanie, hi." I take in the woman's fair skin dotted with freckles and light brown hair falling in waves past her shoulders, immediately recognizing her from her profile picture. "Is this a bad time?" Odd, since this is the time we planned to meet.

"No, please." She opens the door wider and gestures us inside. "Come in."

I glance at Natalia, who offers the couch with a reluctant wave of her arm, before taking a seat in the armchair beside it. Krystal and I take seats on the couch next to each other. We're cramped even closer together when Stephanie takes a seat on Krystal's other side.

"This is my friend Krystal," I say to Natalia, who barely looks up. "We actually went to the Tower of the Americas a few days ago because I wanted to show her the mural you painted. It's beautiful." *Was.* But I'll get there. "It's actually how I discovered you. I've probably spent hours going through your online portfolio."

"I already told her you're a fan of her work," Stephanie says from the other side of the couch.

"You wanted to show your friend *that* mural?" Natalia's head snaps up.

"That's the one." I nod as Krystal's knee shakes slightly, pressing her thigh even closer to mine.

"But you've already seen it." For a moment, I don't realize that Natalia's gaze has slid over to my side, and that her next words are directed at Krystal and not me.

"Wait, when did you see it?" I turn to Krystal in surprise, but she doesn't seem to have heard me. I recalled how I caught a flash of recognition in her eyes. I thought I'd imagined it.

"That reminds me." Natalia turns her back on us and makes her way over to the desk shoved in the corner of the living room. "I came up with a suitable replacement for you after all."

"What is she talking about?" I ask Krystal once Natalia's back is turned. Her face is impossibly close to mine. When she turns to me, we're practically breathing the same air.

"Remember the mix-up I told you about?" I nod at her. "The piece she gave me—"

"I'm in a bit of a slump, so you'll have to forgive me. I don't make a habit of being six months late on commissions," Natalia calls out as she riffles through a filing cabinet. "Here it is. Sort of a twin to *The Woman in Wanting*, you could say."

She hands Krystal an eight-by-ten print of the most breathtaking piece of art I've ever seen, aside from the mural I've grown abnormally attached to. The same colors and overall style are used in this piece, but the woman in it is undoubtedly different from the one depicted in the mural. The features of her face are different, her hair sleeker and straighter, but her expression is…sad. Her eyes are closed in anguish. A delicate hand is raised over the outline of a beating heart inside her chest, as if shielding it.

The Woman in Waiting, the title below it reads.

"It's beautiful," Krystal says, staring at the print in awe. Then, as if shaking herself out of a trance, she says, "Thank you." She's in the middle of digging through her purse when Natalia raises a hand.

"Six months late, remember?" She shakes her head. "This one's on me."

Finally, Natalia turns to face me. "If Stephanie is to be believed, I guess this belongs to you, then." Her hand dips back into the filing cabinet before she hands me a print, the same size as Krystal's. It's an exact rendering of the mural that was washed away, only in clearer, more vivid detail. *The Woman in Wanting*, the title above it reads.

"You're giving this to me?" I ask, even as my fingers clutch it tighter. I may not know why she's giving me the print so easily, but there's no way she's getting it back from my greedy hands if she changes her mind. "I don't understand."

"You were right," she says, but not to me. "It wasn't yours after all."

"That's the one she gave me originally." Krystal nods to the print in my hand. "She gave me *The Woman in Wanting*."

"She *did*?" I glance down at the print in my hand, then back at her. "That's why you recognized the mural. I wasn't sure, but I thought…" I shake my head. "Why didn't you tell me?"

"You told me how much that mural meant to you," she explains. "It didn't feel right to tell you about the way I grimaced when Natalia first showed it to me. It's not that I hated it or anything, just that it…didn't resonate with me."

Meanwhile, it resonated with me so strongly it led me all the way to Natalia's apartment.

"I don't usually allow for do-overs, especially not for that particular round of commissions," Natalia says.

"The *All the Ways to Be Queer* series?" I ask. Both Krystal and Natalia nod. "I heard about it, months after the fact, but still. People submitted a paragraph detailing their experience to queerness, and then got a specialized art piece. I read about how one person even got a blown glass frog. I would've loved to commission something from that series."

"Well, congratulations." Natalia smiles dryly as she takes her seat again.

"The mural might've been washed off, but I thought you should still have a piece of *The Woman in Wanting*," Stephanie says. "Not that it's any consolation prize, but—"

"No, it's *better*," I protest, looking between them before landing on the artist in question. "I can't even begin to thank you."

"I'm happy you like it," Stephanie says. "Natalia—"

"Let's cut to the chase, then," Natalia interrupts. "I know why you're here. You're the content creator who thinks it's a good idea for some godforsaken reason to date the entire internet."

"That's one way to put it." I let out a nervous laugh. "But I'm concentrating more on the scavenger hunt right now. I thought it might be a great way to meet other queer people in town and ultimately have my first kiss. You know how much your art means to me."

"So I've been told." She glances at Stephanie and a look crosses between the two that I can't decipher. "She's been talking about you all week."

"Because it's the perfect way to get you out of your rut," Stephanie says. "I thought if you could just hear her out—"

"Don't get me wrong, your story is very compelling," Natalia says over her friend, turning back to me. On Krystal's other side, Stephanie crosses her arms over her chest and mumbles something I can't hear. "It would have to be for you to have amassed the kind of following in the amount of time you have."

"Thank you?" I exchange a look with Krystal, confused about where this is going, but the pit forming in the base of my stomach knows the truth before I do.

"I'm afraid Stephanie invited you here under false pretenses," Natalia says. "I can't help you."

"If you would just listen to what they have to say—"

"You know how this story goes just as well as I do," Natalia tells Stephanie, shaking her head slightly before turning back to me. "I can't help you with the scavenger hunt, but I can give you some advice. I'm sure you've heard all about what happened to me by now."

"I've only read articles about you alluding to...what happened, but I don't know the full story," I tell her. "I get it, though. People are so miserable that when they see you thriving and happy online, they have to take you down. I get messages like that all the time."

"You *don't* get it." She rises from her seat. "What you're experiencing now is only a taste of what's coming the second you stop giving your audience what they want. Quit before they tear you apart. That's my advice."

"You want me to quit?" I burst from my seat, and then we're eye to eye. "I can't do that. I'm sorry about what happened to you, but that's not—"

"Not going to happen to you?" She huffs a laugh even as her eyes narrow. "If you really believe that, you're a fool. The signs are already there. There are rumors circulating online about your past."

"Rumors about my..." I take a step back from her, stunned. "*What?*"

"Men who you've supposedly dated and flirted with and ghosted, claiming the story you've created online is all a fabrication. Oh, you didn't know about that?" She raises a brow.

"Then there's the woman you brought with you. I don't believe you've mentioned Krystal at any point in your videos."

There are no words to explain how completely bizarre it is to hear about my history of flirting with men and infatuation with Krystal from a perfect stranger. She's not totally wrong, except for the fact that there was only one guy I ever dated, not that I count it as "dating" at all.

"We're just friends," Krystal says, rising to put herself between me and Natalia. "I'm helping her put on the scavenger hunt. Why would I do that if we were something more?"

I'm still wondering why she'd go through the trouble myself, especially after what she told me about her past relationships. If she really believes love isn't for her, why is she so interested in whether I find it or not?

"Where did you hear these rumors from?" I ask Natalia.

"For better or worse, my For You page is now a fan of any topic relating to you. There are people claiming to know you in some capacity making videos about you now. For good measure, I searched your name on Reddit and found even more bullshit."

"They're not true," Krystal says. "Obviously these people will say anything for their ten minutes of fame."

"You really think these people care about the truth?" Natalia lets out a sharp laugh. "Anyone familiar with comphet can put two and two together to explain the way Angela has interacted with these men in the past. As for whatever's going on here"—she waggles a finger between me and Krystal—"maybe you're friends, maybe you're something more. What I do know is there's nothing that breaks down a parasocial relationship faster than even a whiff of deception."

"How am I deceiving my audience by being friends with Krystal, exactly?"

"I don't know. How many friends do you hold hands with and make moon eyes at?"

Oh no. Do I have a habit of making moon eyes at Krystal without even knowing it?

"I get it, okay? You smell smoke, and that's why you don't want to help me. You've been through your own internet dog-piling already. I can imagine you don't want anything to do with another in the making. I'm sorry to have wasted your time."

"You still don't get it." She shakes her head before I turn to leave, and when she looks up at me, her eyes are shining. "I'm not your enemy here. I'm not saying you're deceiving anyone." Natalia steps forward as I step out from behind Krystal's back. "I wasn't either, but they still came for me."

"This is ridiculous!" Krystal protests, crossing the room to face Natalia. "Are you really this bitter over what happened to you? The internet has the memory of a gnat when it comes to stupid shit like this. Are you really gonna let it ruin your spirit like you let it ruin your career?"

"Hey!" Stephanie steps in front of Natalia. "You're going to need to watch your tone. This isn't what I invited you here for."

"What *did* you invite me here for anyway?" I ask her. "I don't get it. I thought Natalia was on board to help with the scavenger hunt. Clearly she has no interest in having anything to do with me."

"Stephanie still has hope for me." Natalia rolls her eyes before facing her roommate. "Which makes her more foolish than you, Angela."

"I may not have liked the way she yelled at you, but Krystal has a point," Stephanie says. "You don't have to let them win. It hurts me to see the way you mope around this apartment. You haven't picked up a brush in *weeks*. Dropping out of First Friday was the last straw. I had to do *something*."

"Wait, you dropped out of First Friday?" I ask her.

"Even if I wanted to help you, I couldn't." She shakes her head. "This slump has been killing me."

"If you would just *try*—"

"Nothing is *working*!" Natalia kicks the coffee table so hard, the glass falls and shatters. The three of us stand here, stunned and silent, until Natalia exits the living room without another word.

"We should..." Krystal looks between me and Stephanie. She nods her head toward the door and her voice lowers to a whisper. "We should probably go."

"I'll walk you out." Stephanie motions us to follow her. Outside, she shuts the door behind us with a soft click. "I'm so sorry about...well, about everything. She's been like this since she quit social media last year. I didn't understand it. She was at the height of her career, but I guess it's true what they say." She holds my gaze, and a shudder runs through my body as she says, "What goes up must come down."

There are so many questions I want to ask, but I don't even know where to start.

"You thought I'd be able to get through to her," I realize. "Sorry to disappoint."

"Don't be sorry yet," she says. "I still think you can."

"But why me? Natalia and I don't even know each other.

What makes you think I'll be able to change her mind?" I ask. "Because of the mural?"

"Because there's nothing that matters more to her than community," she explains. "There was a time when she would've jumped at the chance to be part of this scavenger hunt. She's not herself, and I…" She sucks in a breath. "I'm worried she won't ever be the same again."

I want to ask her again, *what happened*? Natalia has already proven she wants nothing to do with me. Stephanie is wrong, and so am I. There's nothing I can do to convince her to be part of this.

"I'm sorry there wasn't more I could do."

Just as I'm about to turn away, she reaches for my arm. "Wait."

I turn back to her.

"Let's exchange numbers at least. I know you're on a timeline, but maybe something will change. I'll let you know if anything does."

"All right." I nod, but inside I'm not as hopeful as she seems to be. Natalia turning me down is one thing, but I still have the rumors she mentioned to look into. As it is, I have to figure out if the scavenger hunt is still salvageable, or if it was DOA from the very beginning.

Fourteen

RECENT COMMENTS:

@Alisha: Any updates on the scavenger hunt yet?
Dying to live vicariously through you!

Replying to @Alisha
@Priya: Same here!

Replying to @Alisha
@Christine: Me too! Dying for a new update!

"So, how'd it go?"

When Julian seems to shrink into himself after he glances at me, it's clear he's able to fill in the blanks. Probably because of my disheartened expression, or the way my shoulders sink at the question.

"Not so good," Krystal answers for me, squeezing my arm in a way that makes my heart sing, despite everything. "She told her to quit."

"The scavenger hunt?"

"Well, yeah, but also TikTok in general," I say. Krystal glances back at me, concern brimming in her eyes. The art print Natalia gave me burns a hole in my purse, its twin hanging from Krystal's fingers. *What does it mean?* Because it has to mean *something*, doesn't it? Despite the colossal failure this venture turned out to be, I can't help but feel as if our fates are tied. Natalia's and mine. Krystal's and mine.

One woman wanting. One woman waiting.

"That's a bummer," Julian says as he starts the engine. "What are you gonna do now?"

Krystal turns to me, the same question shining in her eyes. She bites down on her bottom lip. I'm unable to look away until she clears her throat. I clear my own before my eyes fall to the woman depicted in Krystal's hand. The prints we were given juxtapose each other the same way we do. There's no hope for us. Isn't that what she was trying to tell me when she said love wasn't for her?

"I don't know." I throw my head back against the headrest and curl my knees up to my chest. "I'm practically back to square one at this point. I need to think."

"Stephanie thinks you can convince her," Krystal says. "There might still be a chance."

I don't know Natalia well enough to gauge if that's a real possibility. But Krystal is right. Stephanie seemed to think there was a possibility I could change her mind. How she thinks I can do that, I have no earthly idea.

"Maybe," I say. "Maybe not. I don't think that's something I can count on."

But scrapping the scavenger hunt wouldn't just let me down. I'd be letting down this online community I've built too. If I haven't already let them down, that is. Maybe they won't even care, if the rumors Natalia mentioned have spread far enough already. One thing is for sure, though. I might have a bigger problem on my hands than whether the scavenger hunt is DOA.

The ride home is silent, but my thoughts are anything but. When we arrive back, I'm still reeling.

"As fun an adventure as this was, I'm laughably behind on grading." Julian salutes us on the porch, calling out a last "Good luck!" as he disappears inside.

Krystal leans back against the porch railing, arms crossed over her chest, eyes trained down at her scuffed sneakers.

"You probably have to head out too," I say, even as I silently hope she doesn't have to go yet. "I won't keep you."

"I'm sorry this didn't turn out differently. What are you going to do?"

"Hell if I know."

"Well, maybe I can help," she offers. "We can brainstorm new clues. This doesn't have to be the end of the scavenger hunt."

"We?" I try for a wry smile, but I'm not sure it has the desired effect. If it comes off more sad than anything else, mimicking my true feelings about this whole mess of a day.

"Yeah," she says as I look away from her, unable to meet her eyes. "If you still want help, that is."

I nod, try to reroute my thoughts in a more encouraging direction, but fail miserably. "Sure. I'd love your help. But maybe we should give planning a rest for tonight. I think I need a break from it for a while."

"Of course. Whatever you need." Her hand falls on my shoulder, squeezing lightly. "You'll have a clearer head about this tomorrow."

"Right." But as soon as she makes her way down the porch steps, I can't keep myself from calling out her name. She turns around and meets my eyes, brows raised in question.

"What is it?"

Good question. What is it with me and this woman? Why does the thought of her leaving make me feel hollowed out? It has to be more than the silence waiting for me inside. For the first time since my parents have been gone, the loneliness plaguing me dissipates when she's around.

"Do you want some company for a while?" She seems surprised by the question, but instead of turning me down like I think she will, she nods. A single dip of her head that turns my bones to liquid.

"Sure." She clicks a button on her keys, unlocking her car doors. "Hop in."

Fifteen

Natalia was right. There's an entire Reddit thread filled with guys I've flirted with and dodged, including a former Havana Bar employee I haven't thought about in years. After a little digging, Krystal finds some videos on TikTok of a few guys grossly exaggerating what our interactions were really like. Luckily they don't have many views and it appears none of my followers have seen them.

"You don't have to respond right away," Krystal says when I open the camera app. "We haven't eaten all day. Let me make you dinner."

"I'll think about it," I tell her. "But I should probably post an update on the scavenger hunt, even if it is a disappointing one."

"All right, you can record here. I'll try not to make too much noise in the kitchen."

I'm sitting on Krystal's couch when I hit record.

CAPTION:
A DISAPPOINTING UPDATE

@ANGELA CLOSED CAPTIONS: After a long week, it looks like I'm officially back to square one on this scavenger hunt plan. I wish I had better news for y'all, but I'm not giving up yet. Until then, I have a few videos scheduled but if you guys want to see content from me aside from the scavenger hunt series, let me know.

Once I'm through filming, Krystal allows me to explore as she cooks something that smells delicious. Her eyes watch me as I inspect the corners of her apartment I didn't get to last time. As I'm taking stock of her music choices, it hits me that she's never once played the radio while I've sat in the passenger seat of her car. The only music she plays is her own, the artists she's collected for herself displayed on this shelf.

"Taylor Swift, Taylor Swift, Taylor Swift." I flick past all eleven studio albums. Krystal chuckles softly from her place on the edge of the barstool. "How did I have no idea you're a Swiftie?"

She hides her smile by taking a sip from her beer. So far mine has sat on the floor next to me, untouched. I don't know why I said yes when she asked if I wanted one. I don't even like beer. But she's an impossible woman to say no to, even in something as irrelevant as a drink request.

"I guess it never came up."

I make a mental catalogue of each vinyl I come across and look up unfamiliar names on Spotify, marking them to check out later. Before I know it, I have an entire playlist full of artists I've never heard of. Before I can analyze what I'm doing too closely, I name the playlist after Krystal and tuck my phone away in my jeans pocket.

It's just a Spotify playlist, I tell myself. *So what if you put a heart emoji by her name?*

"What else don't I know about you?" I rise from the floor, ambling toward the kitchen. She hops from the stool and follows close behind.

"That I make a mean chicken alfredo," she says. "It's a lot simpler to make the sauce than people think. It's just cream, butter, and a shit ton of parmesan."

My stomach grumbles from the yummy, artery-clogging description, and we both laugh.

"I'd offer to help, but I fear I'll only hold you back. I'm a disaster in the kitchen."

"Look at us, learning more about each other." She smirks. "Your turn now. Tell me something I don't know about you."

"I think you know pretty much all there is to know about me."

"That can't possibly be true," she says, dumping nearly an entire container of parmesan into the pan she's working in. "I saw you reading a historical romance a few weeks back. What do you like about them?"

"About romance books?" I ask, surprised that she remembers, and she nods. "Living vicariously through made-up people's romantic lives, probably. Guess I have that in common with a lot of my followers."

"Why historical in particular?"

"This might sound reductive, but I like reading about women who are still virgins," I tell her. "It's one of the only times I can actually relate to a character in romance. In contemporary, there seems to be this unwritten rule that leading women who are still virgins in adulthood are at best unbelievable, at worst un-feminist, so you rarely see them as much anymore. I think we can all agree that the 1800s was one of the worst eras to be a woman in, but I think it's kinda nice to see the female characters in these books fight back against the rules that constrain them, including the whole virginity equals purity thing."

"I never thought of it like that," Krystal says, grabbing two plates from a cabinet. "I remember getting into an argument with my mom over the plot of one of those books."

"What was the plot?"

"I hated how women were described as 'ruined' after having sex out of marriage, or even *perceived* to have. I can't imagine my whole future being taken away from me after one kiss in the garden all because some nosy busybody was out trolling for gossip."

"And now they're forced to be married. You'd probably hate to know that's one of my favorite tropes." Her eyes bug out at me as she hands me a plate. "But the heroine can gain freedom after being ruined too—as long as it's by the right man willing to strike the right deal, that is. And then they surprise themselves by falling in love in the process."

"Does reading these romances ever make you want one for yourself?"

"More like it quenches my thirst for one," I explain, twirling my fork in the pasta. "It works for a while, anyway. Makes me feel a little less alone."

We don't want you to be lonely.

My mother's words come unbidden. *Am I lonely?* A few weeks ago, definitely. But that hollow feeling in my chest gets a little bit smaller the more Krystal and I hang out. If there's no longer a scavenger hunt, does that mean we won't see each other as often anymore?

"Are you okay?" she asks when I've been silent a moment too long.

I glance back up at her. Heave a long-suffering sigh. "It's a long story."

"I like long stories." She flashes an encouraging smile, taking a bite of food as I explain.

"My parents went to San Juan a couple of weeks ago," I tell her. "They seemed worried about leaving me."

"Why would they be worried?"

"Before they left, they said something I can't get out of my head, about them not wanting me to be lonely."

"Are you?" She looks at me beneath her lashes. "Lonely?"

I close my eyes and take in a deep breath, but it does nothing to thwart the sudden stinging sensation in my eyes.

"Yeah." The reply comes out breathless, like it takes every spare breath I have to get the single word out. "Yeah, I guess I am."

I can't stand her looking at me the way she is, the concern and pity swimming in her eyes beneath her creased brows. But she won't leave me alone. Krystal follows me to the sofa, both of us leaving our food behind, and takes a seat beside me, so close there isn't an inch of space between us.

"I'm a good chameleon," I say. "It's how I got through college without anyone knowing I've never been kissed. I figured the kind of shit people would say if they knew, so I did everything I could to bury the truth. I hid in plain sight."

"I remember." She nods. "You had Jacob wrapped around your finger when he worked at the bar."

Jacob worked at Havana Bar around the time Marcela and I graduated college. He was cute, with his boy band haircut and easy grin. Huge flirt too. After a bit of back-and-forth, we made a deal that for every free drink he put in my hand, he'd earn one digit of my phone number. Unfortunately for Jacob, the ninth drink resulted in his termination.

"He was in the Reddit thread we found earlier. I'd totally forgotten about him until then." Krystal shoots me a disbelieving look, and I shrug. "What? It's not my fault he was forgettable."

"Did you end up giving him the final digit?" she asks. "He did risk his employment for you."

"About that." I bite down on my bottom lip. "Aside from the area code, I was giving him random numbers the entire time."

"*Angela.*" Her tone is quelling, but her mouth is wobbly from holding back a grin. She gives a single shake of her head before bursting out a loud laugh. "Poor Jacob."

"Poor *Jacob*? He's currently telling anyone who'll listen that I led him on and got him fired!"

"Angela…" She pats my arm. "You *did* lead him on and get him fired."

"I never told him to ply me with free drinks; he made that choice himself." I let out a sigh when her expression doesn't change. "I know I'm partly to blame, but in my defense, I never know what to do when guys come on strong. I just wanted to flirt a little, not actually date the guy."

"No angel, despite your name." She laughs when my mouth drops open.

"I took the chameleon thing too far," I concede. "But I guess that wasn't the first time either."

"What do you mean?"

I've avoided my cousins for too long. I'll have to deal with them at some point, clean up the fallout, but I don't know where to start. Maybe talking about it is the first step. I've told her most of what happened, but I still haven't gotten my feelings off my chest.

"I'm sick of my cousins," I confess. "I get that I'm the one who fucked up. I lied to them instead of telling them how I really felt. I thought it'd be a better way to get my cousins to back off than the truth, and I was right."

"I can't say I blame you," Krystal says, punching a fist into her palm. "And I'm more than willing to teach them a lesson for you."

"As nice as it is to have someone willing to fight my battles for me, I haven't even gotten to the worst part." Her brows furrow, eyes narrowing dangerously. "When I lied about the guy, they were so...*happy*. I couldn't figure out what it was then, but now I think they were relieved to finally have me figured out. I wasn't someone they could understand or relate to before. It's funny." I huff out a humorless laugh. "Well, maybe it's more sad than funny that the first time we got along like family is supposed to it's because of a lie."

It's been exhausting, keeping up the facade. Pretending to know what I'm doing when guys flirt with me. Brushing them off at the end of the night. Unintentionally getting them fired for serving one too many free drinks. Merely playing at playing hard to get. Coming out alone couldn't erase the years of comphet. Changing my wardrobe little by little has helped, as well as being honest with myself about the type of romantic relationship I want and who I want it with. That's not something I see my cousins ever understanding. And ever since Natalia brought it up, I can't help but wonder if my followers will understand either.

"Briana and Esme think I'm lying to thousands of people on the internet." I shake my head. "That's what's believable to them. That's the version of me they prefer. The version *everyone* prefers. At least then I'm someone they can understand. But now…"

I wish I knew then what I know now. I wish I grew up with the community I've built online. Maybe then I wouldn't have thought it was so shameful to be as inexperienced as I am. I wouldn't have felt the need to keep up this facade for a third of my life.

"You're not the person you worked so hard to convince everyone you are."

"Yeah." I rest my head in my hands, blinking back the sting of tears. "Yeah, that's exactly it." When she puts it like that, it's no wonder Briana and Esme are so confused. They thought they knew who I was, but the truth is they never had a clue. No one did. Not even me, until last year. Is that what the source of this ache is, this hollow feeling inside my chest? Did I do this to myself?

Sixteen

'm not trying to defend them in any way," Krystal explains, raising her hands. "Your cousins don't deserve the amount of grace you've given them throughout the years. It's just that I understand trying to fill a role other people made for you."

"I didn't think you were," I assure her. "There's no excuse for the way they treated me when we were younger. But you're right. I only came out to a handful of people before I made that video because I didn't want the hassle of coming out over and over again. I wanted to skip to the end. Be the healthy, well-adjusted queer person the internet thinks I am. The truth isn't nearly as pretty."

"It never is." Her smile is dry.

"What role were you trying to fill?" Her shoulders stiffen slightly before she lets out a sigh. "Is this about your ex?"

"Our moms were best friends," she tells me. "I'm pretty sure they were more ecstatic than we were when we finally got together."

"What happened?" I'm scared to even voice this simple

question. I know what happened, even if it's only the tight-lipped version she told me yesterday. Maybe now she feels comfortable enough to share the details.

"He was my best friend." She circles her ring finger with a thumb and forefinger. Her movements are absent-minded, tracing over a remembered weight. "We grew up together. Saw each other at our best and worst, you know? I loved him, but I wasn't in love with him. And I hate myself for it."

"Did you think you were better off as friends?"

"When he asked me out our sophomore year of college, it felt like the natural thing to say yes," she explains. "Our friends always suspected there was something between us, the same way our families did. There was something different about him that year. He was bolder, unafraid to go after what he wanted, and he'd decided he wanted me. I don't know, it was an attractive quality. It made me want to give us a shot. See if everyone was right."

"What happened then?" I ask, taking a sip from my beer, swallowing down a wince along with the bitter taste. She notices and grabs the bottle from my hand before turning into the kitchen.

"We went from friends to full-blown relationship," she says as she turns her back on me, gathering ingredients from the fridge for my usual at the bar. "There was no easing into the transition. It made sense in some ways because of how familiar we already were with each other. I didn't expect to skip to the end with him when I agreed to try dating, but I'd already fallen into it before I even knew what we were doing."

"If you loved each other, I don't see how that's a bad thing,"

I tell her. "Then again, there are different ways to love someone. Romance isn't for everyone, despite what the world would like us to believe. Not everyone wants to fall in love, get married, and have kids."

"I'll cheers to that when I finish making your drink."

"Have you ever thought you might be aromantic?" I ask as I return to my seat at the bar where our untouched plates are sitting and watch as she twists open a bottle of Malibu. I'm still hungry, so I eat as she makes my drink.

"I don't think so, no," she says. "I've experienced sexual and romantic attraction. And not always both at the same time for the same person. That wasn't an issue with Isaac, though. I was attracted to him, but when it came to love—romantic love—he was years ahead of me and didn't give me any time to catch up. Our relationship was great at first, don't get me wrong. It was just…fast. As friends, we saw each other every day, spent the night at each other's place most weekends. After our first date, we were practically living together. Within the span of a few months, we were bickering like an old married couple."

"So when you say you and Isaac skipped to the end, what you really meant was you skipped the honeymoon phase and went straight to the we've-been-together-for-years phase."

"The honeymoon phase lasted approximately two days before we apparently became official." She nods, handing me the drink she's finished crafting. When I furrow my brows, she says, "That's when Isaac says we became a couple, not that he asked me to be his girlfriend in any official capacity."

"And that's when all the excitement died?"

"I guess, but that wasn't the issue either. It was all the small ways we failed to meet each other's expectations. I didn't like staying at his place when his roommates were home, but he didn't like going to sleep alone the nights I worked, or being woken up in the middle of the night when I came in. I hated coming home to a sink full of dirty dishes he always promised to wash but never did. He hated that I was more concerned about the dishes in the sink than grateful for the meals he left in the fridge for me to heat up when I got hungry during the day. When it was clear our lives didn't sync, my solution was to slow down—his was to move in together. I let him and everyone else convince me his idea was better. Slowing down would mean an eventual breakup, and neither of us wanted that."

"That sounds…intense," I say. "If you had your doubts about the relationship early on, why stick around for so long?"

"I might've had doubts, but they weren't fully formed yet. There wasn't a real, concrete reason to break up with him. Just a bunch of tiny, nagging reasons that added up to some big-time resentment. But when I said them out loud, those reasons sounded so much smaller than they felt," she explains. "Anytime I vented to my mom or other friends, they told me all serious relationships were like this. I needed to compromise more, be willing to share my life with another person if I wanted to make it work. Funny that aside from my mom, I don't have a relationship with any of them anymore. Isaac and I may not have made it down the aisle, but breaking up was like a divorce. He got the friend group; I got the house plants." She gestures around her, to yet another hanging plant above her head and two more framing either side of the sink.

"We lost so much when we broke up. Decades of friendship.

I lost the rest of my friends and my mom's respect. Breaking up was—" Her palms slap the counter so suddenly, I can swear I feel the force of it on my chest. Her head bows and there's a long, anguished sound at the back of her throat. "A complete and utter mess we still haven't recovered from."

I wonder how long this story has been sitting on her chest, waiting to be told. I want to comfort her somehow, but how can I when I can't even relate to her? I can't imagine going through what she went through.

She sits down on a barstool beside me, close enough that our arms brush, and then our knees as we turn toward each other. My skin erupts in goose bumps at the touch, my stomach fluttering with inconvenient butterflies.

"He was my best friend, the boy I loved. The one person I could talk to about anything without judgment. I convinced myself that he was still in there—disguised as the pushy, judgmental boyfriend I couldn't for the life of me understand how I wound up with."

"Judgmental?" I crack my knuckles, readying for a fight the same way she did for me. Krystal merely shakes her head with a small smile.

"I told myself I was being too sensitive, but yeah." She blows out a breath. "He had this weird insecurity about my job. He used to tease me all the time for sleeping in despite knowing how late I came in the night before. Then there were these comments he'd make implying my job wasn't as important as his. They always cropped back up during a fight. And we had plenty of them when he started planning these surprise, over-the-top romantic dates that he always scheduled during the nights I worked."

"That's so shitty," I tell her. "He probably did it on purpose. If you were practically living together, there's no excuse for him not to know your schedule."

"That's what I told him," she says. "I don't know why I ever thought getting married would fix our problems. Once we got engaged and started making plans for what our life together would be like, I realized we were still on two completely different pages. He expected me to quit Havana Bar and get a desk job so we'd finally be on a similar work schedule and see each other more often. Then we'd buy a house and start a family once he got promoted and started making more money. It wasn't the life I wanted, and what's worse is it was preplanned without me. When I made it clear I had no intention of quitting my job, now or in the future, I'm surprised we didn't break up then and there."

"What was your vision for your life together?"

She hesitates for a beat.

"Sorry. I didn't mean to put you on the spot—"

"It's not that," she says. "It's just that I haven't told a lot of people this, and the last time I did, it didn't go over well. It wasn't really a vision for our life, but *my* life. Another clue that I wasn't in this relationship as much as he was." She takes in a breath. "I want to run my own bar one day."

"Really?" I sit up straighter. "That sounds awesome."

"Thanks." She smiles slightly. "I still have no idea if it's an achievable dream. I don't know the first thing about securing the loans I need to get a place up and running, because my savings account is lacking to say the least."

"You'll figure it out." I wave away her concerns. "Where there's a will, there's a way, right? Does this bar have a theme?"

"I've cycled through a few ideas over the years. I've been on plant apothecary for the past few months, but that just might be all the extra oxygen in here." She laughs as she waves at the array of house plants again.

"That would make for some cute drink names," I say. "Belladonna. Wolfsbane. Foxglove."

"Aren't all of those deadly flowers?" She raises a brow at me. "Am I opening a bar or a mortuary?"

"Well, you wouldn't *actually* be poisoning people. Besides, wolfsbane's only deadly to werewolves, right?" I roll my eyes. "You're the one with the apothecary theme. I was just trying to give you some inspiration."

"You do know apothecaries are meant for *healing*, not killing, right?"

I give her a blithe look.

"We'll workshop this later. Besides, we're off topic."

"Right." I nod. "I take it Isaac didn't like this idea?"

"He thought it would set our relationship back. We'd have to say goodbye to owning our own home, not that that was ever a dream of mine. I'd have no hope of starting a business if I couldn't get a loan, and even then, there was always a chance it could fail. Plenty of new businesses do. He never outright said he didn't believe I could do it, but…" She shrugs. "He didn't have to. And maybe he's right. I always thought I would've started it by now. Instead, I'm almost thirty and still working at the same bar I have since college."

"There are no age limits on life achievements, you know," I tell her. "Relationships aren't supposed to hold you back. Your lives didn't sync, but that was far from the only problem. You spent an awful lot of time with someone who rushed you into something you weren't ready for, had no respect for what you do for a living, and let you do all the compromising rather than do any himself."

"He's not a bad guy," she says. "Running my own bar is just a dream. It's so wildly far out of my reach, it can't even be called a goal. And I didn't do nearly as much compromising as you think. Ask anyone. Ask my mom. It's bad enough that I didn't love him as much as he loved me. I had to go and break his heart in the most devastating way. I did that to him by being half in and half out for years."

Her eyes are glassy, and I can't help but think this isn't how it's supposed to be. She's been holding so much of herself back, at least until now. *This is why she doesn't think she's capable of love.* She didn't just lose Isaac when they broke up—she lost an entire group of friends. Her family doesn't understand how smothered she felt by their expectations. It's not that she doesn't believe in love. She's been made to believe she isn't capable of it by other people. Because if she didn't love Isaac the way she was supposed to, who could she possibly fall in love with?

"Sounds to me like you're still trying to fill a role other people made for you," I tell her. "You couldn't fill the role of Isaac's wife, so they made a new one for you."

"And what role is that?" she asks, tired.

"Villain," I say. "Incapable of love, romance, and serious relationships. And you're letting them, aren't you? You broke Isaac's heart, and everyone convinced you that you're a terrible person for it. That's why you told me love isn't for you, right? That idea didn't come from you. It came from other people."

"It doesn't change the fact that it's true."

The first tear falls, streaking down her cheek before stopping at her chin. *The Woman in Waiting* comes to mind, the singular tear track down one cheek, eyes shut in anguish. For the first time, I wonder what Krystal wrote for her commission essay for Natalia to have clocked her so well.

"Let's talk about something else." She clears her throat, wipes at her cheeks with the back of a hand. "Preferably not something so emotionally heavy."

"Sure. Of course." I nod. "What do you want to talk about?"

Her gaze settles on me. "You."

Seventeen

M e?" I blink slowly, confused by this abrupt topic change. My chest hurts watching her wipe the tears from her face. She straightens, composing herself and clearing her throat. Tucking away this new, vulnerable side of her before I can get a closer look.

"I've been doing a lot of research since I found out about your identity," she says, surprising me all over again.

"Really?" I'm stunned, but also touched that she would take the time to do that. Earlier, she described her romantic and sexual attraction so succinctly. I wonder if her research had anything to do with it.

"Yeah. There was a lot I didn't know about the asexual spectrum, and I thought if I was going to help you with the scavenger hunt, I should know more about your identity. I wondered if you were wanting to find a partner who's also ace-spec."

"Not necessarily," I tell her. "But I guess I worry sometimes about being misunderstood by an allo partner."

"I get that," she says. "What would you want them to know about you?"

"The usual, I guess. That just because I've experienced little to no sexual attraction in my life doesn't mean there's something wrong with me or that I'm not as into them as they are into me. And that sex isn't everything, even if I am sex favorable. At least, I am in theory rather than in practice. That's something I'm still trying to work through."

"You don't have to have it all figured out right away."

"I know that." I turn my head to her. "But in some ways, it feels like I do. Sex is make or break for so many people. I don't want to put myself in an uncomfortable position like that just to break up because it turns out I don't like having sex after all."

"Okay, so let's talk through it. What makes you think you're sex favorable?"

"I'm not sex-repulsed or averse," I say. "That's why it took me so long to realize I was ace in the first place. I've never been disgusted by the idea of sex, but I can't say I've ever desired it to the degree other people seem to."

"Okay." She nods. "This is good. Keep going."

"Lately, I've been wondering if I might be graysexual or cupiosexual," I tell her. "You're actually part of the reason."

"Me?" Her mouth drops open in a perfect O.

"Well, you and Sophia Bush." I laugh. "There have only ever been two women that have made me question whether I've experienced sexual attraction before, and you're one of them." She's silent for so long, I start to wonder if I've shared too much. "Is it okay that I'm telling you this?"

"Yeah, it's okay." She nods, voice low. "It should come as no surprise that I'm *extremely* attracted to you too."

It shouldn't, given that I still remember the way she stared at my chest my first time in her apartment, playing nurse to my injuries. Hearing confirmation from her lips, however, fills me with an enormous amount of relief.

I'm not alone in this, whatever this *is. She's right here with me too.*

"Do you want to share what specifically led you to thinking you might be graysexual or cupiosexual?" she asks. "Cupio is when you identify as ace but still desire a sexual relationship, correct?"

I nod. "So, the way I explained it in one of my videos is that sex primarily exists in my head, right? So when I fantasize about sex, it's usually not with a specific person, and it definitely never includes me. Except for two very specific instances. The first was Sophia Bush in *One Tree Hill*, specifically when she wore that red lace top for some of the promo shoots."

"An iconic look." Krystal nods sagely. "I can see how it would've enamored you."

"It did a lot more than enamor me the weekend I discovered those pictures, I'll tell you that." I laugh. "The second was actually when you were taking care of my injuries."

"Was that the first time you felt attracted to me?"

"As far as sexual attraction goes...yeah." I nod. "I don't think I'd ever felt that way about you until then. Romantic attraction is another story."

"So both times, it was a specific instance that triggered feelings of sexual attraction."

I nod at her assessment.

"Has it ever gone away?"

I shake my head. "Brooke Davis is going to be my TV

girlfriend until the end of time, I fear. And how I feel about you…I don't see that going away any time soon either."

Her gaze is molten, rendering me incapable of looking away. It's intense, whatever this pull is between us. Sexual attraction? Something more, mixed with all the romantic feelings I've never been able to shake when it comes to this woman?

"Graysexual fits," I say. "Leaning more toward ace than allo, since sexual attraction is something I've so rarely experienced. I'm not sure that alone makes me sex favorable, though. Generally speaking, I've wondered what sex would feel like, but it's not and never has been the reason I want a relationship with someone."

"That makes sense. Could you be sex favorable if the sex you had incorporated your fantasies?"

"Maybe." My brows furrow in thought. "I think so."

"Okay, then." The way she's smirking at me has butterflies swirling in my stomach. "Now, let's hear about those fantasies."

I swallow hard. I'm not used to being the cornered one, but there's something about Krystal's curiosity that has my pulse racing. Something about her hooded eyes traveling down my body that has me shivering on the barstool next to her.

"You mean, like, positions or…" I trail off, squeezing my thighs together.

"Whatever works for you." She tries to play it cool with a shrug, but her shoulders are tight. I have a feeling she's more invested in my answer than she's letting on. Her throat works on a swallow. I only notice because she keeps touching her hand to the crook of her neck. My eyes follow the movement of her hand, trailing down to the delicate bones of her clavicle. "For example, one of mine would be…light bondage."

"Really?" I clear my throat when the one word comes out gravelly. "Are we talking fuzzy handcuffs, or is that too hardcore?"

"I'd start with silk ties." She bites down on the pad of her thumb. "But I'm pretty much into anything that has my hands pinned above my head."

Interesting.

I imagine doing what she's described, pinning her wrists above her head, the way she'd look up at me with that pretty blush coloring her cheeks, eyes wide in shock. If I kissed her, I'd have more control of her movements. I could lead the pace, figure out what suits me without the pressure of her hands roaming before I'm ready for them.

"Your turn."

For a moment, I think about where to start. "There are kind of a lot, but there's one I keep going back to. You know those guided masturbation audios?"

"Yeah." She nods. "They definitely come in handy every now and then."

"Right." I try to laugh, but it comes out hoarse. "Well, I don't really use them for me. I use them to imagine someone else doing what the narrator says to do."

"So you imagine someone else masturbating?" She cocks her head. "Someone else taking instruction?"

"Well, I can't say being the one doing the instructing doesn't intrigue me. Sex is foreign territory for me. I feel like I'd need rules or some sort of guidance in order to navigate it, since I don't like the idea of being the one to give up control. But that's not really relevant to the guided masturbation fantasy. It's more that I want to feel as good as the woman in my head does, if that makes sense."

I bite down on my bottom lip. This conversation is making my libido go into overdrive. Now that she's put the thought out there, I can't help the sudden *need* building inside me. I don't know what it says about me that just talking about sex has me all hot and bothered.

That you're a stereotypical horny virgin, that's what.

"So what I'm hearing is, you want someone to give you a show?" Her smirk is razor-edged. As her eyes darken, shiny pink lips parting on an intake of breath, all I feel is the undeniable edge of desire pooling low in my belly.

"If they're willing," I hedge, shrugging tense shoulders. "Who am I to turn them down?"

My blood heats at the picture she's put in my head. Of Krystal putting on a show for me. Touching herself the exact way I tell her to. I'm almost tempted to ask for a demonstration here and now, despite how wildly stupid of an idea that would be. Except right now, with her staring at me the way she is, I can't recall a single reason why.

"Oh, yeah?" Her mouth quirks up at the side. "So you're saying you wouldn't turn me down?"

"Who in their right mind would turn you down?" The words just come blurting out of me, no thought to the consequences.

Her body rises from the stool, eyes trained on me as she whips off her top in the space of a ragged breath. My eyes immediately fall to her lace bralette, sheer enough to make out brown nipples through the fabric.

Good fucking lord, what is this woman doing to me?

"What—" No amount of throat-clearing in the world can surpass the lump lodged at the back of my esophagus. "What are you doing?"

"Bringing your fantasy to life." She chucks off her jeans. "Consider it a test. If this works the way I think it will, you'll have a clearer idea if you're sex favorable. Does that work for you?"

For a long moment, all I can do is stare at her. From her heavy breasts to the soft rolls of her body to the skimpiest pair of red panties I've ever seen. *Does that work for me?* What a stupid question. It's taking all the self-control I can muster not to squirm in my seat, *that's* how much this works for me.

And yet...

There's a wild, unhinged part of me that wants to see this ludicrous idea of Krystal's through. To see more of her than I've ever seen of another person in the flesh. If there's anyone I'd feel comfortable enough to act out one of my sexual fantasies with, it's her.

"Or I can put my clothes back on." She crosses her arms over her chest, suddenly self-conscious.

"Don't you dare."

Surprise touches her features, that pink blush coloring her skin again before her mouth transforms into the most radiant smile I've ever seen. I rise from my seat, carefully moving her arms to uncross over her chest. I take her in from a closer vantage point, sucking in a shallow breath. God, she's gorgeous. So gorgeous, it's unfair. I lick my dry lips, clocking as her gaze moves down my face to watch the movement.

"Just to be clear…" She shivers as I whisper into her ear. "You want me to tell you what to do?"

She nods.

"You want me to tell you how to run your hands down your body? How to get off?" I ask. "You'll do everything I say, exactly the way I tell you?"

She bites her bottom lip, then nods again.

"Okay, then," I say. "Take me to your bedroom."

Eighteen

She points to the door behind her, and then we practically sprint the whole way there. I chuckle to myself, but my palms are sweating.

Are we really going to do this?

The dark room casts half her body in shadow, the light from the hallway lighting the expanse of her tan legs as she sits on the bed. She crosses them at the knee as the mattress dips under her weight, exposing more of the skin beneath her thigh. Every breath comes out harder the longer I stare at her. Anticipation heats my skin, warming me from the inside out as I wonder what she'll do next. Will she start by undressing the rest of the way, or wait for my direction?

But just below the excitement thrumming through my veins is anxiety, making my hands shake. What if I'm not good at this? It wouldn't be the worst thing in the world if my fantasies were meant to be just that—*fantasies*. As curious as I've been about what sex with another person would be like, I've never felt unsatisfied by what only I can give myself. I don't need sex to have a fulfilling relationship with someone. What does it mean that I may want it anyway?

"I'm not sure what to do." Krystal gives a nervous laugh that deflates all the tension in my shoulders. "Is this a good position to start in?"

"If you're comfortable," I say, and she tells me she is. "This is a bit weird, isn't it?"

"No." She shakes her head after thinking a moment. "I'd say it's new, but not weird. It's normal for something we've never done before to take some adjusting."

I'm relieved she feels that way. It makes me less anxious about moving forward. She's right. There doesn't have to be anything weird about this. It's…an adjustment. It's us getting to know each other in a new way.

"You're right." I let out a breath, easing a shoulder against the doorway. "This is…new. It's okay if there are a few bumps at first. We'll get through them."

"You say stop, we stop," she says.

"And vice versa," I add, and she nods. "Well, in that case, I have a couple ideas to get us started." Her eyes go dark, and her thighs clench tighter. "Lie back on the mattress."

She does as I say, settling herself higher on the bed. Her hair fans over the pillow, dark curls I ache to sink my fingers into.

"Good."

I let my eyes skate over her body. The curves of her waist, her thick thighs, her flushed skin. I imagine what she'd look like beneath the last remaining layers, how her hands would move over her body, the kind of sounds she'd make.

"Take off your bra."

The thin material slides off her chest before falling to the floor. It doesn't matter that I could practically see everything through her bra. Without it, she's a fucking masterpiece. She arches her back, pushing her breasts forward and smirking at how dumb my face must look right now.

Breathe, Angela.

"Like what you see?"

"Uh…" I have no idea what the right response to that is, so I settle for a nod. Then I let out an awkward laugh, resisting the urge to cover my red cheeks with both hands. "You love embarrassing me, don't you?"

"Only when it helps my ego." Her smirk goes crooked.

"I'll get you back for that," I warn with a tsk. "I didn't give you permission to talk."

Her mouth closes, even as her eyes sparkle with intrigue.

"Panties next." She does as I say, sliding them down her long legs, but not before I catch sight of the wet spot in the center of the fabric.

Fucking Christ, she's as turned on by this as I am.

Her thighs close as soon as her underwear hits the floor, hiding that perfect view I almost got of her. Maybe it's better this way. I shouldn't be this close to combusting when we've barely even started.

"How do you feel?"

Her chest falls with a deep breath. "Good."

"Comfortable?"

"Exposed," she responds with a shaky laugh.

"Do you want to keep going?"

She nods, and even though I'd be more than happy to stop if that's what she wanted, there's no hiding the relief that washes over me.

"Close your eyes, pretty girl," I tell her. "Imagine you're alone."

Her eyes flutter closed.

"It's just you and the voice in your ear, guiding you." She gives a subtle nod as if to herself. "I want you to run your hands down your body. Wherever feels nice. Your inner thighs, your stomach, your breasts."

Her fingers drag up her full stomach, along her waist, up to her breasts. She uses both hands to pinch her nipples. A moan falls from her lips as her fingers work, teasing and pulling. *So this is how she likes it.* I'll have to remember—

This is just practice, I remind myself. No matter how much my mind is already coming up with excuses for a repeat. But still, I can't help but wonder if nipple-pinching is really what does it for her or if there's something more that could help her along.

"Are you doing that for me? Pinching your nipples like that?" Her eyes flit open. "Or because it makes you feel good?"

"Does it matter?" She halts her movements. "This is your fantasy. This is about your pleasure."

"Of course it matters," I say. "My pleasure isn't at your expense. It starts and ends with yours."

"Oh…okay." A flurry of emotions I can't name cross her features before she finally gives in with a sigh and answers my first question. "It does sometimes. Usually not at my touch alone."

"Okay." I nod. "That's good to know."

"What do you want me to do?"

"How do you get off when you're alone?"

"That, um…" She fidgets in place. "Requires a bit of battery-powered assistance."

The thought of her using a vibrator is almost enough for me to see stars. I clear my throat, trying to look unaffected when an idea occurs to me. "Can you come without it?"

"I can," she hedges, nose scrunching. "But it's faster with a vibrator. I can't remember the last time I just used my hand."

"Interesting," I say. "You're used to getting your way, then. Used to getting off quick and easy at the touch of a button."

She stares at me for a long beat. "I know what that evil smirk of yours means, Angel."

Said evil smirk spreads wider. "Nothing angelic, that's for sure."

She hitches a breath as my hand closes around her ankle. It's the most innocent part of her to touch, considering all the glorious naked skin splayed out before me. I use the pad of my thumb to stroke circles against the fragile bone on the outside of her ankle, reveling in the way her breathing sharpens at my touch.

"Hands where I can see them." She raises her hands before setting them palm-up on the pillow above her head. The movement pushes her breasts up, and it's taking all the willpower I possess to keep my eyes focused above her neckline. "I just want to look at you for a while. Is that okay?"

She nods shakily, staring up at the ceiling.

"Krystal." My fingers skate up her calf as I come to the

head of the bed. My hand closes on her chin, gently pulling her face down. "Eyes on me."

I can't read the emotion behind her eyes. Is it nerves, or is she just as scared as I am about what this will do to our friendship? This has to be crossing a line, even though we're barely touching and one of us is fully clothed. But there's no one I'd rather do this with than her, no matter the cost.

"Can you do that for me?"

She nods again, a deep breath sinking her chest. It's a reminder for me to take one too. To loosen the tension in my shoulders, though it does nothing for how fast my heart is racing.

My eyes rake over her body, looking my fill. I can't deny that this is doing all sorts of pleasurable things to me, though now I'm not sure how that ever could've been a question. If I stuck a hand down my shorts right now, it'd take three rubs max to make me come. Maybe less. If this was more than a test, if I was allowed to touch her past the boundaries we created, there's no doubt this would be the best sex of my life. I'd want more from her—I'd want to do this again and again.

"Spread your legs for me."

She does as I ask without a word, her thighs widening on the mattress until she's baring herself to me. Through the dim light from the hall, I can see how wet she is. The evidence of how much her idea is working a little too well for both of us.

"Do you need to touch yourself?" She nods rapidly as she lets in a ragged breath. "Show me."

She doesn't waste time. Krystal goes straight for her slick folds, dragging a finger through her arousal before circling her clit. She lets out a soft little sigh that turns into a moan as her fingers move faster. Her back arches off the bed, and I know none of it is for show this time.

And it's the hottest damn thing I've ever witnessed.

"Tell me when you're close."

"I'm close," she breathes. "Oh god."

"That quick, huh?" I can't help the gravelly chuckle that comes out. "We can't have that. Stop touching your clit."

She does as I ask, but not without a whimper of protest. Her eyes stay on me, chest rising and falling fast with her quick breaths.

"Where's your light switch?"

"What?" she asks, confused. "Please tell me we're not done."

"Don't worry, Krystal. I'm nowhere near done with you," I promise as I find the switch on the wall behind me. "I want to see you better. Is that okay?"

She nods and I flip the switch, filling the room with light. It's almost too much, this unencumbered view of Krystal sprawled on the bedspread—the swirls of ink on her right upper arm, the sweat beading her skin, her flushed chest rising and falling with quick breaths. Her brown nipples are hard, beaded points, and for a moment all I can think of is what she said earlier about feeling good when other people touch them.

Would my fingers be enough, or would she need suction from my mouth? Is that something I want to do? Suck those hard nipples until she's crying out for more? Work my way down her soft, needy body to her wet pussy?

Well, I'm certainly not opposed.

"You're fucking perfect."

The words slip past my lips unintentionally. That's when I notice the agony twisting her features, the lower half of her body squirming, and I remember—

"Don't just leave me hanging here." She bites down on her bottom lip hard enough to leave teeth marks. "Angela, please."

"Was there something you needed, pretty girl?"

"I need to touch myself," she says desperately. "I was so close."

"You can continue," I tell her, and her sigh of relief fills the entire room. "But you're not allowed to come yet."

She makes a noise of dissent, but that doesn't stop her from touching herself like I've allowed. It was one thing to watch her in the low light coming from the hall, but this—*this*—her fingers furiously working her clit, the way her lips form around a moan, the way her legs can't stop shaking—

I. Will. Never. Recover.

"*Fuck.* Angela." I've never heard her voice this high before, but I've never seen her like this before either. Unraveling right before my very eyes. "Please. I'm so close again. I need to—"

"Stop."

She squeezes her thighs together and rolls onto her side, biting into the fabric of the pillowcase to muffle a frustrated cry. I'd laugh if I wasn't enduring a different form of tortured agony, all of my own making. There's nothing I want more than to watch her orgasm, to unbutton my shorts and shove a hand down my panties and turn this into a mutual masturbation session.

"Something wrong?" I stare down at her with what I hope is a blithe look. She returns it with narrowed eyes and a disbelieving scoff.

"I'm giving you a new nickname after this," she hisses. "Once I'm...thinking straight again. You're no Angel."

"Was there something you needed?" Her eyes bug out at me. "If there's something you want, all you have to do is ask."

She licks her lips and stares up at me. "I want to come, Angela."

So do I.

It's killing me, holding out for as long as I have. Edging isn't normally a habit of mine, but I'm not ready to stop yet. I want to prolong the fantasy she's brought to life for me for as long as I can, but that's not the only thing motivating me. It's a power trip, controlling Krystal's pleasure like this. I'm already addicted to driving her to the edge just to take away her satisfaction and watch her keen for it. How much more can she take? How much longer can I put her through this?

"Hmmm," I pretend to consider. "Beg me."

She rolls her eyes heavenward.

"That's not very nice of you, Krystal. There's a time and place to be a brat." I tsk. "And from the way you're squirming, I don't think you can handle any of the punishments I'll come up with."

She inhales, bites her lip down on any sassy remarks I'm sure she has teed up. From the way her blush deepens and eyes glitter, I know she likes this bossy side of me more than she's saying.

"Angel, please." Her voice turns into a whine I like the sound of way too much. "I need to come. Please let me come, Angel."

"There's that nickname you think I don't deserve." I smirk. "You must be desperate for an orgasm to please me like that. Since you asked so nicely, I'll let you come...this time."

She sighs in relief as her hand resumes its movement. It doesn't take very long for her to work herself back up to that same frenzy, moaning and writhing at her touch. I shut my eyes, back against the wall, and gather the courage I need to pull down my shorts.

"Oh *fuck*." I was right. Once I start touching myself, it doesn't take long at all for me to fall over the edge. The tiny room is filled with the sound of our ragged breathing, and I've never heard anything hotter. I can't catch my breath as the quickest orgasm of my life brings me to my knees.

"Oh my god," Krystal finally says. "I can't believe we just did that."

That makes two of us.

"Me neither," I agree, my voice still breathless. I'm tempted to join her on the bed, not for another round, but because it only seems natural to lay myself down beside her after what we just did. For her face to fill my vision as we exchange shy smiles, to make out the sweat glistening her reddened cheeks. Instead, I'm awkwardly kneeling at the foot of her bed trying not to stare at her naked body.

"Come here," she says, and all that awkward tension releases from my shoulders as I'm flooded with relief. As I reach the bed, Krystal kicks at the duvet beneath her body and then sits up to cover us both with it. We're turned toward each other, just how I wanted us to be, but there's nothing shy about the way she's smiling at me right now.

"Hi." Her nose grazes mine, radiant smile filling my vision, and it's even better than I imagined.

"Hi," I say back, and I could almost laugh from how absurd this situation is. I've orgasmed in the same room as Krystal, but

I've still never been kissed. "I guess that answers the question. I am most definitely graysexual and sex favorable."

"Glad to be of service." She mock-salutes me. "Feel free to use me as practice anytime you need, because *oh my god* was that amazing."

I try to return her grin, but I can't quite manage it over the sudden hollow feeling in my chest. Something about what she's said doesn't sit right with me.

Practice.

There's nothing about the use of the word I can fault her for. It shouldn't bother me, not when I agreed to let her enact one of my sexual fantasies as a test to gauge whether I'm sex favorable. Because that's what this was, ultimately. That's what we agreed to.

But thinking about what we did in those terms cheapens the whole experience for me. Like there's nothing real between Krystal and me, when to me, what we just did solidifies my feelings for her. No matter how much I've tried to deny it. Would she have agreed to do this if she knew my feelings for her weren't anywhere in the realm of friendly?

"God, I wish I could kiss you right now." It takes a moment for what she's just said to register. Then, every inch of my skin heats in a new way. In a way that has my heart beating into overdrive. Her fingers trail my cheek, smoothing the strands away from the side of my face.

There's nothing I want more than that...and yet.

"Maybe giving up the scavenger hunt doesn't have to be a bad thing," she says. "We could...I don't know. Keep doing what we did tonight. More, if you want."

The thought of more with Krystal is too much to bear,

because it's never been clearer to me than right now that we have different definitions of the word.

I'm such an idiot.

Whatever Krystal feels for me, if anything, it can't go anywhere. She's made that clear from the start. It'd be fair enough if she didn't want to fall in love, but I know the truth now. It's not really about what she wants, but what she believes herself capable of. What her family and former friends think of her.

"In the name of practice, you mean." I turn away from her, staring up at the ceiling.

"Sure." The lightness in her tone grates on my nerves, even if it doesn't take her very long to sense the distance between us. "Angela?" She places a hand on my shoulder, eyes widening when I flinch at the touch. A knee-jerk reaction I can't hold back, thanks to all the thoughts burdening my brain. "Did I...What's wrong?"

"Nothing." It's such an obvious, bald-faced lie. I take in a deep breath, but it does nothing to calm me down. "I should probably head back."

"You don't have to," she says, confusion scrunching her brows. "Unless...you want to?"

Good lord, we never should've done this. How can I possibly explain that the thought of us as "practice" is depressing enough for me to shut down as soon as the word left her mouth?

"I want to," I say instead, because at least that's the truth.

"I'll drive you back." I hate the disappointment in her voice almost as much as I hate myself for being the reason it's there. For ruining what was almost a perfect night, all because I like her way more than I should.

Nineteen

She insists on packing up what's left of the chicken alfredo for me to take home, which ends up being the biggest Tupperware of food I've ever seen. I doubt she left any for herself, given the weight of the container in my lap. We're silent the whole way to my house, but every now and then I catch Krystal glancing over, that same confusion from earlier written all over her face. Once she parks outside my driveway and kills the engine, I finally give in and stare back at her.

"It's something I said, isn't it?" When I don't say anything, all but confirming her question, she continues. "I shouldn't have called what we did 'practice.' It was stupid and thoughtless of me. I'm so sorry, Angela. I didn't mean—" She cuts herself off with a curse.

"It's fine," I say, another placating lie. "There isn't exactly a more appropriate word for what we did together, right?"

"But it obviously hurt you." My eyes shut with a shudder. The truth of her statement burns through me, and once again I hate how she can always seem to see right through me when she hides so much of herself away. "I don't know what the right word to use is, but that was the wrong one. I'm sorry."

I don't trust myself to speak, especially not when inexplicable tears water my eyes. Good fucking Christ, of all times now is not the time to cry.

"Talk to me." Her hand closes around my wrist. "Angela, please. I don't know what you're thinking right now."

"Too much," I admit, shaking my head as I remove my arm from her gentle grip. "I don't really want to get into it right now. It's not logical." Nothing about what I feel for this woman is logical. Krystal and I are so far from together, it's laughable. It'd be so easy to fall for her, and that's the last thing she wants.

"Okay," she says, but if anything she looks more confused than ever. "If I crossed a line tonight, I'm sorry. I didn't mean to push you."

"It's not that," I assure her. "I don't regret anything we did. If there's anything you don't need to be sorry about, it's that."

"What do I need to be sorry for, then?" she asks. "Tell me."

Fuck it. We've come this far. What'll it hurt for her to know the truth?

"If we're not calling what we did 'practice,' then we're calling it 'casual,'" I finally say. "Is that a fair assumption?"

"I guess," she says. "Is there something wrong with that?"

"Not for some people. But for me…yeah." I let out a sigh. "There is. Flirting is one thing. It's banter. Getting to know each other without strings. I've done it all my life and never felt a thing." Except with Krystal and to a degree, Leti. "But I don't think I can be a casual sex kind of person. What we did together—that's not something I can do with just anyone. Not because I'm graysexual. Not because it was my first sexual experience. But because I *know* me." Because I know *her*, just like I know *casual* is something I'll never be able to do with her. "I love what you did for me, Krystal. It's not meaningless to me."

"It wasn't meaningless to me either, Angela," she says, her voice so low I can barely make out the words. "It meant something to me too."

I can't describe what her words do to me. The balm they provide to my battered insides, even if I can sense the *but* at the end of that statement from a mile away.

"But you know I'm not good at this," she continues. "I told you all about how my last relationship went. I don't have it in me to go through that again."

"I figured you might say something like that." I shake my head. "I'm not going to push you into something you're not ready for. I just wish that you could give yourself more grace."

"You're the only one who says that kind of stuff to me." She huffs a laugh. "I gotta admit, it's nice to have someone on my side for once."

"Anytime." I smile sadly at her.

"I don't think 'casual' is the right word for us either," she says after a beat. "Can't there be something in between? You started planning the scavenger hunt to dip your toes into the dating pool. You said yourself that you're not expecting to find the real thing right away. The purpose was to get a feel for dating, to have fun. I guess I just don't understand why I can't be that for you instead."

Of course the difference isn't clear to her. But I'm fully aware that this persistent crush I've had on her for years has never gone away. If anything, it's spiraled so far beyond my control I may never get a hold on my feelings for this woman. We're beyond casual, beyond whatever in-between Krystal is asking for, but there's no way forward for us to go. Not with all her reservations and my yearning for so much more than she's willing to give.

"Maybe I lied," I say instead, a version of the truth I've kept to myself until now. "Maybe I purposely kept my expectations low because I was too scared to hope for more. I don't want *fun*. I want the real thing. That's what I want more than anything, okay? I'm not even sure I really believe in soulmates, or true love, or the one, but maybe I do believe in *my* one, you know? Maybe it's stupid to think I could be that lucky, to think it could ever possibly happen for me on the first try, but that's what I want."

It's a subtle shift, the way her expression changes. Her shoulders straighten as she turns away from me, something in her face closing shut behind a locked door. We are two different people. One wanting, one waiting. Though what Natalia thought Krystal was waiting for, I have no clue. It's more like she's stalled herself. Frozen, too afraid to move. To breathe. To *live*, even. If we continue down this path, that's what will hurt me in the end. The fear holding her back from even trying.

"It's dumb, I know." I wipe at the rogue tears that have fallen down my cheeks. "Ever since I came out, I've tried to tell myself I don't need a partner. I don't need romance or sex or any of the other bullshit I've been programmed my whole goddamn life to think I need because it's what everyone else wants for themselves. Like maybe it makes me less ace to want all of that for myself too. What my parents have. What Marcela and Theo have."

"It's not dumb." I'm not sure how much I believe her when she can't even look at me.

"Right." I let out a sigh. "I guess I'm just sick of being left behind all the time, you know? It's lonely not being able to relate to anyone. Like maybe there's something wrong with me, even though I know now that's not true. But it's hard to believe when I don't have anyone in my life to relate to. It's…"

We don't want you to be lonely.

"It fucking sucks."

"Angel, no one's leaving you behind." She grips my hand again, resisting this time when I try to pull away from her. "You're not alone. You're *not*, okay? I'm here. Your friends are still here."

"Friend," I amend with a sniff. "I really only have Marcela now, and even with her it feels like I only have half of her because of Theo."

"So, bring him into the circle," she says, as if it's that easy. "Julian too. Don't shut them out just because you think they don't need you. In my experience, being in a committed relationship can be more lonely than not being in one. I mean, look at me now. I lost most of my friendships when Isaac and I broke up. I'm lucky my coworkers still like me, but that's only because we can't get rid of each other.

"It's funny." She huffs out a humorless laugh. "You think growing up means settling down. Getting married and starting a family. That's the only option we're given, isn't it? You said it yourself—it's what we're programmed to believe. Our whole lives are built around one end goal, but it's not one-size-fits-all. That kind of life isn't for everyone, and it shouldn't have to be."

"Yeah," I agree over a fresh wave of tears. "It shouldn't be. And it shouldn't be this hard to go against the grain either. To wonder if what I want is *really* what I want, or just what other people want for me."

"Yeah," she agrees, wiping a tear beneath my eye with the pad of her thumb. "I get that. You have no idea how much I get that."

"I'm sorry for crying." I pull away from her when a thin layer of snot threatens to leak past my nostrils. "You don't have any tissues in here, do you?"

She opens a compartment and pulls out a small, unopened pack of tissues. I tear through the packaging and blow my nose with the first one I grab, hoping I don't look too disgusting doing it.

"We should be friends." She squeezes my hand, interlocking our fingers. "Not the bullshit kind that talk about hanging out but never do. The kind that makes time for each other no matter what else is going on in their lives. It sounds to me like we both could use one."

"Friends? *Really?* After we…" I trail off, liking the way her cheeks turn pink a little too much. After delighting in the way she flusters at the memory from earlier tonight, I think over her suggestion. "You know, I thought it was complicated at first, the way the ace community breaks down attraction. Now I'm thinking there are probably a lot more ways the relationships we have with other people can be broken down too. Nothing fits for what we are."

"Is that why queerplatonic relationships became a thing?" she asks.

"QPRs became a thing because our society doesn't value strong friendships in place of romantic relationships. But you make a good point. 'Friend' feels too small a word for someone you love, even if it's not romantic love."

"'Friend' also feels too small a word for someone who's seen you orgasm." She laughs at the way my mouth pops open. "You're probably right. It'd be good if the ace community could come up with a couple more categorizations."

"In that case, Krystal, I think you might be my very best friend." I laugh. "Just don't tell Marcela I said that."

"I won't." She takes in a deep breath. "So, we're friends again."

"Yeah," I say over the twinge of disappointment in my chest. "I like that idea. I think we can do that."

As I stare down at our clasped hands, I wonder if that could really be possible. If my heart will let me be friends with this woman without wanting more than she's willing to give.

From the porch, I watch her drive off, headlights disappearing down the road with the rest of her, before I go inside to another lonely night.

Twenty

ACTUALLY, I'M A GRAYSEXUAL LESBIAN?

@ANGELA CLOSED CAPTIONS: There have only been two times in my life, at least that I can recall clearly enough, where I've experienced sexual attraction. The first was easy enough to discount because unfortunately, I have not and will never meet Sophia Bush in person. And I mean, yeah, I've had other celebrity and fictional crushes before, even on men, but none of them compare to Brooke fucking Davis.

I won't go into detail about the second time, but it's safe to say it happened fairly recently and sort of threw me for a loop. After giving myself the time to contemplate and explore this side of myself I never fully realized was there, I have an answer. Because I experience sexual attraction so rarely, I'm actually graysexual rather than ace like I once thought.

All of this is to say, this is your reminder that labels aren't one-size-fits-all. Identities can be fluid—something that fit you five years ago might not necessarily fit you now, and that's okay.

COMMENTS:

@Alisha: We're both discovering things about ourselves at the same time because I realized recently that I'm demisexual!

@LetIlsTrying: Okay, but Sophia Bush is HOT I'd be confused too

@HavanaGirl1015: 🖤

⁂

"Something happened with Krystal last night."

Marcela's desk chair whips around. In a red body-con dress that falls off her shoulders, this is the most gorgeous I've ever seen her. Her lipstick and the rose in her hair match the dress. It's not the most appropriate look for a librarian for teens, but it's book club tonight and I recognize the signs of Rosalinda from *Sinner's Isle* when I see her.

"Tell me." She claps her hands. "Tell me tell me tell me—"

"Okay, first off, calm down. All this excitement is making me anxious."

Truth be told, I've been anxious since I came in this

morning. If Erika hadn't asked me to withdraw the five boxes of library materials as soon as I entered the office, I would've bombarded Marcela with this news *hours* ago. Plus, anytime I'm not working, I'm on my phone texting Krystal. I haven't logged in to complete a single assignment today, so I'll probably have loads of schoolwork to catch up on when I get home from work.

What are you up to tonight?

The text had come in after I got through withdrawing two boxes of material. I smiled to myself, thankful that no one could see me through the stacks of books surrounding my desk.

It's book club tonight at the library. Everyone's dressing up and there will be plenty of snacks. You should come!

I didn't think twice about inviting her. We're friends, right? There isn't anything weird about asking her to come, no matter how excited the idea makes me.

Is there a theme? I've never had to come up with a costume on the fly. Ugh, I'm already stressed out.

What time should I be there?

Don't feel you need to come in costume,
it's mainly just to get the kids excited.
But if you want to, you can dress as whoever you want! We start at seven 🙂

"How long have you been hanging out?" Marcela asks me now. "Did she ask you out? You have no idea how long I've been waiting for it to be your turn to talk romance."

"Probably about as long as you've known me." I grimace. "We've been hanging out…awhile."

Marcela slaps a hand on her desk. "Why didn't you tell me?!"

"Because it's not a big deal," I say. "And no, she didn't ask me out. We're just friends."

She visibly deflates. *If only she knew.* Krystal asking me out seems tame compared to what we did instead.

"Okay, so what happened, then?"

"We…" I glance around the office. There's one other assistant back here, Andrew Thomas. He has headphones in, but he's been known to wear them to eavesdrop on conversations. My voice lowers to a whisper. "It's not exactly safe-for-work conversation."

Her eyes practically bug out of her skull.

"But you're just friends?" Her smile is smug. "I've heard this story before, you know."

"When are you taking your lunch break?" I glance at the clock on her desk, which reads a minute to noon. We both stare at it, willing the digit to move. When Erika emerges from her office and finds us having a staring contest with the clock, she practically shoos us out of the office.

Fifteen minutes later, Marcela pulls into a parking space from the drive-through and turns the car off.

"Just like old times," I say as I hand over her order. "Feels like just yesterday we were here talking about you and Theo."

"And your accidental adventures in thirst trapping." She laughs. "By the way, I finally got ahold of the new library assistant at the school."

"Oh yeah?" I ask. "Is she cool? What was her name again?"

I make the mistake of biting into a chicken tender at the same time she says, "Very. Her name's Leticia Maldonado." Her eyes glitter. "And guess what? She's ace-spec."

Marcela is oblivious to the bombs she just dropped on me. Leticia? *Ace-spec?* There isn't a single doubt in my mind she's talking about Leti. I try to swallow down my food, but my throat is too dry. And then Marcela isn't so oblivious to my turmoil anymore when I start choking on a particularly thick piece of breading.

"Here!" She hands me her water bottle. "Angela, drink!"

I do, breathing a sigh of relief when nothing is clogging my throat anymore.

"She doesn't happen to go by Leti, does she?"

"I think so?" She raises a brow. "How did you know?"

"I may have...met her already. Online, at least."

"Oh, dear." Marcela lets out a long sigh. "She wouldn't happen to be one of the many women you've been flirting with through TikTok, would she?"

"There aren't that many." Not anymore, at least. I stopped responding to a lot of them when the scavenger hunt stalled and Krystal and I started hanging out more. The only reason I keep talking to Leti is because I genuinely like her.

If it weren't for the Krystal of it all, I could see us being something more. Brunch on Sunday mornings, meeting her family and winning them over with my charming personality, kissing on the couch as a movie we're clearly not watching plays on. Maybe I'd even develop sexual feelings for her, though it wouldn't be the end of the world if I didn't.

"Do you like her?" Marcela asks. "The same way you like Krystal?"

"It feels wrong to compare them," I say. "Especially because I haven't met Leti in person yet. But I do like her, a lot. That's why everything's so complicated now."

"I'd be more excited for you if it wasn't for Krystal. Which brings us back to the reason we're here." She gives me a pointed look. "What exactly led you to believe mutual masturbation was a good idea?"

We'd talked through current events on the drive here. She almost ran a red light when I dropped that particular bomb on her, and my life flashed before my eyes.

"It made sense at the time. Plus, I think I understand my boundaries better now when it comes to sex. Things I'm willing to do and things I'm not." I smirk to myself. "Turns out I'm graysexual, and not opposed to much. At least when it comes to Krystal."

"Did it go much further than mutual masturbation?" Marcela asks, brows creased like she thinks I'm hiding something from her.

"I touched her ankle," I divulge. "And there may have been some dirty talk in the form of guided masturbation. I surprised myself with that, let me tell you."

Who knew my kink was being bossy in the bedroom? Certainly not me, but it makes sense. I like the sense of control it gives me. Sex is still a somewhat overwhelming idea, maybe because it's something I've never experienced. But when the power's in my hands, it doesn't feel so nerve-wracking. Quite the opposite, really.

"Not the ankle fetish," she mutters to herself. "No wonder you like those historical romances so much."

"Shut up, Marcela." I laugh. As great as last night was, the way we left it is still burned in my mind. I wouldn't mind canceling the scavenger hunt if Krystal felt the same way I do. I'd do it in a heartbeat, even if Natalia changed her mind about helping. But she hasn't, and I'm back to square one regardless of Krystal's feelings for me.

"Does this change your plans for the scavenger hunt?" Marcela asks, reading my mind somehow.

"I'm not sure," I answer, still thinking about Krystal. "I'm still being bombarded with comments asking for an update on when it's happening. Leti would participate for sure, and based on her competitive streak alone, she'd probably win."

"And then you'd be two librarians in love." Marcela's eyes sparkle. "I kinda like the sound of that."

"I feel like I'm cheating." I frown into my bag of fries before pulling one out to munch on. "I'm not dating Leti *or* Krystal and I'm already confused and exhausted."

"Welcome to the dating pool you created for yourself." Marcela laughs. "You wanted options, you got options."

"I take it all back. I should've joined an app." After I demolish my fries, I turn back to her. "How did you know it was right for you and Theo to do the casual thing before becoming something more?"

"We couldn't handle anything more than casual. Not at first. It's not like we expected to ever want something more with each other."

"What made you change your mind?"

She thinks over the question as she bites into her burger. "It wasn't just one thing, you know? My feelings for him changed slowly and so unexpectedly. Even then, I worked overtime to deny what was happening. I didn't give in until I knew I could trust us to make it work."

I nod to myself, even though I knew all this already. I was just hoping if I heard it from her a second time, some part of her story would resonate with what I'm going through with Krystal.

"It's probably different if the person you can't trust is yourself." What will it take to change Krystal's mind? What will it take for her to forgive herself? "When you've been made to believe that you're not a good person. How do you get over something like that?"

"Who told you you're not a good person?" Marcela's brows crease as I realize the mistake I've made.

"Um..." As much as I'm dying to tell Marcela everything, telling her this much about Krystal feels like a betrayal. "Never mind. I'm just thinking out loud...about nothing in particular."

She doesn't look like she believes me, but she lets it go for the moment. "Did Krystal say something about wanting a casual relationship? Is that why you asked me?"

"Yeah." I nod. "We want different things. No shocker there. Unrequited love never works out in the end, does it?" Except, I'm not convinced it's as unrequited as I thought. Maybe that's why I still can't let this go.

"That sucks." Marcela's mouth turns down in a frown. "Did she say why?"

"It's…it's not my place to say." Marcela's expression doesn't change. "Seriously, don't push this. We agreed to just be friends, previous encounter notwithstanding."

"*Friends*. Right." She shakes her head, and dread settles in the pit of my stomach. "Because that always works out exactly how you think it will."

Twenty-One

CAPTION:

WHO ARE YOU GOING HOME WITH AT THE END OF THE NIGHT?

VIDEO DESCRIPTION:

A clip of Angela in a blue dress and red lip with her hair down that transitions smoothly into a clip of her with hair slicked back and no makeup, wearing an oversized button-down open at the collar.

COMMENTS:

@Alisha: Both, please!

@LetIlsTrying: How do you look so damn good as both WOW

@Christine: 🔥 🔥 🔥 🔥

@HavanaGirl1015: Good lord, Angela. I've never been more jealous of a comment section in my LIFE

Even though it was my idea, I'm always amazed when every single kid comes dressed up as a book character. I'm circling the table, taking pictures for the library's social media, when a hand falls on my shoulder and Marcela comes into view.

"This is the last time I post my outfit before book club." I'm confused by this seemingly random announcement until Andy steps up beside her. A laugh bubbles up from the back of my throat. The two are dressed exactly like Rosalinda from *Sinner's Isle*. Andy's even more of a mini-Marcela in their matching outfits, down to the rose tucked above their left ears.

"Don't act like this isn't the type of shenanigans you love, Miss Ortiz." Andy smirks at her, where she stands with her arms crossed over her chest. She has a point. This is *exactly* the type of shenanigans we've come to expect from Marcela's favorite teen patron.

"How come no one ever wants to copy my outfit?" I huff, staring down at Andy with accusation. "I know she's your favorite, but can't you at least pretend to love us equally?"

"I thought you just used book club as an excuse to work in your pajamas."

"*Ouch.*" I rub at my chest with a hand like the kid delivered a physical blow there. She might as well have from the way she called me out. It was a lucky coincidence when I found a pair of yellow lounge pants with cat heads printed on them at

Marshalls. I paired it with an oversized Wellesley College shirt tied in a knot and simple tennis shoes. Now I'm rethinking the entire costume.

"Do I really look like I just rolled out of bed?"

Marcela looks me up and down, a judgmental purse to her lips and a gleam in her eyes.

"I'm so done with both of you. I bet you don't even know who I'm supposed to be."

"Jo from *Dear Wendy*." For a moment, I forgot who I was talking to. Bored of me, Andy turns back to Marcela. "Is your boyfriend coming again?"

As if Andy's conjured him, Theo turns a corner into the YA section. Ever since Marcela gifted him a Captain America outfit, he's spent the last three months cycling through Marvel heroes. Today, the bow and arrow set gives him away as Hawkeye.

The group settles soon after, and Marcela leads the discussion on this month's pick. I snap a few more photos when motion from the corner of my eye makes me look up. I'm not the only one who notices. When the teens break into small groups, Marcela nudges me with an elbow.

"Did you know she was coming?" Her smile falters slightly as Krystal edges away from the group, ducking behind a bookshelf. As if I could so easily miss her presence in my workplace, no matter what kind of chaos she's walked in on. "Do you want me to ask her to leave?"

"What? No!" My mouth pops open, aghast that she would ask me that. Whatever I said earlier, it was obviously the wrong thing if Marcela believes I need protecting from Krystal. After book club, I'll have to correct her opinion. "I invited her. She's probably here for the free snacks I was bragging about."

"Just let me know if you need backup." Marcela crosses her arms over her chest. "Theo and I got you."

"Much appreciated, but not at all necessary."

I rise from my seat and make my way to Krystal. She's staring determinedly at a row of nonfiction, glancing up only when she senses my arrival. Her hair is styled in two braids that fall over her shoulders, and she's wearing a black dress with a white collar, along with white knee-high socks and chunky black loafers. Her makeup is darker than usual, no trace of the colorful bold lips she usually wears.

She dressed up.

I'm giddy for no goddamn reason, except that she's *here* and in costume.

"Hey, *friend*." The white powder on her face does nothing to hide her pink cheeks. It feels good to be the one flustering her for a change. I'd never thought of Krystal as shy before, but there's no other reason for why she's hiding from a bunch of teenagers behind a bookshelf. "Or should I call you Wednesday?"

"Is my costume okay?" she asks, smoothing her dress down like she's flustered. She looks up and her eyes go wide when she sees the overflowing snack table behind me. "Oh no, I should've brought something! Dammit, I *knew* I was forgetting something."

"Are you kidding me? That rickety table's one bag of chips away from the apocalypse. You're all good."

"Is it cool for me to be here even though I'm not a teen?"

Her gaze dips past my shoulder, then down the length of my outfit. My skin heats under her perusal, and for the second time tonight I'm kicking myself for not choosing something more dressy.

The trouble is I hate everything in my closet these days. Dressing as my old self for the transition video felt like taking a huge step backward, despite how visually satisfying it was to see the final result come together. A perfect before and after, side by side. I've had the video sitting in my draft folder for almost a week before finally hitting post an hour ago. I even ended up changing the caption to "Old Me vs. New Me." Now the New Me just needs a new batch of semi-formalwear to complete the picture.

"If Marcela can bring Theo, I can bring you." I grab her hand. "Come on. I'll introduce you."

The group activities vary each month. This time, we set out paints and watercolors for the teens to create an alternate book cover. As the kids are hard at work, I introduce Krystal to Erika and bring her around to greet Theo and Marcela before directing her to the snack table. Just like dressing up, bringing in food is optional but from the spread of sweets, I don't think a single person came in empty-handed.

"The main character's a baker, if that wasn't apparent." I pick up a knife to slice us both a piece of tres leches cake. She nods idly, taking in the decorations.

"How long does book club usually go for?"

"We close at nine, but people usually start heading out by eight thirty," I tell her. "Why?"

"Fiesta starts today. I thought maybe it'd give you some

inspiration to continue the scavenger hunt. That's why I texted you earlier. I thought we could go today or tomorrow. I have a rare weekend off."

"Fiesta." I hadn't even considered that. It's a brilliant idea, if my heart is still set on salvaging the scavenger hunt. I'll at least have one willing participant, a girl I've never met in person who shares my identity. There's potential with Leti. More than there is with Krystal, anyway. I haven't made up my mind yet, but maybe that's why I should give Krystal's idea a shot. "Tomorrow sounds perfect. I'm in."

"Cool." She glances around again, eyes lighting in excitement. "You know, for all the times you and Marcela have seen me at work, I've never seen you two in your element. It's a nice change of pace."

"You pour drinks, we dress up as fictional characters and eat." I laugh. "She's—"

Right in front of me.

"Marcela!" Krystal jumps in surprise as she turns around.

"I hope you're taking care of my best friend here." Marcela walks around her to stand next to me, all the while never taking her eyes off the other woman. "You're not getting her into any trouble, are you?"

"More like the other way around." Krystal laughs, sharing a knowing look with me. "I'm looking out for her, though. No worries there."

"I hope so," Marcela warns. "You two have been spending a lot of time together. I'd hate for anything bad to happen to her...intended or not. Do you get what I'm saying?"

Oh, good lord.

The last thing Krystal needs to hear right now is Marcela's equivalent of the "you hurt my best friend, I hurt *you*" speech.

"Marcela—"

"It's okay," Krystal cuts me off, not even flinching away from Marcela's stare-down. "I get exactly what you're saying. And I have no intention of hurting her. I'd never do that."

"Well, like I said," Marcela says. "Intended or not, there'll be hell to pay."

And with that ominous note, she leaves us.

"Don't mind her," I start to explain. "She's just—"

"Cautious," Krystal finishes for me. "As any best friend would be. I get it."

"I didn't tell her what you told me," I say, needing to get this much off my chest. "About Isaac and your feelings on love and relationships. But she senses I'm not telling her something, and now she's on her guard. I'll tell her she has no reason to be."

She's quiet for a moment. Takes a bite of cake with a plastic fork. Over my shoulder, the teens are still painting on their easels. Marcela flashes me the timer on her phone. They have eight minutes until we call time and move on to the last activity of the night.

"You can," Krystal finally says. "If you want to, you can tell her. Don't keep any secrets from Marcela on my account."

"It's not my story to tell." I shake my head.

"She's your best friend. No secret is safe from a best friend." She smiles, but it's a sad smile. "Thanks for inviting me. I should let you get back to it. See you tomorrow?"

"Sure." I nod. "Yeah."

We say our goodbyes, and I watch her back as she walks out of the building.

Twenty-Two

Downtown is buzzing with activity. Krystal and I pass through a throng of people as we look around. Vendors are lined up on every corner selling street food and other goods, carnival rides are set up in the distance, and musicians perform Tejano music live from various stages where crowds have gathered.

Krystal and I walk down the street arm in arm, cups of elote in hand as we peruse the downtown scenery. It's hard, pretending I'm not overthinking the friendliness of our linked arms while also acting like I'm not replaying the other night on a constant, never-ending loop in my brain. Every luscious curve out on display for my viewing pleasure, our shared sighs filling her tiny bedroom, the orgasm that no other orgasm has any hope of measuring up to.

"Are you still thinking about what Natalia said?" Krystal asks, concern shining in her brown eyes. *Not at all.* "I'm sure we can figure out an alternative. I mean, look around." She throws out her free arm holding the cup of elote, gesturing to the festival around us. "You couldn't find a better backdrop for a scavenger hunt than this. We don't even have to start over, at least not completely."

"I don't know." I smash my spoon into the smooth layer of cheese, mixing until the hot sauce and corn are visible and evenly incorporated. "I'm not sure if I can go through with it anymore, no matter how many willing participants I have."

"What?"

Krystal stops in her tracks, forcing me to look up at her.

"Remember that harmless online flirting I've been doing?"

"Is that something you're still doing?" she asks, expression unreadable.

"On and off, and really it's only been with one woman for a while now," I tell her. "Apparently, she not only lives in town but she's also the school's new library assistant. She wants to join the scavenger hunt, and she's desperate to win."

"Oh." Her shoulders deflate, and a flash of something like hurt crosses her features. "Not so harmless anymore, huh?"

"I…like her." I force the words out, no matter how hard it is to admit them to Krystal, someone else I like. A whole hell of a lot more than I should. "She's looking for a relationship too. Mostly to get her family off her back, I think, but aside from that it's something she genuinely wants for herself but hasn't been able to find up to this point."

"I see," she says, taking in a deep breath. "Have you met her? In person?"

"Not yet. We have something planned for next weekend with Marcela. Her new project has been finding people to expand our friend group. Might be kind of awkward given that

Leti and I have been flirting with this scavenger hunt idea as well as each other for a while now, but Marcela's determined for us to see it through, anyway."

"Why haven't I received an invite to the friend group?" It's hard to tell if her tone is teasing or hurt.

"That's probably my fault."

She's about to ask me why, but instead of stumbling through what could barely be called a reasonable explanation, we're interrupted by an older woman selling teresita crowns. Krystal asks me which color I prefer, insisting it's her treat when I reach for my wallet. I wear a small smile as I point toward one with white and purple flowers. Krystal reaches for a traditional multicolored crown for herself.

Once she pays, she leads me to the grass where we're out of the way of passersby. She smooths my hair down and sets the crown atop my head, arranging the thin trail of curled ribbons over my left shoulder.

"Now do mine," she says, handing me her crown.

I place my arm through the wide circle and reach up to fix the strand of hair displaced by the wind. Her curls are soft and lush between my fingers. There's just so much of it, wild tendrils falling past her shoulders. At first I thought our hair was the same color, but up close I notice hers is lighter than mine, especially at the ends. Notes of amber and copper mingled together, darkening at her roots.

The dizzying scent of her coconut shampoo wafts into my nostrils until I'm spellbound. I can't stop myself from sinking my fingers through the thick strands, twining it around my fingers—

It isn't until she clears her throat that I remember myself. *Good lord, what the hell am I doing?* She no doubt thinks I'm some sort of weirdo, playing with her hair needlessly like this and neglecting my crowning duties.

"Sorry," I choke out before quickly placing the crown on top of her head, adjusting the ribbons to fall behind her hair. When she raises her head, she's grinning.

"Not a problem." She reaches out to tug an errant curl of mine between her fingers. I feel the jolt of her touch throughout my entire body. A blush heats my face, and I only hope she can't see it beneath the dusky sky. "You're not the only easily distracted one here."

For a moment, I forget how to breathe. Our faces are so close, I'm eye to eye with the freckle dotting the edge of her mouth. All I can think about is the other night, her flushed skin glistening with sweat, telling me the one thing I've dreamt of hearing from her for years.

God, I wish I could kiss you right now.

I clear my throat to clear the tension I'm sure only I can feel, then hold out my arm for her again. She takes it, guiding us down the street.

"What do you want to do first?" she asks. "I'm guessing the Ferris wheel is out of the question, given your…" She trails off with a knowing smirk.

"Fear of heights," I supply, smiling dryly. "You haven't forgotten, I see."

"If I promise to protect you, can we go?" She bats her eyes at me, biting down on her bottom lip.

"Fine." I roll my eyes with a grumble, though I have to

admit that the idea of Krystal "protecting" me is highly appealing, despite the fact that if I need saving from anything, it's *her*. This crush can't go anywhere, but try telling my heart that. She's heartbreak waiting to happen. "On the off chance our carriage goes careening off its hinges, I'm using you to break my fall."

"Ye of little faith." She tugs my arm closer, until the right side of my body is pressed against her. "Come on."

The lines aren't long yet. We've arrived at the perfect time. Perfect if you're not like me and terrified of heights, that is.

"Why do people *do* this?" I shut my eyes when our carriage lurches upward. Krystal reaches for my hand, squeezing in what's probably meant to be reassurance and nothing else. Only with each new brush of her hand, I have to make a concerted effort to remind my brain she doesn't feel that way. She wants to be *practice*. She's not capable of anything else, or so she thinks. The wrong relationship suffocated her. Would a relationship with me do the same?

"What is it?" she asks, sensing my unspoken anguish.

"Nothing," I say too quickly. She tilts her head at me, eyes squinted in a knowing look. "Okay, fine. I'm in my own head again."

"What else is new?" She shoulder bumps me. "If this is about the other night—"

The carriage lurches to a sudden stop. I jump, bracing a hand over my chest and muttering to myself. Krystal laughs under her breath before placing a hand on my shoulder that does nothing to comfort me.

"I'm not sure if you know this already, but I've had a massive crush on you for years." I look past her out at the skyline, brilliantly lit up beneath the sunset. She sucks in a breath, the only sound filling my ears. "Pretty sure I came close to admitting as much two years ago."

"I…didn't know," she says. "You were drunk. I didn't think you meant much by it, but I did take it as a great compliment."

Mankind has never seen a more beautiful face, I'd said at the time, drunk from five too many vodka shots. *I mean, god, would you look at yourself? Krystal, you're not looking—you're not looking at your face. Somebody give this woman a mirror.*

"I meant it," I mumble, unable to look away from her. "Every foolish word out of my mouth that night was nothing but the truth."

Her cheeks turn a perfect shade of rose.

"Isaac broke up with me that night," she says, and for one dumbfounded moment, all I can do is stare at her. "Before I went in for my shift. You made my day brighter."

Her warm smile makes my chest ache. I hadn't known at the time she was seeing someone, not that it mattered. I was never going to make a move on her.

"What do you think about using the top of the Ferris wheel as an alternate location?" She swiftly changes the subject while I'm still processing what she told me. "There's nothing quite as romantic to me as a fantastic view."

"Do you want to be part of the scavenger hunt?" I ask. "I'm not above cheating, you know. Especially if it gives you the means to win. If you win the whole thing, it means I get to kiss you."

"You shouldn't say things like that to me." Those dark

eyes sear into mine. "Not when I already can't stop thinking about it."

"About what?" I ask her. "Joining? Because that's what I'm saying. You can—"

"No." She shakes her head. "Kissing you. Sitting here, looking at you, the sunset making your skin glow like a fucking angel I don't deserve, all I want to do is kiss you."

The air has been sucked from my lungs, and we're not even touching. I can't look away from her. I've imagined this moment far too many times to count. Of our heads leaning forward until our noses graze, until we're breathing the same air, until our lips finally touch.

I'm about to get what I want. All I have to do is move. I can get away with one kiss before the scavenger hunt, can't I? If I don't have a plan in place yet, it might not even go on at this point, so there's no issue. Right?

"Angela." Her breath is warm against my cheek. "Are you sure you want to do this?"

I'm sure. My heart is pounding and my palms are slick with sweat, but I've never been surer of anything. Just as I'm about to nod, make the plunge, do *something*, our carriage pitches forward, breaking the spell and bringing us both back down to earth.

We're silent for the rest of the ride. As much as I try to tell myself it's better that we didn't do it, regret fills every inch of me. This was my chance, and I blew it. Hesitated with the lurch of the carriage, too afraid to take the leap. I almost turn my head to look at her, conjure that moment back, but instead I wipe my sweaty palms on my jeans and breathe out a sigh.

It's for the best. Maybe I won't even like kissing, despite all the daydreams I've had romanticizing the act. Maybe it'll be too much tongue and saliva for my liking, and hating it will disrupt our relationship so much that we never talk to each other again. Or maybe I'll like it too much, the same way I like *her* too much. Maybe I'll kiss her and be completely ruined for kissing anyone else.

To have my feelings returned is like someone starting a wildfire inside my chest. I'm burning with want. I could so easily fall in love with her, if she'd let me.

I want her to let me.

I want everything I shouldn't.

"What are you thinking about?" she asks once we're back on the sidewalk, concern brimming in her brown eyes. Does she regret admitting as much as she did? As much as we both did?

I shake my head, clearing away the regret over our second almost-kiss. It would've complicated everything. This is better. We have no business kissing when we want completely different things. It's not even worth bringing up.

"I was thinking about your thing for views," I say instead.

"*Okay.*" She chuckles slightly. "What about them?"

"That must mean you have a favorite."

"Hmm." She raises a perfectly arched brow. "You think you're worthy enough for that?"

I scoff at her, more playful than accusing. "Did I not just risk my life for you by willingly stepping into that metal death trap?"

She throws her head back and laughs. "All right, Angel. You win. I'll show you my favorite view in town."

Twenty-Three

The drive is longer than I anticipated it would be. On the highway, Krystal takes the I-10 ramp to the north side of town. A song from her Spotify playlist plays softly from the speakers. I recognize the melody from the time I hurt myself falling off the BCycle.

"What are you doing?" she asks when I grab her phone from the console, but she doesn't protest when I unlock the screen with her face when she turns her head toward me.

"Snooping through your music," I answer, putting her phone down after following her Spotify account from my phone. "You have some bangers."

"Thanks." Her eyes train on me for a moment, glittering black pools I could drown in. She places a hand on my thigh, and my whole body warms at her touch.

I close my eyes and let the music and the warmth of her hand wash over me. I'm hoarding every memory I have of her so I can pull them out when I have need of them. When all this is over. When Julian moves out and Marcela and Theo get married and I have no idea what my life will look like after the scavenger hunt. The gentle timbre of her voice, the dark curls falling over her shoulders, the tattoos swirling over her skin, her touch radiating heat at every point of contact.

I'm not sure if I can trust her promises yet. Not when I'm already bottling up every scrap of her I can get my hands on. It's too easy to envision an ending before we've really begun.

A while later, she takes the exit for the UTSA campus and crosses the intersection.

"Where are we going?" I already know this question is no use (she ignored me the last two times I asked), but this time she surprises me by flashing a brilliant smile.

"We're almost there."

We drive up a steep hill until we're cloaked on both sides by trees. If this is part of campus, it's not one I recognize. Finally, she comes to a stop when we reach a small parking lot at the very top of the hill. She turns off the ignition and sends another giddy smile my way.

She unbuckles her seat belt, and I do the same. I glance around, hoping for some clue, but alas. Despite being parked on top of a particularly steep hill, there's nothing of note at the bottom but more trees, overgrown grass, and a paved road I can only assume leads to campus.

"Over here," Krystal calls from the back of her car, where she's sorting through the layers of blankets in her trunk. She tosses a pillow at me before climbing inside. I catch it with a surprised *oof*, holding it to my stomach.

"I'm confused," I tell her. "Where—or *what*—is this view supposed to be?"

"You'll understand in a second." She pats the space beside

her that's covered in a thick layer of blankets. "Come here and look up. It's starting soon."

"What's starting soon?"

She doesn't answer, only pats the blanket harder. I heave a sigh before climbing in beside her. The absurd thought that this is almost like camping comes to mind.

Or a *date*. If I'm being honest, this whole night has felt like a date. The kind of first date that feels like the hundredth.

The best kind of first date.

Not that I would know. Not from any previous experience anyway. But she's setting a pretty high bar if this is meant to be a non-date.

I glance up at the near-black sky, and then back at her. "Well?"

"You comfy?" she asks instead, adjusting the pillows at my back and placing yet another blanket over my lap. They just keep appearing, and I have no idea where they're coming from. "Want any snacks?"

I gape at her. "You have *snacks* back here?"

"Oh yeah." She reaches behind her for a storage organizer I hadn't noticed earlier. "I have Cheez-Its, Goldfish crackers, hot Cheetos—"

A loud popping sound startles me out of my wits. The car shakes slightly under us from the movement. I place a hand over my chest, heart racing beneath my palm.

"Oh! They started early!" She shoves the box away and nudges me with an elbow. "Look up!"

I already am. A blast of red fireworks lights the sky, so close I can fool myself into believing I'm able to reach out and touch them. Another blast, this time white and green. A shower of colored sparks directly above our heads.

"Wow," I breathe. "Wait, where are the fireworks coming from?"

"Six Flags." She shrugs, but her eyes are twinkling. "I haven't been here since they opened the park back up for the season. You reminded me when you asked about my favorite view in the city. Well"—she glances back up at the sky as another round flies into the air, this time pink and purple—"here it is."

"This is incredible," I tell her, awestruck.

"I know." She smiles, showing her teeth. "There are probably a number of good spots around here to watch them from, but this one's my favorite. The parking lot's almost always deserted."

"I didn't know you could see them so clearly from here."

"Isaac had a night class here once. He didn't have a car at the time, so I used to pick him up when the shuttles stopped running. That's how I found out about the fireworks. I came back one night when he didn't have class and drove around until I found this spot. Then I parked, hopped onto the hood of my car, and just…watched the firework display."

"Wow." The sky is full at this point, sparks raining down as new shapes replace them. "So you found yourself a secluded, comfortable spot to watch the fireworks show for free. And with snacks." I shake my head at her, but I'm smiling far too widely. "You little rebel."

"This is like the upgraded version of sneaking outside food into a movie theater." She laughs. "My mom would be proud. Which is exactly why she can never know this spot exists."

A laugh bursts out of me. "This would make a great first date spot, actually. Especially when the nights get cooler, and you can cuddle up with your absurd amount of blankets." I use one to cover my shoulders. "Who else have you taken here?"

She goes quiet for a moment. Then, without looking at me, she says, "You're the first, actually."

"What?"

"You're on hallowed ground, Angel," she says lightly, but her eyes are burning with an intensity that clogs my throat. "I don't show this place to just anyone. It's too…personal."

Something charged fills the air when she looks at me now, and I'm overcome with an emotion I can't name. It's a lot like that moment in her bed, lying side by side, both of us breathing hard. The one at the top of the Ferris wheel, the dying sun setting her hair on fire and her calling me an angel with no amount of teasing whatsoever. Now, beneath a shower of sparks, hidden away in a place she hasn't shown a single soul but me.

"But you don't mind sharing it with me?"

She doesn't answer the question, but she doesn't look away from me either. This is somehow even more romantic than the top of the Ferris wheel at sunset, maybe because of how special this place is to her. If I tip my face forward, would we pick up where we left off?

For the second time tonight, I wonder what it would feel like. The brush of her lips against mine, the sweep of her tongue, the graze of her teeth. My pulse races at the possibilities. My arms are shaking, jittery from nerves, but it's not an altogether bad feeling. I hardly know what I'm doing when I start to lean toward her, our faces a mere inch apart, and then—

"I've decided I'm not going to kiss you," she says, almost reluctantly. It's the last thing I expect her to say when our faces are this close together. If there was ever a time to kiss someone, it'd be now, wouldn't it?

"What?" I blink at her. "Why not?"

"This is your first kiss, Angela. I can't be the one to take it from you," she explains. "Your first kiss should be yours to give freely. If you decide to give it to me, I'm honored to have that moment with you. If not, that's okay too. It's your choice. That was the whole purpose behind the scavenger hunt, wasn't it?"

My heart feels so full that she understands what the scavenger hunt means to me. Even so, part of me can't help but resent myself for coming up with the scavenger hunt idea in the first place. But it was my choice to take charge of my dating life, to discover what possibilities were out there for me. Nothing is going according to plan, but one thing is clear: until I decide what is happening with the scavenger hunt, I can't kiss Krystal. No matter how much I may want to.

"I really hate how right you are." I lean away from her until my back hits something solid. Then I stifle a groan. "You would've kissed me when we were on the Ferris wheel."

"You're right. I would have." She nods, sighing softly. "But I'm glad I didn't. It gave me the chance to really think about where you are in all of this. What you need from me." She pauses a moment, choosing her words. "You asked for my help in setting up the scavenger hunt. No matter what happens or how I might feel about you, I'm going to ensure everything goes according to plan. Even if that means you end up with someone else at the end of it."

Even though I know she's right, there's still one detail I can't get past.

"How you might feel about me," I repeat, and she glances away. "How do you feel about me, Krystal?"

Is that too direct a question to ask? She still won't look at me, even though I can't take my eyes off her. But I'm not letting her off the hook, even if it's the polite thing to do. Even if ultimately we want different things.

"How do you feel about Leti?" Her tone is even, not throwing the words at me like a jab I'm not expecting, even if that's ultimately how they land. "You know what? Don't answer that. It's not fair of me to ask, and I probably don't deserve to know anyway."

"Everything is confusing," I tell her. "I just…I wish things were different. Nothing is clear to me anymore."

"Well, at least we both can agree on that." She smiles sadly. "I don't want to hurt you. I can't. Not you, Angela."

"Because you think you're not capable of love."

"It's not about what I think." She sounds frustrated. "It's what I know."

I wish she could see what I see. How her friends and family manipulated the situation, made her out to be the villain for daring to want more than the life she had with Isaac. To want someone who really saw her.

I see you, I wish I could say. *Right now, I see you running.*

"You're capable of anything you want," I say instead. "And you can talk to me, you know. I'm not him. I'm not the friends and family who took his side over yours. I wish you felt like you could talk to me without shutting down."

"This is hard for me." She glances down at her hands. "If it helps, I've told you more than I've told most people."

Knowing how isolated she is from the people who were supposed to care about her, I believe that. Maybe I'm the only one who gave her a chance to explain her side without judging or making her out to be a villain.

"But you're still holding back. Because you think if we get any closer, you'll hurt me like you hurt him."

"Even if I was capable of love, *true* love, the kind of love you deserve from someone better than me"—her eyes burn through me—"I still come with a lot of baggage. We're in two completely different places. Your first romantic relationship shouldn't destroy you. I wouldn't mean to, but I would."

"I don't believe that."

She softens, a sigh deflating her shoulders.

I let out a long sigh too. "You're right about the scavenger hunt. It does mean a lot to me. But you mean a lot to me too." I grab her hand. When she doesn't move away, I intertwine our fingers. Her skin is warm and smooth, and her touch eases something in me the way her words didn't.

"Life is long, you know," she says. "Who knows? Maybe a few years down the line, we'll be ready for each other. You'll have experienced all your firsts, and I'll be healed enough to believe in love again."

"Or someone else will destroy me for the possibility of love, and we'll be back to square one," I joke as she gives me a quelling look. "Kidding. Kind of."

"I'm not ready for you yet," she says in a whisper I almost don't catch. "I wish I was, Angela. Believe me. But…I'm not there yet."

She rests her forehead against mine. We remain like this for a moment, hands touching, breathing each other in, staring at each other. The sky is awash with bursting, brilliant light all around us. And, for a moment, it's almost enough.

Twenty-Four

DM EXCHANGE:

@LetiIsTrying: I can't believe we're finally going to meet in person soon!

@Angela: I can't believe the new assistant librarian Marcela has been stalking is YOU! Talk about a small world.

@LetiIsTrying: Incredibly small, but I'm not fighting it. It's like we were meant to meet one way or another

@Angela: It sure seems that way, doesn't it?

After spending my Sunday morning completing this week's assignments and getting started on coursework due in the next

few weeks, I text Marcela asking if she and Theo are free today. The only time I ever hang out with Theo is during book club, and if I'm befriending him, as Krystal suggested I do, that means hanging out with him more than once a month. Julian has the day off from work, so I figure I can cook a friends' dinner for us all. It'd be nice to fill the house with more than two people at a time. And while I'm on a roll, I text Krystal too.

What are you up to today
on your free Sunday?

Nada. Why,
what'd you have in mind?

Do you want to come over
for dinner? Everyone will be here.

And by everyone you mean...?

Marcela, Theo, and Julian.
I'm taking your advice about
bringing them into the fold.

You're not gonna want to
miss out. I'm cooking!

...or learning how to cook, at least 🙈

Sounds fun, I'm in!

When I was growing up, my parents hosted every family event here. Birthdays, anniversaries, even my quince was here. My mom would set up folding chairs around the patio furniture, and my dad would get the grill started and cook enough food for the entire block.

All my brightest childhood memories were formed in this house. Running around with my cousins, playing hide-and-seek, taking photos in front of the staircase with my damas.

All my worst memories were formed here too. Esme and I sitting at the bottom of the stairs when I told her I'd never been kissed. Briana was outside beneath the old oak tree when Esme told her. If I squint, I swear I can still see them outside the window, smirking conspiratorially at each other.

I lift one of the small picture frames from the side table downstairs. It's one of me and Julian when I was twelve and he was nine. He's smiling up at the camera, two front teeth missing. That was the year he lost two baby teeth after biting into a chocolate egg on Easter Sunday. Our hair is flecked with colored confetti from an afternoon of throwing cascarones. I smile to myself at the memory.

"Oh no." I glance up at the sound of Julian's voice. He points to the picture frame in my hand. "I *knew* your parents still had that picture. My mom swore she lost it."

"You were so adorable back then," I tease. "What happened?"

He tries to snatch the frame from my hand, but I hide it behind my back and take a big step away from him.

"I think I'll hold on to it," I say. "It's perfect blackmail material, don't you think?"

"I'll remember this. Particularly the next time Krystal comes over. I'm not the only one who took embarrassing childhood photos."

He shoves past me to the side table, inspecting it for blackmail material on me. His frown deepens when he doesn't find any.

"You're forgetting I've never taken a bad photo a day in my life." I flip my hair off my shoulders. "I doubt you'll find anything."

"We'll see about that." He purses his lips, but his expression twists when he finds one of the few pictures we have of his father. Before I can think about what I'm doing, I set the frame face down on the table. He glances at me, raising one singular brow.

"That won't help." He lifts the frame from the table, cradling it in his hands as he looks down at his father. The photo was taken at least ten years ago. I can tell by how little gray is in my father's hair, though Manuel's was already starting to streak with silver. They're standing shoulder to shoulder, smiles wide and faced straight to the camera.

"There's no chance of him coming around, is there?" Julian's expression hardens, and I kick myself. "Sorry. Stupid question."

"It's not stupid. Impossible, maybe. But not stupid." He sets the frame back on the table with a sigh. "My mom doesn't believe in divorce, but she hasn't stopped considering it since I came out."

"I didn't know that. I don't think my parents did either."

"You know better than anyone how quickly secrets become

public knowledge in this family." *Boy, do I.* "I told her if she's going to do it, she should do it for herself. Not for me. I feel guilty enough knowing how well and truly I upended our family."

"You're their child. You didn't upend anything." He doesn't believe me now but I hope he realizes someday that it's true.

"It could be worse, I guess." He rolls his shoulders back. "No one's told Buelo and Buela yet."

"That's probably a good thing." Our grandparents are in their early seventies, but they've already gotten into the habit of saying, "This isn't our world anymore" every June when the pride parade shows on TV. And yet they never think to turn off MSNBC. It's wild coming from a Democratic conservative family. They hate Republican politicians for everything they stand for except stricter abortion policies and rampant homophobia. After many long conversations, my parents have come around on their own time but the same can't be said for the rest of my family. "Their hearts won't be able to take it with two of us around."

He flashes a grin. "No, probably not."

"By the way, you only have a couple hours to find that blackmail material," I tell him. "Krystal's coming over for dinner, and I fully expect you to be on your best behavior."

"Today?" He goes white with panic. When I give him a questioning look, he says, "Well, the thing is, Briana and Esme kind of invited themselves over."

Oh, fuck no.

"You *invited* them here?"

"No, no." He holds up a finger. "I want to make it very

clear that I tried to ward them off, but they weren't having it. Especially not when they found out I'm staying with you."

"You didn't tell them you were living here?"

"Are you kidding?" His eyes go comically wide. "I told as few people as possible. I don't even think my dad knows I'm staying here. Briana and Esme only found out because they ran into my mom at H-E-B."

"And now they're coming over." I smother a groan with both hands. "I'm not cooking for them."

"I'll be sure to tell them that." He stares down at his feet, hands in the pockets of his shorts. "Your parents still have photo albums upstairs, don't they?"

"If you think I'm letting you anywhere near potential blackmail material when you invited them over here without telling me—"

He bounds up the stairs at a run, and my hands curl into fists. I don't have time for this. Apparently, I have dinner for seven people to prepare.

Twenty-Five

What do you cook when the woman you orgasmed in the same room with and the cousins who tortured you all throughout high school and are currently avoiding like the plague come over for dinner? According to Marcela, pasta is always a winner. Especially when you don't really know how to cook to begin with.

"Did Julian say when they were coming over?" she asks as she dusts a pinch of salt into a pot of water.

"Nope." I hand her the box of penne noodles. "But Krystal should be here in about"—I glance down at the stove clock—"thirty minutes."

"I'm here for whatever you need when they arrive. Heck, I'll even use Theo as a diversion if I have to. Do your cousins care about football?"

"They probably won't recognize him, but Theo's hot and Briana and Esme are straight, so that should give me a solid half hour of peace. How long does the chicken go in, again?"

Her eyes flick to the oven's screen. "You know you have to preheat the oven first, right?"

"Shit. How long does it take to preheat?"

"Here." She knocks my hand away, pressing buttons until the timer is set. "We won't be ready by the time Krystal gets here, but maybe we'll have it together by the time your cousins show up."

She's at least half right. When the doorbell rings a half hour later, I allow myself to step away from the kitchen to call out, "Come in!" As the door swings open, it occurs to me I have no idea who will be behind it. I cross my fingers until the side of Krystal's head comes into view, hands in the pockets of her jeans, her bright yellow top like a beacon and brown sandals at her feet.

"You made it!" The relief in my tone is obvious.

"Any reason why I wouldn't have?" Her expression shifts as her eyes scan me up and down. "What's wrong?"

How does she *do* that?

Before I can give her the recap, Theo rises from the couch and juts out his hand. "Nice meeting you again, Krystal."

"So polite, isn't he?" Julian has appeared by my side as if by magic. I didn't even notice him leave the couch. Marcela emerges from the kitchen to greet Krystal, their arms encircling each other tentatively. My best friend is still wary of Krystal, and I haven't found a moment to try and convince Marcela otherwise. "Feels like I shouldn't be here."

I glance over at him, surprised. "What? Why would you say that?"

"This is practically a double date. I'm fifth wheeling, at least until the cousins crash. I would've tried harder to ward them off had I known everyone would be here."

"It's not a double date." But it comes out half-hearted,

maybe from how much I suddenly want it to be true. "And it definitely won't be by the time Briana and Esme get here."

An expression I can't read passes over his features. Guilt, maybe? I know it's not his fault the same way I know my cousins. They would've found another way to walk all over us. They always do.

"Any chance we can sic the big guy on them when they get here?"

I let out a laugh. "It's been discussed."

Krystal meets my gaze across the room and breaks away from my best friend. "So, what's for dinner? Need any help in the kitchen?"

Oh crap. I have no idea what's going on in the kitchen right now. Over Krystal's shoulder, Marcela meets my eye and says, "I got it," before going to check.

"Should I be concerned about what'll end up on our plates?" Krystal teases. "You weren't kidding about the cooking thing, huh?"

"It's been a long day." I shrug. "But it's looking up."

I hook an arm around Krystal's shoulders, smiling too wide at all my favorite people assembled together in the same space.

"Don't talk to me about long days until you start coming home at one a.m.," Julian groans, flopping back onto the couch.

"Are you a bartender too?" Krystal asks, taking the seat next to him as I plop down beside her.

"Until I graduate." Julian nods. "At this point, I'm counting down the days until I can finally get a solid eight hours of sleep. I'm exhausted all the time. I don't know how anyone does this."

"At least you know what you want to do with your life," I tell him. "You haven't had to change careers yet. I almost became a teacher until my last semester of college made me realize I had no idea what I was thinking."

"I'll cheers to that," Theo calls out from the kitchen bar. "It's a real bitch shifting careers, especially in your thirties. What's worse is I'm not sure I'm set on coaching for the rest of my life."

"Really?" I ask, surprised. "Do you have something else in mind?"

"A friend of mine is opening a bar in Dallas. He retired from the team this year and asked if I wanted to invest. I gotta admit, I'm tempted. If I hadn't moved, we might've been opening it together."

Krystal and I exchange glances, and for the first time in my life I experience what it's like to have one of those silent conversations you can only have with someone you've known for years.

Tell him. My eyes widen at her. *Tell him about your idea.*

I can't. She looks back at me like I've lost my mind. *I barely know the dude.*

What can it hurt? I slap at her knee until she shoos me away.

"Is that so?" I ask Theo.

"I minored in business finance." He takes a swig from his beer. Huh. I didn't even know I had beers in the house. "Not that that means I have any idea what I'm doing. There's a lot of trial and error that goes into opening a small business, but it's less daunting when you're doing it with someone you trust."

"What about someone you could grow to trust?"

"Okay, what is going on over there?" It took Theo a lot longer than I thought it would to sense the weirdness between me and Krystal, but now that he has, he raises a brow at us.

Tell him, I mouth at Krystal before slapping her knee again. She grumbles, but finally stands abruptly to face him. "She wants me to tell you that I…" She heaves in a deep sigh. "I actually want to open up my own bar one day."

He looks at Krystal as if with new eyes. "What kind of bar?"

"I don't know." I kick at her feet. Apparently, the only way I know how to show encouragement is through violence. She casts me an annoyed glance before looking back at Theo. "Something unique. When I first started at Havana Bar, I loved the lounge feel to it. The dark, moody furniture. All the candlelight."

"Her theme is a plant apothecary," I tell him. "With cute cocktails named after poisonous flowers."

"Or a greenhouse," she says, like the idea just came to her. "Imagine a building with floor-to-ceiling windows that mimic a greenhouse, lots of trailing vines, bright neon signs—"

"And poisonous drink names." His smile spreads wider. "Any ideas for a location?"

"I'm open to whatever price is reasonable, to be honest. As ideal as downtown is, I'm not sure how feasible it'd be."

They talk through ideas for a few more minutes, until finally Theo asks to exchange contact info. When he returns to the kitchen to help Marcela, I sling an arm around Krystal's shoulders. She lets out a flabbergasted noise into my chest.

"I think you just snagged a business partner." Krystal

shakes her head at me but doesn't say a word. "Do you want a tour of the place?"

"Yes, please."

The living room is sparse except for the faded couch and framed family photos. She picks up each one, asking me to name family members and point myself out to her in group photos. "You were so adorable." She stares down at my third-grade photo. "You still part your hair the same way." She fingers the edge of my curls, thumb trailing down my forehead. I resist a shiver at the touch.

"I tried giving myself emo bangs in sixth grade." I shudder for a different reason now. "You won't find that photo anywhere, and for good reason."

Julian makes a coughing sound from the couch. I narrow my eyes at him, remembering his little hunt for embarrassing pictures. There's no way he could've found them. I destroyed them as soon as the order came in over a decade ago. My parents grounded me for two weeks, but it was worth it.

I cast one last glare at him before leading Krystal upstairs. A diagonal line of even more photos greets us—a portrait of my grandparents, a smaller one of my dad and his siblings when they were my age, a group photo of cousins from my mom's side.

"We should take pictures," Krystal says, stunning me. "After the tour. Maybe we'll end up on the wall one day."

"I'd like that." I smile at the thought, staring at the pictures on the wall again. "There are a lot of good memories here. The only trouble now is most of my family members have either moved away or made themselves out to be terrible people."

"What do you mean?"

I glance down at the first level when we reach the landing. Julian is sitting on the couch downstairs, eyes trained on the blaring TV. Theo is helping Marcela in the kitchen, so I don't feel as bad for abandoning her to make dinner on her own. I'll make it up to her later.

"How did your family take it when you came out?"

She nods, understanding dawning in her eyes. "My parents were surprisingly okay about it. Other family members…not so much."

"Julian came out before I did, so I got a firsthand look at what would happen when it was my turn. Once I started to realize I was queer, I couldn't stop thinking about the shit he went through. But he ended up making the path easier for me to come out. The last thing my parents wanted was more discord, but they made it clear that they supported me no matter who I loved."

"It must've been hard for him, being the first," Krystal says. "Is that why he lives with you now?"

I nod. "His dad's an asshole. His mom supports him, but it's not enough when his parents are still together. They can't live peacefully under one roof."

I lean my arms against the railing. "My parents used to host all our family gatherings here, but they stopped last year when a fight broke out between our dads. My dad essentially told his brother he needed to get over himself and take Julian back. Tío Manuel made some wholly distasteful remarks about Julian, his own son, in front of our entire family. I saw everyone's true colors that day. It didn't take them long to pick sides."

"I can't even imagine what that must've been like for him," Krystal says. "When I finally came out to my mom, she thought that was the reason I broke up with Isaac." Her mouth twists into a half scowl, half dry smile. "I think she needed a more concrete reason than the one I gave her."

"Did you ever come out to him?" I ask her. "Did he think the same?"

"I told him a year before we got engaged. That was never a problem for him. My parents and certain family members were the last ones I came out to. I knew how they'd react, which is why I waited for as long as I did."

"Oh no." I wince. "Was it really bad?"

"I expected worse." She shrugs. "My parents are supportive in their own way, but we're not that close anymore."

"Really?" I ask her. "Because of what happened with your ex?"

"Yeah." She lets out a sigh. "I see them every few weeks. We catch up, I get a free meal, and then I leave before they get a chance to bring up my failures. The degree I don't use, leaving Isaac, why I don't have a real job yet, et cetera." She waves a hand. "I stopped paying attention a long time ago."

"Ah." I tip my head in a commiserating nod. "I get that. Mostly from my mom, wondering when I'll start dating and find someone to be with long-term. My dad's always been content to leave me be, figure out what I want in my own time."

We don't want you to be lonely.

Right now, I'm far from that. My heart feels as full as it's ever felt, flooded by this makeshift family I've found for myself. Marcela and Theo, Julian, and Krystal. If Leti's as cool as Marcela says she is, perhaps her, too, once I've figured out my shit when it comes to the scavenger hunt.

And then the doorbell rings.

Twenty-Six

J ulian answers the door. I watch from above as Briana and Esme make their way inside. They exchange greetings and hugs, Briana's voice carrying all the way up the stairs. She lifts her head, spotting me immediately.

"Bitch, get down here!" Her arm waves me forward. "I haven't seen you in ages!"

"She seems friendly," Krystal mutters under her breath, but her eyes are assessing. She knows everything about Briana and Esme, how small they've made me feel over the years. "Are they—" I nod grimly before she can finish, and she gives a sympathetic wince.

"They wore Julian down, apparently." I let out a long sigh. "All right. Let's go get this over with."

Her hand catches my wrist, stopping me from taking the stairs back down. "Are you okay?"

"I will be," I say, and I almost believe it. "I'll be fine."

The last time I hung out with Briana and Esme was a year ago, before I came out to my parents. From a cursory glance, they haven't changed much since then. Briana's dark hair is straightened, falling to the middle of her back. She pulls me into her arms in a strong

hug. I'm always surprised by her strength, given that she's even skin-
nier than me despite having two kids. But also because this is the
kind of bone-crushing hug you give someone you miss, not someone you're mad at for lying to you. Over her shoulder, Esme and I
wave to each other. She's never been a hugger like her sister.

"It's been way too long!" Briana pulls away slightly to get a
better look at my face, her grip strong on my shoulders. "How
have you been?"

I'm not sure how I get through the small talk, but somehow
I manage. At least, until the doorbell rings again. Krystal and I
exchange confused glances as Esme bounds to answer the front
door.

"That would be the boy toy of the month," Briana answers
my unspoken question. "Well, it's been more like three months
at this point, which is approximately two months and three
weeks longer than I thought he'd last, so props to him."

Great. Now I have three unexpected mouths to feed.
The portions are going to be so small, it'll be like eating at a
Michelin-starred restaurant except far, far worse.

"Finally! What took you so long?" Esme's voice rings out
from the hallway.

"I know, sorry. I swear I recognized the car out—" A white
man around my age turns the corner into the living room, eyes
wide like a deer in headlights when they immediately lock on
Krystal.

"Isaac? What's wrong?" Esme pulls at the sleeve of his shirt
with furrowed brows.

"*Isaac?*" I lower my voice, glancing between the three of
them in bewilderment. "As in—"

"Yeah." Krystal finally tears her eyes away from the man to look at me. "My ex."

He's different from what I would've imagined for her. Tall and lanky, with overlong hair and glasses too big for his face. They keep falling down his nose. Hell, he's even different from Esme's usual type. So iron-clad was her typical guy that back in the day, she used to cycle through virtually the same-looking dude every other week. All buff gym rats with biceps that could crack my head open like a nut. Isaac is nothing like them. He sticks his hands into his flannel jacket, eyes staring determinedly down at the floor.

"Who's your friend?" Briana steps forward, eyes assessing Krystal's guilt-ridden form. The way she can sense something wrong before her sister is uncanny. Idly, I wonder if it's some sort of mom intuition bursting within her, the need to protect Esme from whatever storm might be brewing.

I step in front of Krystal, blocking Briana's view of her, but only slightly.

"We've got a full house. Come on, I'll introduce y'all to everyone." I pull Briana into the kitchen by the wrist, hoping Theo will be enough of a distraction for her.

By the way her eyes bug out of her skull when she spots him, a relieved sigh deflates my shoulders. I practically push her into the other man's chest. To his credit, Theo hides his discomfort well, only exchanging apologetic glances with his girlfriend when Briana and Esme crowd him. That leaves me with one problem, but lucky for me it's one I'm equipped to handle.

"Let me show you some pictures of Esme as a kid." I guide Isaac out of the kitchen by linking our arms. "I think I have a few from the great food fight of 2011. As beautiful as your girl-friend is, she does *not* wear cafeteria spaghetti well."

Isaac raises a single brow at me but doesn't fight when I guide him back to the living room. Over my shoulder, I catch Krystal's eye and give her an encouraging smile. *I've got this*, I silently convey to her. I don't think much when her face turns pale and she opens her mouth as if to speak, but nothing comes out. They probably haven't spoken since the breakup. I under-stand her panic, but this could be a good opportunity for them. Maybe all they need is closure. Maybe then, Krystal will be able to forgive herself for how things ended with Isaac. If he can forgive her, she'll be able to forgive herself.

I point out some mildly embarrassing photos of Esme, along with some pretty great ones. Isaac's tense shoulders loosen with every turned page of the photo album. Soon enough, so does his tongue.

"She's not my girlfriend," he confesses after a while. "I mean, I'd like her to be, but Esme's a bit harder to convince."

"I can't remember the last time she had a serious relation-ship, to be honest," I say. "But we're not that close these days, so what do I know?"

He hesitates a beat before he asks, "How do you know Krystal?"

I look up at him, surprised he brought her up so easily. I've been gearing up to ask him about her, but no question I've landed on so far has been subtle. It's better this way, though. This is a conversation to ease into, lest he shut down too soon.

"We're friends. I'm a regular where she works."

"She told you about me." It's not a question, just something he's figured out for himself. He takes in a deep breath. "How is she?"

"She's…" I trail off, wondering how much of the truth to

admit to him. "She feels awful about what she did to you." He tenses up again, eyes scrunched in a wince before a wall closes over his expression. He might be with someone else now, but he's not over what went down with his ex. "She hasn't forgiven herself for hurting you."

"Yeah, well, I'd find it hard to forgive myself, too, if our roles were reversed," he says, tone hard. "Leaving someone at the altar isn't an easy thing to forgive."

The air stills, or maybe it's just me frozen in time. I stare at him for a long moment, my brain working overtime to make sense of what he's just said.

"I...What?" An unintelligible sound leaves my lips, something like a manic, disbelieving laugh. "Left at the altar? There was an actual *wedding*?"

"She didn't tell you about that?" He turns to face me fully now. "It was back and forth with her for *months*. Ever since I put that ring on her finger. First, we couldn't agree on anything for the wedding. Then when we did, she said the planning was getting to her. Finally, she said she'd rather elope instead. It was the last thing I wanted, but I agreed because it was what *she* wanted. I knew I was losing her. I *felt* it. All I wanted was to make her happy, even when it came at the cost of my own happiness. I thought if we just got married, without all the pressure from our families, we could get our relationship back on track.

"And then she changed her mind again." He scoffs. "I found out she wasn't coming through a voice message. She couldn't do this, she was sorry, and we'd talk later. That should've been the end of our relationship right there, but I was too stupid to see that she wasn't in it anymore. It was so obvious when I think back on it, but I didn't see it. I didn't *want* to see it. She was my first love. First and only, I used to think."

She left him at the altar. I thought I knew the full story, but she kept the biggest piece to herself. Why didn't she tell me? Did she think she couldn't trust me? I'm so naive, thinking if I just talked to Isaac I could convince him to forgive Krystal. That maybe if he and Krystal got the closure they needed, she'd finally be able to put her past mistakes behind her.

"I'm sorry," I take in a deep breath. "I didn't know. She didn't..."

He lets out a humorless laugh, the side of his mouth quirking in a knowing smirk. I don't like the look of it at all, even if he is the wronged party. Over by the dining area, Julian and Krystal are helping Marcela set the table. Every once in a while, I catch Krystal's eyes on us. Her expression is unreadable, but I can tell she's anxious from the way she can't keep still.

"I'm not surprised," Isaac says. "Listen, I don't know you. I don't know what your relationship with my ex is like. All I know is my side of things. I never really knew how she felt about marrying me until we were breaking up. She strung me along until her mind was made up. She didn't love me, and there was nothing I could do about it."

I can't believe she didn't tell me.

It all makes sense now—why she lost so many people when Isaac broke up with her, why she believes so strongly that she'll only hurt me if we take our relationship any further. I understand Isaac so much more than I want to. Not because he was left at the altar, but because of what he said about Krystal guarding her feelings until her mind was made up. There's a reason she didn't tell me the full story. She's guarding herself from me too.

Twenty-Seven

D inner is tense, though I'm not sure if the others can feel it the way I can. The way Krystal and Isaac can, too, judging by the way they make a concerted effort to avoid eye contact despite being seated straight across from each other. I'm not being a very good hostess either. I'm still rattled by everything Isaac told me, turning over this new piece of information in my head.

She left him at the altar, and she didn't tell me.

Marcela picks up the slack, handing out plates of chicken and pasta and asking what everyone wants to drink. Once everyone has their drinks, we lock eyes across the dining room and she mouths, *You okay?* I'm not sure how much she's pieced together, but she must sense something wrong. I shake my head, mouth, *Later*, and take my seat next to Krystal.

She hasn't said a word to me since her ex arrived with my cousin. I should've checked up on her sooner, and I would've if Isaac hadn't thrown that curveball at me. If he hadn't made me reevaluate everything I thought I knew about this woman.

"So, how do you two know each other?" Esme motions

a hand between Krystal and me. The question is innocuous enough, but there's an edge to my cousin's tone that wasn't there when we greeted each other in the foyer. There's no way she doesn't know who Krystal is. Isaac had to have filled her in as the table was being set, if not long before they entered this house. Esme's gaze flits to the other woman and stays there, assessing with a calculating eye.

"We met at the bar where she works," I answer, squeezing Krystal's knee beneath the table. I try to give her an encouraging look, but her eyes stay trained on her plate. "But we only started hanging out recently."

"Are you guys seeing each other?" Briana asks on Esme's other side, seemingly oblivious to the elephant in the room. She's a bit harder to read, occupied with cutting into the chicken. "You never updated TikTok on the scavenger hunt. Is that over?"

I blink at my cousin for a moment, stunned. "You...you watch my videos?" I could've sworn I blocked her and Esme after the group chat fiasco.

"I watch on Diego's phone when he's cleaning," she answers, spearing her fork into a penne. *Dammit. I forgot about her husband.* "I still can't believe you blocked me. Was that really necessary?"

"My page is meant to be a safe space." I sink into my chair, wishing we could drop this conversation. Or that I could suddenly become invisible. One of the two. It was naive of me to believe she wouldn't bring up the conversation I've been avoiding for weeks at the table in front of six other pairs of eyes, but that's my cousin for you—steamrolling right over anyone in her path. "I didn't just block you and Esme. I blocked plenty of people from high school and homophobic family members."

"Esme and I aren't homophobic," Briana says before squaring her eyes on our cousin. "Are we, Julian?"

"Leave him out of this," I say, giving Julian enough time to stuff his face to avoid having to speak. "This isn't about him. It's about me."

"Then why have you been ignoring me?" Briana's silverware clatters onto her plate with a loud crash. "Because I'm not 'safe'? Whatever the fuck that's supposed to mean."

"You're the reason she *needs* a safe space to talk about what she's built her platform on," Krystal interjects. I blink over at her in surprise. Moments before, I thought she was shutting down on me. That coming face-to-face with Isaac was too much for her. Turns out I was wrong, because she's all fired up now on my behalf. "God knows you and your sister bullied her enough times for it in high school. Why are you so surprised she doesn't trust you?"

"Oh, come on. You can hardly call what we did bullying," Esme retorts. "We only teased her a little bit. It was harmless. She knew we were just joking around."

"No, I didn't." I shake my head. "What was harmless about humiliating me *countless* times in front of all my friends and family?" I ask her. *Them.* Both of them. "Or reducing me to tears I fought to hide until I was alone? Or making me feel like a fucking weirdo just because I didn't want to kiss anyone I went to high school with?"

"You lied to us—"

"Because I *had* to!" My fist bangs against the surface, rattling the table. "You left me no other choice. All I wanted was for you guys to get off my back. That's why I lied about having a fling. Not because I thought it'd make you like me more."

Esme shakes her head, dismissing my outburst with an eye roll that has me seething. "What kind of person makes up a boyfriend?" She looks me up and down like *I'm* the problem. "That doesn't even make sense."

"And making fun of her for not having been kissed does?" Krystal's voice is low, but it thrums with barely contained rage. Her hands form white-knuckled fists beneath the table. "She was a teenager, for god's sake! Not to mention you giving out her number to every creep she went to high school with. She could've been harassed, assaulted, or worse!"

Briana's face has taken a greenish tinge. She places a hand over her mouth like she's about to be sick, but Esme remains unaffected, rolling her eyes again.

"Were we really that bad?" Briana's brows scrunch together. If I didn't know any better, I'd say she was...concerned. For the first time, I wonder if their memories are different from mine. If they truly never understood how much they hurt me over the years.

"You were worse." Krystal looks Briana right in the eye as she says it. "Whatever you're realizing right now, you were so much worse than you think."

"You never said anything," Esme says to me, still skeptical. "If we really hurt you that bad, why didn't you tell us?"

"You wouldn't have taken me seriously." I cross my arms over my chest. "You guys never took anything I said back then seriously. Even my parents dismissed me after a while. I only forgave you so many times because they asked me to. Because family isn't supposed to hate each other the way I used to hate you two. And maybe I was worried if I told you how much all the teasing hurt me, you'd know how much power you had over me, and the whole situation would only get…worse."

"Is that really what you thought of us? All this time, even after high school and we became friends?" Briana's eyes are shining with tears I can't fathom. "Were we really *that* cruel to you?"

Julian clears his throat from the end of the table, mouth no longer full. "I remember hiding out with Angela plenty of times around here when the whole family got together. You guys were more brutal than you think."

"'Brutal' is putting it lightly," Krystal scoffs, looking Briana dead in the face. "You oughta be ashamed of yourself. Growing up and figuring out who you are is hard enough without your own family tearing you down. You attacked her simply because she was different from you. It wasn't until you thought she was like you that you started treating her like a human being. Don't you see how fucked up that is?"

"You want to talk about who should be ashamed of who?" Esme rises from her chair, towering over Krystal's seated form. "Who the hell do you think you are inserting yourself into a conversation that has nothing to do with you? Who even *are* you, aside from the woman who left my boyfriend at the altar?"

Krystal's face turns white.

"That's enough." I stand up after my cousin, walking around the table until we're eye to eye and inches apart. "I'm not doing this with you. You're not going to attack my friends after I welcomed you into my home."

"It's your parents' house," she scoffs. "They don't even make you pay rent."

"Doesn't change the fact that neither of you were invited."

My arms cross over my chest as I glance between Esme and Briana. "And I won't allow you to talk to Krystal that way."

"What about the way she talked to me and Briana?" Esme rages. "We're your *family*."

"Nothing she said was a lie." I take a step closer. "And after everything you put me through, you can't convince me you don't deserve it."

"What I said wasn't a lie either," she huffs. "How can you be friends with someone capable of hurting Isaac the way she did?"

Briana rises from her seat next, quickly followed by Julian, Marcela, and Theo. Julian stops Briana from whatever she's about to say, lowering his voice to a register I don't catch. My best friend makes her way around the table until she's pulling me into the kitchen, away from the commotion of the dinner table.

"Are you okay?" she asks. "Scratch that. Stupid question. What do you want us to do?"

The dining room has devolved into full chaos now, with Esme shouting something over her sister's shoulder, an accusing finger pointed at Julian's chest. Not even Isaac can seem to calm her down. She shakes off his hand on her arm like she's shaking off a gnat. Theo is slowly backing away from the table, eyes skating the room like he's unsure what to do.

All the while, Krystal is eerily still in her seat, staring down at her full plate as everyone else argues all around her. Even after she hid this huge secret from me, I hate myself for unknowingly putting her in this situation to begin with.

"I have no idea." I shut my eyes against the scene. "God, this is a *mess*. I never should've avoided Briana and Esme for so long. This never would've happened if I faced up to them sooner."

Speaking of, Briana breaks herself away from the group and stalks toward us. Without a word, she pulls me from the kitchen by the wrist and leads me outside. Marcela tries to stop her, but Briana practically bites her head off with a look. I give a silent nod to my friend, assuring her I'll be fine before following my cousin to the backyard.

"Angela, I'm so sorry." I'm startled when she pulls me into her arms in that same bone-crushing hug so familiar to her. Only this time, her grip is even stronger than it was in the foyer. Not in a bad way. In a reconciliation kind of way. "I'm so incredibly sorry, okay? I didn't realize how much I hurt you back then, but I should have."

My eyes burn with an onslaught of tears I don't expect. From the apology I never expected to receive from her.

"I mean it, okay?" she says once she pulls back slightly. "I know we don't get to see each other as often as we used to, but that doesn't mean I don't want you in my life. We're family. We haven't always stuck by each other in the ways we should have, but I don't want you or Julian to feel like you have to avoid me because I won't accept you for who you are."

"It wasn't just that." I wipe at the tears tracking down my face. Briana notices the wetness on my cheeks, and her face falls. "I was never afraid you wouldn't accept me. You stood up for Julian against his father. I still remember the way you laid into him."

"I guess it's that protective instinct that kicked in." She laughs. "Motherhood changes you."

"I'm sure it does." I chuckle lightly. "I knew you'd accept

me. I guess I was more worried you wouldn't be able to under-stand me. Especially given that lie I told you and Esme after senior year, and everything I've said and done since."

"You don't owe me an explanation." She waves a hand. "I've seen enough of your videos to get the idea."

It's a bit of a relief to hear that, but even still I want her to hear it from *me*, not the version of me I send to the internet, now that she's given me the space where I feel safe to do so.

"I lied to get you and Esme off my back, and that's the truth. I was never trying to trick you guys or willingly deceive you. But I won't lie, it hurt that it took a lie like that to get you guys to finally treat me like a friend. When I started college, I made a vow to myself to start over. To never put myself in a situation like the one you and Esme put me in again. I only ever told one person the truth, and that was after I knew I could trust her without a doubt."

"I'm sorry we made you feel like you weren't good enough to be our friend." Briana's hand closes over mine. "And that you felt like you had to hide who you are because of it. God, I was an even bigger bitch than I realized, wasn't I?"

"Looks to me like you're growing out of most of it." I smirk. "Once I came out to myself, I wanted to jump to the end, you know? All I want is to live my life the way I should've been this whole time. I knew how confusing that would be for the people I didn't come out to, which is why I avoided you and Esme for so long."

"Can you forgive me?" Briana squeezes my hand, eyes imploring.

"Of course I can forgive you," I say, surprising myself by how easy that was.

For one cousin, at least.

Twenty-Eight

It's quiet by the time Briana and I return inside. Isaac and Esme are standing by the front door, the former glancing around anxiously while the latter taps her foot impatiently. Her sigh is loud, as if the foot tapping didn't make it clear enough that Esme's ready to leave.

"Let me talk to her." Briana nods her head at her sister before bounding over to her. I don't have much hope where Esme's concerned, and her new boyfriend is only half the reason. I should be used to her dismissing my pain. It's easier for her to believe that I'm the problem. I'm the liar. I'm the one blowing past hurt out of proportion. Anything to exonerate herself. I knew she would be this way. I thought both of them would be, but Briana surprised me.

Krystal is sitting on the couch by herself, arms crossed over her chest. She glances up when I plop down next to her, jaw tense. For the thousandth time tonight, I wonder what's going through her head. What's it like for her to see her ex after all this time? In a new relationship, no less. Does she have any regrets?

"Hi." It's not the best way to cut the tension, but her shoulders relax nonetheless.

"Hi." Her smile is tight, leg shaking anxiously next to mine. "Tough day, huh?"

I glance across the room at Briana. Her hands are moving as she and her sister talk beneath their breath. I can't make out a single thing they're saying, but Esme's pinched brow and single shake of her head is enough. Briana may have surprised me today, but her sister won't.

"How are you?" I ask Krystal, something I should've done the second Isaac walked through the door. How could I have been so thoughtless to not check in on her until now? "It couldn't have been easy seeing Isaac again. Are you okay?"

"I'm fine." When I give her a look, she shakes her head. "I'm the one who broke his heart, remember? Someone should be asking him that."

"I'm sure Esme has." I blow out a breath between my teeth. "How weird is it—your ex dating my cousin?"

"Super weird," she agrees. "Are you mad at me?" Her voice is so low, I barely hear her. I've never seen her like this before, bottom lip trembling, eyes that can barely look me in the face. I haven't had time to process today's many revelations. From Krystal's lie of omission to Briana watching my videos to making up for eleven years' worth of bottled-up hurt, I'm still not past the whiplash this dinner party's given me.

Before I can answer her question, a commotion from the front door snaps me out of my thoughts. Esme is cackling at something on her phone screen, and Briana is chastising her in hushed tones. It's exactly what I expected, despite Briana's insistence to get her sister to come around. And then there's Isaac, who looks like he's been gut-punched, staring across the room at me. No, at *Krystal*.

But she doesn't notice him staring at her. She quickly turns from them and asks me if I'm okay. Esme's laugh echoes off the walls, bouncing back at me. I get déjà vu to eleven years ago, that same laugh echoing in my ears as she tells Briana the secret I relayed to her in confidence. I can't hear what she's saying, but my ears burn just the same. Only this time, I'm not that same helpless girl anymore. I don't need anyone to stick up for me. I can do that my damn self.

I rise from the couch, hands balled into fists at my sides, but before I can confront her, Esme's back turns on me as the front door swings open. Once she steps outside, all I can do is watch as Isaac follows close behind her. Briana and I lock eyes, hers as helpless as I refuse to feel.

"Go." I wave her off. "Don't worry about it."

"She'll come around." *Doubtful*, but still, I nod and let her go. "I'll talk to her again. We'll work this out."

"Maybe." I shrug, try to come off unaffected. When a horn blares outside, Briana scowls at the door. "Seriously, I'll be fine. I've got my people. You can go."

"I'm texting you when I get home," she vows, arms tightening around my shoulders. "You better answer this time."

"I will," I assure her. "I promise."

And I actually mean it this time.

⤌⟶ ⟵⤍

After my cousins and Isaac leave, I lead Krystal to the back-yard. I feel bad for leaving the pile of dirty dishes untouched when Marcela did all the cooking, but she told me she'd get the guys to clean up. Tonight has to be confusing for her—there's so much I kept from my best friend. Between my cousins and Krystal's ex, I wonder how much she's been able to piece together. I thanked her with a bear hug and vowed to tell her everything soon before heading back to Krystal.

The back porch is a wasteland compared to the summer barbecues of my childhood. I don't know how to use the lawn-mower, so we're up to our ankles in grass as we make our way to the garden bench beside a Guadalupe statue.

"What did Isaac tell you?" Krystal's arms are crossed over her chest as she sinks onto the stone bench beside me.

"More than I would've told a perfect stranger." I shake my head. "I should've listened to you, but I thought I could help. That maybe if you guys had some closure, he would forgive you and you'd both be better off."

"He's not as bad as I thought if he's dating again," Krys-tal says. "I'd be happy for him if his girlfriend wasn't such a grade-A bitch to you. Even if he still hates me for everything."

"I guess that's something." I nod. "He said you strung him along. He seemed…angry. I saw the way he looked at you. Even when he wasn't staring at you, it was like someone punched him in the gut." He seemed less angry than heartbroken, actually. That man is definitely holding on to some lingering feelings.

"I don't blame him. I deserve it," she says. "He's right. I dragged out our relationship in this needless way because I was so afraid of hurting him. It was easier to say yes to a ring I had no intention of wearing. To say yes to an elopement I had no intention of showing up to and a life I knew in my bones I didn't want. I told myself I was trying to make our relationship work, when in reality that was the last thing I was doing." She blows out a breath. "I did the worst thing of all by not doing a goddamn thing, and I hurt him so much worse in the process. If I were him, I'd never forgive me."

"Is that why you didn't tell me?" I ask her. "Because you thought I'd look at you the same way everyone else in your life does?"

"Angela, this is the worst thing I've ever done in my entire life. Anyone who looks at me like I'm a heartless monster is right to. I could barely admit to myself what I'd done. I didn't have the words to express how I was feeling, or *why* I was feeling the way I was when it was always clear how much he loved me. It's only now that I've had some distance that I can properly articulate why Isaac was so wrong for me, and what I would do differently if I could go back. But I can't." She shakes her head. "It's too late."

"Listen, I don't blame you for the mistakes you made with Isaac," I assure her. "I know how heavy this burden is for you. If you were truly a monster, you wouldn't feel any remorse at all. Changing your mind about someone doesn't make you an evil or malicious person, even if Isaac was the best boyfriend in the world. Even if you didn't have a good enough reason for changing your mind about him."

"For the first time, I'm finally starting to believe that." She's staring at me in this inexplicable way. In a way that renders me unable to swallow past the lump in my throat. "You don't think less of me, then?"

"It was a shitty thing to do," I concede. "I'd think less of you if you hadn't acknowledged that. But I don't think less of you, Krystal. I think I'm starting to understand you more."

"Really?"

"I understand why you've been holding yourself back from romantic love of any kind." *And me*, I think, but don't dare voice aloud. "I finally get why you think you're such a terrible person for the way your relationship ended. Isaac might never be able to forgive you for what you did, but that's his choice."

"I told you, Angela." She stares down at the grass covering her feet. "I'm no good for anyone."

"If I haven't told you before, then I'm telling you now—I don't believe that." She doesn't say anything for a long moment. "Maybe you should reach out to him. See if you can get that closure after all."

She's quiet as she contemplates the idea. At first I think she's going to shake her head, tell me there's no way she can do that. A few weeks ago, maybe she would have. "What if he turns me away?" she asks instead, voice low. "You saw how we were in there. He couldn't even look at me."

"Yeah, I did. He'd have every right to, I guess." I shrug. "But just because he can't forgive you doesn't mean you can't forgive yourself. In fact, I think you should. Whether he turns you away or not."

She takes in a deep breath. After what feels like minutes, she finally nods. "Okay."

"Okay?" I glance at her, surprised she gave in so easily.

"I'll reach out. I'll try. Maybe you're right. Maybe it'll be good for us to get some kind of closure. And if it's not the right thing for him, I'll respect that. It's about time I start moving forward, you know?"

"Yeah." I'm speechless for a moment before I get my bearings back. "I'm happy for you, Krystal. I hope he hears you out."

"Thanks." She smiles softly. "We'll see what happens."

Twenty-Nine

CAPTION:

THIS EVER HAPPEN TO ANYONE ELSE?

@WILLWORKSOUT CLOSED CAPTIONS: Anyone else date a girl in high school who turned out to be a lesbian? I just came across her page the other night and I'll admit, I was taken aback. But from what I can tell, she seems to be doing really well for herself. I'm happy for her, especially since I was a complete jerk when we went out. So, Angela, if you're watching this, I'm sorry about what happened, and wishing you all the best.

COMMENTS:

@Angela: Well, this is certainly a throwback. Sorry our date was such a flop but as I'm sure you can see now, we never would've worked out 😆

Replying to @Angela
@Alisha: Wait, but I thought you've never dated anyone before?

Replying to @Alisha
@Christine: I'm also lost here

Replying to @Alisha
@Esme: Not your lies catching up to you 💀

Replying to @Alisha
@Angela: We went on one date our senior year and I spent the entire night on my phone. He tried to kiss me at the end of the night and accused me of leading him on, which is what I'm assuming he meant when he said he was a jerk when we went out.

Replying to @Angela
@WillWorksOut: You assumed correct. I'm really sorry about that, btw. You didn't deserve any of that.

Replying to @WillWorksOut
@Esme: So did you two hook up or not? I'm still trying to get all my cousin's lies straight...

⊰⊹⊱

Monday night after work, I return to the drawing board. Krystal was right about one thing—Fiesta would make the perfect backdrop to the scavenger hunt. After a few hours of brainstorming, I discover that there are plenty of downtown locations that would make perfect scavenger hunt locations and cut down on driving time. I'm not sure I'm totally in love with my replacement for Natalia's art piece, but I don't know if she'll see me again either.

After making some calls on Tuesday night to secure a few places for two weeks from now, I catch sight of *The Woman in Wanting* hanging from my wall. Her eyes seem to pierce through me, questioning how I can solidify a date for the scavenger hunt without Natalia. "Don't look at me like that." Great, now I'm talking to digital art prints. "Natalia isn't going to help me. She told me so herself."

The print doesn't respond, because it's *paper*. "You want me to prove it?" I grab my phone and scroll to find Stephanie's contact. "I'll show you."

She answers on the third ring. "Angela, hey." Stephanie sounds breathless, like she's been running. "How's it going?"

"Good, for the most part," I respond. "Is Natalia available to talk?"

"Sure thing, she's right—" There's a bit of shuffling. I can just make out voices mumbling back and forth. It goes on for so long, I think about hanging up. I glance back at *The Woman* and mouth, *Told you so*, when a new voice finally comes on the other end of the line.

"What do you want?"

"Natalia." I didn't think she'd actually take my call. "How are you?"

"The same." I wait for more words to come, but that seems to be it.

"Oh, well…I'm sorry."

"Why are you calling?"

It's obvious she hasn't changed her mind about helping me, and it almost feels like adding insult to injury to ask again. If she's not showcasing anywhere, asking for her involvement could potentially mean asking her to create a whole new art piece, which is a huge ask on its own even without considering her slump. I should hang up and apologize for wasting her time. Instead, I'm staring at the art print Natalia gave me and wondering how off base I am in my interpretation.

"What does *The Woman in Wanting* mean?" The question comes bursting out of me without forethought.

"What do you think it means?" I cross my arms and slump in my desk chair. Figures Natalia would answer a question with a question.

"I know what *I* think it means," I tell her. "I've been applying my own false meaning to it since I spotted it from the Tower of the Americas. I poured so much of myself into a mural I couldn't even touch, and then it got washed away. Just like that."

"It spoke to you," Natalia says. "What's always drawn me to art is that there's no right answer really. There's no one telling you your interpretation is wrong. You use your senses to explore what an art piece means to you, how it makes you feel, what emotions it provokes. It obviously provoked something in you."

"I guess you're right." As unsatisfying of an answer as that is, it's all she's willing to give me. Not that she owes me any kind of explanation. Maybe it's better this way. I get to keep applying my own meaning without the artist's intention influencing me one way over another.

"I'm sorry, by the way," she says. "I shouldn't have told you to quit TikTok. If anyone had told me back then to quit sharing my art online, I wouldn't have listened. I shouldn't have acted like I knew better than you about what would happen. You're not me, even though meeting you felt like history repeating."

"It's okay, Natalia. I think I get it now. You were just looking out for me, even if it came out..."

"Like I'm a raging asshole?"

"I was going to say aggressive." I laugh. "Is it okay to ask you what happened?"

A deep sigh fills the phone static.

"The same bullshit, over and over, until I couldn't take it anymore," she says. "It started when one user asked me if I was queer. This was before I had an answer—when I was exploring how I felt about myself and queerness through my art. You know the nature of the internet; they don't like when an answer isn't tied up with a neat little bow."

Isn't that the truth. Ever since I commented on Will Mora's post about me, I've been getting more questions than ever. A few people even migrated back to my most recent video to demand answers.

@Christine: Why say you've never dated before when you clearly have? Even if it was just one date with @WillWorksOut that didn't go anywhere, it still counts.

Replying to @Christine
@Katie: Wait, someone catch me up. What happened?

> Replying to @Christine
> @Alisha: Did you see what her cousin commented? I don't know what to think to be honest...

> Replying to @Christine
> @TheGreatAcecape: I'd hardly say it counts if she wasn't attracted to him.

I'd left another comment explaining the situation much like the one I'd left on Will's video, and that was the end of it. At least for now.

"And then when I finally had an answer, they didn't like that either," Natalia continues. "Apparently, being asexual isn't queer enough. Or I'm lying, or confused, or making up my experience to feel special. It wore on me. Especially when the people who once praised me and my art turned around and made their own platforms dedicated to destroying mine."

"Jesus. Natalia, that's terrible. I'm sorry that happened to you."

"I guess you could say influencing, content creation, whatever you wanna call it"—she scoffs—"it didn't work out so great for me. But maybe you'll be different."

"I'm not sure," I admit. "I think I just got embroiled in my first online scandal. Maybe it comes for us all eventually, if we're determined to share our lives on the internet."

"What happened?"

I tell her about Will's video and the questions that came out of it, including my cousin stoking the flames.

"I see. What are you going to do?"

"It'll blow over," I say. "I've already explained what

happened. Twice, actually. It's their choice whether they believe me or not." She's silent for so long, I'm not sure she's still on the line. "Natalia?"

"Just promise me you'll be careful," she says. "And if the shit hits the fan again, call me."

"You mean call Stephanie?" A beat later, an incoming text from Stephanie lists ten digits. "Wow. And here I thought you hated me."

"I don't hate you, Angela," she says. "I've just…been through this before. I'd hate to see what happened to me happen to you."

"You think it will?" She's silent long enough for me to realize I don't really want to know the answer. "You don't think I'm stupid for putting on an entire scavenger hunt just to have my first kiss and broadcast the entire experience online for hundreds of thousands of people to witness?"

"You're taking control of your life," she says. "There's nothing stupid about that. I only wish I could do the same."

"Thank you for saying that. And thanks again for the art print. It's lovely." *It's haunting me.* But I don't tell her that, because I think Natalia has enough ghosts of her own to contend with.

When I hang up, I'm not dissuaded from moving forward with the scavenger hunt. If anything, I'm even more determined to see this through. So what if I've had a few setbacks? I can still pull this thing off and have my first kiss the way I originally planned to. Maybe even date around afterward, figure out who I am inside of a relationship. With Leti, or with someone else. It's what I want. It's what I'm ready for.

Besides, Krystal has made it clear numerous times that she's not ready—not *capable*—of something more, which means I have to move on. I can't make her change her mind, no matter how much I may want to. That's something she has to figure out on her own.

I spend a few hours online after posting an update on Tik-Tok, check my email for sponsorship requests (I guess I'm a real influencer after all), and then open a few message requests from followers in the San Antonio area.

The next week and a half passes in a flurry of planning and messaging potential participants back and forth. By Wednesday, I have five final locations secured with a few phone calls. By Thursday, I'm DM'ing women in town I've already been casually talking to online in order to confirm that they'd like to join in. Including Leti, I have at least seven women willing to participate in the scavenger hunt.

I should be excited. The scavenger hunt is nearly all planned out, I have more than a handful of willing participants, and I'm even planning an after-party at my house for everyone to get to know each other in a more casual way. But I still can't get Krystal out of my head. I can't help but wonder what we could be if she chooses to forgive herself. If she decides that she was wrong about love and that I'm partially the reason.

Stupid. Hopeless. And yet...

She's still in the forefront of my mind on Friday night, when I have plans to meet up with Marcela and Leti. I'm hoping that afterward, I'll feel reinvigorated about the scavenger hunt like I was when I first came up with the idea. I'm the first to arrive at Havana Bar by nearly an hour. Krystal is pouring drinks for a group of twentysomethings, smiling idly at them until she spots me. Her grin spreads, making my pulse jump. The group heads to a table once they have their drinks, and I quickly take their place at the bar.

"Hi." She pushes a stray strand of hair away from her face. "This is an unexpected visit."

"I'm meeting Marcela and Leti, but I wanted to say hi," I tell her. "And I also wanted to let you know I won't be needing your help anymore."

The glass in Krystal's hand overflows with liquor. When the liquid sloshes over the rim and puddles around the shot glass, she curses beneath her breath and makes a grab for a rag behind the counter.

"What do you mean?" she asks when she returns.

"I finished planning the scavenger hunt. I still need to make a couple calls before everything's set in stone, but it's done."

"Good." She nods, but something about the motion is agitated. "Did Natalia change her mind?"

"No. I called her the other night, and I don't think it's going to happen." I shrug. "But after some brainstorming this week, I decided I could pull it off without her. So far I have five locations secured, a decent number of participants, and a date. Two weeks from now."

"That's...that's great, Angela." Her words don't match up with her expression. She glances behind me and then down at the shot glass on the counter. "That group forgot a drink." She picks up the glass and nods to the table behind me. "Sorry, I need to deliver this."

The bar isn't as packed as it usually is for a Friday, but Krystal still manages to avoid me half the night. Not that it matters, because I came here to see Marcela and Leti anyway, but it stings nevertheless. They arrive as I'm ordering my second drink of the night from another bartender, and we take the upholstered chairs in a corner.

The first thing I notice about Leticia Maldonado is that she's stunning. She's wearing a dark dress with cutouts along the sides that show off her curves and a small handbag with a gold chain crossed over her body. As we take our seats, multiple heads turn her direction and outwardly stare.

"*Wow*, Leti. You clean up nice."

"So do you." Her eyes sparkle as a smile takes up her entire face. "It's so nice to finally meet you in person."

"All this time, how did I not know you're a library worker too?"

"We never mentioned where we work, I don't think," she says. "I didn't know that about you either."

Marcela leaves to order a second drink fifteen minutes in, and then mysteriously disappears. She's not slick. I know exactly what my best friend is doing. I'd appreciate the gesture more if I didn't have a perfect view of Krystal over Leti's shoulder. But there's no hope there. With Leti, there might be.

I learn that Leti's not much of a reader despite her profession, but when she does, she prefers audiobooks and graphic novels. She's taken her side hustle as a cozy gamer on TikTok to Twitch as well, and we're able to commiserate about our time spent largely in online communities. An hour passes, and I hardly notice.

"So, what do you think?" I ask. "Still want to join the scavenger hunt?"

"Of course I do." She places her hand on top of my mine. "I know we were mostly joking in the beginning about saying we should date each other, but it feels like fate that we're in the same city with the same connections, doesn't it?"

"It was certainly a surprise." Her soft hand warms my palm, and though it's not an unpleasant feeling, something about the contact feels...wrong. I pull my hand away and cover by grabbing my drink. "And remind me again, are you single?" My brows waggle as she rolls her eyes, but her smile is fond. "Because it's sort of a requirement that you have to be single in order to participate. You wouldn't go through the trouble of winning my first kiss just to break my heart, would you, Leti?"

"Funny." She takes a sip from her drink. "And no, Angela, I wouldn't do that to you. Lucky for you I'm *extremely* single. So single, in fact, I'm the last single sibling in my family. Last of them to have my life figured out, really."

"I don't have any siblings, but I get it. I'm living with my parents until I graduate and find an open librarian position."

"I just moved out of my parents' place," she says. "We have so much in common already."

"We sure do." For the first time since Leti walked in, I catch Krystal's gaze across the bar. Her eyes quickly dart away as she turns and disappears into the back. Shaking my head, I continue. "Say you win the scavenger hunt." Leti mimes raising her arms in victory. "What would the next step look like? Would you say you're looking for a relationship?"

"That would be the goal, yes, if we agree there's a connection here. I'd say it's looking pretty good so far. Wouldn't you?"

A crash from the bar saves me from answering. Krystal is

mumbling beneath her breath as another bartender returns with a broom.

"Sounded like a bottle broke," Leti says before turning back to me. "Anyway, where were we?"

"Um…" I blink a couple times before turning away from the bar, where Krystal is cleaning up whatever mess happened back there. "Right. Dating. Aside from messaging accidental thirst trappers on TikTok, have you been dating anyone recently?"

"Not at all." Her mouth purses. "I haven't been on a date in four years. After the worst first date in history, I pretty much gave up on dating until I figured out my identity. I'm trying not to be a cynic about dating, or the idea of returning to dating apps, but it's hard not to be when you know what's out there."

"Yeah, I'm a little happy not to know what's out there yet." I laugh. "Aside from you, but I doubt anyone would become a cynic after dating you."

She smiles shyly, casting her eyes down, and I wait to feel something. Some sort of spark or connection like she mentioned earlier. But that's not why we're meeting up. This isn't a first date, and romantic feelings don't happen instantaneously for me. They grow over time—slowly, inconveniently, until they swallow me whole.

Leti leaves soon after, and Marcela quickly takes her vacant chair.

"Well?" she asks, looking far too excited for her own good. "How'd it go?"

"She's going to join the scavenger hunt." When Marcela's expectant look doesn't change, I sigh. "What?"

"That's it? That's all I get?" she yelps. "This was your first time meeting your flirtationship in person! What did you think about her? Is there something there?"

"I don't know," I say honestly. "Maybe. It's too soon to tell, but I…" Krystal has finished cleaning up whatever mess happened behind the bar and is now taking orders when a group of women enter. "Is it wrong of me to go through with this if my head is somewhere else?"

Marcela turns to where my gaze has landed, and then looks back at me. "That depends. Is it your head or your heart that's elsewhere?"

"I…don't know."

"Come on, Angela." She shakes her head slightly. "We both know that's not true."

"You're not gonna try to convince me to give Leti a chance?" I raise a brow at her. "I thought you weren't on Team Krystal anymore."

"Are you kidding me? After the way she stood up for you to your cousins?" I'd given Marcela as much of an explanation as I could after the worst dinner party ever when Krystal went home and Julian and Theo hung out upstairs to give us some space. She had given me permission to tell Marcela about Isaac, and my fraught feelings for Krystal were starting to eat me from the inside out. After that, we did a deep dive on my cousins and our high school history. It felt good to finally get everything off my chest after keeping so much about my cousins to myself. "If I'd known the full story, I wouldn't have fed them."

"I'm sorry I didn't tell you sooner," I tell her, and not for the first time. "For so long, I didn't want to talk about them with anyone. I still have a lot of pent-up shame from the way they treated me in high school."

"Krystal's right. They're the ones who ought to be ashamed, not you." I know she's right, but it still brings a sense of relief to hear her say it. "As for Krystal, I'll be honest. I'm still conflicted. Leaving Isaac at the altar and then waiting for him to initiate a breakup?" She grits her teeth in a grimace.

"That's why she doesn't think she's capable of falling in love. She doesn't want to get into a new relationship because she's scared of making the same mistakes. And I get it. I really do. She doesn't want to hurt me the same way she hurt Isaac."

"But she's hurting you by not being with you the way you both clearly want to be," Marcela says, and that's pretty much the crux of it. "What are you going to do?"

I let out a sigh. "I have no idea."

Thirty

Marcela doesn't stay for much longer. I should head out, too, but I want to say goodbye to Krystal, especially since she's avoiding me. It doesn't feel right to put even more space between us without figuring out what she's thinking. Another bartender takes my order while she's gone, a man with close-cropped hair and a flirty grin that does absolutely nothing for me.

"I hear these are your usual." He deposits a Malibu sunset onto the bar. "Extra Malibu, on the house," he adds with a wink.

I take a sip and nearly sputter from the burning sensation clawing at my throat. "How much extra are we talking, here?"

"Not sure." The side of his mouth quirks up. "I don't measure alcohol for friends."

Another cheesy wink. I glance over my shoulder, where Krystal is busying herself with wiping down tables. I don't return the bartender's advances, but I do down the drink in three gulps. He sets another beside my empty glass. It's not as strong as the first but has twice the amount of grenadine it should. I wince at the taste, but he doesn't seem to notice.

He's leaning over the bar, a leering smirk on his admittedly handsome face, when a shadow falls over us.

"I can take her from here." Goose bumps prickle the hair at the back of my neck at Krystal's voice. When I turn around, her stony-eyed gaze is trained on the new guy.

"That's okay," he says, looking back at me. "I'm good here."

"It wasn't a suggestion." Her stern voice sends chills running up and down my spine. "Go take inventory in the back."

"I already did that when I came in." Krystal stares him down until he finally breaks. "Guess I'm doing inventory again."

"Who was that?" I ask once he's gone. She doesn't answer my question as she clears away my three empty glasses and grabs a fresh one from behind the counter. She opens the tap, filling it with water before handing it to me.

"Drink up," she says, her tone brokering no argument. I do so, if only because I'm kind of a fan of this bossy side of her. Is she…jealous? "I can't leave you alone for a second. How much did he give you to drink?"

"Just what you cleared away." I wave her concern away. "I'm good. Ish. We'll find out when I try to stand up."

She curses beneath her breath. "I'm gonna kill that guy."

"He was just doing his job." I shrug. "I can't expect you to hang out with me all night. You were doing your job too."

"And you were occupied for half the night yourself," she reminds me, her expression torn. Finally, she asks, "How was your date?"

I rear back. "I'd hardly call it a date."

"I'm not accusing you of anything, Angel. You can do whatever you want. We agreed to just be friends, remember?"

"Still, it wasn't a date," I insist. "After the scavenger hunt, who knows? If she wins, maybe we'll see each other again. Or maybe we won't."

"Do you want her to win?" she asks, holding my gaze. "You told me you like her, after all."

I do like Leti. Under very different, Krystal-less circumstances, yeah, I'd probably be rooting for her to win. We want the same things. Hell, we're both graysexual. She's pretty and smart and incredibly interesting, but at the end of the day, she's not *Krystal*. I take a sip of water instead of answering. After a beat, Krystal sucks in a deep breath.

"I texted Isaac," she says out of nowhere, surprising me. "He hasn't replied yet and I don't know if he's going to."

"That's still good," I tell her. "You never know, right? He could surprise you."

"Maybe. But I'm not holding my breath."

"Still. I'm glad you texted him."

"Yeah?"

I nod. "Do you know what you're going to say to him if he replies?"

"I keep going back and forth in my head about it." She pushes a stray curl back from her face. "If I'm apologizing for the wrong reasons, is it still worth saying 'I'm sorry'?"

"That depends more on whether he wants to hear it," I say. "Plus, how wrong can your reasons for apologizing be?"

"Maybe it's selfish," she says. "Aside from last weekend, we haven't spoken to each other since we broke up. Actually, I'm not sure we spoke at all."

"Maybe that's exactly why you two need to talk," I tell

her. "If you hadn't seen each other at my house, neither of you would've bothered to reach out. Now you have an opening. It might be a hard conversation to get through, but maybe it's needed."

"You're right." She groans. "I'm just nervous."

"At least wait until he replies to be nervous." I smile dryly. She pushes at my shoulder, but there's no force to it. "It'll work out, regardless of whether he wants to see you."

"You really believe that, don't you?"

"I believe you're capable of forgiving yourself," I say, if only because I so desperately want that for her. "With or without Isaac."

"That makes one of us, at least." She looks up at me from the floor, and for the umpteenth time, I'm sucked into her orbit. "You're a good friend."

Those words can't negate the pounding in my chest or my inability to breathe properly in her vicinity. I may be inexperienced, but not so much that I don't know friends aren't supposed to feel like this for each other. But at this point, I don't see any other option for us.

"We shouldn't try to be more than that," I tell her. Tell *myself*, because I need to hear it more than she does. "At least, not until after the scavenger hunt is over."

"Right." She bites her bottom lip, my eyes immediately pulled to her mouth. "We still have that rule."

"Someone thought it'd be a good idea, not that I can remember why." Not when she's looking at me the way she is now.

"Well, you've had a couple drinks," she reminds me with a stern look. "You'll remember in the morning."

I hop off the barstool, and *boy* is that a mistake. The room spins for a moment until I'm able to right myself by grabbing on to the bar. "Malibu, why hath thou betrayed me?"

"Angela?"

"That stupid boy threw off the portions in my drink." I rest my forehead against the wood as my head starts to pound. "Too much grenadine, then too much booze. Or maybe it was the other way around. Too much booze, and then too much grenadine."

"Who are you talking about?" She walks around the bar and pulls me into her arms. "The bartender who served you?"

"Isn't it in the job description that a bartender has to know how to make a damn drink the correct way?" I'm spewing complete nonsense at this point. "Oh god, I think I'm gonna be sick."

She power-walks me to the bathroom, where I hurl into a toilet bowl just in time. After pulling my hair back into a chongo, she tells me to stay here while she closes the bar, as if I was capable of moving off this floor by myself. Luckily, my stomach seems to be feeling fine after one barf session and I'm not nearly as dizzy as before.

Once the building is locked for the night, she returns to the bathroom to lead me to her car and helps me into the passenger seat. I reach for the seat belt above my head but can't seem to find it for some reason. Krystal's chest rises and falls with a long sigh. Just as I find the buckle, her hand closes over mine.

I glance up and holy shit her face is so much closer than I thought it was. The upper half of her body is bent over mine, her right hand braced on the seat beside my thigh. There's that feeling again, like something's clogging the back of my throat, preventing me from breathing.

"There we go." She pulls down the seat belt and buckles it in place over my lap. She sounds as breathless as I imagine I'd be if I was capable of speaking, but she recovers quickly. "You feeling okay?"

All I can manage is a nod, and not even because of the alcohol. When she closes the door, I'm finally able to catch my breath. Krystal walks around the car until she reaches the driver side.

"Let me know if you start to feel sick," she says as she starts the engine. "I might have a plastic bag you can barf in if you need to."

"I think my stomach settled after the one."

"Good, but I'm still taking you back to my place," she says. "You can't drive back home like this."

I'm too tired to argue with her, because she's probably right. I'm in no state to drive myself anywhere. But the two of us under one roof, with all our unresolved feelings? That doesn't sound too smart either.

Thirty-One

After loaning me an old T-shirt and pajama bottoms to sleep in, we fight over who gets the couch. Krystal, apparently, is too polite to let me take it, even for a night, but the last thing I want to do is put her out. "We're both adults," I finally say, too tired to continue arguing but not enough to give in. "Your bed is big enough for two people."

Which is how I end up here, lying next to her, our shoulders brushing on her full-size mattress. But the extra Malibu had one hell of an effect on me because without even meaning to, I'm asleep before I know it.

Sunlight pours in through the gauzy curtains covering her window, waking me long before I'm ready. I'm warm and comfortable, tangled in Krystals arms.

Wait a minute.

I blink against a bare shoulder, barely registering my arm slung around her back.

"Krystal," I whisper her name, gently shaking her arm.

"Mm-hmm." Her eyes are still closed, but a hand at my

waist tightens slightly. My heart races so hard, I can hear the sound of rushing blood in my eardrums. How in the world am I waking up in her arms when we weren't so much as touching last night?

Stop complaining and enjoy it while it lasts.

"We're cuddling," I tell her, in case she's half asleep and somehow unaware. If she was thinking clearly, maybe she'd want to extricate herself from my body. "Should we—" When I try to roll away from her, she pulls me back into the curve of her body.

"What time is it?" she mumbles, her hand moving up to stroke my arm. Blearily, her eyes blink open.

The clock on her nightstand reads 7:35 a.m. When I tell her as much, she grumbles and sinks back into me. Distantly, I can recognize the trouble I'm in. Cuddling isn't nearly as innocent as it sounds, not when her arms feel like the safest place I've ever been. Not when I'm counting her breaths to fall back asleep like I'm counting sheep. Not when I'm lulled into the best sleep I've ever had by the warmth of her embrace.

The second time I wake up, I'm alone. I smell freshly brewed coffee wafting from the kitchen, telling me Krystal didn't go very far. My head pounds in protest when I try to sit up, and last night's drinking comes screaming back to me. Something catches my attention at the corner of my vision, and I turn my head to the glass of water and bottle of Advil sitting on the nightstand. I pick up the bottle with a ridiculous grin on my face. Why does she have to be so thoughtful? I can't afford to like her any more than I already do. I won't survive it. I palm two pills and wash them down with the glass of water before getting out of bed.

"Oh good, you're up," Krystal says, turning to me with two mugs of coffee in hand as I make my way into the kitchen. She hands me one when I reach her. Her hair is down, falling past her shoulders in gorgeous brown waves. There's a softness to early-morning Krystal, her face clear of makeup, sleepy eyes half closed until her third sip of coffee.

I try and fail not to stare at her thin pajama set. She doesn't notice the strap of her see-through tank top fall off one shoulder, but her breath catches when I tug it back in place. For two blissful seconds, my fingers brush her soft, smooth skin. Goose bumps erupt at my touch, and I can't help but wonder if that's my effect on her. If that's the case, I like it way too much.

"How'd you sleep?" she asks, looking away from me.

"Better than I have in weeks," I say honestly. "Sorry we ended up...you know."

"Don't apologize." She smirks. "I wouldn't doubt I'm the reason we woke up like that. Sometimes I wake up strangling my body pillow. Living alone has made me touch-starved."

"I didn't know you made a habit of cuddling in your sleep." I delight in the way her cheeks turn pink. "It's cute."

"Shut up," she grumbles into her mug. "If I ever become manager, I'm firing Luis."

"Who's Luis?" She gives me a look that says, *You can't be serious.* Then it comes back to me. The flirty bartender plying me with drinks while Krystal's back was turned. "Oh. Right."

"It'd be more money. And more benefits, not to mention more experience if I want to open my own bar one day. Like firing handsy bartenders who don't have a clue."

"But he never touched me."

"I can't fire him for being flirty. That's half the job description."

"So you'd make up a fireable offense because you're jealous?" Her mouth pops open as if to deny it, but not a word comes out. "I'm flattered."

"I *was* jealous," she admits in a low growl that makes my toes curl. "Twice in one night. Even though I know you don't like men. How pathetic is that?"

"It's not pathetic." I bump her shoulder with mine. "Ego boosting for sure, but not pathetic."

"You don't need any help in that department." I let out a guffaw, but she just laughs in my face. "Am I wrong?"

"Only a little." Her brows furrow in question. "It's a facade. Back when I thought I had something to prove, I flirted with lots of guys. Maybe it's comphet, or maybe my cousins fucked me up more than I even knew. I thought my world would fall apart if people found out I'd never been kissed. I did anything to counteract the damage Briana and Esme caused. Anything but actually kiss someone."

"You weren't ready," Krystal says. "I hate that they pressured you like that, and then made you feel like you weren't enough as you were. You shouldn't have had to become someone you're not just to appease them."

"I think I would've been ready a lot sooner if it wasn't for them," I confess. "Ever since I figured out my identity, I keep thinking about all the time I lost trying to prove to everyone how straight I was. I like who I am now, but my family doesn't get it. I stopped wearing makeup and feminine clothes, and my parents thought I was depressed. I can just imagine how they'd look at me if I did what I really want to do."

"What do you really want to do?"

I burst off the couch before the question is out of her mouth.

"How good are you at cutting hair?"

"Decent, but there's a reason I'm a bartender and not a hairdresser," she says. "Why?"

"Want to give me a haircut?"

Her stare lingers on me for a moment before I realize what she's doing. Her hand reaches out to push my hair back from my shoulders as her head tilts, assessing.

"Let's do it." Her smile spreads. "Scissors are in my bathroom drawer."

I barrel past her to the bathroom, barely registering as she calls out, "Wait!" when I reach out to pull open the first drawer I see below her sink.

"That's a lot of vibrators." I feel Krystal standing over me, waves of mortification coming off both of us. She kneels beside me, moving my hand from the drawer and shutting it with a loud *thump*.

"Let's just pretend this didn't happen, all right?" Krystal clears her throat and finally looks at me. "Let me grab the scissors."

She seats me on top of the toilet seat and wraps a bath towel around my shoulders, tying it at the back of my neck. Her fingers sink into my hair, massaging my scalp. Her touch is exquisite and does nothing to clear my mind from what I spotted in the bottom drawer.

"The bathroom is sort of a weird place to store...*those*."

"I thought we agreed to pretend you didn't see anything,"

she says, and for a moment I think that's the last of it. She fills a spray bottle with water, wets my curls, and brushes through them with a comb. "Those are my waterproof ones. I…take a lot of baths in here."

"Oh…*oh*."

Before I can ask any of the myriad questions that come to mind with that little tidbit, she asks, "How short were you thinking?"

"The shorter the better," I reply quickly. "I didn't know they made waterproof vibrators. Are they designed for…bath play?"

I hear her suck in a breath behind me. "They're not technically vibrators. And they're made to use in or out of the bath."

"What do you mean they're not vibrators?"

"I guess the more appropriate term would be…suction toys."

Holy shit.

I don't have much time to react to this knowledge before she asks me a few more questions about the length. I give her a quick rundown of the style I have in mind, wondering at her many talents when she doesn't so much as bat an eye at my request. Even though I've always been tempted to chop off my hair, I never have. I've gotten lots of compliments for my long hair over the years. I always thought my hair is what made me pretty. But if I'm being honest, I think I'm done with pretty.

"What does it feel like?" I stare down at the floor, watching more and more of my hair fall to the tile. "Using one of those things."

She stops cutting for a moment. "A vibrator or suction toy?"

"I don't know." I bite down on my thumbnail. "Either?"

"Have you never used one before?" She doesn't sound surprised, merely curious.

"I live with my parents." I roll my eyes. "The walls are paper thin. Believe me, I've been tempted to buy one, but I've never wanted to chance it."

"They do have silent ones. I can give you some recommendations for those." I nod, and she resumes cutting. "As for how it feels..." My blood heats in anticipation. "Well, I've always had a preference for suction. It doesn't feel the same as oral with a partner, obviously. There's a circular tip that pulls air to create a suction feeling."

"That's the one you use in the bath?"

"Mm-hmm."

Unbidden, the thought of her using one of those suction toys on herself pops into my head. I only caught a glimpse of the silicone device before she snapped the drawer shut, so I hardly remember what it looked like. Not that that's any deterrent to the dangerous thoughts churning inside my brain. Not when I've already seen what Krystal's body looks like mid-orgasm. The way her mouth drops open in an O, the flush of her skin. Replace the bedsheets with a clawfoot tub and bubbles covering most of her body, and the image shouldn't be nearly as arousing but somehow it's more.

And then my thoughts veer into even more treacherous territory. How good would it feel to use one of those devices on myself? How would the soft silicone feel on my skin, where I'm most sensitive? I cross my legs just thinking about it, squeezing my thighs together to quell the growing ache.

"What are you thinking about?" Her voice is innocent

enough, but her timing is uncanny. She's in front of me now, snipping some framing pieces. She has to know what kind of thoughts are circling my brain after this conversation.

"I'm thinking that's a lot of sex toys for one person." It just comes bursting out of me, no tact. "There were at least five in the bottom drawer alone." I clamp my mouth shut when I realize I sound judgy without meaning to, guilt niggling in my chest when Krystal's face turns a shade redder. "How many more do you have?"

"There's maybe one or two in my nightstand. There was a sale last time I was online, and I kinda went a little wild."

"Isn't there a law against owning this many sex toys in Texas?"

"I'm pretty sure that's dildos. Either way, I doubt they really care that much about a bogus law. Besides, what the government doesn't know won't hurt them."

"It shouldn't matter to them, period. We're allowed to own more guns than sex toys. What kind of a sick joke is that?"

"Let's pretend that's why I own an obscene amount of sex toys at the moment." Krystal smirks. "This little collection is my small protest. I'm sticking it to the man by...sticking it to myself."

The room is quiet for a long beat. Then we both look at each other and burst into laughter.

"Do you want to see what your hair looks like so far?" She shakes out the remaining length of my hair, which now barely grazes my shoulders. I stand from the toilet seat and glance in the mirror. The difference is stark, and when I try to remember the last time I cut my hair this short, I come up blank. In college, guys would always comment how much they liked my long hair. Though I was never attracted to them physically or romantically, I always swelled at their praise. Sucked it up like a sponge. Wore my hair down every time I went out and reveled at the result of turning heads.

"I want to go shorter. Do you have hair clippers?"

She shakes her head, brows creasing. "Should I be worried about you, Angel?"

"No." I shake my head in the mirror and watch the short curls fly. They're tighter now that all the extra length isn't weighing them down. My head feels light. "You know in the movies when women cut their hair after a breakup to signal a breakdown or radical transformation?"

"Sure." Her brows crease, wondering where I'm going with this.

"I think I'm in my radical transformation era." The truth is, I've come a long way since discovering my identity. Hell, I've come a long way since coming out to three people and then feeling frozen in my life, so afraid of what people I know will think when they find out. I don't care about any of that anymore.

"Radical, huh?" Her fingers skate the ends of my freshly cut hair. "I think you'd look pretty hot with short hair, or even a '90s boyfriend look." My eyes shut and for this short moment, I sink into her touch. At least I'm prepared for it to be short, but when I open my eyes, our faces are an inch apart. I suck in a breath, stunned. Something like anxiety or excitement shoots through my veins until I remember what she told me last weekend.

She's not going to kiss me. She's going to wait for me to

make a move first—something I'm not even sure I know how to do. My eyes flick down to her lips, pink and plush and parted on a breath, and then I move my head down to meet her. Our foreheads touch, noses grazing. My heart is jumping in my chest like it's searching for an exit route, stilling my progress. Are we really about to do this? In her bathroom with my hair scraps at our feet?

We're breathing the same air, staring at each other for surely what's longer than necessary as I get my thoughts in order. Just as our lips graze—the most incremental of touches as my bottom lip rubs against hers—I divert course completely and rest my forehead on her shoulder.

Kissing her now would feel wrong with the scavenger hunt hanging over my head. Even though kissing her is the only thing I want to do. But nothing's changed. As long as she believes she isn't capable of love, we can't go anywhere. But none of it is strong enough to stop me from wanting to kiss her anyway.

"I can't kiss you yet," I mumble into her skin. Her nails graze my scalp in the most delicious way, and it's almost tempting enough to change my mind. "I just can't. Not until I cancel the scavenger hunt."

She freezes for a moment beneath me. "Is that what you want?"

"I want to kiss you," I tell her instead, because it's the truth. "I want you to be my first. But I can't in good conscience do that, not right now."

"I understand," she says, freezing again when I plant a kiss on her bare shoulder. I don't even mean to; it's just that when she's this close, she's even harder for me to resist.

"Sorry."

"Don't be sorry," she sighs. "I'm the one who'll take any first you have to offer like the greedy bitch I am."

As if I've been possessed—or maybe it's her confession spurring me on—I kiss her in the same spot again. Longer this time, letting my teeth drag against her sensitive skin. She sucks in a ragged breath, the sound overloud in my ears. I move my way up the slope of her shoulder to her neck, leaving open-mouthed kisses with just the barest of suction across her skin along the way. Her head arches back, giving me ample access to her. I revel in this first, in the taste of her, all the while taking stock of her every reaction.

When my arm wraps around her waist to pull her body closer to mine, her hand tightens on my head, keeping me pinned to her. Her other hand tugs at my shirt as I kiss and suck her neck, finding a rhythm that drives her up the wall the fastest. The first involuntary moan comes the second time I use my teeth, and again when I kiss away the sting.

"Is this okay?" I ask between kisses. When she gives a wordless nod, I'm pushing her against the wall and grabbing her wrists. "What about this?"

She heaves a breath as we're chest to chest, her arms in the air as I pin her wrists above her head. Those gorgeous brown eyes glitter up at me. "What are you— *Oh.*" Her breath hitches as a knee makes its way between her thighs, pushing up until the warmth of her core seeps into my pajama pants.

"I may not be able to kiss you," I tell her, "but I have a few ideas for what we can do instead."

Thirty-Two

W hat kind of ideas?"

Bad ones. Ones that have her splayed out and naked on her bedsheets, much like the last time we did something as monumentally stupid as we're doing now. But I don't care. I can't find it within me to care, even when I know how this ends.

"Ones that involve what's in that bottom drawer you're too afraid to show me." She practically whimpers as I grind my knee against her. Her arms move to escape my grasp, and for a moment I almost let her until I remember her light bondage kink. I tighten my grip on her wrists as she writhes against my thigh. I hope I'm not hurting her, but I can't stop staring at her face twisted in equal parts agony and pleasure, can't stop being amazed that *I'm* the cause. I want to know everything about this woman, but right now what I want more than anything is to know what it feels like to make her come. "If that's okay with you?"

"Everything's okay with me," she says. "Do you want me to show you how to use it?"

I release her wrists, but neither one of us moves. When her

hands grasp at my shoulders, I grip her waist as she continues to grind down on me. I can tell she finds a pace she likes because her nails are starting to dig into my skin.

"You'd have to let me go for that to happen." I huff a laugh as my fingers play at the waistband of her sleep shorts. She doesn't let go. If anything, she holds on to me tighter as I drag them down as far as they'll go with my thigh between her legs. Once the purple lace of her panties is visible, I sink my fingers beneath the thin fabric at her sides.

"Fuck, Angela, you're killing me." She finally stops squirming for a moment, but by the way her lips purse I can tell it's with reluctance. Then she looks up at me with wonder for a moment. "Are you sure you're okay with this?"

"I'm sure." I've never been surer of anything in my life.

Sooner than I want, I pull away from her and get down on my knees to reach the drawer. There are so many options, I don't know where to start.

"Which one's your favorite?"

She motions to a small blue device with a circular tip. It takes a moment for me to find an angle that fits comfortably in my hand where the button is within easy reach. I haven't done much research on vibes or suction toys, but from the look of it alone I have no idea how it's supposed to be used. All I know about sex toys are the gigantic, hot-pink, phallic-shaped dildos that movies like to sensationalize. Even in the porn I've watched, I've never seen a device like this before. Then again, I generally make it a rule to avoid videos that use sex toys. It's never been something that's turned me on. Until now, at least.

"The tip creates a suction." Krystal readjusts her shorts and falls to her knees with me. "You can place it somewhere on your body you'd like to feel suction, like a nipple or your clit, and it feels good."

I press the power button, expecting a loud buzzing noise. Instead, the sound is more of a low hum that steadily gets louder as I play between the three different speeds. I place my thumb over the hollow tip and let out a yelp as the suction pulls it in. I feel a jolt low in my belly, and suddenly I'm imagining what the device would feel like on other places of my body. Krystal laughs softly at my reaction as she shuts off the device. I shake my head. Me and my damned curiosity about her toys. I need to focus.

"Do you use lube with this?" She nods, opening the drawer again. I spot the bottle and take it out. "Can you show me how you use it?"

Her cheeks turn pink, but she nods. "Maybe we should move to the bedroom."

Her floor isn't exactly comfortable or clean thanks to my hair scraps, but I'm growing impatient. And by the way she's pushing her thighs together, she's just as impatient as I am. I raise a brow at her as my eyes coast over her body. "You sure you can wait that long?"

"It's what, five paces?" Her voice is shaky and her breaths are coming out in rasps. "Okay, fine." She gives in so fast, I have to laugh. "How do you want to do this?"

"Well." I cough, turning on the device. "I'd like to make you come with your suction toy. Would you like that?"

Her nod is enthusiastic.

"Lie back on the bath mat." She does as I say, using the over-sized mat as a cushion. I lift her tank top over her chest, freeing her bare breasts to the cool air. Her nipples are already hard, beaded points. "You've used this device on your nipples before?"

"Once or twice. It doesn't always do much for me."

"Can I try?" She nods as I place the tip over her left nipple. She doesn't react to the low suction, or when I raise it to the second highest setting. When I readjust the device against her and set it to the highest setting, however, she lets out a gasp. "Do you feel that?"

"Yes," she says, the word almost a moan. Then again when I place my other hand on her right nipple, working the tip between my fingers. "Fuck, Angela."

"Which feels better?" I ask, not because I'm hoping she says me, but because I want to know what's working for her. When I give her nipple a light pinch between my thumb and forefinger, her lower half is squirming again.

"You." There's no mistaking the flush that washes over me. "Your touch feels better."

I turn the device off for now and play with her nipples. Another moan falls from her lips. Lord, the sounds this woman makes. They only get better when I put my mouth on her, sucking and licking her. Her hand grips the back of my neck, those nails grazing my scalp in a way that has me humming like a cat against her skin.

It's not as nerve-wracking as I thought it'd be, touching her this way. Kissing my way down her sternum to her peaked brown nipples.

I could get used to this.

I already am. I watch her face for a reaction as I reach her shorts, pulling them down her legs when she gives me a shaky nod. It's a heady feeling, placing myself between her spread legs. Running my fingers up her inner thighs. Watching her shiver from my touch.

"Are you ready for the suction toy again?" I ask as I push her panties to the side and use my fingers to spread her open. Her head tips back against the edge of the tub when I spread her arousal around her clit. It's a strange sensation to be doing this to another person for a change. I know exactly how to use my fingers on myself to get off. I could apply the same technique to her if we weren't using the suction toy.

She nods. "Yes, please."

I open the bottle of lube and squeeze some onto my fingers, ensuring the toy is nice and ready for her. Then I turn on the device and start at the lowest setting, watching her face to gauge her reaction as I press the slick, circled tip against her clit. When that doesn't have the desired effect, I kick it up a notch. She hitches a breath at the second highest setting, her eyes shutting closed in contentment.

"Should I move it, or—"

"No," she gasps, squirming. "Right there is good."

"Okay." I let out a breath as I continue to hold the toy steady against her. After a moment or two, I ask, "How does it feel?"

"It feels nice." She sighs. "I— *Fuck*."

The expletive comes when I use my other hand to play with one of her nipples. She lets out a moan, her thighs beginning to shake. "What…what are you doing?"

"I got bored." Careful to keep the device against her steady, I bend down to lick her other nipple. "Is this okay?" I ask against her skin. "I like doing this to you."

"Y-yes." Her body trembles as I suck the peak into my mouth. "Oh, Angel. I'm about to come."

"Then come for me, Krystal." I bite down on her nipple, and her moans turn into a keening whine I like the sound of way too much. "I won't stop you this time. Promise."

I feel her thighs tremble around the hand using the toy on her. When the pressure is too much and she starts pushing my hand away, I turn the device off and use my fingers to soothe her down from the orgasm. She looks up at me in wonder, or maybe even awe. When her mouth opens, I don't expect the next words that come out of it.

"Can I return the favor?"

I squirm a little at her request. Then I stare down at the device I just used on her as she makes a grab for it. She rises to her knees, practically stalking over to me. "Only if you want to. Otherwise, I feel like I get so much more out of this than you do."

"That's not true," I assure her, staring at her mouth. "But I'm not gonna lie, I have been wondering what your little toy would feel like on me."

"Lie down." We swap places until she's hovering over me.

It's a little unsettling to have her undivided attention on me as I slip off my pants and underwear. Do I look weird wearing a shirt and bra and nothing below? *Fuck it.* I sit up and pull off both before lying back down, my heart racing. No one's ever seen me naked before—not as an adult at least. Krystal's eyes scan me up and down, every inch of exposed skin on fire.

This feels weird. I bite back the urge to say the words aloud, afraid if I do that she'll stop. And I don't want to stop. I want to experience this closeness with Krystal. I want to experience *everything*.

"Can I touch you?" she asks, biting down on her bottom lip. When I nod, her fingertips skate my skin—sliding up my hips to my waist, my belly, until she's cupping my small breasts. "Angela, fuck you're so gorgeous."

"Really?" I don't have to see myself to know my cheeks are pink. "With my choppy haircut and bits of hair clippings sticking to my arms?"

"Hey," she admonishes. "Are you insulting my barber skills?"

"Not at all. It's just I've never had short hair before. I didn't think I could feel pretty this way."

"You're not just pretty." Her right hand moves up to my cheek. I suck in a breath when her thumb traces my bottom lip. "You're beautiful, Angela." She moves in closer, her voice a hot whisper in my ear. "And I bet you'll look even more beautiful when you're coming apart on my fingers."

As if I wasn't already a puddle of goo at that statement, her lips trail a path over the shell of my ear. I'm already shivering at the touch when she bites down on my earlobe.

Fucking hell, this woman.

There's another jolt low in my belly, making my legs shake. When she soothes the bite with her tongue, I'm a goner.

"*Krystal.*" I don't register when I started clutching at her bare shoulders, only that I'm holding on to her for dear life. One hand smooths up my inner thigh. She looks into my eyes, silently asking for permission, which I give when I spread my legs wider for her. Her fingers find me soaking. I'm nearly dripping onto the bath mat when two fingers sink into the wetness to spread up to my clit. "Oh, fuck."

I'm trembling all over again. We're not going to have enough time for the suction toy if she doesn't stop soon. "Krystal, please, the toy—"

"One on my fingers first." Her thumb works fast circles on my clit, and hell, I'm about to come apart this second and give her exactly what she wants. "Then we'll have some fun with the toy."

Approximately five seconds later, my thighs are shaking around the most intense orgasm of my life. I'm breathing hard as I stare up at her ceiling, willing my heart rate to go down. No such luck, because Krystal is far from done with me.

"I was thinking," she says as she grabs the device from the floor. "You've only ever used your fingers to come. Is that right?"

"Yes?" I'm not following where this is going.

"You've never used a sex toy before." She opens the bottle of lube before using her slick fingers to spread me open and expose my clit. "And no one's ever licked this gorgeous pussy of yours."

My eyes shut at her dirty words and the effect they have on me. She's already kneeling between my spread legs, her hands on my body. What would her mouth feel like...*there*? I've always wondered what oral would feel like, the sensations they'd cause, lips and tongues and sucking where I'm most sensitive. Would it feel better than my hand, or would I be too self-conscious to fully enjoy the moment?

"And before about thirty seconds ago," she continues, "no one's ever used their fingers on you. So I'm curious about something." I die a little when she presses the power button and gently places the circular tip against me. It's like nothing I've ever felt before, so it takes me a moment to get used to the suction feeling. But when I do...

Oh.

"What?" I barely remember to ask, biting my lip as she raises it to a higher setting. *Holy fuck.* The suction is intense, but it feels so good against my clit. "What are you curious about?"

"I'm curious which one you'll like better," she says, her left hand pinching my nipple. I let out a gasp. It's so easy to feel overstimulated by all these new sensations at once. The pressure building on my clit, her fingers thrumming the tip of my breast. It's hard to concentrate on what she's saying. "My hand, the toy, or my mouth."

A second orgasm is quickly cresting, especially when she switches to the highest setting, but I'm not sure if I'll be able to give her a third. As high as my sex drive is, I've rarely given myself three orgasms in a row. One or two is usually enough.

I fly apart when her mouth kisses a trail up my shoulder. She shuts off the device and strokes me softly with her fingers as I come down, all the while licking and sucking my neck. What started out as gentle, soothing kisses and touches quickly turns to more as she kisses the top of my breasts. I'm getting wet again when she starts sucking my nipples, and her fingers move just a bit faster against my clit. Getting me ready for her mouth, I realize.

"I'm gonna have you sit on the edge of the tub for me," she says against my right breast. "Whenever you're ready."

"Mmm, what you're doing now feels nice," I tell her as her hand strokes me. "Maybe just a little longer?"

"Sure, Angel." She lets out a low laugh. "I think you'll agree my tongue will feel nicer, but we'll do whatever you want."

I'm sure I will, but I'm still slowly building my confidence up to that. The lighting in here is bright. There'll be no hiding anything from her. After a moment, though, I acquiesce and rise to the edge of the tub. She positions herself on her knees, spreading mine until her face is eye level with my pussy. I'm shaking with nerves more than desire as she stares at me for what feels like the longest moment of my life.

"Are you feeling okay?" she asks me. "If you want to stop—"

"No," I say quickly. "I don't want to stop. I just—" I swallow. "I'm nervous."

"Hey, it's okay." Her hands smooth up and down my thighs. "It's okay to feel nervous. If you're not into it, tell me and I'll stop. We'll use my detachable shower head instead." She smirks slightly, and I resist the urge to turn around because I did *not* know she had one of those in here.

"Deal." I take in a deep breath.

When I nod at her, she takes it as permission to explore my body more closely. She eases me into it, her lips kissing up my inner thigh and then switching to repeat the process on the other side when she reaches my crease. She takes my legs and settles them over her shoulders, pushing me *that* much closer to her face.

I try not wriggle as she starts licking me but *fuck*, it's hard to stay still. Harder than the previous two times on her fingers and the suction toy. She's driving me completely wild with those long, sweeping licks against my clit. I bite down on a moan, but I can't take it anymore when those gentle, coaxing licks turn to sucks on my clit. My hand sinks into her hair, gripping the back of her head as the pressure builds and builds. She's barely started, and I already feel a third orgasm creeping up.

"Krystal, I think I—" I lose my train of thought as she

alternates between deep sucks and long, wet licks that dip just a bit lower than they should. *Fuck, why do I like this?* Like the maddening goddess she is, she gauges my reaction and teases the hole with a finger as she sucks on my clit. I'm squirming against her and crying out before I remember I was about to tell her something. "What was I saying?"

Her lips release my clit with a noisy pop. "I don't know." She looks up at me, her eyes glazed with desire. "Should I stop until it comes back to you?"

"Don't you dare." She smirks up at me before her mouth is on me again. Working me up to that familiar frantic pace, until I'm gripping the edge of the tub so hard I'm in danger of developing carpal tunnel. She holds on to my thighs through my orgasm, letting me ride it out on her face.

How have I been missing out on cunnilingus for my entire life? What am I going to do when I'm horny and alone in the middle of the night and my hand isn't enough anymore? Could that happen?

"Oh my god," I say as Krystal rises from her knees. My legs feel like jelly, so I don't think I'll be standing up anytime soon. "That was amazing."

"I'm glad you think so." Her smirk is smug, and rightfully so. She grabs my hands as if to help me up. "Come on. We should clean up."

"Together?" Her eyes glitter in answer. "Good idea. Maybe you can show me how to use that detachable shower head of yours."

I'm never getting over this woman, and you know what? I'm not even mad about it.

Thirty-Three

M y fingers are wrinkled and pruny by the time we finish up in the shower. We lost track of time in each other all over again, taking extra care to avoid kissing each other's lips. But aside from that, nothing else was off-limits. It was freeing in a way I didn't expect, to touch her the way I want to, to watch my fill as she came apart beneath the spray of water at her pussy, to be the reason she could no longer stand up straight.

I'm on top of the world by the time we're both dressed and clean. Elated and invincible. As much as I wish we could spend the rest of the day together, I have some calls to make. Krystal readily agrees to drive me back home, but I can't stop smiling, and I certainly can't hide it either. When Krystal catches sight of whatever ridiculously giddy expression is on my face right now from the driver's seat, her lips tug upward to mirror my own. Just as I start to think there's nothing that could possibly bring me back down to earth, I jinx myself. Her Bluetooth screen pings with an incoming message, flashing a name that should come with alarm bells.

One new message from Isaac.

I glance away from the screen displaying the contents of the message. It's not for me to know, unless she wants to share it with me. Her hand darts out to close the notification, but other than that she doesn't outwardly react to Isaac's text. It takes every ounce of willpower I possess not to ask her what he said. *She'll tell me when she's ready.* So I bite my tongue and wait for Krystal to explain, but nothing comes.

"It's cloudy," I say dumbly, because it's the only thing that comes to mind after staring out the window for five minutes grappling for something to say. "You think it's going to rain?"

She lets out a sigh, ignoring my rambling. "Angela, it's okay. We both saw the message."

"You don't have to tell me what he said." I continue staring out the window, afraid to look at her. "I want to give you the time you need to sort everything out with him."

"I've had enough time for that," she says, but before I can ask what she means, she continues. "He wants to meet. That's what the message said."

"Oh. Are you going to meet with him?"

"I am." She takes in a deep breath. Lets it out slowly. "It'll be good for us to get some closure. You were right. Maybe it'll help us both move forward."

"I'm glad." But if that's true, why does the idea of them meeting up make my heart race? *Maybe because he still looks at her the same way I do. Like she hung the moon and sun and every other goddamned thing in the universe.* Not that she needs to hear any of that from me. "We should talk about what happened."

"We should," she says carefully, eyes still on the road. "Angela, I—"

"I don't want to put any expectations on you." I cut her off quickly. "I know you're not ready for a relationship, and I want to respect that. Even though I'm canceling the scavenger hunt, I don't want you to think I'm doing it for you."

"You're not?" Her brows crease.

My heart isn't in it anymore. If I'm being honest with myself, it hasn't been for a really long time. The only reason I've been so determined to see this series through is for my followers. I want to give them a happy ending. Wrap up the series on a good note. For anyone like me to realize they still have time to fall in love and experience romantic firsts, if those are things they actually want for themselves.

It doesn't make sense to go on with the scavenger hunt if I've already found what I set out to find. Not just romantic or sexual first experiences, but so much more than I banked on. I thought I was done with self-exploration when I came out, but I've learned so much more about my identity through Krystal.

I fell for her long before I meant to. But I still don't know how she feels about me, or if her feelings on romantic love will ever change.

"I guess I technically am." I let out a nervous laugh. "But you're not the only reason. Ever since the mural washed off and we met Natalia, I've been thinking—"

My phone buzzes in my back pocket. When I pull it out, Natalia's name lights up the screen. For a moment, all I can do is stare down at it. When Krystal asks who it is, I snap out of it and swipe the screen to answer the call.

"Fine. I'll do it," comes the terse voice on the other end of the line, without so much as a greeting. *Huh?* "But you have to meet me at my studio and tell me how I can help. *And* I want my art featured in at least three videos."

"Natalia?"

"Who else would it be?" I knew it was her; she just surprised me. There's a muffled sound over the speaker, and then a whispered grunt before Natalia comes back on the line. "You are still doing the scavenger hunt, aren't you? Your last update was three days ago."

"Right. I…it was." I rub the side of my temple with a hand. What an inconvenient day for Natalia to change her mind. Krystal mouths, *What is she saying?* and all I can do is shrug.

How do I begin to explain to a near stranger what's happening in my love life right now? Or the fact that for the first time in my life I actually *have* a love life, and it's impeding my plans to start having one. It would be so easy to say no. That the event is off, and I have no reason for Natalia's help anymore. Instead, what comes out is, "Some things are up in the air right now. Can I call you back?"

She's silent for so long, I begin to think she's hung up. A surge of panic floods my veins, as well as the need to backtrack on my ambivalence. I don't know what will happen with Krystal. I don't know what she wants from me, if anything. Am I an idiot to throw out weeks of planning for a person who might not feel a fraction of what I feel for her?

"I don't like waiting." Before I can think of a reply, she hangs up.

"Did she change her mind?" Krystal asks as she pulls into my driveway. I glance around, surprised. I was so lost in my own thoughts, I didn't register that we'd already arrived back at my house.

"I…" I trail off, stunned. *What the hell just happened?* "I think she did, yeah."

"That's…" She looks just as shocked as I feel. "That's amazing news, isn't it? This is what you wanted."

"It's not…I mean, it *is*, but it's god-awful timing, isn't it?" I shake my head. "Can we please talk about us first? Everything that happened between us before we got into this car? I can't handle the whiplash."

"It's been a lot for one day, hasn't it?" Krystal's chest falls with a sigh. Relief, maybe. "First Isaac, now Natalia."

"No kidding." I sink into my seat. "Krystal—"

"I'm not going to hold you to canceling the scavenger hunt," she says. "How could I? You've wanted Natalia to be a part of this scavenger hunt from the very beginning. Plus, you still have Leti to consider."

"Leti isn't the one I want to be with," I burst out. "You're the one I want, Krystal. *You.* Nobody else."

Finally, the words I've been holding back for so long are out in the open.

"Angela, I—" Her eyes shut like she's in pain, and I can hear the words she's about to say before she even says them. *Angela, I can't. You know I can't.*

"Don't." I put up a hand to stop her. "I can't do this right now."

"Angela, don't leave like this."

But I'm not listening anymore. I pull open the door, half hoping she'll stop me. Prove me wrong. But I make it all the way to the door, up the stairs, and to my room without a single protest. It's all the answer I need.

Thirty-Four

Later that night, I scroll through my newest notifications for a dopamine hit, but it doesn't do the trick of making me feel any better. If anything, they fill me with a strange sense of dread. It doesn't feel right going on with the scavenger hunt, even though Krystal gave me her blessing. I also don't want to disappoint my followers when I've already stretched out this series for two months, but is that a good enough reason to go through with it?

That dread only grows bigger when I come across a cryptic video on my For You page. A creator I don't recognize is angry about something, but that's no different from any usual day. What's different this time is they're talking about someone in the aro/ace community. I haven't checked my phone all day, so I'm not familiar with any new drama or discourse that's happening currently.

"You know what I'm sick of?" the creator asks. "I'm sick of constantly being lied to by influencers and content creators. But it's even worse when it comes from someone in your own community—or who claims to be, anyway."

I watch the rest of the video with a sinking sensation. They don't give any context to the situation or even so much as a name, but that's also not unusual. The creator is going on the assumption that their audience will know who they're talking about. The dread builds in the center of my chest until my hands are shaking.

Something is wrong.

Two more cryptic videos appear as I'm scrolling before another creator finally gives me some sort of clue as to what's happening.

"The thing about this whole Angela situation is—"

I sit up immediately upon hearing my name. I don't register a single word out of their mouth past that. How the hell did I become the aro/ace community's villain of the day? I return to the last video I posted, wondering if I accidentally said or did something that could be considered problematic or harmful, but it's just me responding to a commenter's question about a date for the scavenger hunt.

I open the comment section, and that's when I really start freaking out.

@Alisha: This is so disappointing. I related to your journey so much and now I feel like a fool for buying it. Esme was right about everything.

@Connor: I knew her story had to be fabricated. No one who looks like her makes it to twenty-seven without being kissed.

@Olivia: Another influencer lying on the internet for clout. What else is new?

"What the hell is happening?" For a moment, I consider deleting the app and calling it a day. Better yet, deleting my entire account. Instead, I return to the For You page to the cryptic video that I now know is about me. But *why*? That's when I spot the search engine question below the video.

What did Angela Gutierrez lie about?

Good question.

I click the link and finally find the source of what everyone's talking about, and *oh my god*. The unmistakable face of my cousin stares back at me. Behind Esme is a picture of me and Krystal on the green screen filter.

"I just want everyone to know that *this*—" She moves her head out of the way until the picture is in clear view. It's from the disastrous dinner party, after all the fighting at the table and my conversation with Briana outside. My hand is on Krystal's knee, and the way we're looking at each other is...enough to make my breath catch. I know myself enough to assume I look at her like the lovestruck fool I am, but the way she's looking at me is as if she's just as lovestruck as I am. How have I never seen it until now?

"This is everyone's favorite TikToker of the moment," Esme says, using her finger to circle around my face, and then the way Krystal and I are positioned close together on the couch. "You remember, the one claiming to have never kissed anyone, let alone been in love before? Get a good look at her. You can't tell me these two haven't hooked up. They're practically eye-fucking each other and trust me, it was a lot worse in person. Let me tell you a little something about the real Angela Gutierrez."

The picture behind her head disappears, and then she spills everything. The fabricated summer fling story becomes public knowledge, but it doesn't end there. My history of flirting with men, the free drinks, getting Jacob fired from Havana Bar—the facade of a human being that comphet turned me into for a large portion of my life. It's all out there, twisted in the worst way imaginable.

"Holy fuck." The video was posted a few hours ago and already has thousands of likes and hundreds of comments. I can't breathe. I can't think of a way out of this. I open the comment section, then think better of it and throw my phone across the room. The loud *crack* it makes against the wall has me on alert for an entirely different reason. "*Holy fuck!*"

I dart across the room and grab my phone from the floor. The screen stays black after I press the power button a million times, but maybe that's a blessing in disguise. I really don't need to see what people are saying about me online anymore. The situation alone is bad enough.

I knew Esme would never believe me, but I never thought she would betray me like this. A sob crawls its way up from the back of my throat as I think about everyone I've let down by falling for Krystal. By not being the person I convinced everyone I was—for the second time in my life.

Thirty-Five

The next morning, I text Natalia to let her know what's going on online, but if anything she seems more determined than ever to help me put on the scavenger hunt. Not that I even know if it can go on at this point. During this time, Briana also texts me to call her, and we have an hour-long conversation over FaceTime.

"Angela, I'm so sorry. I told Esme not to post the picture. I had no idea she was going to go on TikTok—"

"You knew about the picture?"

"I did." She nods, looking about as remorseful as I've ever seen her. Even more than when she apologized to me outside after dinner last weekend. "I saw her take it. I didn't know what she planned to do with it, but I could've guessed. I've tried talking to her so many times, but I can't get through to her."

"She thinks I'm a liar," I say. "Which I am, but not for the reasons she thinks. Maybe I should've just talked to you guys as soon as I started posting, and then I wouldn't be in this mess now."

"Maybe. But maybe not. There's a reason you were so hesitant to talk to us. You had a gut instinct about the way we would've reacted to hearing the truth from you. Maybe it was protecting you."

Later that night, I think over her words. Maybe I *was* trying to protect myself. Esme's reaction at dinner last weekend wasn't a surprise. It was the same cruelty and dismissal as high school, the same disbelief for what she can't understand. I thought Briana would've acted that way too. It feels good to have her on my side for a change, but it can't erase the damage Esme is causing to my online reputation.

At around three a.m., I break down and wake Julian up so I can use his phone to see what people are saying about me on TikTok. I justified the decision by telling myself I needed to see if the scavenger hunt was still salvageable, but I just end up torturing myself instead.

"You told me you got to meet someone in person who was interested in joining, didn't you?" Julian reminds me, hair askew from sleeping. "Contact them in the morning and see if they're still interested. You can explain your side of the internet shitstorm and let them decide how they feel." It's a brilliant, reasonable idea, and it stings slightly that it's the half-asleep one who came up with it.

"You're only twenty-four. You're not supposed to be smart yet." I force a smile and put his phone back on the nightstand. "Fine. You win."

"Great." He rolls over. "I'm going back to sleep now."

After getting a new phone after work (thank god my phone was insured), I avoid the array of missed messages that come in and text Leti to ask if she's seen what's been going on online. As I'm waiting for a reply, my thumb hovers over the TikTok app. How many times will I keep torturing myself with other people's opinions of me? It's not like knowing what other people think will help me change their minds. I already have a response drafted in my notes app. I just need to film and post it, and pray it'll be enough to clear the air.

My phone lights up with a call before I can torture myself some more. Krystal is calling. At least when I was ignoring her messages last night, I had the excuse of a broken phone to avoid her. There's no avoiding her now. I hit answer.

"Hey."

"Angela, I've been calling you all night," she says, sounding anxious. "Are you okay?"

"I broke my phone," I explain, which is hardly an excuse. I'm not even sure why I spent the night avoiding her. On second thought, I know exactly why. Because I have enough to hurt myself with already without adding my feelings for this woman to the equation. "So I take it you saw my cousin's video."

"I can't believe she would do this to you. This girl's getting a piece of my mind the next time we cross paths. She better watch her back."

I make a noise somewhere between a laugh and a sob.

"Seriously, though. I can come over if you want. We'll get through this. People online are already questioning Esme's story and waiting to hear from you before forming an opinion."

I saw some of that last night. A few of my mutuals stuck up for me, including Leti and @TheGreatAcecape, risking their reputations and outraged comment sections to defend me. Even

Will Mora made another video to dispel the story Esme was spreading about us. But rather than make me feel any better, somehow I felt even worse after watching their videos. Because while my cousin had the worst of intentions, part of her video was right. I never told my audience about Krystal, how much I've been falling for her these past few weeks. I never told them about my history of flirting with men for validation, or any personal stories aside from figuring out my identity and lack of a love life. And I surely haven't told them about the firsts I've experienced with Krystal.

I wouldn't go as far as saying I've lied or willingly deceived people but combined with Esme's video, the truth is far from a good look. After building a following based on being real about my experiences as a late bloomer and coming into my identity, I've hidden so much of what's been going on in my life behind the scenes. No matter how you look at it, I betrayed them. I kept so much from them while I was lying to myself about getting in too deep with Krystal, and I have no one but myself to blame.

"I don't know what to do," I admit, cringing at the way my voice wobbles. I'm dangerously close to tears. "I'm a terrible person. This is exactly what Natalia warned me about in the first place. I betrayed thousands of people."

"Angela, what are you talking about? You did nothing wrong—"

"I did, though." I take in a deep breath, cutting her off when she tries to defend me again. "Who the hell are we kidding, Krystal? We're not friends. We never have been."

"I know." She hesitates with a held breath. "We're not just

friends, Angela. You're right. We were only fooling ourselves to think so."

"You'd think I would know by now where lying to myself gets me." A sob shakes loose, and I'm unable to hold it back this time. The tears are free flowing, and I'm grateful we're not on FaceTime for this conversation. I hate the amount of times she's seen me cry already. But more than that, I hate that I can never seem to hold back my emotions. "I built my entire platform as a twenty-seven-year-old who's never done anything. Never been kissed, never had sex, never been in love—or at least the closest I've ever come to feeling it. Only one of those is true now."

For a long moment, the line is nothing but silence. I think I hear Krystal's breath catch, but it could just be static.

"I have to go."

"Angela, wait—"

But I don't. I hang up, unable to face confessing a truth I'm not ready for. I haven't just fallen for Krystal. I'm face-planted on the cement for her. Head over heels, burn it all to the ground and destroy your life in love. And I have no idea what to do about it, because I know she'll never feel the same way I do.

I've known that all along, haven't I?

Thirty-Six

This is what I want.

I'm reminding myself this three days later at Natalia's apartment as we're discussing options for a replacement for the mural that was washed away. Part of me wondered if I should tell Krystal I've decided to go on with the scavenger hunt, but I decided against it in the end. Talking about the scavenger hunt would lead to talking about *us*, where we stand, and where we go from here after pretty much confessing that I'm in love with her—all the things I'm not ready to hash out yet.

The only bright side, if any, is that I finally get to see Julian a week before the scavenger hunt as we're both getting home at eleven p.m. on Saturday. He looks ragged under the porch light. His hair is a mess, and the bags under his eyes are more prominent.

"You look rough."

Julian rolls his eyes. "Thanks. The bar let me go early for the same reason."

"Seriously, how are you holding up? This is the second time I've seen you so exhausted."

"You mean aside from waking me up in the middle of the night?" he asks. "That's the price you pay when you work two jobs but only one of them pays you." He rolls his neck in small, circular motions. "I don't know how much more of this I can handle."

"So, quit."

He sends me a glare that chills me to the bone. "I can't. One gives me money, the other gives me a future. Which exactly are you asking me to quit?"

"The bartender gig." I place a hand on his shoulder. "I know you're sending money to my parents for rent. They're tearing up the checks." It came out when my parents called me last week during my lunch break.

His cheeks redden, but he's far too stubborn to budge. "I'll start depositing them in your bank account. I found all the papers in your dad's den."

"You will do no such thing." I shake him this time, but not as hard as I want to. "And I'm locking that room."

"You have to let me do *something*," he says, his voice growing more desperate this time. "I'm so sick of being a burden to people. If you don't want rent, maybe I can help with utilities. Or groceries. Just…let me help somehow. *Please.*"

"Julian, you're not a burden." I grab his arm, practically shoving him onto the couch. "Come on, sit down. Talk to me."

He sits down, but the words don't come. Instead, he buries his face in his hands with a long-suffering groan.

"You're *not* a burden," I tell him again, more slowly this time. "It doesn't matter if you believe me or not. The only thing I really wanted was to spend more time with you, but you've barely been home."

He looks up at me now, brows creased.

"We're family," I remind him. "You don't owe us anything. If the job is stressing you out—"

"It's not just that," he interrupts me, blowing out a breath between his teeth. "I still have loans I need to take care of, teaching jobs to apply for, a new apartment to find once I graduate. It's all coming up so fast. I only have a month and a half left to figure out where I'm going to be in August, and no idea how it's all going to come together."

His hands rake through his hair, before forming tight fists at the sides of his head. I thought Julian was better off than me because he knew teaching was what he wanted to do. That it would all work out because he's exactly where he's supposed to be. How did it take me this long to realize the reason he's not okay is because he feels like he doesn't have a support system?

"Stay as long as you need to," I tell him. "No one's kicking you out after you graduate. Take as long as you need to get it all sorted."

"And what happens when your parents get back?" He looks at me like he's not convinced staying here is a viable option either. "My dad is *this* close to finding out where I'm staying, and guess who'll be his first call when he does."

"Is it really so bad that my parents want to stick up for you?" I ask him. "It's not your fault that your dad is a raging asshole who refuses to accept you. He's the one who's supposed to protect you from people like him. My dad knows that. It's why he wanted you to stay here in the first place."

"It's also why he's fighting with his own brother." His hands are covering his eyes, which is why it takes me a moment to realize he's crying. "He literally fled the city because he knows when my dad finds out, another fight will break out and it'll be my fault."

"Julian, look at me." He doesn't until I pry his hands away from his face. "None of this is your fault. Are you hearing me? *None of it.*" Tears are prickling my own eyes just looking at him. I've never seen my cousin this helpless before. His face is red from unshed tears, his eyes as glassy as I've ever seen them. Hell, I don't think I've ever seen him cry before.

"How can you say that?" he bursts out in an angry rush, but I know it's not really me he's mad at. "Of course it's my fault. I didn't even try to ease the family into it, and I made everyone pick sides. Maybe if I'd picked the right moment, or pulled him aside to tell him privately—"

"I hate to tell you this Julian, but there's no right way to come out to someone who's as bigoted as your father is." I shake my head. "Nothing you can possibly say is going to be powerful or meaningful enough to make him see you. Just like there's nothing I can say to Esme to make her see me. Once you finally realize that, it kinda takes the burden of changing other people's minds off your shoulders. What they think isn't up to us, just like their actions aren't our responsibility. It's a tough pill to swallow, but there's something freeing about it too."

"There's nothing freeing about this." He hangs his head in his hands, and my heart aches for him. "Not when I'm going to be homeless in a month."

"No one's kicking you out," I reassure him again. "And if you try to move out on your own, I'll call Theo to stop you. He's the only person I know who's big enough to barricade the front door."

He chuckles slightly at that.

"Are you sure about this?" he finally asks. His shoulders deflate like a weight's been lifted off of him.

I nod. "You're always welcome here, Julian. And if there's anything I can do to help, you know I'm here for you. You have a lot on your plate. That's a lot for one person to carry alone."

"I appreciate it, Angela. Really." He lets out a relieved sigh. "Wait, why are *you* coming home so late?"

"Taking care of some last-minute details for the scavenger hunt." My sigh is a more tired one this time.

"So that's still happening?"

"Apparently, yeah." I shrug at his questioning look. "Lucky for me, it seems like the only people who hate my guts live on the internet. Aside from Esme, I guess." After I explained the whole story to Leti and the other participants, they assured me they were still interested in joining the scavenger hunt and that they were on my side.

"I really hate that she did this to you." For a moment he seems conflicted, and then he says, "I'm surprised you're still going through with it, though. It looked like there was something going on with you and Krystal."

"For the first time in my life, I'm experiencing the *it's complicated* relationship status," I say, resting my chin in my hand. "I don't think I like it very much."

"It's the worst," Julian agrees. "Do you wanna talk about it?"

Desperately. But it's getting late and I know he has an early morning tomorrow. I don't want to pile on any unnecessary additions to his overflowing plate.

"No," I decide, shaking my head. "That's okay."

"Fine by me, but you'll be missing out on some good advice," he says. "Last year, I gave my best friend advice that made his current girlfriend agree to go out with him. If you'd like a reference, I'm sure he'd be happy to—"

"You're not job hunting yet, Jules." He makes a face at the nickname but doesn't correct me. "And I'll take a raincheck on the advice if it makes you feel better."

"It does. Thanks." He nods, rising from the couch. "Well, if you don't need anything from me, I'm gonna go to bed. I nearly forgot how exhausted I am."

He has a point. I nearly did too.

But when I lay my head to go to sleep, I can't keep my mind from racing. Not knowing where I stand with Krystal is going to haunt me the longer we don't talk.

Thirty-Seven

H ow's everything over there?" My dad's on speakerphone as I'm getting ready for work. "Is Julian doing okay?"

"He had a mini breakdown last night, but I think he'll be okay." I tell him about the stress Julian is under, excluding fears about what Tío Manuel will do when he finds out Julian's been staying with us. My dad's smart enough to read between the lines. "He'd probably feel better if you call and assure him he's welcome here for as long as he needs."

"That boy's as stubborn as his father is." I wince at the comparison, even if my dad has a point. Being stubborn must be a family trait, because they're far from the only ones afflicted with it. "I've been telling him that from the beginning, but he's so unwilling to ask for help. I'll talk to him again if you think I'll be able to get through to him."

"He's this close to caving, so I think you will," I tell him. "Do you and Mom know when you're coming back yet?"

"That's why I'm calling," he says, and I glance up from the mirror. "We'll be back next week."

"So soon? That's great!" I smile to myself at the news. I've missed my parents—it's been weird spending any amount of time at the house without them.

"Don't tell Antonia's girls. I don't want word getting around yet, and Antonia told me you saw them recently."

Oh shit.

"You heard about Briana and Esme crashing, huh?" I haven't told my parents about the TikTok videos I've been making. The one blessing about them being away for a few months is it's easier to hide all the trouble I've recently gotten into from them. "What did Tía Antonia say?"

"For starters, that you're seeing someone you haven't told us about." His tone is teasing, and I know I'm in for it now. "You don't keep secrets from us, mija. Why haven't you mentioned her to us yet? It's embarrassing to hear about your daughter's girlfriend from someone else."

"Oh my god, she's not my girlfriend!" I groan. "She's…she's just—"

We're not friends.

My last words to her haunt me. And then, as if I've summoned her, my phone vibrates with two incoming messages from Krystal.

Met with Isaac yesterday.
Can we talk?

My heart beats out of my chest. I don't know if I should be nervous or excited about this. If I've learned anything from living vicariously through my friends' relationships and romance books, it's that a *can we talk* text is rarely followed by something good.

"Listen, I've gotta go," I tell my dad. "I'll call you later."

He gives me some trouble at first, but once we hang up, I finish getting ready and head out. I'm so rattled by Krystal's text that I don't notice I'm twenty minutes early until I'm in the parking lot outside the library. Oh well. At least I can bother Marcela while she's working until it's time to clock in.

"You're so *early*. And your hair is short!" Marcela brightens at her desk as I walk in. Once she notices my storm-cloud mood, however, her brows furrow. "What's wrong?"

"What does it mean?" I ignore her question and shove my phone in her face. She glances down at Krystal's text and winces.

"Angela, it's too early in the day to jump-scare me with a *can we talk* text." She does a full-body shiver in her chair. "How'd you leave the last conversation you guys had?"

"I might've let it slip that I'm falling for her."

Marcela's mouth falls open. "Oh, Angela."

"And then I sort of hung up on her immediately after." I cover my face with my hands. "She's about to let me down easy, isn't she? I didn't let her a few days ago, and now she wants to meet up so there's no possible way for the message to get misconstrued."

"Why do you assume she's letting you down easy?"

"Uh, hello? Have you not been paying attention?" I glance back at the door behind me. Any minute now, Erika's going to emerge from her office and exile me to the break room until it's time to clock in. "She doesn't believe she's capable of love, and I practically told her I'm in love with her."

"Just because she's not there yet doesn't mean she's going to reject you," Marcela tells me. "She met with her ex to get closure, right? Maybe part of the closure she got was realizing that what she once believed about herself is no longer true."

"That's what I hoped would happen." I sigh at the full cart of returns. "I have to clock in soon and check these in."

"Do some at your computer." Marcela helps me sort some piles to take to my cluttered desk. "Listen, don't assume the worst before you know the facts. Krystal could surprise you."

"Maybe." But I'm not so sure. Now that my online reputation is tarnished, I'm getting used to catastrophizing before daring to hope for a positive outcome. "I guess we'll see."

"Do you really love her?" Marcela asks.

I let out a long sigh. It's a good question. One I'm not entirely sure I can answer yet. The more I got to know Krystal, the more my feelings for her grew. But it hasn't always been as happy and amazing as people make it seem. It's been painful too. Anxiety inducing. Living with this constant fear of getting hurt, of having the rug pulled from underneath my feet when I least expect it.

"What do I know about love?" I ask instead. "Romantic love, anyway. How do I know I love her if I've never been in love before?"

"I don't think romantic love is all that different from other kinds of love," Marcela says. "It's not a feeling. It's a choice."

"What do you mean?" I ask her. "Is that how you feel about Theo?"

Before she can reply, Erika's office door opens.

"Angela." Her tone is grave, and a sinking feeling grows in the pit of my stomach. "My office."

I exchange a look with Marcela, but she seems just as surprised as me. Once I cross the threshold, Erika tells me to close the door, which is how I know whatever she has to say to me can't possibly be good.

"Am I in trouble?" I ask her. "I haven't made any more thirst traps if that's what this is about." Not any that can be misconstrued as inappropriate anyway.

"You're *dating* the internet?" She raises a brow at me.

Fucking hell.

"Right..." I swallow, hard. "About that..."

"There is only so much inappropriate internet behavior I can defend to the board," she says, rubbing her temples. "Here's what's going to happen—"

"Oh no." My eyes sting with the sudden onslaught of tears. "I'm fired for sure this time, aren't I?"

"Of course not." Erika shakes her head. "At most, the board wants you to shut down your TikTok but I called discrimination and managed to talk them down from that."

I blink up at her. "You did?"

"These are the videos the board would like you to delete." Erika hands me a paper. I'm expecting the list to be a lot longer than it is, but I'm surprised that only three videos are listed. My initial scavenger hunt video, as well as my application to be your internet girlfriend parts one and two. "And it goes without saying that any future videos of you...offering yourself to the internet will result in consequences a lot less lenient than this."

"Offering myself?" My brows crease until I realize what she's talking about. "Do you mean the scavenger hunt?"

"As one board member put it, this isn't a season of *The*

Bachelorette." She shakes her head. "I would've loved to have seen how it turned out, but I'm afraid the board isn't having it."

"So, that's it, then." An entire week of crunching, of getting Natalia on board and making sure I still had people willing to participate, all for nothing. At this point, I'm not sure what I feel. Bummed? Relieved? It's almost laughable that I'm slapped with this news at what feels like the very last moment.

I spend the rest of the morning focused on checking in returned items and other tasks. It's my hour for the circulation desk when I realize I forgot to text Krystal back, I stare down at my phone, racking my brain for a reply, when the glass doors whoosh open and I no longer need one, because she's walking in. I hate how good she looks, with her hair tied at the back of her head in a high ponytail, her face clear and open and glowing. She spots me at the front desk immediately.

"Hey," she says as she reaches me, hands in the pockets of her baggy jeans. I zero in on the sliver of skin peeking out between her crop top and the waistline of her pants, evoking memories of when I've seen her in less. "Did you get my text?"

"I did." I finally have the common sense to tear my eyes away from her exposed skin and look up at her face, but it doesn't do me any better. She bites down on her bottom lip and fidgets with the bracelet on her wrist. *She's nervous.* Is it because of me, or what she has to say to me? I was already nervous about texting her back, but now I'm not sure how I feel. Somewhere between anxious, horny, confused, and unbearably sad, all mixed into a giant ball of...*yearning*.

"I'm sorry I haven't had a chance to reply." I look away from her face when staring becomes too painful. "It's been...busy."

She looks over her shoulder to scan the empty library. Other than her there's only one patron inside, an older man with today's newspaper checked out. Mr. Johnson is napping in the armchair by the windows, the paper splayed over his face to block the light. She turns back to me with a raised brow.

"What time do you get off for lunch?" she asks instead of commenting on my obvious lie. "I'll buy this time."

"I brought my lunch from home," I say, and of all things, it's the stupidest excuse I could've come up with, and not even a true one. "It'll go to waste if I don't eat it today. Plus, I have some coursework to catch up on." That at least is partially true, but I only have two finals left to complete before the end of the semester and plenty of time, even with all the scavenger hunt madness that's been going on.

"If you're trying to avoid me, you could at least do me the favor of coming up with a better excuse." Of course she sees right through me. She always has. "I want to talk to you."

As if the universe is set on my humiliation and demise, another assistant librarian emerges from the back and dismisses me for my lunch break. With a sigh, I head to the back and tell Marcela we'll talk later, then meet Krystal by the entrance. One thing is abundantly clear after yesterday—we're not friends, and we can't continue pretending we are.

A weight settles over me as I climb into her car. As much as this conversation is needed, it couldn't have come at a worse time. My online safe haven has been disrupted and the scavenger hunt is DOA for the last time. The community I've spent the past few months cultivating is in tatters and I have no idea if it'll ever be the same again. The same way I have no idea if Krystal and I will ever be the same.

Very soon, our relationship to each other is going to change. I'm just afraid it'll be for the worse. That after today, we'll be nothing at all. I've already lost so much this week. How much more can I stand to lose?

Thirty-Eight

We're quiet in the car. I spend half the drive wondering if I should rip the Band-Aid off and ask about how her meeting with Isaac went or wait until we're at the restaurant. In the end, curiosity wins out. "How was seeing Isaac again?"

"Awkward," she answers as she turns at a green arrow light. "Awkward and awful. But I was finally able to get a lot of stuff off my chest that I'd held back when we were together, so that's something." She's silent for a while, thinking. "I'm still not sure he understands my side. Maybe he never will. But I think we both got what we needed from seeing each other a final time."

"Closure?"

"Closure." She nods. "Plus, I yelled at him for what his stupid girlfriend did to you. He's not on TikTok, so apparently he had no idea about the video she made."

"You didn't have to do that."

"It's not about what I have to do." A left turn, and then we're in the restaurant parking lot. When she parks and shuts off the engine, she makes no move to get out of the car. "How are you? *Really*, Angela."

I open my mouth to assure her I'm fine, then think better of it. I'm not fine. After the onslaught of criticism, more and more people are starting to come to my defense and reach out to check in on me. Last night I had a full-on sob fest reading through the comments and messages from friends, mutuals, and strangers alike. I haven't responded to anyone—I still feel like I don't deserve their kindness, but I'm closer to getting to the place I need to be in order to come back.

"I'm angry," I admit. "At Esme, but mostly at myself. I keep thinking if I'd talked to her and Briana sooner, I could've avoided this. And then I remember what they put me through in high school, and I think *fuck that*. They don't deserve an explanation. Not even Briana, though I think I'm starting to trust her."

"Just say the word and I'll find Esme through Isaac and—"

"Krystal, please." There's no bite to my voice. Just fond adoration, because apparently that's the only thing I'm capable of feeling for this woman, even at my worst. "We should go inside."

As soon as we're seated, I regret not answering her messages sooner and making plans to meet somewhere a little more... private. Because there's only one thing we haven't addressed yet, and I'm not sure how I feel about being rejected in front of the deli lunch crowd. Which is only about two tables' worth of people, but still.

"I need to tell you something I should've realized a long time ago." Krystal fidgets with the place mats, avoiding eye contact the same way I have been since she arrived at my job. "I just…" She takes in a deep breath and lets it go slowly. "God, why is this so hard for me?"

I don't think I was meant to hear that last part, which she mutters to herself in a rush of breath so low I almost don't catch it.

"What is it?" I ask as a waiter delivers our food.

"My parents always loved each other," Krystal says. I'm confused what her parents have to do with this, but I let her go on. "To this day, they still have their nauseating lovey-dovey moments. It's why my mom was so devastated when Isaac and I didn't work out. We were a way of connecting all the people she loved together forever. Breaking up with Isaac didn't just hurt him. It hurt my mom too."

She takes in a deep breath before continuing. "What hurt her even worse was the distance I put between us after we broke up. She means well, but she's a meddler. I got sick of her always trying to control my life, of her believing she knew what was best for me better than I did. I had to do it for my own sanity. My parents hate that we barely see each other anymore, so I guess I was feeling guilty after I met with Isaac, because I decided to pay them a visit afterward."

"Oh." If her mom made her feel bad about how her relationship ended, I'll go to bat for Krystal the same way she did for me against my cousins. I reach for her hand and squeeze once, my heart singing at the way Krystal automatically intertwines our fingers. "Are you okay? How was it?"

"I'm okay," she assures me, her thumb stroking over my hand like it's the most natural thing in the world. "I told them about seeing Isaac again, and then I…" Another deep breath halts her progress. "I told them about you."

"You…did?" I blink at her, stunned. "Why would you tell them about me?"

"My dad reminded me of something I'd forgotten a long time ago," she continues, ignoring my question. She breaks contact with my hand before rooting around her purse to pull out a wallet. "When he and my mom started dating, he asked for a picture of her to put in his wallet. He still has it, yellow and frayed at the edges with time, but he still looks at that damn picture the same way he looks at her now. Like a man in love."

When she unzips her wallet and dumps out the contents, I'm more than a little bewildered. "What are you—" She pushes our untouched lunch aside as what looks like confetti flutters down onto the plastic table. On closer inspection, I realize they're cut up rectangles of copy paper.

Each piece has a printed picture of me.

"Julian gave me this a few weeks ago." From the card compartment of her wallet, she pulls out the only picture that wasn't printed on copy paper. It's my seventh-grade yearbook photo.

"Oh my *god*." I cover my mouth with a hand as I take in my thirteen-year-old fringe. That was the year my mom yelled at me for dyeing my hair black with her box dye when she was at church. The height of my emo phase, which was the closest I'd ever come to a rebellious teenager, only lasted a year before I realized the hairstyle did *not* suit me. "I'm gonna kill him."

"Don't." She catches my wrist in her hand. I notice her expression for the first time since dumping the pictures from her wallet, and for a moment I'm confused all over again. Her eyes are soft with fond adoration, and I'm reminded of the damning photo Esme took of the two of us. "He's the one who sent me all these pictures of you. Before I knew what I was doing, I was arranging them in a Word doc, printing and cutting them into perfect rectangles, and putting them in my wallet like a corny 1950s husband."

"Or a serial killer." I raise a brow at her, but my smirk tells her I'm only kidding. "Seriously, how many pictures did Julian send you?"

"That's not the point." She stares down at the table, at the twenty or so pictures of me, and surprises me all over again. "The point is I'm not like this. Or at least, I *thought* I wasn't."

I shake my head, hoping it'll be enough to chase the hope growing in my heart, but she only devastates me further.

"I think about you all the time. This whole week, I've been so worried about you. I hate what Esme did to you. Hell, I hate *her* more than I've hated anyone in my entire life. I've seen people say the most heinous shit about you online and it makes my blood boil. I hate not knowing if you're okay, and I hate that you felt like you had to avoid me while you've been going through this alone when I want to be the person who comforts you through all of it. I know that that's my fault, and I'm sorry, Angela. I'm so fucking sorry you have no idea."

It's on the tip of my tongue to tell her she has no reason to be sorry. She told me from the very beginning what she was capable of. I'm the one who didn't listen. I'm the one who fought through every wall she put up, hoping against hope that I could make her change her mind.

"I'm even sorrier for not realizing this sooner, but I can't keep it inside anymore. I tried holding it back—hell, I've tried for weeks *not* to feel this way about you, but, Angela—"

No part of me saw this coming, the words she's about to say, what I can't stop her from saying...

"I think I'm in love with you." She lets out a humorless laugh. "No, I am. I know I am. The evidence is staring me in the face—literally. You're probably the only one who knows how scary and impossible this is for me, and I don't know if that makes it better or worse that you're the person I fell for. And it's been killing me to hold myself back and watch as you prepare to find someone else when I..." She trails off, but nothing more comes out except a tiny whimper from the back of her throat.

"You...what..." She's not the only one left speechless. "You changed your mind about me?" My voice is so much louder than I mean for it to be. I only wanted clarification, but the question comes out sounding idiotic and baffled. Someone from the next table over turns to look at us. Krystal's cheeks redden, and her head dips down so she can cover her face with her hair.

"I changed my mind about a lot of things, but I never had to change my mind about you," she says, finally looking at me. "The truth is, I knew a long time ago how easy it would be to fall in love with you. I knew it two years ago, the moment you told me I was beautiful."

It's a cruel kind of irony that we've been pining for each other for years without ever knowing how the other felt. Of course, I did fall for her first. Five years ago, long before I truly realized I was romantically attracted to women, she caught my attention right away. That riot of curly hair pinned to the top of her head. The way the red light at the bar made her skin glow like a fucking goddess. The way I stammered over my words when she asked for my name. The brilliant grin that would take over her whole face whenever I came in.

"I wanted to ask you out," she admits. "Say fuck it to all my insecurities about love and relationships and put myself out there for a change. But night after night, I watched you turn everyone away. I told myself there's no way I'd have a chance with you. I assumed some lucky person already had you locked down. That you'd bring them in one day, and I wouldn't be able to contain my jealousy."

She's never told me any of this before. The thought that we felt the same way, pined for each other from afar the same way for *years* and never knew how the other felt...it's too much for me to conceive. It's unbelievable.

"How do you know you love me?" I ask. "After everything you've told me about being incapable of love and not wanting to put someone through what you put Isaac through. I don't understand."

"With Isaac, I was always half in and half out. It's not like that with you. It never has been. When I'm with you, I'm in. I'm all the way in," she explains. "I wasted so much time try-ing to convince myself Isaac was right for me when I knew he wasn't. That if I'd communicated how I was feeling better or compromised more of myself, our relationship could've turned out differently. But none of that is true. We just weren't a good fit for each other, and that's okay. I can forgive myself for the way I hurt him because I don't plan on making the same mis-takes with anyone else. Especially not you.

"I love you." The words come bursting out of her, and

somehow they're not any less shocking than they were the first time. "I'm in love with you, Angela. I think I have been for a while, no matter how hard I tried to deny it."

Krystal's eyes stay trained on me, but I can feel her leg shaking beneath the table. For a full minute, I'm completely speechless. I can't force what she's just said to make sense in my brain. I can't make myself believe that I'm about to get everything I want during what has undoubtedly been the worst week of my life.

"I thought you were going to let me down easy," I say, because it's the only thing I can think of right now. "Because of what I said to you on the phone."

"Angel, I have about a thousand pictures of you in my wallet that I've been carrying around for nearly two weeks. You're not the only one who can surprise people." She tries to smile, but it comes out stiff. I watch as she gathers up the pictures littering the table with reverence before carefully placing them back inside her wallet. "What are you thinking?"

"I…" I shake my head. "I don't know."

It's the worst possible response to someone after they tell you they love you. The disappointment on her face is immediate and crushing and all my fucking fault. I open my mouth to clarify, to take it back, to tell her I feel the same way, but how do I *know* that I do? Isn't this the question I've been asking myself all week since I slipped and told her I was falling for her? I need to say something. Anything is better than leaving it at *I don't know*. What kind of dumbass am I?

"I mean— *Fuck*." I shut my eyes. "You're right, Krystal. I do know how hard it was for you to say those words to someone new, let alone *me*. Even though this is what I've been hoping for since I can hardly remember how long. It's just…everything I've trusted in for the past two months is falling apart. *I'm* falling apart."

"I wish I could do something," Krystal says. "Please, Angela. Let me help you."

"You can't." I shake my head. "I don't even know how to help myself. All I've wanted since I started posting was to talk to other people like me, and now they're all turning on me. And just when I thought I could salvage the scavenger hunt, my boss told me to cancel it or my job could be in danger—"

"Wait, *what?*"

"Nothing is turning out the way it's supposed to," I continue. "Now I can't say 'I love you' back, and I'm going to lose you too."

"Angela, I don't need you to say anything," she says, grabbing my hands. "I just wanted you to know how I felt. And that I'm not going anywhere." Her eyes glint with something like determination. "Lord knows I've spent weeks giving you nothing but mixed signals. I'd be an asshole to react badly to a less-than-positive response to 'I love you.'"

"I'm sorry," I say, desperately blinking back tears. "I wish I could give you a better answer than this."

"I should take you back," she says instead of responding to me. She stands up and then hands me my untouched sandwich still in its wrapper. I'll stuff my face at my desk when I get back. I open my mouth to say something, but nothing comes out.

"It's okay," she tells me. "Really. Just…think about what I said, okay?"

I will. I don't think I'll be able to think about anything else for the rest of the day.

Thirty-Nine

The next day, I call Natalia and ask if I can come over to talk about canceling the scavenger hunt. "I thought you weren't going to let those fuckers win."

"I wasn't." I sigh, thinking of the people tearing me apart online at this very moment. "It's my job. Apparently, the library board doesn't like the idea of one of their workers whoring themselves out to the internet."

"Is that what we're calling kissing these days?" she huffs. "Fuck them too. We've come so far just to cancel the scavenger hunt. What else can we do?"

For a moment, I'm flummoxed by the direction this conversation has taken. Natalia didn't want to be part of the scavenger hunt in the first place, and now she's convincing me not to quit?

"Let's talk about it," she says. "I'm home all day, come over anytime."

An hour later when I arrive, she answers the door to her place. I cross the threshold to her studio, glancing around at the amount of finished projects scattered around the space. She showed me a couple of new pieces the last time I came over when we went over her role in the scavenger hunt. I'm not sure when her burst of inspiration happened, but it's clear she's finally over her slump. When her back is turned, I take a peek beneath the tarp covering her newest project.

"Are you excited about the art showing?"

After calling me out of the blue, Natalia told me the McNay museum accepted her residency application. She'd applied for it last year before her slump hit, and she wasn't sure if she was going to take it at first. The museum's program begins with an artist showcase, and after a bit of finagling, I figured out a way to incorporate it into the scavenger hunt. At least, before Erika told me it couldn't happen.

"You know what? I actually am." When she turns back around, I immediately straighten. "So, what are we doing about the scavenger hunt?"

"You mean besides giving up?"

"It doesn't have to be about experiencing your first kiss or even dating, you know," she says. "If the original purpose no longer serves you, why can't you just change it?"

"To what, exactly?"

"Oh, I don't know," Natalia says in a tone that tells me she does, in fact, know. "A fun event to meet new people and make friends but also rebuild the community you worked so hard to cultivate these past few months?"

"I...hadn't considered that." I tilt my head at her, thinking over the idea. "I'd have to talk to my boss to make sure, but I think that could work."

"Problem solved, then." She smirks. "Besides, I've already

come up with a replacement for the mural, so there was no way I was letting you back out."

I let out a laugh at that.

"There's one problem resolved, at least." I let out a sigh. "If only the rest of my issues could be so easily fixed."

It's weird avoiding the app I've spent the past few months on hours at a time. I love talking to other people like me and making new friends online, but I'm never sure how close the other person thinks we are. After the shitstorm Esme caused, a few mutuals I thought I knew really well unfollowed and blocked me. I saw from other mutuals that those same creators were making videos to condemn me. It was gutting, but maybe it's also what I deserve.

"I'm sorry." Natalia grimaces slightly, twisting her body until she's fully facing me. "I never wanted what happened to me to happen to you too."

I'm not sure if it's the rare kindness in her tone or the careful way she tilts her head at me, but I can't contain the floodgates anymore. When the tears come, they burst free of their own volition.

"I'm sorry." I heave in a deep breath, but it does nothing to calm me. "I'm so sorry. I—"

Natalia is stunned for a moment, and then I'm surprised when her arms wrap around me and my head settles over her collarbone. I shut my eyes and let myself feel everything I'm feeling for a moment. This pain I never realized was inside of me, finally set free.

"It's just that...I didn't want to be this person, you know."

She glances down at me, eyes narrowed at the corners in question. "The one who's understood more by people on the internet than people I know in real life. It's..."

"Sad?"

"Lonely." The feeling hits me square in the chest the moment it leaves my mouth. My eyes sting with an onslaught of fresh tears. I try to blink them back, but it's no use. Natalia doesn't seem to mind, patting my head awkwardly as she waits for me to pull myself together.

I breathe in, thinking it'll help to center myself, but when I breathe out, what comes out instead is a choked sob. "I've never felt lonelier in my whole life than when I realized I was ace-spec. Is that normal?"

"'Normal' is relative. But yes, unfortunately I know exactly how you feel."

"Does it ever go away?" I bat away the box of tissues she tries to hand me, only to make a grab for it when she sets it on the coffee table. After using one to blow my nose (she graciously ignores the obnoxious sound my snot makes), she finally answers me.

"There's only one thing that can help." She smiles a rueful smile. "Finding the people who do understand and doing anything and everything you can to hold on to them."

"The only people who understand me are people *like* me. And after what Esme said, they all hate me." I dab a clean tissue beneath my eyes. "And the ones who don't...I can't face them because I feel like I've failed them."

"What about your friends?" she asks. "Your family?"

"I don't really talk about being ace-spec with them," I admit. "The only person I've talked to in depth about my identity is Krystal. And the internet, I guess. That's what TikTok was supposed to be for. I thought if I came out on social media, I wouldn't have to keep coming out over and over again."

"You wanted to skip a step." Realization dawns in her expression. "Not that I'd classify coming out as one singular step. It's several steps you make with anyone you deem important enough to know, including new people who enter your life. It was the same with you, once. Weeks, months, or even years of gathering all the information you could to figure out who you are. That journey was yours, but it wasn't theirs."

"That's why I started posting in the first place. To share my journey. And it backfired in the worst way. Everyone turned on me. Not everyone, but…" My eyes burn again. "There's no coming back from that."

"Fuck them," Natalia says, like it's that easy. "Seriously. The people who turned on you can go to hell. They don't matter. But the people in your corner—what makes you think they care so little about you that they wouldn't happily take the time to get to know this side of you?

"Coming out isn't enough," she continues. "You can't expect the people who don't know enough about your identity to be immediately caught up with where you are inside of it. Posting about your journey online isn't enough. All it does is create a barrier that gives you the illusion of safety, but take it from me—that so-called safe space you think you've created for yourself?" She shakes her head. "There's nothing safe about it."

"Yeah." I let out a long sigh. "I learned that the hard way."

"You have to be honest with the people who care about you. They may not be able to relate to you, but there are ways you can make them understand where you're coming from."

Why does she have to make so much sense?

"You're right." I heave a sigh. "But it's not as easy as it sounds."

"Nothing ever is." She shakes her head.

"How did you get over the dogpiling that happened to you?"

"I'm far from over it," she confesses. "It took so much from me. Some days I'm not sure I'll ever fully move on. Especially on days when I consider giving up art altogether. For all the good it's done me, it's also nearly destroyed me. Deteriorated my mental health. What's the point in putting myself through hell for something that doesn't serve me anymore? I gave up social media for the same reason. So why not this?"

Could I give up social media like she did? It's done me a world of good—at least in the beginning. It brought me that connection I so desperately wanted from other people like me. It led Briana to understand my identity and apologize for the past. It brought me and Krystal together after years of pining for each other from afar. Would we have ever found a deeper way into each other's lives if it wasn't for the scavenger hunt?

"Why haven't you?"

"Because it wasn't always like this," she answers. "I think I was at my happiest when my art was just for me. When I didn't care what anyone else thought. If I was talented enough, or queer enough, or making enough money to pay rent. I didn't have any expectations or undue pressure. Only passion. Drive.

This itch beneath my fingers to pick up a brush, or whatever I could find to create with."

I'm no artist, but I'm not unfamiliar with the feeling. Back when my first video reached an obscene amount of numbers, I was overflowing with content ideas. I itched to talk about my experience more, to connect with other people like me. The scavenger hunt was supposed to be for me, but now it feels out of my hands, especially with Erika's final request that I shut it down. Everything I've done has been in fear of disappointing the people following me, but that happened anyway.

"I don't think I'll ever forgive myself," Natalia says, eyes shining, "for being incapable of choosing anything but *this*."

My throat swells until all I can think about is her. *Krystal.* Is that what love becomes over time? Good until it's great—great until it fails? Even when you think you've found the one? Is that the reason Krystal gave up on love in the first place? I don't want to fail before I even begin, but I don't want to live in this constant fear of an outcome I have no control over either.

"Is that how you fell into a slump?" I ask, ignoring the sheen in her eyes.

"It's part of the trap when you're paid by commissions. People tell me what they want, and I create it for them. Sure, some pieces surprise me by how much of myself I pour into them. Usually it comes out unwillingly, and giving over the final product becomes a harder act." She's silent for a moment, contemplative. "I didn't give you a real answer about *The Woman in Wanting.*"

My back straightens as I regard her. "I figured that was on purpose."

"It was." She smirks, but her eyes are still haunted. "*The Woman* is me, ten years ago when I told everyone I wanted to be an artist. Before I made a name for myself, before my talent turned on me, before the mental breakdowns and online discourse and all the other bullshit that comes with monetizing your passion. When I was so sure of what I wanted—so sure that nothing else would do."

Behind my closed eyelids, I can see it. A younger Natalia, full of hope and wonder and pride. Unknowingly tearing her heart from her chest and offering it up to the world, not knowing what would happen next. A self-righteous naivete that comes with the territory when you're seventeen and think you know better than everyone else.

"More and more, I find myself missing the days when I hoarded my art. When every brushstroke belonged to me and me alone. But therein lies the catch." She raises an index finger. "You can't be an artist without an audience."

"Is it the criticism that gets to you?"

"It's far from the only thing that gets to me," she says. "Some days, it feels like I betrayed myself. Or rather, like my dream betrayed me. It's not possible to do this full-time and support myself on my own, and even if it were, I'm sure I'd find new ways to get sick of it. Every so often, I have to make myself take a step back from the thing that once brought me nothing but joy. I waste sleep worrying over how a client will react to a certain piece, what I'll do if they hate it. I start the project over in my head completely before they ever receive it. Ways to make it better, more what they want."

"That sounds like a lot of pressure to put on yourself."

"My best friend said the same thing," she says. "She's the one who suggested I take a break."

"And how is that going?" I ask. "Get any clarity yet?"

"Nope." She shakes her head before looking back at me. "I don't think I was very helpful. I'm sorry if I couldn't give you the advice you were looking for."

"You were more helpful than you think," I tell her. "I hope we can stay in touch when the scavenger hunt is over."

"You really want to be friends with a struggling, reclusive artist whose life is falling apart?" She raises a brow at me.

"Only if you want to be friends with a library assistant–slash–canceled influencer who lives with her parents."

"Sure." She laughs, and it's the first real one I've heard from her. "I could always use more friends just as lost as me."

Forty

"W hat's wrong?"

"Nothing," I lie to Julian, even as many indicators give me away. My wobbly voice, the tears running down my face, the snot threatening to touch my top lip. I'm still reeling from my talk with Natalia, everything we shared, how unbelievably lonely I still feel. I suppose this is what happens when I bottle up all my bad emotions instead of letting myself feel them.

I feel them now, all right. If Natalia could see me at this very moment, she'd say something like, *See? I told you I'm not helpful at all.* It might not look like it right now, but she was. She opened up something in me I've spent nearly an entire year trying not to feel.

"Is it your hair?" If the question is meant to make me laugh, it works. Seeing as I've spent all day crying in bed, I can only imagine what my short hair looks like right now. I let out an unexpected chortle that has mocos raining down onto my bedspread. Julian's face twists in disgust before he hands me a tissue box from the nightstand. "It's not that bad. I'm sure a hairdresser can save it…somehow."

"I can't believe you're just noticing it *now*."

"Forgive me, I've been kinda stressed out lately."

"Fair. Remind me to book an appointment asap," I tell him before plucking a tissue from the box and blowing my nose. "I met with Natalia today, and I don't know. I guess it brought up a lot of unresolved stuff for me."

"Like what?"

"How awful was it to be the only queer member of the family before I came out?" He looks surprised by my question. "Is it still awful even though you're not the only one anymore?"

"It was definitely isolating," he admits. "But it was more isolating before I came out. I don't have any regrets, even if I never have a relationship with my father again. It's better than hiding who I am."

"Yeah." I nod. "You're right about that."

"Come on." Julian pats down the duvet beside him, carefully avoiding the snot stains. "Tell me what happened."

I sit down in the middle of my bed, facing him.

"What if no one ever understands me?" I ask him. "What if I don't even understand myself, and it makes any romantic relationship I have that much harder?"

He's quiet for a long time. Long enough for the dread to sink in that maybe I'm right. Krystal loves me now, but what if the feeling fades and she decides I'm not worth it anymore? What if my identity changes a third time and I decide later in life that I never want to have sex again?

There's always been this fear in the back of my head that I'm wrong—that I announced myself to the whole internet without thinking it through. And then I get angry thinking of the hundreds of people online this very moment questioning the validity of my identity, because I'm the only one who gets to decide who I am.

Which is it, then? Righteous anger or constant indecision? You can't have both.

"I watched all your videos, you know," he says finally. "Pretty soon, the algorithm caught up and my feed was full of other ace-spec creators. I haven't told anyone this yet, but for a while I've been questioning if 'bisexual' was the right identity for me. Coming out the first time was a fucking circus, and not the fun kind I want to repeat anytime soon."

"Oh." I had no idea Julian was feeling this way. "Did you get any answers?"

"I think I'm demisexual," he says, his smile small. "A biromantic demisexual. Not that anyone in this family aside from you is going to understand that, so I get it. Believe me, whatever internal conflict you're going through?" He falls back against the mattress and lets out a sigh. "Me too."

I lie down next to him. "Krystal told me she loves me, and all I could say back was 'I don't know.'"

"Oh," he replies. "Do you not love her?"

"It's not that simple," I tell him. "Or maybe it is and I'm overthinking it."

"What's the problem, then?"

"The scavenger hunt was supposed to be my grand entrance into the dating world," I explain. "I was going to get my time to play the field. Have fun. I was finally going to have the chance to do everything I was supposed to have done years ago. *That's* what I'm supposed to want." I shake my head. "But I don't. I don't think I ever did."

"Because of Krystal?"

"Partly, yeah." I let out a long sigh. "Krystal obviously has no idea what she's gotten into by falling in love with *me* of all people. I don't know what it feels like to love someone. I haven't done anything! Everything I *have* done has been with her. Don't get me wrong, I care about her. *A lot.* So much it hurts sometimes just looking at her stupidly beautiful face, but would you call that *love*?" I shake my head, this time with conviction. "I've never been in a relationship. I've still never been kissed. What do I know about loving someone? How am I supposed to know for sure that that's what I feel?"

"I've never been in love either, you know," he reminds me.

Maybe I should've gone to Marcela. We never finished our conversation the other day at the library. I should've asked her when she knew Theo was the one. She was so scared to commit to him, even when she knew undoubtedly how she felt about him. I didn't understand it at the time, but now that I'm in her position, I do.

After a moment, my cousin says, "But I think I can give you some advice."

"You're the perfect person to be giving relationship advice. I know because that used to be me." I nod at him. "You're a rare, unbiased opinion." He's a late bloomer, too, though unlike me he at least has had minimal experience with dating.

He chuckles lightly at this. "I think it's just that our advice comes from reading romance novels."

"You may have a point there." My eyes slide to the bookshelf in his room visible through the open door, where an entire row of mass markets taken from my room sit. When he asked to borrow a book last month to read during spring break, I never expected him to rob me. "By the way, I'd like some of those back one day."

"Not a chance." He lets out a loud *oof* when I punch his shoulder. "Ow! Fine, all right. Geez."

Once we've settled the issue, he grows serious. "Did you always know you were different? Before you realized you were ace-spec?"

I consider his question, thinking back to the days when Briana and Esme and my other friends first started talking about boys they liked. "On some level, yeah. I think so. I always tried to shove that feeling back, find some other explanation for it. But it was always the reason I avoided dating anyone for so long."

"I did that too." He nods. "But I couldn't avoid how I felt forever. I didn't want to, but I knew what it would mean to tell other people. Especially my dad."

"I wish there had been some way out of it for you."

"It's okay," he says, even though we both know it's not. "When we came home that night, after my dad had his whole tirade and left, my mom made me sit down and talk to her. She asked me a lot of questions to better understand my identity. She was very understanding about it. More than my dad, even more than some of my closest friends. I saved coming out to the family for last, and by that point I was starting to feel really...lonely. No matter how kind or supportive everyone was, I never felt understood by any of them. Especially when they'd say they knew I was queer all along and were just waiting for me to say something." He shakes his head.

"How could they know when *I* didn't know?" he continues. "Anyway, the point is I never banked on feeling understood by either of my parents. But my mom must've sensed some of the doubts I was having. So I told her how I felt. The whole circus of coming out, let alone what dating would be like. She just smiled and said she couldn't wait for the day I fell in love. 'The fight will be worth it,' she said, 'when you find the person who looks at you and sees the sun.'"

I smile to myself, picturing Soledad with her son, pushing him into a chair to give him the best kind of lecture a mother can give.

"So? Is the fight worth it if you get to be with Krystal at the end of the day?"

I've spent years pining over Krystal. Her face has been burned into my brain since the moment I first saw her. How could I have spent weeks getting to know her without cataloging the changes? How did I miss the moment she started to see me differently? The moment she looked at me and saw the sun?

I only began to realize it when my cousin exposed that picture. It's since circulated online in the worst possible way, proof of my betrayal, but maybe it's proof of something else— something that's been between me and Krystal for much longer than either of us knew. Even now, when I close my eyes, I can see her face in that picture.

Of course she's worth the fight. How could I be so stupid to ever think otherwise?

"Oh my god." I'm not sure if I only think the words, or if I say them out loud. When Julian breaks out into a knowing grin, I have my answer.

I love her.

Now I have to fight for her.

Forty-One

When my parents arrive home Wednesday evening, they're a little stunned when I run down the stairs and practically throw them to the wall in a bear hug. I don't notice I'm crying until my dad's voice pitches in alarm.

"Mija? What's wrong?"

"I'm sorry." I try to pull away, but my mom stops me by tightening her grip around my shoulders. "I can't seem to stop crying. It's been happening all week."

"Angelita, why have you been crying?" My mom pushes my hair back, seeming stunned by the length. "You cut your hair."

"My friend helped me. I actually want to go shorter," I tell her, trying not to take it personally when she gasps. "I'm really glad y'all are home."

"You're starting to scare us," my dad says. "Tell us what's going on before I have a heart attack. Is everyone okay?"

"Everything's fine," I say before I think better of it. "Well, physically I mean. You guys missed a lot since you've been gone."

"Is this about Esme?"

I rear back, not only by the fact that they know, but also by the hard tone in my father's voice.

"You know about that?"

"We only found out this morning," my mom answers. "We had to switch seats when Antonia called. Your dad was so worked up I thought he was going to kill us on the road."

"I don't know what this family is coming to," my dad says, barely looking at me as he stalks into the kitchen. When I tell him the coffee is ready, he grumbles a "thanks" before pulling out a mug from the cupboard to warm in the microwave. "This isn't who Amá taught us to be. We don't put *anything* before family, least of all personal belief."

He spits *personal belief* like the words are acid in his mouth. I wonder if those are the words Tía Antonia used to defend herself. She wasn't outwardly nasty to Julian when he came out last year, but later on I heard she was telling anyone who would listen that *Julian* ruined her birthday party and that his father's actions were justified. I'm just glad I never had to face her myself, because we would've had *words*.

"So I take it she knows about me, then." Word will likely spread like wildfire about the second queer family member, if it hasn't already. I wonder how people will take the news that there are two of us. I'm just glad other people are breaking the news for me. Now I know who to avoid. And if they can't be avoided, who to be careful around should I ever encounter them face-to-face.

"We knew we'd have to deal with them sooner or later," my mom says, carefully sipping the mug my father hands her.

"Don't worry about what anyone has to say. Keep posting your videos. We'll take care of them."

The words only bring more tears to my eyes. I knew my parents had my back, but to hear them say so means more than I can say.

"You could've given us a warning this was coming, at least," my dad says. "I hate having to hear everything from my sister. You didn't tell us about your girlfriend—"

"Again, she's not my—"

"You didn't tell us about your videos," he goes on like he hasn't heard me. "And you didn't tell us about what Esme did to you. Angelita, you know we love you, but we can't protect you if you don't talk to us."

A wave of guilt rushes over me even as my heart warms. I may be an adult, but my parents will always do anything and everything within their power to protect me. I'm not even sure why I didn't tell them. But I saw the fear in the looks they exchanged the day I came out to them. They knew the storm we'd have to weather from the rest of our family when everyone eventually found out. Maybe, unwittingly, I was trying to protect them from that by letting everything fall on my shoulders.

"I'm sorry I didn't tell you." Good lord, I'm getting choked up all over again. "I thought I could handle it on my own. You have enough to put up with from Julian's dad. I didn't want to add to your plate."

"That's not for you to decide." His hand falls on my shoulder.

"Your father is right." My mom leans her head on my other

side. "We love you, and we worry about you carrying so much without any help. We never wanted that for you."

We don't want you to be lonely.

Is that what they meant when they told me that all those months ago?

"You look so happy in those videos you put online," my mom adds, her eyes shining. "I watched some on the way home."

"I do?" I blink at her. "You did?"

"I think that girlfriend of hers has something to do with it." My dad chuckles. "I know, I know," he says before I have a chance to correct him. "She's not your girlfriend. Not that I know what you're waiting for."

He gives me a knowing look, and for a moment, all I can do is balk at him. What *am* I waiting for?

"Well, in the spirit of telling you guys stuff, I actually have an idea," I say, hoping to distract them from a conversation I'm not ready to have with them yet. "I could use the help if you're up for it."

"Of course," my mom says.

"Anything," my dad adds.

I take them at their word. Ever since I got back from Natalia's, her idea has been brewing at the back of my mind. She was right. It'd be a waste to cancel the scavenger hunt, but what if I changed the incentive? What if I changed the reason for putting on the scavenger hunt entirely?

After talking over the idea with my parents, I only have three more things I need to do this week. Late Thursday night, I finally post the long-awaited response video. It's tempting to limit the comments, but in the end I decide not to. I want to create an open space to talk. Negative comments will be ignored or deleted if they get too out of hand.

I finally make it to the salon on Friday, just before closing. My hair is in desperate need of a fix, and I can't put it off any longer. When I glance in the mirror, I hardly recognize myself. The top is longer than the sides, the only hint to my natural curls. I can just imagine the heart attacks I'll give everyone when they see me for the first time. I smile to myself, because I don't care. I think I like this new version of me.

Later that night, after my parents have gone to bed, I stare down at my phone debating whether it's too late to call or if I should text her instead. *Fuck it.* This is too important for a text, but her phone rings twice before going to voicemail.

"Krystal, hey. I'm not sure if you're ignoring me or not. I'm sorry if I hurt you when I couldn't say it back. I still don't know why I couldn't when I…" I shake my head. "I don't want to say it over the phone. We should talk—*again*, I know—in person. Come to the scavenger hunt. I changed the rules, so anyone who wins that isn't you won't get to kiss me. You're the only one I want to kiss, Krystal. You're the only one I want to be with."

I hang up and stare at the ceiling until I fall asleep, wondering if I'm too late.

Forty-Two

CAPTION:

ACTUALLY, I'M NOT SORRY.

TEXT IN LEFT HAND CORNER:

Ten minute video

@ANGELA CLOSED CAPTIONS: When I was sixteen, I made the mistake of telling my cousin—yeah, that cousin—I've never been kissed. All of my friends were starting to have their first relationships, and it was making me feel self-conscious. I felt like I was so far behind my peers, but looking back I'm sad that I put all this undue pressure on myself. I was only sixteen. I shouldn't have been worried about crushes or boyfriends or kissing, but I was—because I thought that's what all teenaged girls were supposed to worry about. Because what would people think of me if they knew I'd never really had a crush before, that none of the boys in school interested me in that way?

So I told my cousin I'd never been kissed. Boy, was that a mistake. Because after I told her, she told *everyone*. All our family members, all the kids at school—there was not a soul left who didn't know that I'd never been kissed. I won't bore you with my teen angst or all the bullying that preceded that event, just know it eventually led me to come up with what I thought was a white lie after my senior year of high school. I was tired of everyone giving me grief, so I made up a summer fling. We even went all the way, this summer fling of mine, because I wasn't about to enter college a virgin and repeat history all over again.

Except, it was a lie. I was still a virgin. I'd still never been kissed. But now I was good at hiding the truth. I was flirting with any and every guy with a pulse. After I turned twenty-one, my friends and I never paid for a single drink when we went out to bars or restaurants. I could've been the poster girl for comphet, that's how good at hiding the truth I was. But I wasn't happy. I turned down every guy who asked me out. I went from being called a prude to a tease, because the patriarchy doesn't let women win once.

It wasn't until very recently that I came into my identity, which is also around the time I started posting. For the most part, I've had no problem being open on here about my identity and my experience because I know so many of you can relate. But I haven't shared everything for a reason. We all know the internet is where nuance goes to die, just like I know there will be plenty of people who still won't believe my story.

Which brings me to one last thing—the woman in the picture. Well, maybe two things. The fate of the scavenger hunt is a bit up in the air. When I first came on here a few months ago and talked about my experience, I was telling the truth. A few months ago, I was a virgin who'd never fallen in love, let alone dated or been kissed. Now, well…maybe some of those aren't true anymore. For privacy reasons, I won't go into detail. The truth I am willing to tell you is, in an ironic twist I never saw coming, while planning the scavenger hunt, I started to fall for someone close to me. Everything I set out to find through the scavenger hunt, I was starting to find with the very person who was helping me set it up.

So, where does this leave me and the scavenger hunt series? If you're still with me, stick around, because I have an idea where that's concerned.

COMMENTS:

@LetilsTrying: I'm so sorry you're going through this, Angela. You don't owe us any details, but it sounds like you found someone really great and I'm extremely jealous but so happy for you! I hope we get to see them in a video one day 😊

@Priya: I so relate to being the poster girl for comphet back when I was "straight." When I came out as a lesbian, no one believed me 💀

@Alisha: Whatever. Do you really expect us to believe that?

DM EXCHANGE:

@Angela: Are you done trying to drag my name through the mud? Should I be anticipating another ambush from you or are you satisfied?

@Esme: Fool the internet all you want, but you're not fooling me. You're still a fucking liar, and your girlfriend is no better than you are.

@Angela: You're right about one thing. I was a liar. I spent most of my life lying to myself. But if I've learned anything in the last year, it's that I don't want to be the person other people want me to be anymore. It's exhausting. You don't have to understand my perspective or take the time to get to know the real me if you don't want to. Hell, you don't even have to know me. Hope you have a nice life.

Are you sure you want to block this user?

Yes   No

Forty-Three

@Angela: I'm so happy you're still psyched about the scavenger hunt despite all the changes. Also, I need to thank you and apologize to you. You stood up for me when everyone was turning their backs on me. Meanwhile, I haven't been fair to you. I never meant to lead you on or hurt you, and I genuinely hope we can be friends after this.

@LetIsTrying: I'll admit, I did get my hopes up that something would happen between us after the scavenger hunt, but I knew you were talking to other women online besides me. For all our joking about dating, I knew it was never serious between us.

@Angela: Still. I hope you know that I really did like you. I wasn't trying to mess with your head.

@LetilsTrying: I get it. You fell for someone else. And you know what? You've given me hope that there's someone great out there for me too.

After spending half an hour getting ready, I don't look like myself. At least, not my usual self. I'm wearing a short-sleeved button-down and close-fitting slacks, but not close enough to show off any kind of silhouette. I even bought a tie especially for this moment, the first masculine accessory I've ever bought that dresses up the outfit just that much more. Along with my newly close-cropped hair and face clear of makeup, it'd be easy to mistake me for a guy at first glance.

It's ironic that my outfit choices these days highlight everything I used to be so insecure about growing up. Now I'm more than happy with my flat chest and lack of a "feminine figure," both easily hidden away by a baggy shirt. Maybe one day I'll return to brighter, feminine colors and incorporate them into masculine fits.

The reaction I get from Marcela and Julian is priceless. I kept my new haircut a secret for an entire day—the most dramatic change to my appearance—and their wide eyes and exchange of shocked glances don't go unnoticed.

"Well?" I do a little faux-curtsy as I make my way down the stairs. "What do you think?"

"You look great." Marcela grins ear to ear. "The short hair really suits you."

"Agreed, and you reminded me I'm due for a trim soon," Julian says, tousling his over-long curls with a hand.

The day of the scavenger hunt has arrived, and I couldn't be more nervous. What if no one shows up? What if it gets awkward? The tie around my neck is starting to get tight as we arrive at the bar.

What if she doesn't show up?

Krystal never replied to my message the other night, or the one I sent this morning. I spent the entire day checking. Even now, I'm checking my phone for any missed messages from her and come up empty.

"Full house tonight."

Julian's right. Inside, the bar is packed. I recognize Leti and a few women I've messaged online, as well as others from the profiles I sifted through a few weeks ago, but most are regular bar patrons.

"You nervous?" Marcela asks, placing a hand on my shoulder. "It's not too late to back out, you know. Best friend drives the getaway car."

"I call shotgun."

"You can't call shotgun if *I'm* the one running away." I roll my eyes at my cousin. "And I'm not running." Though the longer I look out at the crowd without seeing Krystal's face, the more I sort of want to. My throat feels so tight, even loosening the tie around my neck doesn't help.

She's not coming.

I shake my head to myself. There's still time for her to show up.

Cristina, the bar manager, gets the crowd to settle down and introduces me. She helps me onto the bar, giving me a perfect view of the crowd. I try to spot Krystal while I'm up here, but I'm nervous and overstimulated and trying not to choke over my words as I explain the rules. If she's here, I don't see her.

"Thanks for coming, everyone!" I call out. "I'm Angela, your host for tonight's scavenger hunt. Just a quick reminder that clues will be posted on TikTok every thirty minutes, so be sure you have the app downloaded and that you're checking for new updates periodically. The first video will go up in"—I check the time on my phone—"five minutes!"

I set a timer on my phone, and then Julian helps me down from the bar. I'm not any less anxious as I try to force myself to stop looking for Krystal in the crowd.

"Are you okay?" Marcela asks when I start biting my nails. "Are you still looking for—"

"Angela." Leti appears in front of me, cutting off Marcela's question. A welcome distraction from having to talk about Krystal, and why she's not here when just last week she told me she wasn't going anywhere. I let Leti pull me into a side hug as she says, "I wanted to say hi before the scavenger hunt began. I'm excited to start."

"I'm so glad you're here! Thanks again for being cool with me changing the incentive at the last minute."

I cut it pretty close when I posted my last update yesterday, but only because I'd needed to check with Erika first. Instead of the winner getting to be my first kiss, they'll get to choose which charity organization I donate the money I earned from my most recent sponsored post.

"Of course," Leti tells me. "I'm happy you found someone. Really."

My stomach sinks even as I look over her head for any sign of Krystal. That constricting feeling tightens my throat again.

"Are you coming to the after-party?" I ask, if only so I don't have to correct her.

"Wouldn't miss it." She smiles. "I'm gonna go line up behind the door with everyone else and wait for the first clue."

A glance behind her shows me she's right—there's a group lined up behind the exit. I let out a laugh and let her go. I step back and almost trip over something on the ground. And then I really start freaking out when a hand on my ankle rights me from falling over.

"*Julian?*" He's on his hands and knees behind a barstool. "What the hell are you doing down there?"

"I dropped my phone," he says as I help him off the floor, but there's something shifty in his expression that stops me from believing him. He looks behind me to the line behind the door, shoulders tense in agitation. "How do you know that girl?"

"Leti?" I follow his gaze to where Leti is chatting with someone in line. "It's…kind of a long story. Why?"

"I know her," he replies, but doesn't explain how.

"Okay, cryptic much?" I cross my arms over my chest. "How do you—"

The alarm on my phone goes off before I can ask him how he knows her. *Time to get started.* I glance back at him and give him a look that says this is far from over before turning to my phone and hitting post on the drafted video.

"The first clue is posted!" I shout, and watch as everyone pulls out their phone.

CAPTION:
ON YOUR MARK...GET SET...GO!

@ANGELA CLOSED CAPTIONS: Hey, y'all. I'm here with your very first clue. In a blue house of rarities, the second clue awaits you.

For a moment, I'm taken back to a few months ago, when the scavenger hunt was still just an idea that came to me out of nowhere. *Find me in a house painted blue, where the smell of aging paper envelops you and books line every wall.* If Krystal is watching somewhere, she'll remember the callback.

Marcela drives us to Cheever's, where we wait for people to arrive. In the car, I lose the tie altogether before we walk inside. How do men even wear these things? I start to feel better as the cool air from the store hits my skin.

The second clue might be my favorite of Natalia's art pieces. Two weeks ago, when she unveiled the faux display of books created especially for me, it nearly brought me to tears. I direct Marcela and Julian to a side room where the display is tucked away beside a stack of worn mass market historical romances.

At first glance, the display is unassuming. The faux books are so lifelike, if you didn't know what you were looking for you'd mistake them for real hardback novels. Until you look closely at the titles and realize they're far from real. The first spine reads *The Woman in Wanting*, followed by *Angela's Ever After*. But the next clue is on the last title, *Ferris Wheel Death Trap*, the cover a perfect rendering of downtown San Antonio during Fiesta. On the bottom of the display is Natalia's signature.

"Angela, this is amazing!" Marcela exclaims. "I can't believe Natalia made this."

"She really outdid herself with this piece," I agree. "And the best part is I get to take it home with me after the scavenger hunt."

We make our way toward the back as I'm checking my phone for the time. They should be arriving behind us any second now. At the ten-minute mark, Marcela splits from us and heads to the front of the store. She'll text me when the first arrivals enter Cheever's.

"While we're waiting, you never told me how you know Leti."

Julian sighs as he leans against a shelf of children's books. "It's a long, awkward story that doesn't make me look very good."

"After I found you hiding behind a barstool, I didn't think it did." I raise my brows at him. "What happened?"

"We met a few years ago." He lets out a long breath. "I don't think she likes me very much."

"Wait a second." Something clicks into place as I stare at his sheepish expression. "She mentioned something about the worst first date in history. Did you *go out* with her?"

His whole face turns pink, and I have my answer. Before he can reply, Marcela calls to let me know Leti and a few others have arrived. "I lost track of some of the participants after a huge group walked in. Either way, I think you're good to post the next video."

"Thanks," I tell her. "You didn't see Krystal by chance, did you?"

"Sorry. I was too busy trying not to get trampled by the newcomers. She could've slipped in, but I have no idea."

"Right. Well, I guess we'll see." Once we hang up, I open TikTok and post the next video.

CAPTION:

@ANGELA CLOSED CAPTIONS: Back again with your second clue of the night. Something is not what it seems inside these walls. Can you spot the difference? I sure hope so, because it'll lead you to the next clue.

"Come on." Julian follows me out the back exit so we don't run into anyone. We meet Marcela by the car, and then we're off to the next location. Clouds are rolling in by the time we make it to Fiesta, but far from being dead the streets are packed with bodies. It looks like everyone's getting their final hours of fun in before they're rained out.

There's so much of Krystal in this next clue, which makes sense given that she's the one who gave me the idea when we were here weeks ago. The line to the Ferris wheel is long, extending all the way to the street, but that's okay. In that way, it was just for us. Besides, the participants don't need to actually ride the Ferris wheel to spot the next clue.

Though we're an entire block away from the Ferris wheel, Natalia's newest mural is in full view. *The Woman in Wanting* stares back at us from the next building over. Even though the details are almost exactly the same as the mural I first saw from

the Tower of the Americas, something is different about this
new mural. Maybe it's my imagination, but this version seems
bolder, more full of life than its predecessor. Beside the mural,
a poster is taped to the wall with information on Natalia's art
exhibit at the McNay museum.

"It's going to get harder making sure everyone's keeping
up with the clues," Julian says after two back-to-back passersby
shove by him. "Do you see anyone?"

I glance around, like I haven't been looking for signs
of Krystal all damned day, but he's right. It's even harder to
make out familiar faces through the droves of people out today.
Luckily I figured something like this would happen and set up
a timer. After another fifteen minutes pass, I hit upload on the
third video in my drafts folder.

CAPTION:
GETTING WARMER...

@ANGELA CLOSED CAPTIONS: Are we ready for the
third clue? My friend has a view for you that can be
seen from the top of a Ferris wheel. Hope you guys are
better at interpreting art than I am.

As soon as I post the video and glance up from my phone,
I spot her.

There. A mass of dark brown curls I recognize by heart,
piled on top of her head. Just to be sure, I move through the
crowd to follow her. Julian calls out my name, but I ignore him.

Turn around, I think frantically. *Just once.*

I'm surrounded. There's no way for me to move faster, to catch up to her. I call her name, but I barely hear myself over the roar of voices. Again. And then, miraculously, her head turns. I only catch her side profile, but it's enough.

It's her. She came.

I'd run to her if I could. Fall at her feet and apologize for being so dense. Because how could I not see then what I so clearly see now? There's no one else for me but her. I love Krystal. I've been slowly falling for her for months. Years, even.

"Angela!" I'm pulled out of the crowd by a hand gripping my arm. When I turn around, Marcela looks anxious. "You can't just run off like that. We almost lost you."

"Sorry, I—" I turn my head back, but if the person I saw in the crowd really was Krystal, I have no way of knowing. She's gone. "I thought I saw her."

"Krystal?" When I nod, she asks, "What are you going to do?"

There's only one thing I want to do—something I should've done a long time ago. Julian and Marcela follow as I ditch the crowds for a grassy lawn outside a nearby building. Once we find a secluded area that isn't too noisy, I press the camera app and hit record.

NO CAPTION

@ANGELA CLOSED CAPTIONS: Krystal, if you're watching this, ignore the last video I posted. I don't know if you got any of the messages I've been sending you, but just now I thought I saw you, so if you are

here—and if you're still in this—meet me at your spot.
You know the one. I like to think of it as our spot now.
Hopefully I see you, and it will be.

"You're really doing this, huh?" Marcela's eyes are sparkling, and Julian is wearing a cheesy grin once I hit post. They
crush me in a hug from both sides, sandwiching me between
them. "I'm so proud of you, Angela."

"Go get your girl!" Julian agrees, shaking my shoulders.

"All right, fine, yes, but we have to hurry!" I say, pulling
away from them. "Can you drop me off at home? I need to get
my car. I have to be alone for this."

They agree, and then we're running back to Marcela's car.
Julian says they'll let me know who wins the scavenger hunt
later, and for a moment a pang of regret hits me that I won't get
to see it through. But only for a moment. Because with every
fiber of my being, I'm praying that I'm right. That Krystal is
really here somewhere, searching for me. That we're not too far
off from our happily-ever-after.

Forty-Four

The sky is dark with gray clouds by the time I reach the deserted parking lot. My hands are shaking as I turn off the ignition. My whole body is shaking, actually, at the thought that she might not show. That the face in the crowd I could've sworn was hers belonged to someone else, and I'll end the day the same way I started it: alone. Not that I'm entirely against the prospect as much as I once was. Krystal is it for me. It's her or no one.

I'm envisioning our reunion like the night she first brought me here—the sky awash in brilliant color, the air cool on my skin, Krystal pulling me into the trunk of her car and wrapping us in one of her many oversized blankets. It's a perfect picture. At least, until thunder rumbles in the distance. I push myself out of the driver's seat, my shoes hitting the pavement at a run. The fireworks should be starting any second now. With a storm on the way, we might only get a few minutes of fireworks before we're rained out.

I check my phone for notifications, looking for her name.

Come on, Krystal. I glance up at the darkening sky when the first drop of rain hits my cheek.

No. No no no—

Against the skyline, a red flurry launches into the air and pops, but fizzles out before it can make its grand showcase. The sound of popping fireworks is replaced with another roll of thunder that's much louder than the first, and then the sky splits open above my head. In mere seconds my hair and clothes are soaked, but that's not what I care about. I barely notice I'm soaked to the bone until I take my first steps, bogged down by my water-logged tennis shoes.

No fireworks. No Krystal. No first kiss.

It's just about what I deserve for being so fickle. But despite how gigantic of a bust this whole scavenger hunt turned out to be, I don't have any regrets. It wouldn't have felt right to lose my first kiss to anyone else. There's no one I'd rather kiss than Krystal. I won't be satisfied with anyone else.

I tip my head back and let the rain hit my face. Take one deep breath in and hold it before letting it out in slow bursts between my teeth. I might have a towel in the back seat, or at the very least a jacket of some sort. Even then, there's no way my seat survives the drive back. These are the thoughts occupying my brain when a flash of headlights break through the fog. My pulse races the closer they get, until I'm just able to make out the silhouette in the driver's side. I'd recognize those curls anywhere.

Krystal's car pulls in beside mine. She wastes no time jumping out despite the pouring rain. "What are you doing out here?" Even though she's shouting, I have to strain my ears to hear her. "Angela, you're gonna get sick!"

"You came." She doesn't hear me. I know because I can barely hear myself, and her stern expression doesn't change. My face breaks into a ridiculous grin I can't contain, that I don't *want* to contain, because *she actually came.*

"Come on." She grabs my arm and pulls me against her. "Get in the car."

"I didn't think the rain would reach this side of town," I tell her. I shout it, really, so she can hear me. "There were supposed to be fireworks. I had all these plans. I was going to kiss you—"

A crack of lightning startles us both.

"Angela, get in the car," she says again, but I'm shaking my head. I can't stop staring at her. My jaw is aching from how hard I'm smiling. "What—"

I don't overthink it this time. It's hard to tell if I'm thinking at all, that's how caught up I am in her. My hands cup Krystal's cheeks, pulling her until our faces are centimeters apart. My lips press against hers, clumsy but sure. Her body tenses slightly with a shocked gasp before she melts into me, lips parting to return the kiss tenfold. I'm actually doing it. I'm *kissing* Krystal Ramirez, and it's already the best thing I've ever done.

Her arms wrap around my back, pulling me into her body as her tongue sweeps inside my mouth. Despite the cold rain coming down hard on us, somehow she's able to keep me warm. I let her lead the pace, and we find a steady rhythm as I repeat her motions back. A gentle suck on her bottom lip, a soft glide of my tongue against hers. It goes on and on and on until we remember to take a breath.

When we finally pull away from each other, she opens the door to the back seat of her car and practically pushes me inside.

Once we're tucked close together on the right and middle seats, she pulls down the left one, her body bending over to grab something from the back. She returns with the blanket we shared the first time she brought me here and wraps it around my shoulders. She uses the other end of it to pat my short hair dry.

"You don't have to fuss over me," I tell her, even as a sneeze chooses this exact moment to undermine me. She gives me a knowing look as she procures a small bottle of sanitizer from her purse, but there's also something about her expression that's familiar. Fond, even. She's always taking care of me after I get myself into trouble.

"Thank you," I say as she deposits a dime-sized amount of gel into my hands.

"No problem. I'm so sorry I'm late. I'd just made it to the McNay when I saw your last post. I wanted to surprise you by winning the scavenger hunt. Earn your first kiss the way you imagined back when you first came up with the idea."

"Is that why you didn't text me back?"

"It was a better idea in my head." She looks away from me. "Instead, I made you wait out in the rain for me for who knows how long."

"You still came. You showed up."

She reaches out to push back the wet strands of hair stuck to my face, and then her hand is cupping my cheek, molding there perfectly like it's right where it belongs, her skin surprisingly warm. "I knew you'd look hot with short hair."

"Yeah?"

"Oh, yeah." She sucks in a breath as I lean into her again. "I can't believe you cut out early on your own scavenger hunt."

"You're more important," I say. "You're the woman I love, Krystal. There's nothing I wouldn't do to be with you."

Her eyes soften at my admission. And then her smile is as wide as mine.

She lets out a sigh, so close I feel the heat of her breath on my lips. Her grip tightens on the blanket, cocooning me in warmth. As amazing as our first kiss was, I have a feeling it's about to get even better now that we're somewhere warm and dry. "This is what it's going to be like with you, isn't it? I'll lose my mind over you every time I'm dragged into one of your harebrained schemes, and you're going to relish every second, aren't you?"

My grin comes full force.

"You have no idea."

She kisses me, and fuck if it gets better every time. I pull her body in closer, wrapping my arms around her head until our chests crush together. I don't know when I started straddling her lap, but she doesn't seem to mind. Far from minding, an arm wraps around my back and settles me more securely against her.

"I love you too." She smiles against my lips, setting my heart on fire. Her tongue runs along my bottom lip, coaxing my mouth open, demanding entrance. I let her in, let her take the lead, her hands holding my head in place. When her tongue touches mine for the second time, I forget how to think and breathe and be. Someone groans. I can't tell if it's her or me. It's probably me.

I pull back slightly, not wanting to lose myself in her too fast. Her eyes flit open, as hazy and dreamy as I imagine mine are. *Is this real? Is this really happening?*

"It's happening, Angel." She answers my silent thoughts, or maybe I asked them out loud. I can't tell anymore. She smiles against my lips. Then she kisses the side of my mouth, her lips trailing down my chin. "Was your first kiss everything you imagined?"

"I couldn't have possibly imagined—" A gasp as her tongue slides against my jaw in a slow, indulgent lick. "*Krystal.*"

"Good, huh?" She's so smug, I should hate her. She's all gleaming eyes and taunting smile flashing white canines. Instead, all I want is for us to shut up so she can keep going.

"So this is what I've been missing out on, huh?" I muse on a sigh, running my fingernails gently down both her arms. She shivers from my touch the same way I'm shivering from hers.

"To think, we could've been doing this a lot sooner."

She kisses me again, and it's all I want to keep doing. It's all I want to do for the rest of my life. Funny how I can already know this after the first time. Here with Krystal, in her car, rain pounding the metal above our heads, is the only place I'd rather be. That is, until Krystal asks:

"Do you wanna get out of here?"

"If by 'get out of here' you really mean…" I send her what I hope is my most suggestive look yet.

"If that's what you want." A hand dips beneath my damp, unbuttoned shirt to pull it off me. Once I'm just in my undershirt, she nips at my bare shoulder with her teeth. I hitch a breath, and her lips kiss away the sting. And then I remember—

"Shit." I pull myself off her lap. "I'm late to my own party."

Realization morphs the dazed expression from her face. I check the time. I'm about half an hour late. *What's another half hour?* the dark part of my brain asks. The part that wants very much to stay with Krystal, in this bubble of bliss we've created for ourselves.

"We should probably go," Krystal says, but she makes no move to leave. When I climb back into her lap instead of getting out of the car, she pulls me in with an arm wrapped around my lower back. Both hands cup her face as I crush her mouth to mine. Our movements are fervent this time, rushed.

She tugs on my undershirt to pull me closer, the damp fabric easily giving way beneath her touch. I let my hands explore, too, from the curve of her neck to the straps of her halter top, fingers dipping beneath the fabric. Her breathing turns erratic when our skin makes contact from one little touch of her collarbone.

She lets out a helpless gasp as my hands roam lower, underneath her top, and lord if I'll get over the little sounds she makes. She bites down on her lip as my fingers trail the lace edge of her bralette. At her enthusiastic response, I gather the hem of her top in my fingers.

"Lift your arms for me." She does, and the top is off her body in one fluid motion. "God, you're beautiful."

Her chest is pushed out, dark nipples visible through the sheer lace of her bra. When she reaches behind her back to unclasp it, the sight of her bare beneath me is more than I can take. I crush my lips to hers, hands already moving over her, cupping her breasts in my hands. She moans in my mouth as my fingers flick her nipples, working them with my fingers until she starts writhing beneath me.

"We don't have time for this, do we?" she asks, temporarily breaking the spell. Only, I'm in no mood to dispel the moment.

"Sure we do." An intake of breath as I unzip her shorts. They're practically plastered to her skin from the rain. "We at least have time to figure out if I'm any good at this."

She laughs softly, her hand curling around the back of my head as my hand slides down her body. I look into her face, gauging her permission. Her head nods so fast, I'd laugh if I wasn't breathing so hard. My hand dips inside her panties, where she's already wet for me. A moan in the shape of my name leaves her lips, the sound almost unintelligible.

"Help me get these off you." She lifts her hips and I pull off her shorts and panties in one sweep. I used to think when this moment came, I'd be more intimidated than I am. I've given Krystal pleasure with verbal instructions and the help of a suction toy, but will I be able to please her without battery-powered assistance? Rather than shy away from the task, I'm more determined than ever to see this through. To have her writhing on my hand and calling out my name, because she just can't help herself. Because I'm *that* good.

Which is why when I return to her lap, I'm savoring this moment with gentle strokes, building her up in a slow burn that has her squirming for more, circling her clit with the patience Krystal makes clear in no uncertain terms she doesn't have.

"Angel, *please*," she moans, rocking her hips into my hand. I'm not hesitant with her this time. I use the upper hand this position on top of her gives me. With my other hand, I pin down her thigh to stop her from wriggling away, reveling in the frustrated cry she emits in my ear. Then I press against her a little harder, a little faster.

I know she's close when her body tenses. I work her clit in

tight circles with two fingers. Finally, she lets go with a moan, her legs shaking so hard, she's in danger of launching me off the seat. Her breathing slows, body splayed out languidly as she comes down from her orgasm.

"Oh my god." The words come out as a sigh. "That was…"

Words elude her. She's far from alone in that.

"Yeah," I finish dumbly. "For me too. And I'm not even done yet."

"What—" She cuts herself off when my knees hit the floor of the car. A gasp chokes at the back of her throat when my arms hook beneath her thighs to pull her forward until she's sitting at the edge of the seat. "Angel, what are you doing down there?"

"I want to be good at this," I say as I open her up with two careful fingers, exposing her to me. "When you did this to me for the first time, *fuck*, Krystal. You have no idea how much I loved it. I want to make you feel as good as you made me feel."

"Oh, Angel." She sighs as I leave a trail of kisses up her inner thighs. "I have no doubt that you'll be very good at this. But if it makes you feel better, I can guide you."

"Deal," I tell her as an idea sparks. "I wore a tie today."

"Uh, what?" Her brows furrow as I pull a navy-blue tie from my pocket. When I tell her to hold out her wrists for me, her eyes sparkle with intrigue.

"I was wearing this at the bar," I explain as I bind her wrists together, careful to make it snug enough without hurting her. "But I took it off when it got too uncomfortable from running around all day. Okay, good," I say after ensuring the knot isn't too tight or too loose. "Place your hands behind the headrest for me."

"Fuck, Angel." She does as I say, nearly panting. She's even wetter when I return to her pussy. "You're not living up to your nickname today, are you?"

"Would you be this wet if I were?"

A scream leaves her throat at my first taste of her. If we were somewhere a little more private without a ticking clock above our heads and this wasn't my first time eating her out, I'd probably tease her more. Take my time, savor the taste of her. Instead, I zero in on her clit, focused on wringing out as much of her pleasure as possible.

"Fuck, right there, Angel."

I alternate between long, sweeping licks and sucking her clit directly into my mouth. Right as she tenses, I replace my mouth with two fingers to keep her open as I glance up at her, and fuck if she isn't the prettiest sight. Her arms are fighting against the silk tie restraining her, eyes shut tight as her body squirms and writhes for an orgasm so close, yet so far from reach.

I meant what I said about not teasing her, so once I'm done enjoying the view, I return to sucking her clit until she's crying out around me. When her legs stop shaking, I climb back onto the seat beside her. Her lashes flutter as her eyes finally open, the picture of sated bliss. I kiss her sweaty forehead, and she smiles up at me. Then she straightens suddenly. "We should—"

"Oh shit." I nod. "Let's go, before we're tempted to go for round two."

She laughs when I climb to the front and stumble down

into the passenger seat. But her laughter quickly turns to panic as she stares down at her shorts soaked from the rain and expresses no desire to ply herself back into them. After making a quick pit stop at her apartment so she can change her clothes and making plans to pick up my car tomorrow, we're finally off.

Forty-Five

The house is full and buzzing by the time we arrive, a whole two hours late. My dad is standing in the foyer as we're coming in, his eyes immediately lighting up as they fall to my hand clasped in Krystal's.

"So this is the non-girlfriend, huh?" His mouth quirks in a grin before he holds out his hand for Krystal. "Nice to finally meet you."

Krystal raises a brow at me before taking my father's hand. "Nice meeting you, too, sir."

"You two should go get something to eat while there's still some left," he says before heading back to my mom in the kitchen.

"*There* you are." Marcela quickly takes my dad's place, breaking away from a circle of friends in the living room. Her grin takes up her entire face. "Do I even want to know what took y'all so long?"

"I think I'll check out what's left of the food," Krystal says, kissing my cheek before she saunters away. Once she's gone, I turn to my best friend.

"I'd say I'm sorry, but I'm not." I grin sheepishly. "If I'm sorry about anything, it's that I decided to throw this party in the first place when we could be finishing what we started in the car—"

"Please dear lord, don't let her finish that sentence." Julian shudders as he appears from behind me. "I'm happy for you and everything, but there are some things a cousin should never know."

Krystal returns quickly with two full plates of food. I thank her as she hands me a plate of barbecue chicken, roasted peppers, Spanish rice, and a folded tortilla. "Looks like you pulled off a great party without actually being here," she says. "The food looks delicious."

"What can I say? My parents know how to host." I tear into the chicken with one hand while standing. With all the twists and turns this evening took, I barely registered how hungry I was.

When I asked my parents if they'd be willing to help host a party with mostly queer guests, they didn't so much as bat an eye. As I look around at all our guests laughing and mingling together in the house I grew up in, it heals something in me I never knew needed mending. So many of my blood relations would hate the sight of my living room right now, but none of them matter.

After I finish eating, I make the rounds and thank everyone for coming. Natalia and Stephanie are sitting on the couch, drinks in hand, and that's where I learn that a woman named Nayeli beat Leti to the scavenger hunt prize by a full three seconds. After rounding with almost everyone, I spend half an hour in the kitchen with Briana, Julian's mom, and my parents to help with some cleanup. It's the least I can do after showing up late.

Leti is by the stairs when I finish tidying up. I pull her into a friendly hug as Krystal waits for me by the landing.

"Heard someone else beat you to the prize by a slim margin," I tell her. "I kinda wish I could've seen your reaction."

"I'm glad you didn't. I nearly told the security guard to go fuck himself when he asked me to keep it down." Her nose scrunches the same way it does when she dies in a *Stardew Valley* playthrough. "So close, yet so far."

"You'll get 'em next time."

Julian catches my eye over Leti's shoulder. When he quickly starts backing away from us, I roll my eyes.

"Hey, Leti, have you met my cousin?"

There's nowhere for Julian to run as she turns around. I'm considering this payback for giving Krystal that embarrassing seventh-grade yearbook photo of me, but the drama I'm expecting doesn't come. Leti smiles politely at my cousin as she extends her hand to him. The panic on my cousin's face morphs to something else as he takes in her blank expression with raised brows.

"Nice to meet you," she says as she takes his hand. "I'm Leti."

"Leti, hi. I'm…" Her attention is pulled away as someone across the room calls her name. She pulls her hand from Julian's grasp and waves at the three of us before hurrying away.

I furrow my brows at my cousin once she disappears into the crowd. "I thought you said she hated you?"

"She does, or at least she *did*." He looks more perplexed than I am. "Does she…not remember me?"

"Why would she hate you?" Krystal asks.

"Apparently they went out on a *really* bad first date," I explain before turning back to my cousin. "She could be pretending not to remember you because that's how much she hates you," I tell him, which only causes another worry line to divot his forehead.

"How long ago was this bad date?" Krystal asks him.

"Three or four years." He rubs the back of his neck. "And it wasn't *that* bad."

"Maybe you're right. It clearly wasn't bad enough for her to remember you." I give his shoulder an affectionate pat. "Well, that's disappointing."

Later that night, once the party has ended and we've cleaned up, Krystal and I end up in my bedroom.

"Should we have the talk now?" I ask as Krystal plops herself on the edge of my bed. When she raises a brow at me, I clarify. "You know, the relationship talk? We said we love each other. Does that mean we're in a relationship?"

"I haven't done the whole relationship thing since Isaac," she reminds me. "I'm not sure how good I'll be at it, but you make me want to try. I love you. I want to be with you, Angela. So if you'll have me…" She reaches for my hands, intertwining our fingers as a cheesy smile lights up her entire face. "Do you want to be my girlfriend?"

I can't help but mirror her grin. "Of course I want to be your girlfriend."

My hand tangles in her hair as I clasp the back of her neck and bend to kiss her. Dare I say it, but I think in the last few hours I've become an expert. She moans into my mouth as my tongue glides against hers. I didn't mean to ramp up the heat between us so fast, but I can't seem to help myself.

"You're a little too good at that." She pulls away slightly, voice breathy. "And you're a little too good at some other things too."

"What can I say? Twenty-seven years gives you *plenty* of time to research." I trail kisses down her jaw. "Plus, I had a great teacher."

"Oh, yeah?" Her eyes darken with desire. "Is that who taught you how to drive me wild with your tongue on my pussy?"

Fuck.

I'm never going to get over Krystal's dirty mouth. She pushes me back against the bed, lowering herself to the floor as she peels off my pants. Thankfully, they've dried out so she doesn't have to exert much effort to remove them from my body.

"*Krystal.*" I bite down on a moan as she works me open with her tongue, praying no one can hear us. I'm full to the brim with love for this woman, and I'm in danger of overflowing. "Fuck, Krystal. I love you so much. I love that every first I have is with you. But you know what?"

It takes her a moment before her tongue stops moving against me. Her eyes have a devilish glint to them, but there's something soft in them too. It's that look again. That look you can only give someone you're irrevocably in love with. "What, Angel?"

I stare down at her, in awe of this woman I get to call mine.

"I hope you'll be my last."

Epilogue

Two Years Later

"A re you ready?"

I glance out the window to the dusty building Marcela and I are parked in front of. From the outside, it doesn't look like much. The glowing neon sign is out of place against the old gray brick, but Krystal seems to like the juxtaposition. After a while, it grew on me too. More so when I realized what building it was.

"Ready," Marcela tells me, undoing her seat belt. "Should we be worried that they refused help setting up?"

"They have a staff for all that." I wave off her concern as we cross the street, making our way to the bar. "I'm just here to drink."

Back when Krystal first showed me the building she and Theo had found for the bar, she had waited for me to get it on my own, eyeing me with patient excitement as I squinted my eyes at the unassuming, abandoned building. Inside, I kicked at the trash on the floor as I made my way around the space for the first time. The wooden beams were nice, but the unfinished ceiling and concrete floor left much to be desired.

"I don't get it," I finally told her. "What am I supposed to be looking for?"

Her smile was giddy.

"This used to be your favorite view," she told me. "But I get why you wouldn't recognize the building from up close or inside. You needed some distance to get the full *picture*." When I still didn't understand the hint she was giving me, it finally clicked when she said, "It looks a little different since they washed off the mural, doesn't it?"

This was the building that started it all. For Natalia. For me. Now, finally, for Krystal. When I met Natalia two years ago, I couldn't shake this feeling that our fates were tied. Now, as the sign Natalia designed and built blinks back at me, it's as if the three of us have come full circle.

There's already a line wrapped around the corner. After a successful soft launch last week, people around town have been rallying for the Elixir Lounge to open for normal hours with an extended drink menu. It's even gotten great reviews and buzz in local and national publications. A security guard waves us through in front of the long line, and even though Marcela and I have met Steven on several occasions, it still makes me feel like a treasured VIP guest when he lets us pass without so much as a blink.

Inside, the place has come a long way from the first time Krystal and I visited. The back wall behind a row of booths has been replaced with tempered glass and gold metal plating that lets in lots of sunlight during the day and gives a greenhouse effect. There are rows of multi-colored neon lights behind the bar that make the place look more like a nightclub when the sun goes down. Plant life is everywhere—on the shelves beside bottles of liquor, hanging in pots above our heads, on top of tiered shelves against the windows. There's plenty of Natalia's artwork as well. Any wall space not taken up by trailing vines holds framed paintings, and an array of sculptures in various sizes are mixed in with the plants by the window.

Krystal and Theo are talking with the staff in a circle, possibly discussing the game plan for tonight. While they're occupied, I make my way behind the bar. Marcela shakes her head at me as Krystal excuses herself from the group.

"What do you think you're doing?"

"Practicing my moves." I grab a bottle of Malibu from behind the bar and toss it in the air. My girlfriend catches it in midair before it can land in my hand. I pout at her glare. "Oh, come on, I'm getting better!"

"You can try at home, not here." Home means her place or mine, but more often than not, we end up at her place. I moved into my own apartment last year when I landed a youth librarian position minutes away from what would become the Elixir Lounge, but I'm still not fully unpacked, which makes my apartment a disaster zone. The last time Krystal stayed over, she spent three hours unpacking my kitchen while I was sleeping.

"Fine," I grumble, but it doesn't last long when she kisses my cheek. I turn my head and catch her lips, because even after two years, kissing Krystal never gets old. "Are you excited for tonight?"

"I'm more nervous than anything," she admits as I wrap my arms around her neck. "What if something goes wrong?"

"Nothing is going to go wrong." She harrumphs like she doesn't believe me. "You worked hard for this, and there's a long line of people waiting outside who are all excited to be here. You got what you wanted, Krystal. Don't forget to enjoy it."

"I guess you have a point," she says, looking at me like she's not sure how she got so lucky. It's a feeling I'm all too familiar with. A hand comes up to cup my cheek and her eyes go soft. "I do have exactly what I want, don't I?"

I'm right—the night goes off without a hitch. Marcela and I watch from a corner booth as customers enter the bar with oohs and aahs, smiling as they order drinks and marvel at the general ambiance of the place.

Before long, everyone I love is inside these walls. Theo finds some time to hide away at a back table with Marcela. Briana and her husband pop by, greeting me with her signature bone-crushing hug that only seems to get stronger each year. No Esme, but I didn't expect her. We may never see eye to eye, but that's fine. She's not someone I need in my life, but I'm glad the same can't be said of Briana.

Julian and Leti show up an hour after opening, hand in hand, smiling at each other like the idiots in love they are. Their relationship has certainly come a long way in two years, but I couldn't be happier for them. Natalia and Stephanie show up around nine for two drinks before heading back. I don't get to see them nearly enough these days—ever since the scavenger hunt and completing her art residency, she's been booked and busy.

"I hope you're proud of all the work you put into this place," Natalia tells Krystal as they hug goodbye. "The bar is amazing. Dare I say, it might even be a new hangout spot for me and Stephanie."

"Bet you feel right at home, what with all your art pieces hanging around here." I gesture to the wall where even more of her work is framed.

"You could call it a perk." She smirks. "I have to visit the statues every once in a while. Make sure they don't miss me."

"Thank you for everything, Natalia," Krystal says. "And thanks for being the first to bring my attention to this prime real estate."

Krystal's arm falls around my shoulders as we watch them leave. It's funny, all the transformations a person can go through with enough time. I couldn't have imagined this life for myself two years ago. I have my dream job and once I get my shit together, a nice, cozy apartment that feels like home. A girlfriend I'm dizzyingly in love with, who returns those feelings tenfold. Not one, not two, but *three* best friends—but if Marcela asks, she's still my number one. Natalia and Leti have rounded out our group quite nicely, especially during monthly brunches when our numbers increase to include significant others.

That once-constant loneliness that dogged my every step? Turns out it was ephemeral after all.

"I do too," I tell Krystal much later, once the bar is closed for the night and we've said good night to everyone. We're in her car on our way back to her apartment. It's three in the morning, either way too late or far too early for my contemplative thoughts.

"You what?" She turns to me, eyes sleepy but still alert.

"I have exactly what I want too." At the stop sign, I cup her face and she leans in to kiss me.

"I love you so much, Angel."

"I never get tired of hearing that." I smile against her lips. "I love you too."

My life is so much fuller than I ever thought it'd be. I guess that's what happens when you're surrounded by people you love, and who love you in return. They fill your heart. They never leave you alone. And, if you ask me, no kind of love is truer than that.

Acknowledgments

Firstly, I have some people to thank from *The Next Best Fling*'s release that got left out of that book's acknowledgment page (publishing timelines are screwy sometimes), so let me rectify that mistake right now by giving the BIGGEST thank-you to Dana and Caroline. Thank you for being superstars and making sure my debut entered the world with a bang. I get a little giddy every time I refresh my inbox to an email from you guys. And thanks a second time for everything you have done and will do for *Kiss Me, Maybe*.

To all the booksellers, librarians, and bookish content creators who pushed *The Next Best Fling* so hard last year. I'd name you all if I could (I really need to start making lists), so sorry if this feels broad and impersonal. When my first book came out, I felt the outpouring of love coming in from all directions. You all work incredibly hard, and to see so many people putting in that effort for my book was an astounding thing to witness. I'm forever grateful to all of you for making my debut year a special one.

Second books are notorious for being the most difficult to write, and *Kiss Me, Maybe* is no exception, which is why I couldn't have done it without so many amazing people to cheer me on. To Junessa, thank you for always understanding my vision and for your dedication to helping make my books the absolute best they can be. I'm so thankful that I get to work with someone I trust so dearly with my book babies. To Samantha, thank you for being the best advocate an author can ask for. Your belief in my writing is what keeps me going at the end of the day. Carrie and Anjuli, thank you for helping ensure I don't embarrass myself in copy edits.

Tobie, thank you for befriending me and always lending an ear when I inevitably get stuck in my revisions. I'm so happy to have you in my writer circle. Natalia, thank you for your constant encouragement and for always pulling me back up when I go down my self-doubt/imposter syndrome spiral. Publishing is hard, but I'm so glad to have writer friends to help pull me through.

Asha, Abby, and Justine, thanks for being the most supportive friends. I don't know where I'd be without you guys, and I don't want to know. Mom, thank you for always coming with me to every single book event I get invited to and being so proud of everything I've accomplished so far. Dad, thanks for the moral support even when you'd rather not be there.

To the readers who've stuck with me. You guys constantly blow me away. I don't reply to every message on Instagram, but I try to read everything, and it warms my heart that so many of you have reached out personally to tell me nice things about my book. To every reader I've had the pleasure of meeting in person, who has showed up to signings and events, thank you thank you thank you. Finally, to the readers only just discovering my books. Thank you for taking a chance on me. I can't do this without you guys, and your support means the world to me.

About the Author

Gabriella Gamez is the *USA Today* bestselling author of *The Next Best Fling*. She writes about incredibly messy, well-meaning women trying their best and accidentally falling in love. She is a former library assistant and has a bachelor's degree in English from UTSA. When not writing, she can be found drinking copious amounts of coffee, wasting time playing video games, and obsessing over other people's books. She currently resides in South Texas.

Find out more at:

» gabriellagamez.com
» Instagram: @gabbywritesalot
» TikTok: @gabbywritesalot